Also by Jay McInerney

NONFICTION

A Hedonist in the Cellar

Bacchus and Me

FICTION

The Good Life

Model Behavior

The Last of the Savages

Brightness Falls

Story of My Life

Ransom

Bright Lights, Big City

HOW IT ENDED

HOW IT ENDED

NEW AND COLLECTED STORIES

Jay McInerney

Alfred A. Knopf New York 2009

THIS IS A BORZOI BOOK
PUBLISHED BY ALFRED A. KNOPF

The following stories originally appeared in book form in *Model Behavior:
A Novel and Stories* (New York: Alfred A. Knopf, 1998): "The Business,"
"Con Doctor," "Getting in Touch with Lonnie," "How It Ended," "The Queen
and I," "Reunion" and "Smoke." These stories, along with "My Public Service,"
"Simple Gifts" and "Third Party," were subsequently published in Great Britain
in the collection *How It Ended* (London: Bloomsbury Publishing Plc, 2000).

Some stories were previously published in the following: "Putting Daisy Down"
in *The Guardian Literary Supplement*, "The Madonna of Turkey Season" in *Image*
(Dublin), "The Last Bachelor" in *Playboy* and "Everything Is Lost" in
The Sunday Times Magazine (London).

ISBN-13: 978-0-307-26805-1

Manufactured in the United States of America

For Barrett and Maisie

CONTENTS

PREFACE

Like most novelists I cut my teeth writing short stories, and that's one habit I've never been able to break. I was lucky enough to study under two masters of the form, Raymond Carver and Tobias Wolff, who were both teaching at Syracuse University when I showed up in 1981 after being fired from *The New Yorker* for being a very bad fact-checker. Like the Talking Heads, I believed that facts all came with points of view. Whether or not I was correct to conclude that fiction was my métier, I clearly couldn't be trusted with the facts.

In fact, I'd gone to Syracuse specifically to study with Carver, whose writing I'd revered ever since I read *Will You Please Be Quiet, Please?* not long after it came out in 1976. I was lucky enough to get Wolff, who had just published *In the Garden of the North American Martyrs,* in the bargain. As a teacher, Ray operated on intuition: He saw himself as a nurturer rather than a critic. His greatest gift was to foster the inner editor in each of us, questioning word choice, querying what he considered pretentious verbiage, underlining or crossing out questionable adjectives and sprinkling question marks in the margins. Besides presiding over workshops, he taught a course called "Form and Theory of the Short Story," in which we read his favorite practitioners: Chekhov, Babel, Hemingway, Welty and the O'Connors, Frank and Flannery. At the beginning of each class he would light up a cigarette and ask, "So, what did you think?" Ray's idea of a good session was one in which these were the last words he spoke. When a student from the English department proper challenged him about this methodology, demanding to know why the class was called "Form and Theory" when there was little of either, Ray nervously sucked on his cigarette and hunched lower in his chair. "Well," he said after a very long pause, "I guess it's like we read the stories . . . and then form our own theories."

Toby was far more analytical, and more critical. He would disassemble a short story before our eyes like a forensic pathologist, labeling the various components and explaining how they worked or, as was the case with most of our workshop submissions, why they didn't. Unlike his distinguished colleague, he didn't suffer fools, or their stories, gladly.

At Syracuse I wrote "In the North-West Frontier Province," which I sent to *The Paris Review*. A few weeks later I was astonished to receive a phone call from George Plimpton, its longtime editor, who told me, in that silvery patrician voice, he quite liked the story and was inclined to publish it but wondered if I possibly had anything else to show him. After rereading my old stories and realizing that they were all pretty much derivative crap, I found a paragraph written in the second person that I'd scrawled after a disastrous night on the town. This struck me as more original, and subsequently I stayed up all night writing "It's Six A.M. Do You Know Where You Are?"—which became my first published story when George brought it out in 1982. At some point I realized I had more to tell about this particular character in this particular voice, and the story became the basis for my first novel, *Bright Lights, Big City*. "In the North-West Frontier Province" eventually found a place, as a kind of backstory, in my second novel, *Ransom;* since it seems to me my first successful story, I've included it here.

My next novel, *Story of My Life,* grew rather more organically out of a short story published under the same title in *Esquire* in 1987. Likewise, "Philomena," published in *The New Yorker* in 1995, later evolved into the novel *Model Behavior*. (Not included here is "Savage and Son," published in *Esquire* in 1993, which became the basis for my novel *The Last of the Savages,* because it seems to me a novella rather than a short story—a question not merely of length but of scope.)

Clearly, I was attracted to the long form, and my short stories—some of them, at least—often turned out to be warm-up exercises. There's psychological as well as practical value in using one as a sketch for a novel; the idea of undertaking a narrative of three or four hundred pages, which might consume years of your life, is pretty daunting. A novel's a long-term relationship. Sometimes it's easier to pretend you're engaging in a one-night stand and see how it feels.

On the other hand, at the risk of contradicting myself, I have always been more than a little daunted by the short story. Whereas even a medium-sized novel—let alone the kind Henry James described as a loose baggy monster—can survive any number of false turns, boring characters and off-key sentences, the story is far less forgiving. A good one requires perfect pitch and a precise sense of form; it has to burn with a hard, gem-like flame.

"Smoke" was written in 1985, shortly after the publication of *Bright Lights, Big City*. It was the first outing for Russell and Corrine Calloway, who have reappeared in *Brightness Falls* and *The Good Life*. In between novels I have continued to write stories, seven of which were published in hardcover in 1999 along with the short novel *Model Behavior*, but since they did not appear in the paperback edition I have included them here: "Smoke," "The Business," "How It Ended," "Getting in Touch with Lonnie," "Reunion," "The Queen and I" and "Con Doctor."

It's strange how the retrospective view highlights the temporal signature of certain stories. "My Public Service," which I somehow forgot to include in *Model Behavior*, was written in 1992, years before Monica Lewinsky became a household name. "The Queen and I" was written at about the same time, when the Meatpacking District was still the center of the industry for which it was named by day, and by night devoted to another kind of meat altogether and populated largely by transsexual streetwalkers and their cruising johns. Those familiar with its current incarnation as Manhattan's glossiest hub of platinum-card nightlife might have a hard time recognizing it here. And speaking of change—I saw no reason not to tinker with these older stories when I thought they might be improved. Nor did I feel compelled to resurrect several stories which seemed, on reflection, to resemble sleeping dogs.

The twelve most recent stories, including "Sleeping with Pigs," "Invisible Fences," "I Love You, Honey," "Summary Judgment," "The Madonna of Turkey Season," "The Waiter," "Everything Is Lost," "The Debutante's Return" and "Putting Daisy Down," were composed in something of a sprint from December 2007 through the late spring of 2008. "Penelope on the Pond," which features Alison Poole, the protagonist of my 1988 novel *Story of My Life*, was also written during this period. (Alison has enjoyed an interesting career as a fictional character: Bret Easton Ellis borrowed her for *American Psycho*, where she narrowly avoids getting murdered by Patrick Bateman, and she subsequently assumed a prominent role in his novel *Glamorama*. Moreover, the woman who inspired this character has recently achieved a certain real-life notoriety, but that's a factual matter which needn't further concern us here.) Corrine Calloway returns in "The March," which I wrote while I was working on *The Good Life*. And the most recent story here, "The Last Bachelor," was finished in May of 2008, though the first few paragraphs were written in the early nineties and then set aside.

As different as these twenty-six stories—written over the last twenty-six years—might be, certain preoccupations and obsessions seem to have endured. But enough of these damn facts. I enjoyed writing these stories, and hope you enjoy reading them.

Jay McInerney
August 2008

ACKNOWLEDGMENTS

It's probably impossible to acknowledge all of those who have helped inspire, improve and meddle with these stories, written over a span of twenty-six years. Still, it would be ungrateful not to try. Special thanks to George Plimpton for saving me from law school by publishing my first short story, and to Raymond Carver and Tobias Wolff for reading and commenting on numerous unpublished narratives that preceded it. Bill Buford, as editor at *Granta* and later *The New Yorker,* helped shape and polish several of these stories. I owe a debt of gratitude as well to Rust Hills, who nurtured and published many installments of my fiction during his tenure at *Esquire,* and to Alice Turner, former fiction editor at *Playboy.* Mona Simpson, Bob O'Connor, Donna Tartt, Julian Barnes, Helen Bransford, Terry McDonell, Bret Easton Ellis, Virginia O'Brien, Jon Robin Baitz and Anne Hearst McInerney are among the early readers who have helped to improve these stories. And I feel very lucky and blessed to have had Binky Urban as a reader and an adviser since the start of my career. Finally, Gary Fisketjon has been my closest reader for thirty years, since we were classmates at Williams College. I showed him my earliest stories not long after we exchanged blows in the name of a romantic rivalry. He's read every line of fiction I have written since then, and I've benefited immeasurably from his advice, even if some of his criticism has reminded me of his right jab.

HOW IT ENDED

It's Six A.M.
Do You Know Where You Are?

You are not the kind of guy who would be at a place like this at this time of the morning. But here you are, and you cannot say that the terrain is entirely unfamiliar, although the details are a little fuzzy. You are at a nightclub talking to a girl with a shaved head. The club is either the Bimbo Box or the Lizard Lounge. It might all come a little clearer if you could slip into the bathroom and do a little more Bolivian Marching Powder. Then again, it might not. There is a small voice inside of you insisting that this epidemic lack of clarity is the result of too much of that already, but you are not yet willing to listen to that voice. The night has already turned on that imperceptible pivot where two a.m. changes to six a.m. You know that moment has come and gone, though you are not yet willing to concede that you have crossed the line beyond which all is gratuitous damage and the palsy of unraveled nerve endings. Somewhere back there it was possible to cut your losses, but you rode past that moment on a comet trail of white powder and now are trying to hang on to the rush. Your brain at present is composed of brigades of tiny Bolivian soldiers. They are tired and muddy from their long march through the night. There are holes in their boots and they are hungry. They need to be fed. They need the Bolivian Marching Powder.

Something vaguely tribal about this scene—pendulous jewelry, face paint, ceremonial headgear and hairstyles. You feel that there is also a certain Latin theme, which is more than the fading buzz of marimbas in your brain.

You are leaning back against a post which may or may not be structural with regard to the building but nonetheless feels essential for the maintenance of an upright position. The bald girl is saying this used to be a good place to come before the assholes discovered it. You do not want to be talking to this bald girl, or even listening to her, which is all you're doing, but you don't have your barge pole handy, and just at the moment you don't want to test the powers of speech or locomotion.

How did you get here? It was your friend Tad Allagash who powered you in here, and now he has disappeared. Tad is the kind of guy who certainly would be at a place like this at this time of the morning. He is either your best self or your worst self, you're not sure which. Earlier in the evening it seemed clear that he was your best self. You started on the Upper East Side with Champagne and unlimited prospects, strictly observing the Allagash rule of perpetual motion: one drink per stop. Tad's mission in life is to have more fun than anyone else in New York City, and this involves a lot of moving around, since there is always the likelihood that you are missing something, that where you aren't is more fun than where you are. You are awed by this strict refusal to acknowledge any goal higher than the pursuit of pleasure. You want to be like that. You also think that he is shallow and dangerous. His friends are all rich and spoiled, like the cousin from Memphis you met earlier in the evening who refused to accompany you below Fourteenth Street because he said he didn't have a lowlife visa. This cousin had a girlfriend with cheekbones to break your heart, and you knew she was the real thing when she never once acknowledged your presence. She possessed secrets—about islands, about horses—that you would never know.

You have traveled from the meticulous to the slime. The girl with the shaved head has a scar tattooed on her scalp that looks like a long, sutured gash. You tell her it is very realistic. She takes this as a compliment and thanks you. You meant as opposed to romantic. "I could use one of those right over my heart," you say.

"You want I can give you the name of the guy did it. You'd be surprised how cheap." You don't tell her that nothing would surprise you now. Her voice, for instance, which is like the New Jersey state anthem played through an electric shaver.

The bald girl is emblematic of the problem. What the problem is is that for some reason you think you are going to meet the kind of girl who is not the kind of girl who would be at a place like this at this time of the morning. When you meet her you are going to tell her that what you really want is a house in the country with a garden. New York, the club scene, bald women—you're tired of all that. Your presence here is only a matter of conducting an experiment in limits, reminding yourself of what you aren't. You see yourself as the kind of guy who wakes up early on Sunday morning and steps out to pick up the *Times* and croissants. You take a cue from the Arts and Leisure section and decide to check out some exhibition—costumes of the Hapsburg Court at the Met, say, or Japanese lacquerware of the Muromachi period at the Asia Society. Maybe you will call that woman you met at the publishing party Friday night, the party you did not get sloppy drunk at, an editor at a famous publishing house even though she looks like a fashion model. See if she wants to check out the exhibition and maybe do an early dinner. You will wait until eleven a.m. to call her, because unlike you she may not be an early riser. She may have been out a little late, at a nightclub, say. It occurs to you that there is time for a couple sets of tennis before the museum. You wonder if she plays, but then, of course she would.

When you meet the girl who wouldn't et cetera, you will tell her that you are slumming, visiting your own six a.m. Lower East Side of the soul on a lark, stepping nimbly between the piles of garbage to the marimba rhythms in your head.

On the other hand, any beautiful girl, specifically one with a full head of hair, would help you stave off this creeping sense of mortality. You remember the Bolivian Marching Powder and realize you're not down yet. First you have to get rid of this bald girl because of the bad things she is doing to your mood.

In the bathroom there are no doors on the stalls, which makes it tough to be discreet. But clearly you are not the only person here to take on fuel. Lots of sniffling going on. The windows in here are blacked over, and for this you are profoundly grateful.

Hup, two, three, four. The Bolivian soldiers are back on their feet, off and running in formation. Some of them are dancing, and you must do the same.

Just outside the door you spot her: tall, dark and alone, half hiding behind a pillar at the edge of the dance floor. You approach laterally, moving your stuff like a bad spade through the slalom of a synthesized conga rhythm. She jumps when you touch her shoulder.

"Dance?"

She looks at you as if you had just suggested instrumental rape. "I do not speak English," she says, after you ask again.

"Français?"

She shakes her head. Why is she looking at you that way, like there are tarantulas nesting in your eye sockets?

"You are by any chance from Bolivia? Or Peru?"

She is looking around for help now. Remembering a recent encounter with a young heiress's bodyguard at Danceteria—or was it New Berlin?—you back off, hands raised over your head.

The Bolivian soldiers are still on their feet, but they have stopped singing their marching song. You realize that we are at a crucial juncture with regard to morale. What we need is a good pep talk from Tad Allagash, who is nowhere to be found. You try to imagine what he would say. *Back on the horse. Now we're* really *going to have some fun.* Something like that. You suddenly realize that he has already slipped out with some rich hose queen. He is back at her place on Fifth Ave., and they are doing some of her off-the-boat-quality drugs. They are scooping it out of tall Ming vases and snorting it off of each other's naked bodies. You hate Tad Allagash.

Go home. Cut your losses.

Stay. Go for it.

You are a republic of voices tonight. Unfortunately, the republic is Italy. All these voices are waving their arms and screaming at one another. There's an *ex cathedra* riff coming down from the Vatican: Repent. There's still time. *Your body is the temple of the Lord and you have defiled it.* It is, after all, Sunday morning, and as long as you have any brain cells left a resonant, patriarchal bass will echo down the marble vaults of your church-going childhood to remind you that this is the Lord's day. What you need is another overpriced drink to drown it out. But a search of pockets yields only a dollar bill and change. You paid ten to get in here. Panic gains on you.

You spot a girl at the edge of the dance floor who looks like your last chance for earthly salvation against the creeping judgment of the Sabbath. You know for a fact that if you go out into the morning alone, without even your sunglasses, which you have forgotten (because who, after all, plans on these travesties), that the harsh, angling light will turn you to flesh and bone. Mortality will pierce you through the retina. But there she is in her pegged pants, a kind of doo-wop retro ponytail pulled off to the side, great lungs, as eligible a candidate as you could hope to find this late in the game. The sexual equivalent of fast food.

She shrugs and nods when you ask her to dance. You like the way she moves, half-tempo, the oiled ellipses of her hips and shoulders. You get a little hip-and-ass contact. After the second song she says she's tired. She's on the edge of bolting when you ask her if she needs a little pick-me-up.

"You've got some blow?" she says.

"Monster," you say.

She takes your arm and leads you into the Ladies'. There's another guy in the stall beside yours so it's okay. After a couple of spoons she seems to like you just fine and you're feeling pretty likable yourself. A couple more. This girl is all nose. When she leans forward for the spoon, the front of her shirt falls open and you can't help wondering if this is her way of thanking you.

Oh yes.

"I love drugs," she says, as you march toward the bar.

"It's something we have in common," you say.

"Have you ever noticed how all the good words start with *D*? *D* and *L*."

You try to think about this. You're not sure what she's driving at. The Bolivians are singing their marching song but you can't quite make out the words.

"You know? Drugs. Delight. Decadence."

"Debauchery," you say, catching the tune now.

"Dexedrine."

"Delectable. Deranged. Debilitated."

"And *L*. Lush and luscious."

"Languorous."

"Lazy."

"Libidinous."

"What's that?" she says.

"Horny."

"Oh," she says and casts a long, arching look over your shoulder. Her eyes glaze in a way that reminds you precisely of the closing of a sand-blasted glass shower door. You can see that the game is over, though you're not sure which rule you broke. Possibly she finds *H* words offensive and is now scanning the dance floor for a man with a compatible vocabulary. You have more: *down* and *depressed, lost* and *lonely.* It's not that you are really going to miss this girl who thinks that *decad*ence and *Dexedrine* are the high points of the language of the Kings James and Lear, but the touch of flesh, the sound of another human voice . . . You know that there is a special purgatory waiting out there for you, a desperate half-sleep which is like a grease fire in the brainpan.

The girl half waves as she disappears into the crowd. There is no sign of the other girl, the girl who would not be here. There is no sign of Tad Allagash. The Bolivians are mutinous. You can't stop the voices.

Here you are again.

All messed up and no place to go.

It is worse even than you expected, stepping out into the morning. The light is like a mother's reproach. The sidewalk sparkles cruelly. Visibility unlimited. The downtown warehouses look serene and rested in this beveled light. A taxi passes uptown and you start to wave, then realize you have no money. The car stops. You jog over and lean in the window.

"I guess I'll walk after all."

"Asshole." The cabbie leaves rubber.

You start north, holding your hand over your eyes. A bum is sleeping on the sidewalk, swathed in garbage bags, and he lifts his head as you pass. "God bless you and forgive your sins," he says. You wait for the cadge, but that's all he says. You wish he hadn't said anything.

As you turn away, what is left of your olfactory equipment sends a message to your brain. The smell of fresh bread. Somewhere they are baking bread. You see bakery trucks loading in front of a loft building on the next block. You watch as bags of rolls are carried out onto the loading dock by a man with a tattooed forearm. This man is already at work, so that regular people will have fresh bread for their morning tables. The righteous people who sleep at night and eat eggs for breakfast. It is Sunday morning and you have not eaten since . . . when? Friday night. As you approach, the smell of the bread washes over you like a gentle rain. You inhale deeply, filling your lungs with it. Tears come to your eyes, and you are filled with such a rush of tenderness and pity that you stop beside a lamppost and hang on for support.

You remember another Sunday morning in your old apartment on Cornelia Street when you woke to the smell of bread from the bakery downstairs. There was the smell of bread every morning, but this is the one you remember. You turned to see your wife sleeping beside you. Her mouth was open and her hair fell down across the pillow to your shoulder. The tanned skin of her shoulder was the color of bread fresh from the oven. Slowly, and with a growing sense of exhilaration, you remembered who you were. You were the boy and she was the girl, your college sweetheart. You weren't famous yet, but you had the rent covered, you had your favorite restaurant where the waitresses knew your name and you could bring your own bottle of wine. It all seemed to be just as you had pictured it when you had discussed plans for marriage and New York. The apartment with the pressed tin ceiling, the claw-footed bath, the windows that didn't quite fit the frame. It seemed almost as if you had wished for that very place. You leaned against your wife's shoulder. Later you would get up quietly, taking care not to wake her, and go downstairs for croissants and the Sunday *Times,* but for a long time you lay there breathing in the mingled scents of bread, hair and skin. You were in no hurry to get up. You knew it was a moment you wanted to savor. You didn't know how soon it would be over, that within a year she would go back to Michigan to file for divorce.

You approach the man on the loading dock. He stops working and watches you. You feel that there is something wrong with the way your legs are moving.

"Bread." This is what you say to him. You meant to say something more, but this is as much as you can get out.

"What was your first clue?" he says. He is a man who has served his country, you think, a man with a family somewhere outside the city. Small children. Pets. A garden.

"Could I have some? A roll or something?"

"Get out of here."

The man is about your size, except for the belly, which you don't have. "I'll trade you my jacket," you say. It is one hundred percent raw silk from Paul Stuart. You take it off, show him the label.

"You're crazy," the man says. Then he looks back into the warehouse. He picks up a bag of hard rolls and throws them at your feet. You hand him the jacket. He checks the label, sniffs the jacket, then tries it on.

You tear the bag open and the smell of warm dough rushes over you. The first bite sticks in your throat and you almost gag. You will have to go slowly. You will have to learn everything all over again.

1982

Smoke

That summer in New York, everyone was wearing yellow ties. The stock market was coming into a long bull run; over plates of blackened redfish, artists and gourmet-shop proprietors exchanged prognostications on the Dow. And on the sidewalks noble dark men from Senegal were selling watches, jewelry and fake Gucci bags. No one seemed to know how or why these Africans had come to town—certainly not the police, who tried with little success to explain in English the regulations governing street vendors and finally sent out a special French-speaking squad, who received the same blank smiles. It was a mystery. Also that summer, Corrine and Russell Callahan quit smoking.

Russell Callahan was not one of those wearing a tie. He had worn a tie to work his first day at the publishing house and sensed suspicion among his colleagues, as if this had signaled aspirations to a higher position, or a lunch date with someone already elevated. The polite bohemian look of the junior staff suited him just fine, and abetted his belief that he was engaged in the enterprise of literature. On clear days he saw himself as an underpaid hack in a windowless annex of a third-rate institution. After two promotions he presided over a series of travel books composed of plagiarism and speculation in equal parts. The current title, *Grand Hotels of America,* was typical: He and his associates plundered the literature in print, sent letters requesting brochures and then wrote colorful and informative descriptions designed to convey the impression of eyewitness reporting. Certain adjectives became severely dog-eared in the process. The words *comfortable, elegant* and *spacious* encountered outside the office made Russell feel queasy and unclean. In May, a month after the current project had been launched, two years after he'd started work, he'd been assigned a college intern, an eager young woman named Tracey Wheeler. As a mentor, he found himself assuming the air of a grizzled veteran, and Tracey's enthusiasm helped to focus his cynicism about his job.

Corrine worked as an analyst in a brokerage house. If she had been a man, she would've had an easier time of it her first year. She nearly quit on several occasions. But once she became comfortable with the work, she found that the men around her were vaguely embarrassed by the old cigars-and-brandy etiquette, and vulnerable to the suspicion that she and her female colleagues possessed a new rule book. Gifted with mathematical genius and a wildly superstitious nature, she found herself precisely equipped to understand the stock market. She felt near the center of things. The sweat and blood of labor, the rise and fall of steel pistons, the test-tube matchmaking of chemicals and cells—all the productive energies of the world, coded in binary electronic impulses, coursed through the towers of downtown Manhattan, accessible to her at any moment on the screen of her terminal. Corrine came to appreciate aspects of a style that had at first intimidated her: She started playing squash again, and began to enjoy the leathery, wood-paneled, masculine atmosphere of the clubs where she sometimes lunched with her superiors, under the increasingly benign gaze of dead rich men in gilt frames.

Corrine and Russell had met in college. They were married the summer of graduation, and in New York their East Side apartment became a supper club for former classmates. As a married couple, the Callahans were pioneers of the state of adulthood, but they were also indulgent hosts. They put out crystal with dinner and weren't appalled if a piece of stemware got smashed toward morning. Men who had found Corrine daunting in college, when she was an erotic totem figure, could now flirt with her safely, while women often confided in Russell, drawing him into the bedroom for urgent conferences. He had been known as a poet in college, his verse tending toward the Byronic. Now people who'd hardly known him at school fished up from the yearbook file of their memories words like *sensitive* and *artistic* when his name was mentioned.

A Memorial Day party had reached the stage at which the empty glasses were becoming ashtrays when Nancy Tanner drew Russell into the bedroom. As she tugged him by his fingers, he watched the thick tongue of blond hair licking the back of her shoulders and the edge of her red dress, and remembered again something he'd thought of earlier—that he'd actually slept with her one night in college.

"I guess you've noticed I haven't exactly been myself tonight."

She sat down on the bed and looked up at Russell, who thought that Nancy had been exactly herself, trolling her scooped neckline under the eyes of his friends, her laugh audible from any corner of the living room.

"My stepfather just went into the hospital with cancer. It's really got me down."

"That's rough." Russell didn't know what else to say, and Nancy seemed to be bearing up anyway.

"He used to take me to the Museum of Natural History. I always wanted to see the Eskimos, and I'd think how nice it would be to live in a little round igloo. I was a pretty ugly kid, but he'd call me his 'beauty queen.'" Actual tears were welling in her eyes, and Russell began to believe that she was genuinely upset, and to feel guilty for having doubted it.

"I haven't told anybody," she said, reaching for his hand, which he surrendered. "I just wanted you to know."

"I find it hard to believe the part about your being an ugly kid," Russell said, finally summoning some conviction. She wasn't nearly as good-looking as Corrine, he reminded himself, impressed with his own loyalty.

She stood up and dabbed at her eyes with her free hand. "Thank you, Russell." She leaned forward and kissed him. In temperature and duration, it was a little beyond what the situation called for.

"Do you have a cigarette," she asked when she drew away.

In the hallway, Bruce Davidoff was pounding on the bathroom door. Seeing Russell, he said, "Twenty minutes they've been in there." Back in the living room, Corrine was talking with Rick Cohen, cupping her hand in front of her to catch the ashes from her cigarette, nodding vigorously, her smoky exhalations dissipating like contrails of her rapid speech. He liked to watch her at parties, eavesdrop on her conversations with other men. At these times she seemed more like the woman he had proposed to than the one with whom he watched the eleven o'clock news.

"Symbols work in the market the same way they do in literature," Corrine was saying.

Frowning earnestly, Rick Cohen said, "I don't quite follow you there."

Corrine considered, taking a thoughtful drag on her cigarette. "There's, like, a symbolic order of things underneath the real economy. A kind of dream life of the economy that affects the market as much as the hard facts, the stats. The secret urges and desires of consumers and producers work up toward the surface. Market analysis is like dream interpretation. One thing stands for another thing—a new hairstyle means a rise in gold and a fall in bonds."

Rick Cohen nodded to mask his incomprehension. Russell moved toward the kitchen to check out the wine situation. Except for Corrine, the perfect hostess, who was splitting the difference, it seemed to him that the publishing people were all talking about the stock market and the financial people were talking about books and movies. By the end of the night everyone would be talking about real estate—co-ops, condominiums, summer rentals in the Hamptons. Igloos on West Seventy-ninth Street. *Spacious, comfortable, elegant.*

After the last guest had been shoveled into the elevator, Corrine and Russell sat on the couch in the living room and had a cigarette before turning in. Russell put a side of Hank Williams on the stereo to wind them down. Corrine said, "God, I'm tired. I don't think I can keep this up."

"Keep what up?"

"Everything." She stubbed out her butt and winced at the ashtray. "We've got to quit smoking. I feel like I'm dying."

Russell looked down at the cigarette between his fingers, as if it might suddenly show overt signs of hostility. He knew what she meant. It was a nasty habit. They had talked about quitting before, and Russell had always believed that someday they would.

"You're right," he said. "Let's quit."

To mark the end of the smoking era, Corrine insisted, they should hunt up all the cigarettes in the apartment and break them into pieces. Russell would just as soon have waited till morning, but he got up and joined her in the ritual, leaving one pack in the pocket of a blazer in his closet for insurance.

As they were loading the dishwasher, she said, "Phil Crane was hitting on me tonight."

"What do you mean, 'hitting on' you?"

"I mean he made it pretty clear that if I was interested, he was, too."
She sounded sad, as if she'd lived in a world where until tonight infidelity
hadn't existed.

"That son of a bitch. What did he say?"

"It doesn't matter." She then added she was sorry she'd mentioned it,
and made him promise he wouldn't say anything to Phil.

Later, in bed, she said, "Have you ever been unfaithful?"

"Of course not," he said, and then remembered kissing Nancy Tanner
in the bedroom.

Russell had first caught sight of Corrine at the top of a fraternity-house
staircase, leaning forward over the banister with a cigarette in her fingers,
looking down at a party that until that moment had seemed to Russell the
climax of his recent escape from home and parents. He'd been drinking
everything in sight, huddling with his new roommates, getting ridiculously
witty at the expense of girls he was just working up the courage to talk to.
Then he saw Corrine at the top of the stairs. He felt he knew her, everything essential in her character, though he'd never seen her before. He sti-
fled his first impulse, to point her out to his roommates, not sure that they
would see what he saw. Russell believed in his own secret aristocracy, a
refinement of soul and taste, which he had learned to keep to himself, and
which much later he would almost cease to believe in. Later he would realize that most of us believe in our ability to read character from physiog-
nomy. But now, while she ignored him from her aerie atop the staircase,
he read intelligence into her eyes, breeding into her nose, sensuality into
her lips, self-confidence into her languid pose. As he watched, a boy he
recognized as a campus icon appeared on the landing behind her, along
with another couple. She turned, and though he couldn't see her expression, though they didn't touch, the air of familiarity and possession between the two was unmistakable; and then both couples disappeared from
view, retreating to the real party, the actual center of the world, an action
that suddenly revealed the event on the lower floor to be a beer brawl, a
congress of the second-rate.

The social and academic accomplishments of his first semester, unknown to Corrine, were committed in her name. He didn't have to sleuth

hard for news of her, since she formed part of the group everyone talked about, which made her seem more desirable and less accessible, as did her liaison with Dino Signorelli. Signorelli was a basketball star and a druggie, a formidable combination. Tall, lanky and slightly bowlegged, he was alleged to be good-looking, although Russell disputed this judgment as he bided his time. He had four years.

Second semester, Corrine was in his English class, and without ever actually meeting, they became acquainted. At registration the next fall he ran into her coming out of the administration building and she greeted him as if they were friends. It was a hot September day. Russell admired the tan slopes of her legs, imagined that he could feel radiant heat from the waves of her long dark hair. He kept waiting for her to say good-bye. She kept talking.

They talked through lunch at the inn, filling the ashtray and emptying beer mugs. They talked about everything, but he couldn't stop thinking about her mouth, her lips on a cigarette, the clouds of smoke that she exhaled seeming to him the visible trace of inner fires. Still smoking and talking, they found themselves in Russell's dorm room, where they suddenly fell on each other—a crisis of lips and tongues and limbs that somehow stopped just short of the desired conclusion. She was still going out with Dino, and he was involved with a girl named Maggie Sloan.

Their romance fell dormant for two years, till Corrine called up one night and asked if she could come over. She said she'd broken up with Dino, although she had failed to make this clear to Dino, who began calling up and then coming over to shout drunken threats across the quad soon after Corrine had holed up in Russell's room. Although he was worried about Dino, Russell savored the atmosphere of siege, which lent an extra dimension of urgency, danger and illegitimacy to their union. He broke up with Maggie Sloan over the phone. Crying, Maggie appealed to the weight of tradition—the two years they'd been going out. Russell, with Corrine at his side, was sympathetic but firm.

Outside the dorm, it was a prematurely cold New England fall; red and yellow leaves slipped from the trees and twisted in the wind. For three days they left the room only to get food, staying in bed most of the time, drinking St. Pauli Girls, smoking Marlboros and talking. Russell had been a party smoker before, but Corrine smoked heavily, and he gradually caught up with her. They smoked before bed, after making love and then in the morning before they got out of bed, while Corrine told Russell her dreams in minute detail. Her imagination was curiously literal. She remembered everything—what people had been wearing, inconsistencies and illogic that seemed to surprise and annoy her a little, as if she expected dreams not to be so dreamlike. Her view of the waking world, though, was somewhat fantastic. Certain dates and names were fraught with unlikely significance for her, and, much more than Russell, the class poet, she believed in the power of words. When, after a week, Russell asked her to marry him, she made him solemnly promise never to use the word *divorce,* even in jest.

He might have taken her acceptance of his proposal to be impulsive, her renunciation of Dino to be precipitate, but he'd been in love with her for three years.

The campus seemed to split down the middle over the issue. Some sided with the new couple, some with Maggie Sloan and Dino, whose senior basketball season was visibly affected. He became a loud and dangerous regular at the pub, and one night, while Corrine and Russell were at a movie, watching French people smoke cigarettes and cheat on each other, he trashed Russell's room. Corrine and Russell developed a repertoire of Dino jokes. The day of their wedding, in June, two weeks after graduation, Dino was in a car wreck that landed him in the hospital for three weeks. Two years after graduation they heard that he was working as a representative for a feed and grain distributor in South Dakota.

The morning after the Memorial Day party, Corrine reminded Russell of their resolution, and for the first time since they'd known each other they had coffee without cigarettes. Russell left his first cup unfinished.

Corrine was staring wistfully at her blue Trivial Pursuit coffee mug. Somebody had given them a set of four for a wedding present—Russell tried to recall who it was. "Remember that Campbell's soup commercial?" she said. "Soup and sandwich, love and marriage, horse and carriage?"

Russell nodded. "They forgot caffeine and nicotine."

"I've heard it helps to drink a lot of water the first few days," Corrine said. "Cleans out the system."

Russell got half a glass of water down before he had to leave for work. "We've got to buy you some new shirts," Corrine said, fingering Russell's frayed collar when they were in the elevator.

"I've got plenty of shirts," Russell said.

"We can certainly afford a few more," Corrine replied.

One of us can, Russell thought.

At a little after eleven, Corrine called him at the office.

"How are you holding up?"

"All I can think about is cigarettes."

"Me, too."

Talking about it made it easier. Or else it made it harder. They weren't sure, but they agreed to call each other whenever they were feeling weak. Tracey Wheeler, Russell's intern, came over with a set of galleys she had proofread, smoking a cigarette; she must have seen him looking at it longingly.

"Do you want one?"

"No," he said. "I've quit. At least I'm trying." He felt sad hearing himself. The words seemed to mark the end of a chapter in his life, and made him feel older, relative to Tracey, in a way he didn't like. It sounded fussy, not at all in keeping with the swashbuckling air he assumed whenever she was around.

After Corrine hung up the phone, Duane Jones, an analyst who'd gone through training with her, came into the office and sat down. Corrine and Duane had made a habit of stealing a midmorning break together. This ritual had developed in part because they had been the only smokers in the training program. The first day of orientation she had done mental caricatures of the faces around the seminar table. Duane was *GQ subscriber, Dartmouth class officer, boxer shorts and jockstraps, lacrosse and skiing.* The fact that he smoked made him seem less buttoned-down. Now they often had lunch together, to the point that Russell was a little jealous. Russell always referred to Duane as "Dow Jones, Industrious Average." Duane called him "the Poet." This morning Duane sat down on the edge of the armchair across from the desk and adjusted one of his socks.

"Got any brilliant hunches this morning? Any dreams that might have a bearing on the Exchange?" He took out a new pack of Merits and slapped it against his wrist.

"Put out a heavy sell call on tobacco issues. We quit smoking."

"Say it ain't so. *You?*"

"Me and Russell both," she said, not certain whether she was being loyal or laying off part of the blame on her husband.

Duane stood up and straightened his yellow tie. "I won't tempt you," he said. At the door he turned and winked. "But if you change your mind . . ."

That night, Corrine cooked a deliberately bland meal of chicken, peas and rice. It was the first time they'd eaten at home in weeks. Corrine had read somewhere that red meat and spicy food aggravated the craving to smoke.

"I think we should try not to go out so much for a while," Corrine said as they ate in front of the television. On a rerun of *M*A*S*H,* Hawkeye was wooing a recalcitrant nurse.

"Have you noticed that on television hardly anyone smokes?" Russell asked.

Corrine nodded. "Moratorium on French movies."

"Absolutely."

"And it wouldn't hurt us to cut down on our drinking."

Russell agreed in principle, even as the ice shrank in his third drink of the evening. After ten hours of not smoking he had arrived home feeling like he'd been beaten up, and had reached immediately for the vodka.

Russell said, "The old soup-and-sandwich theorem."

"The thing we've got to realize," Corrine said, "is that you can't have 'just one cigarette.' If you break down once, you'll do it more easily the next time."

"Right." Russell was trying to watch *M*A*S*H.* Corrine had absolutely no television etiquette. She would talk through the first twenty-five minutes of a show and then ask Russell to explain what was going on. Her questions were a little maddening at the best of times. Tonight he was ready to hurl her out the window. Either that or grab the pack of smokes he'd left in his blazer in the closet.

"Russell?"

"Yeah?"

"Please listen just for one minute. This is important."

He looked at her. She was wearing her earnest, small-girl-wanting-to-know-why-the-sky-is-blue expression. He normally found this look devastating.

"Did you ever," she said, "when you were a kid, pretend that something really bad would happen to you if you did or didn't do something? You know, like if you didn't stay underwater till the far end of the pool, then somebody would die?"

"All the time," Russell said. "Thousands died."

"I'm serious. Let's pretend, like that, that something really bad will happen to us if we start smoking again."

"Okay," Russell said, turning back to the TV.

The next day, Corrine screamed at Russell for leaving his dirty socks in the bathroom sink. He got mad at her when he went to the kitchen and found the cupboards bare: How was he supposed to quit smoking if he couldn't have some toast or cereal to keep his mouth busy? She said the shopping wasn't her responsibility—she certainly brought home her share of the grocery money. Corrine stormed out of the house without saying good-bye, forgetting her briefcase. At the office, Russell bummed a cigarette from Tracey and almost smoked it out of spite, as a way of getting back at Corrine. He finally broke it in half and threw it in the wastebasket.

That night, when Corrine got home, their fight was not mentioned; they were both shy and solicitous, as if helping each other through a tropical illness. They cranked up the air conditioning and collapsed into bed at ten. Russell woke up at seven with a keen sensation of guilt. Corrine was not in bed; he heard the shower running in the bathroom. Gradually he began to recall a dream: He'd been at a party, and Nancy Tanner was beckoning to him from the door of an igloo. The purpose of the invitation was unclear. Russell walked toward the open door. It was surprisingly distant, and with each step he told himself he should turn around and run. When he finally reached her, she held out a cigarette and smiled lewdly.

Corrine came into the bedroom wearing a towel twisted around her head and another secured beneath her arms.

"We've got to do something about this water pressure," she said, sitting down at the vanity. Lying in bed, Russell could see her face in the mirror as she began to apply her makeup. She caught his eye and smiled. "What are you so serious about?"

"Nothing."

"I had the weirdest dream last night," she said.

"What else is new?" he said, glad that she was accustomed to his not re-membering his own dreams.

"I dreamed about cigarettes. Sneaking a smoke, like when I was a kid."

Applying a tool shaped like a miniature toothbrush to her eyebrow, she said, "Have you dreamed about it?" Her eyes zoomed in on his for just a moment, and reflexively he answered, "No."

"I guess I'm just perverse."

The next night, Corrine dreamed that she was standing on the side-walk, waiting for someone. The street was entirely deserted, though it was Park Avenue. Not another soul on the sidewalk, not a car on the street. A black limousine appeared several blocks down, cruising toward her slowly, finally pulling up and stopping by the curb in front of her. The glass was smoked; she couldn't see inside the car. The back window slipped down; a man's hand emerged from the open window, holding out a pack of cig-arettes. She looked up and down the street, then climbed into the limo. She couldn't make out the figure beside her in the backseat, but as the car pulled away from the curb, she saw Russell looking down from a window in an apartment building high above the street.

In the morning she didn't mention the dream. Getting Russell's attention had been difficult lately anyway.

That week was the first real scorcher of the summer; the humidity brimmed to the verge of rain, without breaking. Walking to the subway the next morning, Corrine could feel her damp blouse sticking to her shoul-der blades. In the station the men in yellow ties looked wilted, the women in their tailored suits defensive, as if they sensed that on days like this the subterranean violence of the city was likely to boil to the surface. She had forgotten to buy a paper, and as her gaze wandered idly around the plat-form, she suddenly met the eyes of a ragged man staring back at her with malevolent intensity. She turned away, staggered by that look, her mind unreeling images of carnage: muzzle flash, neon blood, filthy hands at her throat, boldface headlines. As the train rattled in, she couldn't help look-ing again; this time she saw a blank face and lusterless, unfocused eyes behind a tangle of matted hair.

A little after ten, Duane Jones stuck his head into her office. "Still being virtuous?"

She motioned him in and whispered, "Close the door."

He raised his eyebrows and pulled the door closed.

"Let me have a couple of drags."

"All this secrecy for a couple of drags?"

"Just light it, will you?"

He shook a Merit out of his pack and held it out to her.

"No, you light it."

Duane was enjoying this. He fired the cigarette with his lighter and held it out to her. "The idea being that if I light it, you won't have actually smoked a cigarette?"

"Humor me." She took the cigarette and inhaled deeply, held the smoke in her lungs. "Funny, it doesn't taste like I thought it would."

"You look great with a cigarette."

She took another, strictly experimental drag. This was more like what she had anticipated, a reunion clinch with a former lover. But she wasn't going to hop into bed. She just wanted to remind herself that she could live without this one passion. Corrine held the cigarette out to him, fortified with a new resolve. "Take it."

"I've got more."

"Take it."

"Okay." Duane noted the faint peach impression of Corrine's lips on the filter. He took a drag.

Corrine was sorting papers on her desk, suddenly all business. "I'm going to be here till midnight if I don't get moving," she said.

"You know where to find me," Duane said as he left.

The stock market was getting hot; Corrine was working ten- and twelve-hour days. With the advent of Tracey, Russell's workload was considerably lighter, but because of Corrine's job, they couldn't get out of the city much. At first he enjoyed being able to meet friends for drinks, watch TV or read at home without interruption, though as the summer wore on, he began to resent her scrupulous fidelity to her job. One hot night when she arrived home after midnight, he made insinuations, mentioning Duane Jones.

At the office he read the *Times* front to back before settling into his official chores, and sometimes he composed fake guide entries for his own amusement. One morning, as the temperature climbed toward ninety and the air conditioning became less and less a source of relief, he was writing one of these when Tracey came in with a new batch of her own vivid compositions.

"I think I've finished Michigan," she said. "What state are you working on?"

He read, " 'The Yukon Sheraton: charming, individual guest cottages constructed by native craftsmen of local materials; cozy interiors, domed ceilings, blubber heat. Year-round winter sports.' "

She forced a faint, nervous chuckle, and then became pensive. "Do you mind if I ask you something? Don't you think what we're doing is kind of, uh, unethical?"

"Think of yourself as a fiction writer."

"I just feel funny about it."

"Why do you think most of the senior staff is alcoholic?" This hard-boiled manner had become reflexive when he was talking with Tracey. He couldn't seem to be straightforward.

An inner struggle was working havoc on Tracey's normally cheerful demeanor. Russell couldn't help admiring the contours of her sleeveless top. "It's just, you're so talented," she gasped, as if delivering a horrible confession. She looked down at the floor. "I'm being a baby." She turned and walked out of the office. Russell stared at the door long after she had gone, then left early for lunch.

Lately, Russell had felt a great shroud of gauze enveloping him, preventing him from touching life and getting hold of it. He felt torpid and cloudy, but he didn't know whether this was a function of the oppressive weather, his decision to quit cigarettes or some subheading under "Changes of Life."

Nicotine withdrawal seemed to dull his mind and sharpen all his senses. The rancid smells of the summer streets had never seemed so acute. The vapors curling from mysterious apertures in the city streets were cruel reminders. Where there's smoke, he thought. He ate four or five times a day. Even his hearing seemed sharper: Noise bothered him, as if he were suffering from an extended hangover. And the women in their summer dresses on the sidewalks excited fantasies more detailed than any he'd experienced since adolescence.

Heading back from the coffee shop, he walked two blocks out of his way to follow a redhead in a yellow halter top. He entertained the notion of striking up a conversation, but then she walked out of his life, slipping smartly into the revolving door of an office building.

"What the hell is wrong with you?" he said aloud, standing in the middle of the sidewalk, drawing scrutiny from several pedestrians who seemed ready to offer opinions.

He absolutely had to have a cigarette.

Outside the newsstand, he stopped and reminded himself that he had already betrayed Corrine once today, if only in his imagination. He walked on, smokeless and repentant.

Waiting for a traffic light, he looked over the display of a sidewalk vendor, one of those West Africans he'd read about in the *Times,* and spotted among the wares a cigarette case made out of python skin. Tracey would be leaving soon to go back to school. He bought the case for ten bucks and took it back to work. Tracey was at her desk, eating a bowl of cottage cheese.

"It's beautiful," she said. "You're so thoughtful."

"It comes with strings attached," Russell said.

She looked up warily.

"Give me a cigarette, for Christ's sake, before I die." He smoked it in her cubicle, and they talked about her courses for the fall. Russell wished he were going back to college, wished that he were embarking on some open-ended adventure, as he savored what he told himself would be his last cigarette.

One morning toward the end of August, Corrine woke up at five a.m. in a terrible state. She'd had a dream: The apartment had gone up in flames. Her breath was short, and she was trembling. At first she wanted to stay home from work, and wanted Russell to stay with her, but Russell pointed out that if the fire was in the apartment building, they were both better off in their offices.

She called after lunch to see if he was okay. As he was leaving the office, he called to remind her about a cocktail party that night. The theme was *La Mort d'Été;* for some reason, all the parties had themes that year, as if conviviality were no longer its own reward.

"I won't be able to make it," she said. "You should go."

"Got a previous engagement?" Russell suggested.

"Don't be an idiot, okay? It's been a bitch of a day already."

"What should I wear," Russell asked.

"Wear a tie. They won't recognize you."

"Remind me what you look like, so I'll recognize you when you get home tonight."

"I'll be the girl with dark circles under her eyes."

After a moment, Russell said. "How's old Dow Jones?"

"The market's up four points."

"I mean the stiff with the starched boxer shorts."

"Duane is very busy, like the rest of us."

"I don't hear you denying my surmise about his undershorts."

"Would you like me to check?"

"No, that's okay."

"I'll see you when I get home. And no smoking."

Russell planned to make a quick appearance, but after two hours the party was just hitting optimal cruise altitude. The invitation had said *Cocktails six to eight,* but food and booze were plentiful and everyone was canceling dinner reservations. Rick Cohen had some blow that he let Russell in on. By ten, Russell had bummed three cigarettes. He felt guilty about the first. The second came after he visited the bathroom with Rick, and obviously that didn't count. Smoking the third, he decided that he was glad Corrine wasn't with him: He could be weak without spoiling her resolution.

Nancy Tanner arrived wearing one of her strapless dresses. She was flashy in a way that reminded him of stewardesses—a stylized, overly wrought femininity that he associated with the service sector. Her obviousness made him feel virtuous. If Nancy were a film, she'd be *Superman II.* Corrine was, say, *Hiroshima Mon Amour.*

Nancy spotted Russell and winked, then caught up with him at the bar. "Behaving yourself?" she asked.

"Trying."

"Haven't seen you since . . . you remember."

For a moment he thought she meant the dream. "How's your stepfather?" he said.

"My stepfather?" She looked baffled for a moment. "Oh, he's fine. He's better. Where's Corrine?" she asked, much as one asks after a tagalong sibling who has finally been given the slip. He felt that if he didn't challenge her tone, he'd be implicated in a developing conspiracy.

"Working," he said.

"All work and no play . . ." She arched her eyebrows and then escaped before he could register his indignation. That was going a little too far. He got a drink and plunged back into the crowd.

"We were just wondering what happened to Dino Signorelli," Rick said when Russell joined his circle.

"Last I heard, he was selling seeds in South Dakota."

"Spilling seed, you mean," Tom Dalton said.

"That guy could fake a guard like nobody's business."

"He could bend an elbow, too," Russell observed.

Russell was listening to Skip Blackman's girlfriend—who had never looked so good—talk about her incredibly boring job when Nancy touched his shoulder.

"Got a cigarette?"

Russell was about to say he'd quit, but he deftly turned the reflex into a negative monosyllable.

"Let's find some," she said, her sparkling eyes seeming to make this simple notion witty and daring.

She took his hand and he followed her, feeling crisp and purposeful in his movements, negotiating the tight throng of bodies and the carpeted floor like an expert skier rounding the poles of a hazardous slalom course.

"I think I've got some in my coat," she said, leading him into one of the bedrooms. She closed the door behind them. He reached for her and drew her face to his, his feeling of precision and control dissolving, the ski slope giving way to a free fall through the clouds.

Shortly before midnight, Russell reeled toward home. His legs were wobbly, but this was a transparent defensive strategy, a white lie on the part of the body on behalf of the guilty mind. It didn't work. His head was utterly clear, an acoustically perfect amphitheater for the voices of accusation. He told himself that it could have been worse; they hadn't closed the deal, those few minutes in the bedroom. But they might have. They were well en route when somebody came in looking for a coat.

He took off his shoes in the hallway, eased the keys into the locks. The apartment was dark. He crept to the bedroom, which was empty. He tried to feel relief, told himself he had a second chance. He couldn't have faced Corrine tonight. She would have seen right through him.

Russell was in bed when he heard the stealthy tick of keys and tumblers. With one eye half-open, he watched the door of the bedroom. The hallway remained dark. Eventually he heard her tiptoe into the bedroom; accustomed to the dark, he could see that she was carrying her shoes.

He pretended to be asleep as she undressed and slipped into bed beside him. He wanted to take her in his arms.

Corrine lay very still beside him. He waited for her rapid breathing to resolve itself into the rhythm of sleep; she could fall asleep on a dime. Instead, her breath became shorter, more irregular, until he realized that she was crying. Somehow she knew. Russell cursed himself for violating this intimacy, which over the years had become so finely tuned that she was able, even in the silent dark, to sense a change in pitch. Then he decided that was absurd. He began to wonder where she'd been all night.

"Oh, Russell," she said. "I'm sorry."

He lifted himself on an elbow and tried to see her face in the dark.

"What do you mean, you're sorry?"

She began to sob. Her back was heaving. She was trying to say something, but her words were muffled by the pillow.

"What?" he said.

When she finally spoke, it was in a dull, featureless voice that he had never heard before. "Tonight," she said, "tonight I had a couple cigarettes. . . ."

She said more, but the sound of her voice was already fading away as Russell lay back on his own pillow, feeling the chill blast of the air conditioner on his face, imagining himself henceforth as a wanderer of frozen landscapes, and in searching for a suitably tragic picture of himself, he came at length, unexpectedly, upon the image of Dino Signorelli, standing alone on a treeless prairie, hatless, leaning into the cold wind.

Invisible Fences

So I come in the front door about one in the morning, after stopping to get some beer and cigarettes, and I hear these sounds from the living room. Two kinds, a low guttural growl that doesn't even sound human and a high-pitched chirping that some kind of distressed tropical bird might make but which I recognize as the love song of my wife, Susan.

"Honey?" I call.

I walk into the living room and this is what I see: Susan naked on the floor, entwined with an equally naked stranger.

"Jesus, Susan."

The man lifts his head from between her legs and regards me with mild alarm.

"You could've waited till I got back," I say.

"I'm sorry," she says breathlessly. "I guess I got carried away."

Meanwhile, the man—I think he said his name was Marvin—puts his hand on the back of her head and directs her back to her task.

Trying to get over my pique, I kneel down on the floor beside them.

"You get those Newport Lights," he asks, thrusting his hips into Susan's face.

Sometimes I think the difference between what we want and what we're afraid of is about the width of an eyelash.

It's amazing what human beings get accustomed to—how quickly the bizarre, the absurd and the perverse can become routine. People have become accustomed to torture, or so I've read, bonded with their tormentors, the wielders of pliers and electricity.

It happens gradually. Maybe one day you get high with another couple and there's a certain amount of joking and talk, and the next thing you know, the guy's making out with your wife and you're kind of freaked-out about it. You and his wife go at it a little, and when you look up, he's massaging your wife's breast. At that point you break it up. Enough is enough. But later you find yourself thinking about the man's hand on your wife's breast. I don't know—could you imagine something like that? I'm just throwing it out as a hypothetical. A possible scenario.

The thing is, I consider myself a pretty normal guy. I manage the bookstore in the Sunset Mall. My parents are still married. My wife, Susan, is a lawyer who works for the city. We have two kids, Cara and Bucky, both of them baptized at the First Episcopal, and while I can't say we go to church every Sunday, we're there for the big holy days. We live in a place where people ask on first meeting what church you go to, a city that has far more churches than saloons. Most of the Bibles in the country are published here, and so are most of the country songs. We also have more strip clubs and massage parlors and adult bookstores than you'd think possible, all tucked away downtown, just off the cloverleaf where the interstate hits the bypass. Locals will tell you it's all out-of-towners at those places, but I'm not convinced. You might even make a case for some kind of correlation between all the pay sex and all these churches, though I wouldn't make it in public, since there's also a hell of a lot of guns around here. I myself have a .38 revolver between the mattress and the box spring and a twelve-gauge Remington pump in the gun cabinet, which would be considered about average. So far I haven't used the .38 for anything, but it makes me feel safer knowing it's there, even though the statistics tell me otherwise. I use the twelve-gauge for ducks; every winter I go with some college buddies down to Reelfoot Lake. We spend four days drinking and shooting, bitching about our wives and our jobs, talking about fish we've caught, and others we should've caught, and occasionally about the girls we've nailed, but more often about the ones who got away.

Sometimes, deep into the sour mash after a morning of freezing in the duck blind, things can get pretty confessional. But in my experience, men are more circumspect when it comes to their sex lives than women are. Susan once let me hide in the closet while she threw a baby shower for her friend Genevra, and all I can say is, it scared me, the shit they were saying. Length and width and how many times. Not that it didn't turn me on, especially when Susan started bragging on me. I'm sitting there next to the dusty-smelling vacuum cleaner with a hard-on. But these women were just, I don't know, clinical, whereas men speak in generalities and hypotheticals. Like, *Hey, tell you what. I'd love to fuck that waitress down at the Trace.* Or, *What about that Penélope Cruz, whooee! I could wear her out.* As for me, I've never been so shitfaced as to share any intimate love details with the boys. Not that I haven't fantasized and even talked with Susan about sharing more than the details with my buddies. Susan gets it—she thinks it's sexy. But there's fantasy and there's reality. Even when you're pushing the frontier between them—especially when you're pushing it—it's important to know where the one leaves off and the other begins. I may be a pervert, but I'm not an idiot. I can't help wondering, though, what happens late at night on their living room floors.

So anyway, on Friday nights Susan's mom takes the kids and we head out on the town. We go different places, often hitting three or four spots in a night. Susan dresses up, puts on makeup and her finest lingerie. Usually I buy the lingerie, or we pick it together out of the Victoria's Secret catalog. "Do you like the pink, or the black and white," she'll ask, standing in front of the mirror. She has a superb little body. Petite but voluptuous—and I don't mean fat. I mean five four, with curves like Daytona. I still can't look at her breasts without my breath catching in my throat. Sometimes I get faint seeing them suddenly. I mean, really. A few of the girls at work have asked her if she has implants, not that they're so big—she sort of fluctuates between B and C—but because they just seem a little too good to be true. Sometimes I can't believe they're mine, so to speak. It must be kind of like marrying money. You think, Whoa, what did I do to deserve these? When I saw guys looking at them, it made me proud. Maybe that was the beginning of something. Sometimes the guys look in a lecherous way, but more often they're secretive and pained, like dogs trying to sneak up on a garbage can. It's like, God, what I wouldn't give to get a good look at those, to stroke them, to put my mouth on those nipples. I admit it: I encourage her to wear tops that show her off, buy her tight little low-cut things.

So, on Friday nights I get home as quick as I can. I'm usually at the house by six, but on this particular night I'm a few minutes late. Darlene, the baby-sitter, is hovering by the front door with her jacket on, all antsy to smoke a cigarette and drive over to her boyfriend's house. My friend Hal always talks about how hot she is and how he'd be happy to drive her home sometime, but I don't know, it's not my thing. She has unnaturally yellow hair and a deep cavernous navel that she displays at all times, winter and summer, beneath short little T-shirts and halters. Sometimes I can't believe I entrust my kids to this little tramp, but so far they haven't broken any bones, collected any tattoos or ingested anything too terribly toxic on her watch. On the other hand, why is Cara lying on the floor, sobbing?

"Bongo saw another dog and he chased it," Darlene says. "I tried to catch him, but he got away."

Appearing in the doorway, trailing her blanket, Cara confirms this. "Bongo run away."

"He'll come back," I say.

Every once in a while he gets so worked up by some dog in the street that he forgets about the Invisible Fence that encircles the property. Getting zapped as he crosses the line makes him even crazier. Fucking Bongo.

"Darlene says he'll get smooshed by a car."

"Where's your brother?"

"Darlene says dogs can't go to heaven."

"Honey, Darlene's no expert on heaven," I say.

Susan's still at work, so I fire up a box of Kraft mac and cheese for the kids, the leftovers of which I eat myself, then pack them up for their big night at grandma's, Bucky with his Game Boy, his Pokémon cards and figures, his SpongeBob pajamas, two pairs of jeans, two T-shirts and two sweatshirts, one that says Vanderbilt and the other UT, equal time for Susan's alma mater and mine. Cara packs her own Hello Kitty backpack: Barbie nightgown, Barbie and Chrissie dolls, the usual stuff.

"Come on, come on," I say.

"I don't want to go to Grammy's," Bucky says.

"Sure you do," I say. "You always have fun at Grammy's."

"Her house smells funny."

"What about Bongo?" Cara whines.

I've forgotten about that. "Okay, let's go find Bongo."

We walk out front and look up and down the street, though I don't really expect to see the crazy mutt—the last time he ran off, we got a call two days later from the next town over. Bongo's a wanderer. He's also a biter, which is why we always make sure he's out in the backyard before we bring anybody over on Friday nights.

"I'm sure Bongo will come home soon," I say, but Cara's still weepy when I drive them over to Susan's mother's house.

"What have you kids got planned for tonight," Susan's mother asks me after we have planted the kids in front of the TV.

"Just going to have a bite and hit the town."

"I think it's great the way you two have your together time. It's important to keep the romance alive. Some couples, the kids come along, they just let the spark go out." I'm afraid she's going to start talking about her ex, Susan's dad, an epic horndog who has achieved sainthood since he succumbed to lung cancer a few years back.

"We're trying to keep it fresh," I say.

"It takes work," she says. "You can't just take it for granted. Buck and I, we had our problems, Lord knows. But every Saturday night he'd take me to dinner at the club."

If I were her, I wouldn't bring up the club; there's a famous story about my father-in-law and one of the waitresses. "He was a hell of a guy, old Buck," I say.

"I'm not saying he was perfect."

She's getting misty-eyed, now, and it's absolutely imperative to change the subject before I get the full-blown eulogy. "He was smart enough to marry you at least."

"I have my faults, too. Believe me, I know."

"Not in my book." I give her a big hug, being careful not to crush her prominent calcium-deficient bones. "You've been great to us."

"I'm only glad I can be here to help."

"You know how grateful we are," I say. "And the kids love it, too."

As if to disprove this assertion, Bucky intercepts me on the front step and attaches himself to my leg, and it takes a good ten minutes to get him settled down again.

Back at the house, Susan is tweaking herself in front of her vanity.

"Turn around."

She puts her arms down and stares at herself in the mirror.

"Susan? Let me see."

She's wearing a low-cut white cotton halter with low-rider Diesel jeans.

Sexy without being theatrical. Her makeup seems subdued. I feel like she could go heavier on the eyeliner. Finally, she stands up and walks to the closet.

"What's the matter?"

She stands at the closet door. "Nothing," she says. "Long day. I'm a little tired."

"We can take care of that," I say, showing her the gram vial I copped at lunchtime.

"Maybe later," she says. She's still standing there, looking into the closet as if at some profound vista.

I walk over behind her, put my hands on her shoulders and rub her neck and her delts. There's nothing to see in the closet except two rows of hanging clothes, hers and mine. "Sure you don't want a little pick-me-up?"

"What the hell," she says, turning around and flashing a wan smile. I tap some onto the fleshy part between her thumb and forefinger. She huffs it up and holds out the other hand. "Have you seen Bongo," she asks.

"He broke out," I say, generously anointing her other hand. "Remind me to turn off the fence so he can get back in."

By the time we get to the Corral, a sprawling C & W dance hall about ten miles west on the interstate, Susan seems to have shaken her funk. We order a couple of platinum margaritas and survey the crowd. We haven't been here in four or five months. Last time, Susan picked up a guy who was a lineman for the phone company, but he was shitfaced by the time she got him out of there and ended up puking in the parking lot, which is where we left him, sprawled over the hood of his truck, drooling on his snakeskin Justins. Earlier, he'd been telling Susan all about the boots, which he'd just bought that afternoon at the outlet in Gallatin.

"Lone Ranger at four o'clock," I shout over Tim McGraw's "Cowboy in Me," indicating a guy down the bar in a shiny orange leather jacket who's been checking her out.

"Let's dance," she says.

"Okay." I finish my drink and lead her out to the floor. We shimmy to Carrie Underwood's "Before He Cheats," or rather, she shimmies and I sway. I look around to see if Susan's got an audience, and sure enough, Mr. Leather Jacket is standing at the edge of the dance floor, watching. At the end of the song, I lean over and whisper in her ear. "Keep dancing," I say. I turn and walk away, heading to the men's room, even though I don't really have to go. I linger there and fix my hair in the mirror, then go back to the bar and order another margarita, forcing myself not to look over to the dance floor until I've paid for my drink and taken a long swallow. Sure enough, now he's dancing with Susan, grinding up against her while Alison Krauss sings "Simple Love." I feel a tingling buzz that's like the first wave of a coke rush.

What can I say. It turns me on watching Susan turn other men on. Is that so hard to understand?

I settle in at a table where I can occasionally glimpse them through the crowd. Susan eventually spots me and maneuvers her partner closer so I have a better view, then starts making out with him. I mean really sucking face. This guy can't believe his luck. Which is, strangely enough, just how I feel.

But then, just to torture me, she drifts back into the sea of bodies until I can't see either one of them anymore. It's making me crazy. I wait a few minutes, then circle the place, but I can't see them anywhere. What the hell? I look everywhere. Did she take him out to the parking lot? On a sudden inspiration I bolt for the men's room. Sometimes she trash-talks about doing some guy in the men's room because she knows it's a turn-on in theory, but in real life that's a taboo, one of the boundaries we've established. When you're playing outside the regular borders, it's important to have rules and boundaries. We've learned that the hard way.

I stop at the men's room door and take a deep breath, trying to compose myself, to think what I'll do if I find them in there. I push the door open. A couple of good old boys in Stetsons, propping themselves up against the urinals. No one in the stalls, which is a relief, I think.

I finally find her at the bar, alone, sucking down a margarita.

"So?"

She shakes her head. "Let's get out of here."

In the car, she says, "He told me he wanted me to meet his mother."

"He must get a lot of pussy with that line."

"Actually, I think he was serious."

"So where to?"

"Let's go to Tini's," she says.

"You sure?" I'm still sober enough to feel some trepidation about Tini's. The last time we were there, somebody got stabbed, although we didn't actually see the fight.

"If we're going to go for it, let's just go for it." Her earlier diffidence seems to have evaporated. "Turn it up," she says, when "Mr. Bright Eyes" comes on Lightning 100.

It's early for Tini's, but the Friday-night house band's already playing. We settle in at a table and order drinks. Mostly old drunks and a few friends of the band so far. A fat mama in a gold bustier calls out, "Tell it!" and "Play it!" in between choruses. It would be easy to imagine these losers are playing the same song over and over, the same twelve bars on an interminable loop, but every once in a while a lyric emerges or the guitarist cuts loose and at some point I make out Sonny Boy Williamson's "Fattening Frogs for Snakes."

Then I see him approaching, rolling like an aspiring pimp, gold chains bouncing on a voluminous white T-shirt. He grabs the empty chair at our table and flips it around, then straddles the back of it. He's not much more than twenty, if that, very dark-skinned.

"I seen you here before," he says.

"That's possible," I say.

"Yeah, I seen you all right."

"I'm Susan, and this is Dean."

It's true: I remember him. We partied with one of his friends.

"I'm dry," he says.

"What are you drinking," I ask.

"Yac and Coke."

"I'll get you one."

"Hennessy," he says, getting cocky.

I look over at Susan to see if it's okay. You need to have signals; you've got to be able to communicate. But she seems fine. In fact, she seems more than fine, with that blurry, lascivious look on her face. How the hell much did she drink at the Corral anyway?

I'm waiting at the bar, listening to "Little Red Rooster," when I hear three little pops. It's like the witnesses always say when you see them on the eleven o'clock news; it's like firecrackers, or maybe somebody snapping a whip outside the door, so I don't even think about it until a young guy with a reddish Afro in a puffy black parka comes running in the bar, shouting, and even though I can't make out a word of what he's saying, the place starts clearing out. Suddenly, Susan and the kid are beside me.

"There's been a shooting in the parking lot," she says. "Derek needs a ride." She doesn't quite wink at me, but she's got that little smirk on her face.

Outside, I catch a glimpse of legs on the ground between the legs of the onlookers, bright white Nikes splayed on the pavement.

"I don't need that shit," the kid says as we're driving away. "You know what I'm sayin'?"

"I hear you."

"You can drop me on Broadway."

"Whatever," I say.

"Or you could come to our place," Susan says. "We could party."

"I got a bottle of Courvoisier," I say.

"XO?"

"I think. It might be VSOP."

"Y'all got any reefer?"

"We've got some fine bud, plus some killer blow."

He seems to be considering the offer, weighing the pros and cons. I try to find him in the rearview, but it's too dark.

"Where y'all's crib?"

"We're over in Green Hills."

He snorts. "More like the white hills."

"Len Simmons lives down the street," Susan says. I turn toward her and roll my eyes, but she's not looking at me. Jesus Christ, I think. But the kid seems impressed that we have a Heisman winner in the nabe.

"Not bad," he says, surveying the house from the vantage of the entry hall.

"Yac and Coke?"

"To start with."

"Susan will show you around," I say, handing him a Baggie with buds and papers.

When I return with the drinks, they're sitting beside each other on the living room couch. Derek is sealing the joint with his tongue.

"What's a crib like this set you back?"

"We bought in '01, back before the big run-up."

He lights up the joint, inhales and hands it to Susan. "I'm gonna get me a house like this."

"It's a great investment."

Susan inhales deeply on the joint while I chop the coke on the coffee table.

Derek nods at me. "We oughta call Len Simmons."

"His daughter goes to school with our little boy."

"That wife of his, she look like she know how to get down."

"She's hot," I say, handing him a length of straw.

"White folks is all about the powder," he says. "Where I comes from, s'all about the rock. You ever smoke that rock?" He leans over and snorts a couple of lines, then hands the straw to Susan.

She gathers her hair behind her head and starts to lean forward. "Would you hold my hair?" she asks.

"No problem." He holds her hair as she crouches down over the coffee table. I've always found this incredibly sexy. When she comes back up, she strokes his arm and kisses him on the cheek. I get the feeling he's just beginning to get a sense of the possibilities.

"What kind of party y'all got in mind here?"

"Just hanging out, getting down," I say.

" 'Cause I ain't into no dudes."

"You're a ladies' man," Susan says.

I shake my head. "Me, neither," I say.

"I ain't ridin' no trike."

"I hear you."

Derek scratches his chin contemplatively. "We need some tunes."

"Coming right up."

I figure *The Black Album* is a pretty safe choice. Marvin Gaye or Al Green might just be pushing it, at least to start. Susan's bending down over the coffee table. Derek takes her hair in one hand and puts the other beneath her breast. This time when she comes up, she starts to kiss him. I hold my breath, standing beside the sound system. This is no time to call attention to my presence. I wish I could say why this thrills me, why I love seeing my wife sticking her tongue in this stranger's mouth, especially when he has skin the color of French-roast coffee. They make out for three or four minutes while I stand there. Then I see Susan going for his belt. By now I have inched a few feet closer, but she has her back to me, blocking most of my view, as she slides his pants down below his knees. At this point I have to remember to keep breathing. Still in stealth mode, I move around the coffee table to improve my angle.

I hear Bongo just moments before I see him; he's barking frantically even before he launches himself at this man who is wrestling with Susan on the couch. The ensuing racket is terrifying, Susan screaming, Derek cursing, Bongo snarling and barking, until he comes flying in my direction, yelping as he lands at my feet. I grab hold of him as he tries to make another run at Derek.

"Motherfucker bit me. Jesus Christ. I'm bleeding. That fuckin' dog bit my ass."

Susan is examining his thigh, which seems to have been the part of his body that actually sustained the wound.

"Fuckin' crazy," he says. "Where'd that racist motherfucker come from?"

"I think we need to get him to the emergency room," Susan says to me. Bongo's still barking and lunging as I clutch his collar.

"You people are way fucked-up," Derek says as we lay rubber out of the cul-de-sac. "What the fuck's wrong with y'all?"

There's not much to say to this, so far as I can see. I hear a sniffling sound from Susan's side of the car and I see that she's crying.

"Fuckin' crazy white folks."

"It's true," she says.

I feel like pointing out that he was down with the program until Bongo bit his ass, but I decide to keep my counsel. I mean, nobody was holding a gun to his head, were they?

Derek can't contain his indignation. "Whassup with you people? You pick up strange white dudes, too, or is this some Mandingo thing?"

"No, it's not." Susan wipes her nose and sniffles. "It's not just—it's both."

She looks over at me, as if trying to read something in my face.

"I think maybe, I don't know, Dean likes it better when it's, you know, a black guy."

"Me? What are you talking about? Don't put that on me. You started that."

"If I did, it was only because I felt like you wanted me to."

"I never said that."

"You never complained, either."

"And that gave you license to go for it," I say. "Which is obviously what you wanted."

"Deeply fucked-up, man."

"Hey," I say, "we never forced anybody."

He leans forward in the backseat and slaps me on the head. "Shut the fuck up," he says. "I want to hear what she say." To Susan, he says, "You into this shit?"

She looks over at me, and I don't like what I'm seeing.

"I don't know. I guess I've gotten used to it."

"Gotten *used* to it?" I can't believe this. She's completely rewriting history.

"You know, after a while it was just . . . something we did."

"Give me a fucking break," I say. "You love getting fucked by strange men. And you really love getting fucked by strange black men."

Derek smacks me again, harder this time. "Shut up and keep your eyes on the fuckin' road. And show the lady some goddamn respect."

We're coming up on the hospital.

"How long's this shit been goin' on?"

Susan is slumped over in the front seat, as if she's suddenly gone boneless. I notice the little blond Kelly doll sprawled, arms and legs akimbo, at her feet. I'm getting fed up with this inquisition. I mean, what the hell difference does it make how long it's been going on, and what does he care?

"I can tell you exactly," Susan says. "It was after Dean . . ." Her voice catches and a sob escapes her pursed lips. "It was after he found out about something I'd done."

"Somethin' you done? Or some*one* you done?"

"Well, yeah, someone I'd slept with."

"What are you talking about?" I say. "What does that have to do with anything?"

"Oh come on. As if you don't remember."

"I don't know what the hell you're talking about."

"I'm *talking* about you finding out about me and Cleve Thompson."

"What the fuck does that have to do with anything? And why are we talking about this now?"

"Come on, Dean. That's what really started this. How long was it between you finding out about Cleve and you telling me to pick up that man at the Last Exit."

"That was like . . . That was way later. And you're the one who brought up the idea of coming on to that guy."

"Oh please."

"Even if it was my idea, which it wasn't, I didn't hear you protesting real loud."

She turns and gives me a look, which is worse than anything that's led up to it. "No, you didn't," she says. "But let's at least all be honest about our motivations here, for a change."

None of us says much of anything as we wait in the ER. I give them my credit card because Derek doesn't have any insurance and it seems we're pretty much responsible for his being here. I'm wondering if the guy who got shot at Tini's came through here. Across from us is a rail-thin country boy in a bloody NASCAR T-shirt, clutching a bloody towel to his neck, sitting beside his fat mother, who's wearing a voluminous pastel sweatsuit. "I done told you," she says several times over the next ten minutes.

Finally, after they take Derek in to be stitched up, I turn to Susan. "You don't really believe what you said back there," I say. "That our . . . little adventures . . . that I'm, what? Punishing you?"

"For Christ's sake, Dean. Wake up."

Forty minutes later, I'm dropping Derek off at a bar on Sixth Street.

"Why'n cha come on with me?" he says to Susan.

To my amazement, she seems to be considering the offer. "I should."

"Give old numbnuts here somethin' to think about."

"I appreciate the offer."

"You know where to find me," he says, climbing out of the back and slamming the door.

I can't imagine what to say now. Neither, apparently, can Susan. We drive past the bright neon signs of one franchise after another in silence. It's a little past one. A gibbous harvest moon hangs over the interstate, leaking an orange glow into the surrounding sky. It's a beautiful sight, even now.

I look across at Susan. A shiny tear moves down her cheek. "What?" I say.

"I was just thinking of the first time."

I almost ask the first time for what, but I don't. That would be hostile. Instead, I pull over in front of the Outback Steakhouse.

"You remember?"

"Of course I do."

"We drove up to your uncle's place on the lake. In that terrible car of yours."

I remember all right. It was a Friday night, the week before graduation. We drove up to Center Lake in my old Subaru, which had a hole in the muffler and smelled inside of gas. The mattress in the bunk bed at the shack smelled like mildew, but my new sleeping bag had a fresh, synthetic smell that was eventually canceled out by the heady, deeply organic funk of our mingled secretions—the first time I'd encountered the smell of sex. I remember the furious creaking of the rusty old bed and the lapping of waves on the shore outside and, eventually, afterward, Susan's muffled sniffles. I didn't know what to think except that somehow I'd failed. "What's the matter?" I'd finally asked. "I'm fine," she'd said, wrapping herself around me in the sleeping bag, her cheek wet against my shoulder.

"You thought I was unhappy," she says now, as if she's reading my mind.

"What was I supposed to think?"

"I was crying because it was perfect, and because it would never be the first time again."

I shake my head and shrug.

"I was crying because I didn't want to ever lose you, but I knew that if we stayed together, sooner or later we would hurt each other."

"You didn't lose me," I say hopefully, reaching over and taking her hand.

"Yeah," she says, wiping the tear from her face. "Actually, I think I did."

"We can go back."

Susan shakes her head and stares straight ahead out the windshield.

I look out, too, trying to remember what made it a harvest moon, and wondering if it was waxing or waning. Of course I remember when I found out about Cleve Thompson. I thought I'd lose my mind. I thought my heart would burst with rage and grief. I couldn't sleep for days. I imagined the two of them in every possible position, in every nuance of lust and carnality. I raged, wept, broke her entire collection of Staffordshire fig- urines, demanded an explanation. She sent the children to her mother's and I took three days off work. I couldn't eat, and when I did, I vomited. I asked if she still loved me and didn't believe her when she said she did. How could she fuck him if she loved me? I couldn't reconcile the two facts. I thought I would die of heartbreak. I'd always believed I would be her only.

So I made her tell me everything. I was tortured by visions of her treach- ery, by my own roiling, filthy imagination. The reality could hardly be worse, I figured. I demanded more and more details. I needed to picture her, with him, in the explicit postures of betrayal. I made her repeat and expand on the sordid details, asking questions, demanding more and more specificity, until I could see it all, or believed I could, as clearly as a porn clip, until I could almost imagine it was something I'd created for my own pleasure . . . until we both realized that the actual circumstances would never be enough to match the images in my head.

I needed more.

2007

The Madonna of Turkey Season

It came to seem like our own special Thanksgiving tradition—one of us in-evitably behaving very badly. The role was passed around the table from year to year like some kind of ceremonial torch, or a seasonal virus: the weeping and gnashing of teeth, the breaking of glass, the hurling of accu-sations, the final nosedive into the mashed potatoes or the shag carpet. Sometimes it even fell to our guests—friends, girlfriends, wives—the dis-ease apparently communicable. We were three boys who'd lost their mother—four if you counted Dad, five if you counted Brian's best friend, Foster Creel, who'd lost his own mother about the same time we did and always spent Thanksgiving with us—and for many years there had been no one to tell us not to pour that pivotal seventh drink, not to chew with our mouths open, not to say *fuck* at the dinner table.

We kept bringing other women to the table to try to fill the hole, but they were never able to impose peace for long. Sometimes they were cat-alysts, and occasionally they even initiated the hostilities—perhaps their way of trying to fit in. My father never brought another woman to the table, though many tried to invite themselves, and our young girlfriends re-marked on how handsome he was and what a waste it was. "I had my great love, and how could I settle for anything less?" he'd say as he poured him-self another Smirnoff and the neighbor widows and divorcées dashed themselves against the windowpanes like birds.

Sometimes, although not always, the mayhem boiled up again at Christ-mas, in the sacramental presence of yet another turkey carcass, with a new brother or guest in the role of incendiary device, though memories of the most recent Thanksgiving were often enough to spare us the spectacle for another eleven months. I suppose we all had a lot to be thankful for, socioeconomically speaking, but for some reason we chose to dwell instead on our grievances. *How come you went to Aidan's high school play and not mine? How could you have fucked Karen Watley when you knew I was in love with her?*

We would arrive Tuesday night from prep school or college, or on Wednesday night from New York, where we were working at a bank while writing a play, or from Vermont, where we were building a log cabin with our roommate from Middlebury before heading up to Stowe at first snow for a season of ski bumming. Dad would take the latter part of the week off, until he retired, which was when things really became dangerous. The riotous foliage that briefly enflamed the chaste New England hills was long gone, leaving the monochromatic landscape of winter: the gray stone walls of the early settlers, the silver trunks of the maples, the white columns of birch.

Manly hugs were exchanged at the kitchen door. Cocktails were offered and accepted. Girlfriends and roommates were introduced. The year of the big snow, footwear was scraped on the blade of the cast-iron boot cleaner outside the door. Dad was particularly pleased with this implement, and always pointed it out to guests, not because he was particularly fastidious about mud and snow, but because it seemed to signify all the supposed charm and tradition of old New England (as opposed to, say, its intolerance of immigrants and its burning of young girls at the stake), although he'd bought this particular boot scraper once upon a time at the local True Value hardware store. But somehow Dad had convinced himself that it had been planted here by the early settlers of the Massachusetts Bay Colony, in between skirmishes with the Wampanoags and the Mohicans. He liked to think of himself as an old Yankee, despite the fact that when his grandfathers arrived in Boston, the windows were full of NO IRISH NEED APPLY signs and they weren't likely to be invited to scrape their boots at anybody's front door. A century and a half later, though, we lived in a big white house with green shutters, which Dad inevitably described as "Colonial," though it was built in the 1920s to resemble something a hundred years older.

Most of the girls we brought—a cavalcade of blondes—were judged by their resemblance to our mother, except when it seemed, as was the case a couple of times with Brian, they'd been deliberately chosen for their controversial darkness. Each of us could see how his brother's girlfriend was a pale imitation of Mom and our own were one-offs who shared some of her best qualities. The girls, for their part, must have been a little daunted at first to discover the patterns of traits they'd cherished as unique. As different as we were, we were all recognizably alike, with the same unruly hair, the same heavy-browed, smiley eyes and all our invisible resemblances, born and bred. Brian, the eldest, kept things lively by bringing a different girl every year; we called him "the Kennedy of the family." The rest of us took after Dad, who liked to say that Mom was his only true love. Mike had been with Jennifer since his freshman year at Colby, and Aidan met his future wife, Alana, before he was twenty. Actually, Brian showed up two years in a row with Janis, whom he eventually married, much to our and then his own chagrin. The second time, she threw the entire uncarved turkey at Brian's head, a scene that eventually showed up in his second play. Another year, he and Foster nearly came to blows at the table when it came out that they'd lately been sleeping with the same girl. It took two of us to restrain Brian.

Brian's personal life, with all its chaos, Sturm und Drang, was the workshop version of his professional life, a laboratory for drama. And of course he wrote about us. Mike said at the time that the phrase "thinly disguised" was too chubby by half to describe Brian's relation to his source material. His first play revolved around the death of a mother from cancer. There seemed to be a number of those that particular season, but his was the most successful. We all went down to the opening night at the New York Theatre Workshop. The play was directed by Foster, who'd been his best friend ever since Choate, and had gone with him to Yale Drama. We sat there, stunned in the aftermath, as the applause thundered around us. It was hard to know how to react. In the play, Brian seemed to be making a special claim for himself with regard to our mother, in that the character who was obviously him had been more loved and more devastated than the others.

Then there was the question of his portrayal of the rest of us. On the one hand, as brothers we wanted to say, *Hey, that's not me,* and on the other, *But wait a minute; that is me.* He'd put us in an untenable position. Brian was a great sophist, and if you complained about the parallels between his life and art, he would start declaiming about the autobiographical basis of *Long Day's Journey into Night* or point out that "your" character had gone to Deerfield, when you'd actually gone to Hotchkiss. And if you complained about inaccuracies—denied that you'd ever, for example, had carnal relations with the family dog—he would cite poetic license or remind you that you'd been banging on a moment before about resemblances and that this clearly demonstrated the fictionality of his masterpiece.

At first, it was hard to tell how Dad felt about it. He put on a brave face and went over to Phoebe's, the bar down the block, to celebrate with Brian and the cast. He seemed to be in shock. But later, in the cab back to the hotel, and in the bar there, he kept asking us, over and over again, some variant of the question "Was I such a bad father?" In truth, he didn't come off all that badly, but we all had a hard time not viewing the play as a flawed family memoir. He also cornered Foster, our unofficial fourth brother, whom for years Dad had consulted as a kind of emotional translator in his efforts to understand Brian.

"Every artist interprets the world through the prism of his own narcissism," Foster told him that night. "He doesn't think you're a bad father. He forgot about you the day he started writing the play. All the characters in the play, even the ones who look and sound like you, are Brian, or else they're foils for Brian." I don't think my father knew whether to be reassured or worried by this. Of course, he'd long known Brian was massively self-absorbed, prone to exaggeration and outright mendacity. But he seemed pleased with the judgment, repeated to us all many times later, that Brian was an artist. At last, he seemed to feel, there was an explanation for his temperament, and his deviations from what my father considered proper behavior: the drugs, the senseless prevarications, the childhood interest in poetry. For Dad, Foster's assessment counted as much as subsequent accolades in the *Times* and elsewhere.

That year, Brian brought Cassie Haynes, the actress, who played his former girlfriend Rita Cosovich in the play, although of course he denied that the character was based on Rita, and we all wondered if Rita would, on balance, be more offended by the substance of her portrait or flattered by its appearance, Cassie being a babe of the first order. She caused a bit of a sensation around the neighborhood that Thanksgiving, husbands coming from three streets down to ask after the leaf blower they thought they might possibly have lent to Dad earlier in the fall. When we heard she was coming, we all thought, Great, just what we need, a prima donna actress, though we couldn't help liking her, and hoping she would come back during bathing suit season.

Brian's play gave us something to fight about at the Thanksgiving board for years to come, beginning that first November after the opening, when the wounds were still fresh. Mike, the middle brother, was the first to take up the cause after the cocktail hour had been prolonged due to some miscalculation about the turkey. Mike's fiancée, Jennifer, had volunteered to cook the bird that year, and while she would later become our chief and favorite cook, this was her first attempt at a turkey, and rather than relying on Mom's old copy of *The Fannie Farmer Cookbook,* she'd insisted on adapting a chicken recipe from Julia Child's *Mastering the Art of French Cooking.* When Dad attempted to carve the turkey the first time, the legs were still pink and raw and the bird was slammed back in the oven, giving us all another jolly hour and a half to deplete the bar. We might have given Jennifer less grief if she hadn't initially tried to defend herself, insisting that the French preferred their birds rare and implying that a thoroughly cooked bird was unsophisticated. When we finally sat down to eat, Brian said grace without letting her off the hook: *"Notre père, qui aime la volaille crue, que ton nom soit sanctifié—"*

Mike interrupted him, asking how he'd like a well-done drumstick up the ass. Dad demanded a truce, and for several minutes peace prevailed, until Dad started to talk about Mom in that maudlin way of his, a recitation that always relied heavily on the concept of her sainthood. Usually we all collaborated in changing the subject and leading him out of this quagmire of grieving nostalgia, but now Mike wanted to open the subject for debate.

"She didn't deserve to suffer," Dad was saying.

"Apparently, the person who suffered the most was Brian," Mike said. "At least that's the impression I got from the play. I mean, sure, Mom was dying of cancer and all, but I never realized it hurt Brian so much to administer her shots the one night that he actually managed to sit up with her. Maybe I'm a philistine, but it seemed to me like the point was the one who really suffered wasn't Mom, it was Brian."

"Okay, okay," Brian said. "I'm sorry I said grace in French."

"That's not really the point," Mike said.

"Oh, but I think it is."

"I don't blame you for trying to change the subject, you self-centered prick. But you know what? We all grew up in the same house. And we all saw the play."

"Now, boys," Dad said.

"You, of all people, know what I'm talking about," Mike said, pointing a fork at our father. "Let's be honest. You were freaked-out by the play."

Dad didn't want to go down this road. "I had a few . . . concerns."

"Don't pussy out, Dad. We've talked about this, for Christ's sake. Why are we all so worried about Brian's feelings? It's not like he lost any sleep worrying about ours."

"Actually," Cassie said, "I happen to know he was very worried about your feelings. I think Foster will agree with me."

"It's not like he shows it," Mike said.

"I think it's wonderful how women attribute lofty ideals and fine feelings to us," Foster said. "But, I'm sorry, if Brian had spent much time worrying about your feelings, it wouldn't have been much of a fucking play."

This quip might have defused the situation, but Mike, like a giant freighter loaded with grievances, was unable to change course. Brian parried his continuing assault with glib little irrelevancies until Mike eventually stormed out of the room, spilling red wine all over the Irish linen tablecloth, but the rest of us considered ourselves fortunate that it wasn't blood. Mike had the fiercest temper in the family, and he was three inches taller and thirty pounds heavier than his elder brother.

The whole exchange was pretty representative. While Brian had always charmed and finessed and fibbed his way through life, Mike had a fierce stubborn honesty and a big hardwood chip on his shoulder, which was in some measure a reflection of his belief that Brian had already claimed the upper bunk bed of life before he came along and had a chance to choose for himself. If Brian were assailing a castle, he would try to sneak in the back door by seducing the scullery maid; Mike would butt his head against the portcullis until it or he gave way. Mike's youthful transgressions weren't necessarily more numerous or egregious, but, unlike Brian, he was inevitably caught and held accountable, in part because he considered it dishonest to hide them. Brian never let the facts compromise his objective, and he seemed almost allergic to them. When he got caught with marijuana, he had an elaborate, if hackneyed, story about how he was holding it for a friend. But when Mike decided to grow it, he did so out in the open, planting rows between the corn and tomatoes in the vegetable garden, until someone finally told our mother, who'd been giving tours of the garden, the true identity of the mystery herb. Back then, none of us could have predicted that Mike would eventually be the one to follow our father to business school and General Electric, that he'd be diplomatic enough to negotiate the hazards of corporate culture. His reformation owed a lot to Jennifer, starting that first year at Colby. It took us a long time to learn to love her—my father was furious over her sophomore art-class critique of our parish church—but there was no denying her anodyne effect on Mike.

The year before Mike nearly throttled Brian, it was Aidan's turn. He was the baby of the family, which seemed to be his complaint—that we treated him as such. That we didn't give him enough respect. The specific catalyst, this Thanksgiving, was obscure. That he was drunk in the manner unique to inexperienced drinkers—he was a senior at Hotchkiss at the time—didn't especially help his case, and sensing this, he became even more frustrated and strident.

"Just because I'm younger . . . it doesn't give *you* guys the right to treat me like I'm a *kid*. Mom wouldn't have let you. If she was here, she'd tell you."

"If she *were* here," Brian said.

"That's *exactly* what I mean. Treating me like a friggin' baby."

We all found it cute that even in his cups, Aidan had used the euphemism rather than the Anglo-Saxonism itself. He wasn't yet ready to cuss in front of Dad. Brian and Mike started sniggering, which further infuriated Aidan, who pounded his fist down on his plate, breaking it in half and cutting his hand on his steak knife, which had been freshly sharpened by Dad that morning. We all agreed that Jennifer was the only one sober enough to drive to the emergency room.

The touch-football games preceding dinner were sometimes an outlet for aggression that might otherwise have overflowed at the table, but it occasionally spilled over, as when Brian accused Mike of unnecessary roughness on the field that afternoon. At Christmas, the sport was hockey, assuming that the pond was sufficiently frozen. Our mother, who believed that exercise and fresh air were essential ingredients of the good life, had inaugurated both of these activities.

We really should have just canceled Thanksgiving the year the movie came out. Anyone could have predicted disaster. Brian spent more than three years working on the screenplay, on his own at first and eventually in collaboration with the director. (His second play, about preppy young bohemians in TriBeCa, had opened to mixed reviews and closed after an eight-week run.) Somewhere in the screenwriting process, the story had acquired a new complication, when the dying mother confides in her sensitive son about her affair with his father's best friend.

In fact, Dad's best friend lived in San Francisco, as Brian was quick to point out later, but still, it made us wonder. Mom had been popular with most of the men in our parents' circle of friends, and one husband, Tom Fleishman, had always seemed almost comically smitten. Now we started to question if it was really a joke, the way Fleishman had always mooned around Mom, or whether Brian had really been the recipient of some deathbed confession. Everyone in town had the same question, including Katy Fleishman, who called Dad in a fury after seeing the movie in September, demanding to know what he knew, and it soon became the talk of the country club. The play had been a distant rumor, but the movie was right there next door to the Pathmark store, in the Regal Cinema multiplex, which had replaced the old downtown theaters where we'd watched *Jaws* and *Summer of '42*. And it was more successful than some might have hoped, buoyed by the performance of Maureen Firth as the wife and mother. The movie played at the Regal for seven weeks. Everyone we knew went to see it.

Brian had warned us, to some extent. On the one hand, he assured us, his vision hadn't been compromised. On the other hand, accommodations had been made, nuances flattened, whispers amplified, subtexts excavated with a backhoe and laid bare. In the play there was a rumor of infatuation.

None of us, Foster excepted, had been invited to the premiere in L.A., or rather, we'd all received a phone call from Brian, who had mentioned in passing "a big industry ratfuck" and said, "I'm not even sure I'm going myself."

And none of us knew quite what to say after we'd seen it. Brian wrote Dad a letter, assuring him that the alleged affair was strictly a Hollywood plot device and had nothing to do with reality. Dad called Foster in New

York and was repeatedly reassured. Mike called Brian, threatening to kick his ass, and while the conversation was hardly conclusive, Brian swore that the affair was just a sensationalistic fiction, and it seemed as if maybe we had all had our say by the time Thanksgiving had come around. We were hoping against hope that the issue would just go away; in an unprecedented move, we even decided to water down the vodka just to keep Dad from getting too maudlin.

And for the first time since any of us could remember, it looked as if we might pass a relatively peaceful Thanksgiving, having made it all the way to the pumpkin pie without major fireworks. But despite the watered vodka, we could see Dad's eyes glazing over with melancholy reminiscence.

"I must have let her down somehow," he said during a lull in the discussion of the Patriots' season.

All of us were smart enough to pretend we hadn't heard this remark, but Aidan's fiancée was still new to the family.

"Let whom down, Mr. C.?"

"Carolyn. I must've let her down. She must have needed something I couldn't give her."

"But why would you think that?" Jennifer asked.

"Oh, for Christ's sake," Mike said, throwing his napkin down on the table. "Look at what you've done, Brian. Now he actually believes it."

"Dad," Brian said, "I told you: It never happened. It's fiction."

"It's slander," Mike said. "I still can't understand why the hell you'd drag our mother's name into the gutter like that."

"It's not our mother. It's not her name. It's a character in a movie."

"A character based on our mother."

"I just must have failed her," Dad said, oblivious to the conversation around him.

"Dad, listen to me. It never happened. I'm sorry. It's my fault. I shouldn't have written what I wrote. It was the director's idea, a cheap plot device. It isn't true."

"I always thought it was harmless," Dad said. "They used to talk at parties, and I knew they had things in common. Your mother had so many interests, art and theater, and I couldn't really talk to her about those things. I knew she and Tom talked. But I thought that's all it was."

"That *is* all it was," Brian said. "At least so far as I know."

"I know she told you things," he said to Brian. "Things she couldn't tell me."

"Not that, Dad. She never told me anything like that."

"After my operation," he said, "I was afraid. I was afraid of physical, you know, exertion."

"Dad, that's enough."

"Are you happy with yourself?" Mike asked as the tears rolled down our father's cheeks.

"Well, who's for a smoke outside?" Foster said, rising from the table. Although Dad was a lifelong smoker, our mother had, toward the end of her life, insisted that all smoking be done outdoors, a rule that Dad himself continued to observe and enforce after she was gone.

A half hour after we put Dad to bed, Mike tackled Brian and got him in a headlock, choking him and rubbing his face in the snow. "Tell the truth, goddamn it. What did she tell you? Is it true?"

"I told you: It's not true. She never told me anything."

But nothing could ever quite dispel the doubt for us. Dad might have been forgiven for lying low, but he was determined to show himself on the local holiday party circuit. A week before Christmas, after three cocktail parties, he crashed his Mustang into an elm tree half a mile from the house.

Mike, who was working in Schenectady, was the first to arrive at the hospital. Dad was in intensive care. Aidan drove over from Amherst, arriving shortly before midnight. Brian and Foster arrived from New York just as the sun was rising and Dad was declared stable. We all spent the day at the hospital and that night traded shifts in the waiting room. Dad looked gruesome when we finally got to see him, his face bruised and puffy and green where it wasn't bandaged, his leg in traction. He was pretty doped up. "Don't tell your mother," he said when he saw us. "I don't want her to worry."

The doctor, who'd tended our mother in her final days, said, "It's the Demerol."

"We could all use some of that," Foster said.

We moved between the hospital and the house for the next ten days, keeping ourselves busy with Christmas preparations. We found a perfectly shaped blue spruce tree in the woods at the edge of the lake and we retrieved the ornaments from the attic in the old boxes from England's department store, closed years before, with Mom's block letters fading on the cardboard: CHRISTMAS LIGHTS, CHRISTMAS ANGELS, CHRISTMAS BULBS. We avoided talking about what had happened or why, concentrating instead on the practical details.

The lake had frozen early that year. After lunch on Christmas Eve, we gathered up our gear, called Ricky and Ted Quinlan next door, and trudged down for the annual hockey game. It was Foster, Ted and Aidan against Brian, Ricky and Mike. Brian's team scored two quick goals. Aidan, who had the fiercest competitive streak of any of us, started to get physical. First he hooked Brian's skate and tripped him; then he body-checked him into the rocks of the causeway. Brian returned the favor the next time he came down the ice with the puck, knocking Aidan off into the bulrushes. He came out swinging, and caught Brian in the helmet with his stick. Then he threw him down and knelt on top of him, ripping off his helmet and punching his face. By the time we pulled him off, there was blood everywhere and one of Brian's teeth was protruding through his lip.

"You bastard," Aidan sobbed. "You selfish bastard."

Brian turned away and limped up the hill, leaving a trail of blood on the ice.

When we got back up to the house, Brian was gone.

Dad came home on New Year's Day. Aidan took winter term off from school to be with him, and Mike came over from Schenectady on the weekends. Brian called from New York to check in. Neither the fight on the ice nor his sudden departure was ever discussed again. From time to time, in his cups, Dad would ask Brian about our mother, and he would always insist that both the affair and the confession were completely fictional. Dad once confronted Tom Fleishman at the country club and he, too, denied it. But Dad could never put the question out of his mind, any more than he could walk without a cane.

Mike and Jennifer had three boys, and he became the youngest vice president ever at GE. Aidan spent a year with the U.S. ski team before marrying Alana and going back to Hotchkiss to teach. Foster, one of the most respected directors in New York, recently married Cassie Haynes, the actress who first appeared at our house as Brian's date. We go down to see his plays from time to time.

Brian moved to Los Angeles a few weeks after Aidan busted his lip. He wrote a TV pilot based on his second play, and became a producer when Showtime developed the series. We can't help feeling relieved that he's not writing about the family, and Dad watches the show every week. Brian is very well paid for his efforts and has been dating a series of extremely pretty actresses. But it also feels somehow like a cheat, a big fucking let-down. After all these years of having to put up with the idea of Brian as a great genius, of knowing that our mother believed in his special destiny, we feel like the least he could do would be to justify her favor and her hopes. Nothing short of greatness could justify the doubt he cast on her memory. Foster believes that he's doing penance and that he'll go back to his real work someday.

In the meantime, we haven't all been together at Thanksgiving since Dad's accident. Now, when the leaves turn red and yellow and the grass turns white with morning frost, we feel the loss all over again. It's like we were a goddess cult that gathered once a year and now our faith has wavered. It's not that we couldn't forgive her anything. But our simple certainties have been shaken. Although we will always be Catholics, we long ago gave up on the Father, the Son and the Holy Ghost. We were a coven of Mariolatry, devoted to the Virgin. Brian believed in art, but lately he seems to have lost the faith. We find it hard to believe in anything we can't see or explain according to the immutable laws imbued in science class. We always believed in you, Mother, more than anything, but we never for a moment thought you were human.

2007

Third Party

Difficult to describe precisely, the taste of that eighth or ninth cigarette of the day, a mix of ozone, blond tobacco and early-evening angst on the tongue. But he recognized it every time. It was the taste of lost love.

Alex started smoking again whenever he lost a woman. When he fell in love again, he would quit. And when love died, he'd light up again. Partly it was a physical reaction to stress; partly metaphorical—the substitution of one addiction for another. And no small part of this reflex was mythological—indulging a romantic image of himself as a lone figure standing on a bridge in a foreign city, cigarette cupped in his hand, his leather jacket open to the elements.

He imagined the passersby speculating about his private sorrow as he stood on the Pont des Arts, mysterious, wet and unapproachable. His sense of loss seemed more real when he imagined himself through the eyes of strangers—the pedestrians with their evening baguettes and their Michelin guides and their umbrellas, hunched against the March precipitation, an alloy of drizzle and mist.

When it all ended with Lydia, he'd decided to go to Paris, not only a good place to smoke but also an appropriate backdrop. His grief was more poignant and picturesque there. Bad enough that Lydia had left him; what made it worse was that it was his own fault; he suffered both the ache of the victim and the guilt of the villain. His appetite had not suffered, however. His stomach was complaining like a terrier demanding its evening walk, blissfully unaware that the household was in mourning. Ennobling as it might seem to suffer in Paris, only a fool would starve himself there.

Standing in the middle of the bridge, he tried to decide which way to go. Having dined the previous night in a bistro that had looked grim and authentic enough for his purposes but had proved to be full of voluble

Americans and Germans attired as if for the gym or the tropics, he decided to head for the Hôtel Costes, where, at the very least, the Americans would be jaded and dressed in shades of gray and black.

The bar was full and, of course, no tables were available when he arrived. The hostess, a pretty Asian sylph with a West London accent, sized him up skeptically. Hers was not the traditional Parisian hauteur, the sneer of the maître d'hôtel at a three-star restaurant; she was, rather, the temple guardian of an international tribe that included rock stars, fashion models, designers, actors and directors—as well as those who photographed, wrote about and slept with them. As the art director of a boutique ad agency, Alex lived on the fringes of this world. In New York, he knew many of the doormen and maître d's, but here the best he could hope was that he looked the part. The hostess seemed to be puzzling over his claims to membership, her expression slightly hopeful, as if she was on the verge of giving him the benefit of the doubt. Suddenly her narrow squint morphed into a smile of recognition. "I'm sorry. I didn't recognize you," she said. "How are you?" Alex had been there only twice, on a visit a few years before, so it seemed unlikely he would've been remembered. On the other hand, he was a generous tipper and, he reasoned, not a bad-looking guy.

She led him to a small but highly visible table set for four. He'd told her he was expecting someone, in the hopes of increasing his chances of seating. "I'll send a waiter right over," she said. "Let me know if there's anything else I can do for you." So benevolent was her smile that he tried to think of some small request to gratify her.

Still feeling expansive when the waiter arrived, he ordered a bottle of Champagne and scanned the room. While he recognized a couple of the patrons—a burly American novelist of the Montana school, the skinny lead singer of a Britpop band—he didn't see anyone he knew in the old-fashioned sense. Feeling awkward in his solitude, he studied the menu and wondered why he'd never brought Lydia to Paris. He regretted it now, for her sake as well as his own; the pleasures of travel were less real to him when they couldn't be verified by a witness. But he'd taken her for granted—that was part of the problem. Why did that always happen?

When he looked up, a young couple were standing at the edge of the room, searching the crowd. The woman was striking—a tall beauty of indeterminate race. They seemed disoriented, as if the brilliant party to which they'd been summoned had migrated elsewhere. The woman met his gaze—and smiled. Alex smiled back. She tugged on her companion's sleeve and nodded toward Alex's table.

Suddenly they were approaching.

"Do you mind if we join you for a moment?" the woman said. "We can't find our friends." She didn't wait for the answer, taking the seat next to Alex, exposing, in the process, a length of unstockinged taupe-colored thigh.

"Frédéric," the man said, extending his hand, seeming more self-conscious than his companion. "And this is Tasha."

"Please, sit," Alex said. Some instinct prevented him from giving his own name.

"What are *you* doing in Paris?" Tasha asked.

"Just, you know, getting away."

The waiter arrived with the Champagne, and Alex requested two more glasses.

"I think we have some friends in common," Tasha said. "Ethan and Olivier."

Alex nodded noncommittally.

"I love New York," Frédéric said.

"It's not what it used to be," Tasha countered.

"I know what you mean." Alex wanted to see where this was going.

"Still," Frédéric said, "it's better than Paris."

"Well," Alex said, "yes and no."

"Barcelona," Frédéric said, "is the only hip city in Europe."

"And Berlin," said Tasha.

"Not anymore."

"Do you know Paris well?" Tasha asked.

"Not really."

"We should show you."

"It's shit," Frédéric said.

"There are some new places," she said, "that aren't too boring."

"Where are *you* from?" Alex asked the girl, trying to parse her exotic looks.

"I live in Paris," she said.

"When she's not in New York."

They drank the bottle of Champagne and ordered another. Alex was happy for the company. Moreover, he couldn't help liking himself as whomever they imagined him to be; that they'd mistaken him for someone else was tremendously liberating. And he was fascinated by Tasha, who was definitely flirting with him. More than once she grabbed his knee for emphasis, and at several points she scratched her left breast. An absent-minded gesture, or deliberately provocative? He tried to determine if her attachment to Frédéric was romantic, but the signs pointed in both directions. The Frenchman watched her closely, yet he didn't seem to resent her flirting. Then she happened to say, "Frédéric and I used to go out," and the more Alex looked at her, the more enthralled he became. She was a perfect cocktail of racial features, familiar enough to answer an acculturated ideal and exotic enough to startle.

"You Americans are so puritanical," she said. "All this fuss about your president getting a blow job."

"It has nothing to do with sex," Alex replied, conscious of a flush rising on his cheeks. "It's a right-wing coup." Though he'd wanted to sound cool and jaded, somehow it came out defensive.

"Everything has to do with sex," she said, staring into his eyes.

Thus provoked, the Veuve Clicquot tingling like a brilliant isotope in his veins, he ran his hand up the inside of her thigh, stopping only at the border of her tight short skirt. Holding his gaze, she opened her mouth with her tongue and moistened her lips.

"This is shit," said Frédéric.

Although Alex was certain the other man couldn't see his hand, the subject of Frédéric's exclamation was worrisomely vague.

"You think everything is shit."

"That's because it is."

"You're an expert on shit."

"There's no more art. Only shit."

"Now that *that*'s settled," said Tasha.

A debate about dinner: Frédéric wanted to go to Buddha-Bar; Tasha wanted to stay. They compromised, ordering caviar and another bottle of Champagne. When the check arrived, Alex remembered at the last moment not to throw down his credit card. He decided, as a first step toward elucidating the mystery of his new identity, that he was the kind of guy who paid cash. While he counted out the bills, Frédéric gazed studiously into the distance with the air of a man practiced in the art of ignoring checks. Alex had a brief, irritated intuition that he was being used. Maybe this was a routine with them, pretending to recognize a stranger with a good table. But before he could develop this notion, Tasha had taken his arm and was leading him out into the night. The pressure of her arm, the scent of her skin—both were invigorating. He decided to see where this might take him. It wasn't as if he had anything else to do.

Frédéric's car, which was parked a few blocks away, didn't look operational; the front grille was bashed in, one of the headlights pointing up at a forty-five-degree angle. "Don't worry," Tasha said. "Frédéric's an excellent driver. He only crashes when he feels like it."

"How are you feeling *tonight*?" Alex asked.

"I feel like dancing," he said. He began to sing Bowie's "Let's Dance," drumming his hands on the steering wheel as Alex climbed into the back.

Les Bains Douches was half-empty. The only person they recognized was Bernard-Henri Lévy. Either they were too early or a couple years too late. The conversation had lapsed into French and Alex wasn't following everything. Tasha was all over him, stroking his arm and, intermittently, her own perfect left breast, and he was a little nervous about Frédéric's reaction. At one point there was a sharp exchange he didn't quite catch. Frédéric stood up and walked off.

"Look," Alex said, "I don't want to cause any trouble."

"No trouble," she said.

"Is he your boyfriend?"

"We used to go out. Now we're just friends."

She pulled him forward and kissed him, slowly exploring the inside of his mouth with her tongue. Suddenly she leaned away and glanced up at a woman in a white leather jacket who was dancing beside an adjoining table.

"I think big tits are beautiful," she said before kissing him with renewed ardor.

"I think *your* tits are beautiful," he said.

"They are, actually," she replied. "But not big."

When Frédéric returned, his mood seemed to have lifted. He laid several bills on the table. "Let's go," he said.

Alex hadn't been clubbing in several years. After he and Lydia moved in together, the clubs lost their appeal. Now he felt the return of the old thrill, the anticipation of the hunt—the sense that the night held secrets bound to be unveiled before it was over. Tasha was talking about someone in New York whom Alex was supposed to know. "The last time I saw him, he just kept banging his head against the wall, and I said to him, 'Michael, you've really got to stop doing these drugs. It's been fifteen years now.' "

First stop was a ballroom in Montmartre. A band was onstage, playing an almost credible version of "Smells Like Teen Spirit." While they waited at the bar, Frédéric played vigorous air guitar and shouted the refrain, "Here we are now / Entertain us." After sucking down their cosmopolitans, they drifted out to the dance floor. The din was just loud enough to obviate the need for conversation.

The band launched into "Goddamn the Queers." Tasha divided her attentions between the two of them, grinding her pelvis into Alex during a particularly bad rendition of "Champagne Supernova." Closing his eyes and enveloping her with his arms, he lost track of his spatial coordinates. Were those her breasts in his hands, or the cheeks of her ass? When she flicked her tongue in his ear, he pictured a cobra rising from a wicker basket.

Then he opened his eyes and saw Frédéric conferring with another man and watching him from the edge of the dance floor.

Alex went off to find the men's room and another beer. When he returned, Tasha and Frédéric were slow-dancing to a French ballad and making out. He decided to cut his losses and leave. Whatever the game was, he suddenly felt too tired to play it. At that moment, Tasha looked across the room, waved, then slalomed toward him through the dancers, Frédéric following behind her.

"Let's go," she shouted.

Out on the sidewalk, Frédéric turned obsequious. "Man, you must think Paris is total shit."

"I'm having a good time," Alex said. "Don't worry about it."

"I do worry about it, man. It's a question of *honor*."

"I'm fine."

"At least we could find some drugs," said Tasha.

"The drugs in Paris are all shit."

"I don't need drugs," Alex said.

" 'Don't wanna get stoned,' " Frédéric sang. " 'But I don't wanna not get stoned.' "

They began arguing about the next destination. Tasha was making the case for a place called, apparently, Faster, Pussycat! Kill! Kill! Frédéric insisted it wasn't open, instead pushing for L'Enfer. The debate continued in the car. Eventually they crossed the river and, later still, lurched to a stop beneath the Montparnasse tower.

The two doormen greeted his companions warmly. They descended the staircase into a space that seemed to glow with a purple light, the source of which Alex couldn't discern. A throbbing drum and bass riff washed over the dancers. Grabbing hold of the tip of his belt, Tasha led him toward a raised area above the dance floor, evidently a VIP area.

Conversation became almost impossible, which was kind of a relief. Alex met several people or, rather, nodded at several people, who, in turn, nodded at him. A Japanese woman shouted into his ear in what was probably several different languages and soon returned with a catalog of terrible paintings. He nodded as he thumbed through it, since apparently this was a gift. Far more welcome was an unlabeled bottle full of clear liquid that a man handed to him. He poured some into his glass. It tasted like moonshine.

Tasha towed him out to the dance floor, wrapping her arms around him and sucking his tongue into her mouth. Just when his tongue felt like it was going to be ripped from his mouth, she bit down on it, hard. Within moments he tasted blood. Perhaps this was what she wanted, for she continued to kiss him as she thrust her pelvis into his, still sucking hard on his tongue. He imagined himself being sucked whole into her mouth, and liked the idea. But without for a moment losing his focus on Tasha, he suddenly thought of Lydia and the girl before Lydia, and the girl after Lydia, the one he'd betrayed her with. How was it, he wondered, that desire for one woman always reawakened his desire for all the other women in his life?

"Let's get out of here," he shouted, mad with lust. She nodded and pulled away, going into a little solipsistic dance a few feet away. Alex watched, trying to catch and follow her rhythm, until he gave up and took her in his arms. He forced his tongue between her teeth, surprised by the pain of his recent wound. Fortunately she didn't bite him this time; in fact, she pulled away. Suddenly she was weaving back up to the VIP area, where Frédéric seemed to be having an argument with the bartender. When he saw Tasha, he seized a bottle on the bar and threw it at the floor near her feet, where it shattered. Then he shouted something unintelligible before bolting up the stairs. Tasha started to follow.

"Don't go," Alex shouted, holding her arm.

"I'm sorry," she shouted, removing his hand from her arm. She kissed him gently on the lips.

"Say good-bye," Alex said.

"Good-bye."

"Say my name."

She looked at him quizzically, and then, as if suddenly getting the joke, she smiled and laughed mirthlessly, pointing at him as if to say, *You almost got me.*

He watched her disappear up the steps, her long legs seeming to become even longer as they receded.

Alex had another glass of the clear liquor, but the place now struck him as tawdry and flat. It was a little past three. As he was leaving, the Japanese woman pressed several nightclub invitations into his hand.

Out on the sidewalk he paused to get his bearings, then started walking toward Saint-Germain. His mood lifted with the thought that it was only nine o'clock in New York. He would call Lydia. Suddenly he believed he knew what to say to her. As he picked up his pace, he noticed a beam of light moving slowly along the wall beside and above him; he turned to see Frédéric's bashed-in Renault cruising the street behind him.

"Get in," said Tasha.

He shrugged. Whatever happened, it was better than walking.

"Frédéric wants to check out this after-hours place."

"Maybe you could just drop me off at my hotel."

"Don't be a drag."

The look she gave him awoke in him the mad lust of the dance floor; he was tired of being jerked around, and yet his desire overwhelmed his pride. After all this, he felt he deserved his reward and understood he was willing to do almost anything to get it. He climbed in the backseat.

Frédéric gunned the engine and popped the clutch. Tasha looked back at Alex, shaping her lips into a kiss, then turned to Frédéric. Her tongue emerged from her lips and slowly disappeared into Frédéric's ear. When he stopped for a light, she moved around to kiss him full on the mouth. Alex realized that he was involved—part of the transaction between them. And suddenly he thought of Lydia, whom he'd told his betrayal had nothing to do with her, which was what you said. How could he explain to her that as he bucked atop another woman, it was she, Lydia, who filled his heart?

Tasha suddenly climbed over the backseat and started kissing him. Thrusting her busy tongue into his mouth, she ran her hand down to his crotch. "Oh, *yes,* where did that come from?" She took his earlobe between her teeth as she unzipped his fly.

Alex moaned as she reached into his shorts. He looked at Frédéric, who looked right back at him, adjusting the rearview mirror as he drove even faster. Tasha slid down his chest, feathering the hair of his belly with her tongue, his vague intuition of danger fading away in the wash of vivid sensation. She was squeezing his cock in her hand; then it was in her mouth, and he felt powerless to intervene. He didn't care what happened, so long as she didn't stop. At first he could barely feel the touch of her lips, the pleasure residing more in the anticipation of what was to follow. At last she raked him gently with her teeth. Alex moaned and squirmed lower in the seat as the car picked up speed. The pressure of her lips became more authoritative.

"Who am I?" he whispered. And, a minute later: "Tell me who you think I am."

Her response, though unintelligible, forced a moan of pleasure from his own lips. Glancing at the rearview mirror, he saw that Frédéric was watching intensely, even as the car picked up speed. When he shifted abruptly into fourth, Alex inadvertently bit down on his own tongue as his head snapped forward, his teeth scissoring the fresh wound there.

On a sudden impulse he pulled out of Tasha's mouth just as Frédéric jammed on the brakes and sent them into a spin.

He had no idea how much time passed before he struggled out of the car. The crash had seemed almost leisurely, the car turning like a falling leaf until the illusion of weightlessness was shattered by the collision with a guardrail. He'd tried to remember it all as he sat folded like a contortionist in the backseat, taking inventory of his extremities. A peaceful Sunday silence prevailed. No one seemed to be moving. His cheek was sore and bleeding on the inside where he'd slammed it against the passenger seat's headrest. Just when he was beginning to suspect his hearing was gone, he heard Tasha moan. The serenity of survival was replaced by anger when he saw Frédéric's head moving on the dashboard and realized what could have happened.

Hobbling around to the other side of the car, he yanked the door open and hauled Frédéric roughly out to the pavement, where he lay blinking, a gash on his forehead.

"What was that about?" Alex said.

The Frenchman blinked and winced, inserting a finger in his mouth to check his teeth.

In a fury, Alex kicked him in the ribs. "Who the hell do you think I am?"

Frédéric smiled and looked up at him. "You're just a guy," he said. "You're nobody."

1999

In the North-West Frontier Province

"And where is your beautiful wife this fine day?" the Pathan asked, when Trey found him at his stall in the bazaar. The woman in question was not his wife, and by his lights it wasn't much of a day—no wind, the sun a degree higher in the sky and hotter than it had been this time the day before, and still no sign of Rudy. The Pathan's question had an ironic tone, as if the man understood all of this. But then, he always sounded that way to Trey, who replied that Michelle was back at the fort where she was relatively safe from lecherous Pathans. This was meant to be a joke, but the anxiety of waiting two weeks in a place where he didn't want to be put a sharper edge on the words than he'd intended.

The Pathan quit smiling.

Something bumped Trey's thigh. He looked down and saw a sheep nosing at his jeans. The animal then turned and waddled off down the bazaar, poking into stalls as if it were shopping.

He had insulted the Pathan, a stupid thing to do. Their sense of honor was extremely delicate, their sense of redress extreme. They killed each other over such matters. Here in the hills between Pakistan and Afghanistan, the code of tribal honor, blood relation and vendetta was the only law that was ever enforced. Pathan tribesmen with Enfield rifles strapped over their shoulders and bandoliers of ammunition wrapped around their baggy shirts strutted past the stall, and the man he was talking to had a revolver holstered on his hip.

"You have heard from your friend?" the Pathan said after a minute.

Trey shook his head, relieved that his indiscretion had been passed over.

"He was not Australian?"

"Scottish."

"Ah." The Pathan nodded. "There is an Australian passport for sale."

It took a minute to sort this out, and to construe the warning. Trey thought he knew where the passport had come from. A few days before, he'd met an Australian in the bazaar who had mined opals in the Outback for two years. He had a dry, brick-red tan against which his green eyes and the gaudy opal pendant on his chest glistened. Over kebabs he told Trey, who hadn't asked, that he was in Landi Kotal to score hash oil. He was going to swallow it, in condoms, just before he flew out of Karachi and then shit out a small fortune when he got back to Sydney. That was his plan. When he finished talking, he beamed as if he were the first person to have penetrated the mystery of demand and supply. Trey felt obliged to tell him that it was an old trick and that people had died in the bargain; any residual alcohol that hadn't been boiled off in the processing of the oil would eat through the condoms, and once that happened it was permanent deep space. But the Australian smiled and rubbed the opal on his chest. "My lucky amulet," he said. Trey had left him licking chili sauce from his cracked lips and yesterday had seen the opal pendant for sale at a stall in the bazaar. He felt awful then, thinking he might have been more sympathetic, more persistent.

It was an object lesson, he told himself. The Pathan was reminding him of what could happen.

"Excuse me," Trey said. "My humor was crude."

The man nodded. "Your wife. She is still sick?"

Trey nodded back. It was a convention of their transactions that Michelle was sick and that the junk was a temporary analgesic. This was, in fact, how Michelle viewed her habit.

"There is anything else I can do for you," the man asked after they'd made the usual exchange.

"How about a fifth of scotch?"

"I am sorry. But you know I am a believer."

Trey nodded once more.

"I hope your wife will be well soon," the Pathan said. "A good woman is a pearl of great price."

Trey had met him the day after they'd arrived in Landi Kotal. Rudy intended to leave for Kabul later that afternoon. The three of them spent the morning in the bazaar. It was Michelle's first time here and she wanted to look at everything. The close-packed stalls displayed bolts of Scottish tweed, Swiss watches, Indian ivories, sundries with the initials of Italian and French designers, Levi's jeans, Japanese cameras and radios, Buddhas in bronze and clay, vintage British cavalry swords and U.S. Army–issue Colt .45s. A hand towel embroidered with the legend *Grand Hotel, Mackinac Island, Michigan* was laid out beside a stack of Tibetan prayer rugs. Smuggling was the region's main industry. Much of the contraband was what it appeared to be, but it was safe to begin with the assumption that the Western-looking goods were Asian counterfeits and that the handcrafts and antiques were mass-produced.

At one of the stalls, Rudy and Trey examined some pale, crumbly hash. Rudy shook his head sadly. It was water-pressed, he explained, the dregs of last season's pressing. He was confirmed in his decision to cross the border and get the pick of the new crop in the mountain villages outside Kabul.

A small boy with a large knife sheathed in his belt stepped into their path waving his arms. "I got stone, man," he announced. "Very hot stuff. Brand-new." He reached into his pocket and drew out a cassette that he pressed into Trey's hand, the blocky roman letters on the inner lining reading EXCITE ON MAIN ST. BY ROLLING STONE. The boy wiggled his shoulders and hips vigorously, then took Trey's arm and coaxed them over to his rock-and-roll emporium. There were more bootleg cassettes, several Japanese cassette players and a Fender Stratocaster displayed in a gun rack at the back of the stall.

Michelle wanted to buy a cassette player. Rudy told her that even if it wasn't confiscated at the border when they went back to India, they'd still end up paying more duty than it was worth. Trey reminded her that their money was tight.

Michelle slammed down the tape she'd been looking at. "Always you and Rudy gang up on me," she said, then turned and stalked off into the bazaar.

Rudy went after her while Trey bargained for the cassette player. Michelle had been clean for three weeks and he wanted to keep her happy. When he caught up with them, he saw they'd gathered a crowd. Michelle's red chamois shirt was on the ground and she was trying to tug her T-shirt up over her head, Rudy trying to restrain her as men and boys in turbans were closing around them.

Earlier in the morning they had counseled Michelle on keeping herself covered no matter how warm it got. She didn't like being told what to do. And she didn't like clothes. In Goa they'd spent the days nude on the beach. But Goa was not Muslim.

Trey pushed through the onlookers. Rudy had her arms pinned. Michelle had a mouthful of her own sleeve and was trying to rip the fabric with her teeth. When Trey grabbed her shoulder she kicked him in the shin.

"Bastards! Beat up on me!"

They each took an arm and pushed her through the crowd.

Michelle was laughing now. "*Fook* these dirty people," she said. "They have never seen *teets* before?"

Trey was hoping no one could make out the English behind her French accent. The crowd followed them, their eyes already hostile. When Michelle tried to wrench herself away, Trey dropped the new cassette player, which had been pinned under his arm. The people behind them hissed and muttered. Trey looked back and saw a man pick up a stone from the side of the road. Others carried rifles. A boy darted forward to grab at the neck of Michelle's shirt; Trey turned and kicked him hard in the knee, provoking many indignant shouts.

"Don't look back," Rudy said.

Michelle was no longer resisting. Her face was pale.

In front of them a man emerged from behind one of the stalls. Trey raised his fist.

"Please follow me," the man said. "This way." He guided them through a narrow passage between two stalls. "Here," he said, holding back the flap of a tent. "They will not come here," he told them, closing the flaps. He then lit an oil lamp and beckoned them to sit.

The first thing Trey noticed about him was that his eyes were blue and the sharply hooked nose seemed to be placed a little too high on his face. He wore a pale-blue turban and had a long, wispy beard that he stroked with his left hand. And the ring finger on his other hand was missing, nubbed below the first joint.

"An accident," the man said, catching his glance. He introduced himself, but Trey missed the name. He said he was of the Afridi tribe of

Pathans, and that it was the code of his people to offer shelter and protection to strangers.

Trey was stroking Michelle's hand, watching her.

"She is your woman," the man asked him.

Trey shrugged.

"I am nobody's woman," Michelle said. "Nobody cares about me." She was pale and her hands trembled.

"She is beautiful," the Pathan said.

Trey put his arm around Michelle and began to knead the muscles in her neck, but stopped suddenly when he saw how the Pathan was looking at her. It was a look he had seen on the faces in the bazaar.

Rudy touched his arm. "We should be pushing on, chum."

They thanked the man, who assured them that he was always at their service. He was a merchant, a broker of commodities, and if they should require anything, anything at all, during their stay in Landi Kotal . . .

To Trey he offered the advice that you did not display a jewel in the bazaar unless you intended to sell it. Then he looked again at Michelle.

They saw Rudy off a few hours later. The taxi stand at the edge of the bazaar had a fleet of fifties Chevys, which rattled off over the Khyber Pass once a sufficient number of passengers had presented themselves. A taxi was nearly ready to leave when they arrived. The driver had seven fares in the cab itself and intended to put four more in the trunk. Four of the passengers were Caucasian. A woman with matted blond hair and dirt in the creases of her face was leaning out the rear window, moaning, the man beside her holding her hair back behind her neck. While Rudy dickered with the driver, she vomited. "That's the way," the man said, "that's the way." Someone else was telling a story about a guy from Ohio who had his balls cut off when the border guards found a ball of hash taped underneath his scrotum. A Pathan with an automatic rifle over his shoulder was securing a canvas bag to the pile of luggage on the roof.

"Well, that's it," Rudy said after he'd paid the driver. "I've got a seat on the observation deck." He indicated the trunk, then turned to Michelle and opened his arms. "How about a kiss for the soldier going off to the wars?"

She allowed herself to be embraced, and kissed him on the cheek.

Rudy hugged Trey and said, "You take care of that lady. That's your only job."

Trey nodded and tried to smile. He was suddenly very nervous. He felt there was something they were forgetting. They'd been planning this for weeks, but now he didn't like the idea of splitting up. The blond girl leaning out of the cab heaved again, and Trey felt his own stomach shrink in on itself. "You'll be back in a few days?" he said.

"A few days, maybe a week. Just as soon as I can."

Rudy had done this before. He liked to buy direct from the tribes in Afghanistan because it was cheaper and the hash was better than anything that came into Landi Kotal. He had a third of the money in his boot heel. Trey was holding the rest. Rudy would catch a bus from the border to Kabul, hire a guide into the hills, arrange the buy and make a down payment. He would come back through customs clean, and they would wait for the Afghanis, who did not believe in borders, to bring the stuff over the mountains. That was their plan.

The taxi driver told Rudy they were ready to go, and he climbed into the trunk and settled himself next to three old men in pink turbans. A cloud of smoke engulfed the rear of the car as the driver gunned the engine. When he popped the clutch, the car lurched violently and died.

More than an hour later, the driver still hadn't managed to get the car running again. Trey and Michelle had waited with Rudy as the sun dropped through the cloudless sky toward the jagged ridge of mountains to the west. He could feel the dry rasp of high-altitude sunlight on his face even as he was slapping his arms and chest for warmth, and Michelle claimed she was freezing to death. Rudy said they shouldn't bother to wait.

"I've been thinking," Trey said. "Why don't you stick around another day, get a fresh start tomorrow." It seemed to him that the signs were not auspicious—the near riot in the bazaar, the sick blond girl, the taxi breaking down. And he was not eager to see his friend leave.

Rudy went to talk to the driver, who had climbed in behind the wheel. When the engine turned over, sputtered and finally caught, Rudy jumped back into the trunk and waved as the car lurched forward. Trey put one arm around Michelle and waved with the other as the taxi disappeared into the dust.

They were staying in a fortified dwelling on the hillside just off the main road. This sort of earthen pillbox was characteristic of the region, designed for defense against bandits. Rudy had arranged for them to stay there, explaining that the family was on a pilgrimage to Mecca. The heavy wooden door on the ground floor opened into a dark space rank with smells, the quarters of the family sheep. A steep stairway led to the second level, where the small, vertical windows admitted little light. There was no escaping the residual aroma of the animals downstairs. *"Le château des pourceaux,"* Michelle said, holding her nose, when they first surveyed the place.

Things had gone sour after the incident in the bazaar. Michelle had seen all she cared to of Landi Kotal and wanted to move on. She began talking about Katmandu, where she and Trey had met. He didn't want to be reminded of Katmandu. They'd spent three weeks together there, Trey having just arrived in Asia. Then one night Michelle went off with an Italian, and he didn't see her again until six months later. She now spoke wistfully of Katmandu's pastel-colored temples and the tall, crooked houses with hex eyes painted on the lintels.

"And the monkeys," he said absently. "Don't forget the monkeys." They were lying on a single pallet in the upstairs room, in the dim light of an oil lamp. Rudy had been gone for three days.

"I hate the monkeys," she said. "Nasty, ugly things. I hate them."

"Sorry," Trey said. There was no telling when some little thing would set her off. He turned onto his side and looked at her. Her face was rigid. He stroked her shoulder; she pushed his hand away.

"It smells like pig in here."

"Sheep. It's sheep."

"*Pig.* Pig pig pig. Big-time, big-deal businessmen. They make a big deal and stay in a pig house. Pig time. Pig deal. Pig guys."

"Michelle."

"Pig!"

He leaned over and kissed her neck. "Once we finish this we'll have money, lots of money. Then we can go anywhere."

"I want to go now."

"We have to wait for Rudy."

"Rudy. Always Rudy. Rudy Rudy—"

Trey clapped a hand over her mouth and she bit him, then resumed the chant, her voice rising until she lashed out at him with her arms and legs. When he tried to cram the blanket into her mouth, she kneed him. He got a handful of her hair and rolled her off the pallet. He thumped her head, hard, against the wooden floor. She stopped struggling and began to cry.

After a while she said, "Do you love me?"

Trey said that he did.

"Do you love me more than Rudy?" she said.

"Do I sleep with Rudy?"

"Maybe you do," she said after a minute.

It was an easy thing for her to think, a quick reduction of whatever was exclusive in Trey's affection for Rudy. They had been traveling together for six months when Michelle showed up in Goa, where they were renting a beach hut for the winter. In Michelle's version of Katmandu, Trey had abandoned her, and when she moved in with them she made him promise he would never run out on her again. For a few weeks it had been idyllic. Rudy liked Michelle, and she liked him. But then she had turned petulant and jealous, quizzing Trey with hypothetical situations in which he had to choose between the two of them.

"I don't go for redheads," he said now. "Now go to sleep."

The next day Michelle stayed in bed complaining of cramps, and he went to Peshawar to check on bus schedules. When he got back she was high. He could see it in the way she greeted him, giddy and languorous, and in the slight drop in register in her voice. She'd had a habit for three months in Goa, and he knew the signs.

"Where did you get the stuff?"

"Come hold me, Trey."

"Where did you get it?" Even as he asked, he didn't know why he bothered. The point was, she had it. But it was the only thing he could think of to say.

"Only a little bit," she said. "To make the sickness go away."

She nodded off before sundown. He stayed with her through the next morning. By noon she was sweating and trembling. He held out until three, when he could no longer stand to watch her. She told him she'd bought it from the Pathan who'd helped them that day. Trey went to find him, and returned an hour later with her fix. There would be time to straighten her out when this business was all over.

He went outside the moment she started to tie off. He might have bought it, but he wasn't about to watch her put the needle in her arm. He looked out over the barren gray peaks. The afternoon sun cast harsh, angular shadows. There was no vegetation in sight. To the west, the road threaded between the jaws of the pass. Three eastbound vehicles crawled like beetles toward the bright mosaic of the town. It was possible that Rudy was in one of them. Trey wanted to think so. But he felt that a landscape like this didn't have anything encouraging to say about the fate of individuals.

He went daily to the Pathan, buying Michelle's fix and checking for news from the border. Afternoons, while she slept, he went back down to the bazaar and lingered over tea in one of the shops. The days were warm and getting warmer.

It was the thirteenth day of waiting when he saw the Australian's pendant for sale in the bazaar. It seeemed like an omen. He went immediately back to the fort, waiting until Michelle was on the declining slope of her afternoon fix to tell her that he wanted her to leave. If there was going to be any trouble, he wanted her to be clear of it. At the same time he wanted to streamline his own concerns. Worrying about Michelle was sapping him. He felt he would have to do something soon, and her presence severely limited his options.

"Listen," he said. "This is important. Do you still have friends in Katmandu?"

She shrugged and smiled. "I have friends in Katmandu, I have friends in Goa, I have friends in Paris, friends everywhere. So many friends."

He took her by the shoulders. "This is serious. Things could get bad here. We have enough for a plane ticket. You go to Katmandu and stay with your friends. I'll meet you there as soon as I can."

She frowned. "You come too."

"I have to wait for Rudy."

"You're wanting to give me the dump."

He shook his head.

"It's true. You don't love me."

"I *do* love you and I *don't* want anything to *happen* to you. I'll come get you as soon as Rudy shows up."

"I stay here with you."

He knew she wouldn't change her mind. He also knew his idea wasn't very practical. She was in no shape to travel alone, yet it seemed more dangerous to let her stay. He'd been having nightmares about the incident in the bazaar.

That night he brought the subject up again, but Michelle put her hands over her ears and began singing whenever he tried to speak.

The Pathan was more discursive than usual on the morning of the seventeenth day. After taking note of the weather and inquiring after Michelle, he began to discuss the business climate. The government was stepping up border patrols. Rival tribes were fighting over the smuggling routes. Trey guessed he was being softened up for a price hike.

"It is especially dangerous for amateurs," the Pathan said. He shook his head slowly and frowned.

Trey registered a new note in the conversation. He felt his heart in his chest, as if it had just started pumping a moment before. "You've got news for me?"

The Pathan raised his eyebrows, as if amazed by Trey's acuity or else by his lack of tact in coming so abruptly to the point. He scrupulously smoothed the baggy folds of his sleeves. "There is a rumor."

Trey waited.

"The men your friend contacted across the border, they are not honest men. They require a payment for his safe return."

"Why haven't I been approached?" Trey demanded, but the answer came to him without any hint from the Pathan, who was gazing impassively over the bazaar as if he'd lost interest in the conversation.

"How much?" Trey said then. He guessed that whoever had Rudy would know exactly how much he was planning to pay on delivery and therefore would ask for a little more. For a moment he felt almost relieved, finally knowing what the situation was, and what was required, but at the same time he didn't feel he knew anything for certain.

"If you wish," the Pathan said, "I can look into the matter."

Trey doubted that any such inquiry was necessary, but he had to ob-serve his broker's ritual. That he appear to trust him was crucial now that he didn't know if he could.

He went back to the fort and read to Michelle, not even broaching his conversation with the Pathan.

That afternoon Trey was told that the kidnappers would settle for noth-ing less than two thousand dollars. He had a little more than eighteen hun-dred in his money belt, and wondered if the Pathan had any way of knowing this.

"I don't have that much."

"Then your friend is dead."

"Tell them I have fifteen hundred." This was the amount Rudy would have promised the Afghanis on delivery.

"I do not believe they will change their minds."

"What if I wired for more money?"

The Pathan laughed. "Where do you think you are?" He was looking at Trey intently now, having shed the bored manner of a man performing an unwanted and unprofitable task.

"I need some proof." He could think of no way to get the other two hundred but felt he somehow had to keep the process moving forward.

"I was asked to show you this." The man reached into a leather pouch on his holster belt and removed a gold signet ring. Rudy's.

"That doesn't prove anything. Why didn't he send a note?"

The Pathan shrugged. "These are not literary men."

"But how do I know he's alive?" Until that moment it hadn't really oc-curred to him that Rudy might be dead. Even if he came up with the money, he had no guarantee except this man's word.

"I believe he is alive," the Pathan said.

"I have to think this through."

"Do you have the money?"

Trey shook his head. "Not all of it."

"Perhaps," the Pathan said, "I could assist you with the balance."

And then Trey realized he had been waiting to say this all along.

"In exchange for what?" he said, then fixed his eyes on the man's face and listened.

Michelle was sleeping on the pallet with her mouth open. Trey knelt down beside her and pushed the hair away from her eyes. He timed her respirations: twelve a minute, low even for a junkie. He watched an insect crawling up the earthen wall above them and wondered if there was a right thing to do.

"Trey?"

"I'm here."

"What time is it?"

"Afternoon."

"I think it is time."

"There's something I have to talk to you about."

"Not now."

"Yes. Now."

She turned to look at him, her face slack. He tried to remember her as she'd been in Katmandu. The outlines of her beauty were still there, but back then this beauty seemed to be projected from an inexhaustible source of reckless energy that kept her always in motion, her eyes full of mystery. When he saw her again in Goa she was showing signs of wear. She'd lost weight and her eyes didn't have the precision he remembered.

"You're crying," she said, then reached up and wiped a tear from his cheek.

Trey said, "Michelle."

"Don't be sad," she said. "Maybe you take a little fix with me."

He shook his head.

"Give me one, Trey. I want you to do it."

"Rudy's in trouble," he said.

She sighed dreamily. "Don't worry. You will think of something, no?"

"I need your help."

"You do what's best."

"Listen to me."

"Please, Trey. Not now. After a little fix." She reached down and stroked his crotch. "Then we make love." They hadn't, not since she'd started shooting up again. The drug had swallowed all of her desire, and he found he didn't want her as she was now.

He pushed her hand away. "I'm trying to talk to you."

"Trey, please."

He had no illusions about his complicity in Michelle's habit, but he felt that some last shred of principle was upheld by his refusal to stick the needle into her arm. Now this seemed a cheap distinction. Michelle was beyond thinking. He had allowed her to do this to herself. For this he had to accept responsibility, and for the rest of it.

"All right," he said. "All right, I will."

She sat up on the pallet and rolled up the sleeve of her shirt. The arm was thin and pale, speckled near the joint with needle marks. Trey took the bandana from around his neck and tied her off. She leaned over and kissed him. He swabbed her arm with alcohol, then wiped off the needle.

"A little more," she said when Trey started to heat the spoon over the flame of the oil lamp. "Okay?"

A little more, then. For the next few hours he wanted her out of it. He didn't want her to know what he'd had to do. He wished her a long, cool rush that would lift her beyond the clammy walls, beyond the gray hills outside to a white, featureless place where there was neither choice nor betrayal. He almost wished he could join her there. He shook more powder from the packet into the spoon, then closed his eyes and opened them.

When the powder had melted, he put the spoon down on the pallet, drew the liquid into the syringe and held it up, looking for bubbles. He missed the vein on the first try, his hands shaking badly. When he tried to pull it out a peak of white flesh rose around the needle. He clutched her elbow tighter. The second time the needle slipped easily into the vein. He raised his thumb and depressed the plunger.

Where he drew the needle out, a tiny red bubble blossomed and burst. Michelle's face unclenched and she sank down onto the pallet with a sigh.

He staggered down the stairs and, outside, got down on his hands and knees and vomited.

He found him in the bazaar.

"You have decided," the Pathan asked.

Trey nodded. There was nothing he could say.

"You have somewhere to go?"

"I won't bother you," Trey said.

The Pathan nodded solemnly, then reached under his shirt and held out a dirty white envelope. "Two hundred dollars," he said, "as a token of good faith. When I return you will have the rest of the money for me, as we agreed."

Trey let him stand there, holding the envelope. The Pathan waited; he would not insist.

Finally Trey took the envelope and shoved it into his pocket. "Two hours," he said.

After nodding again, the Pathan turned and walked off through the bazaar. Trey imagined rifle sights on the receding blue turban.

The sun had just dipped behind the mountains in the west. The bazaar was closing down. Trey was sitting at a table in front of a tea shop. The old man who had served him came out to look at him, then went slowly back inside.

Someone was talking to him but at first Trey didn't hear what was being said. The man who was speaking had his bushy hair tied back in a ponytail and wore a gold ring through his left nostril. He was waving his hand in front of Trey's face.

"Hey, man, do you read me? Anybody home in there?" He unstrapped his backpack and took a seat across the table. He put his index finger to his ear and said "Bang!" then patted his shirtpockets. "Got a smoke?"

Trey shook his head.

"Got a voice? No, don't answer that. I know how it is. Some days, what's to say. Am I right? Silence is golden. I got this friend in some monastery, he's taken this vow of silence. Which is entirely cool." He held his hands out between them and cracked his knuckles. "Speak to me, man. I'm going crazy. Five fucking hours at the border. They tear my pack down. They strip me. Check my asshole. Under my toenails. Behind my ears. But I'm clean. Jesus, I'd kill for a toke right now. Swallowed my last half gram on the bus. Once that hit I thought the Khyber Pass was going to *swallow* me alive. What a place. Journey into Hades. So tell me, what's the scene around here? These dudes toting guns. They got a war going on?"

Trey saw the Pathan approaching briskly, then stopping a few yards short of the tea shop, taking his pistol from the holster and leveling it at him. Trey's companion quit talking and followed his gaze, then dropped to the ground and rolled under the table.

The Pathan seemed to be trembling. "We had an agreement," he said, his voice very strange.

"What happened?" Trey said.

"Perhaps you think to make a joke."

Trey opened his mouth to speak but couldn't catch his breath. The pistol was following the motion of his head.

The Pathan said, "My offer was more than generous."

"Where is Michelle," Trey asked.

"Where? Do not worry about where. She is where you left her." He stepped forward and examined Trey's face. "You do not know, then?" He shook his head, spit on the ground between them and, stepping forward, went through Trey's pockets with his free hand. He found the envelope, put it in the sleeve of his shirt, then left.

The man with the ponytail got to his feet and put his arms around Trey's shoulders.

Trey looked at the ring through his nose, wondering if it had hurt to have a thing like that put in.

"Jesus Fucking Christ," the man said. "That was close, man. Somebody could've got killed."

It was almost dark, and Trey thought of telling him something Rudy had said—that it was dangerous to be in the bazaar in Landi Kotal after dark. Looking up at the huge gray sky, he could see the first faint stars. He could feel the planet turning and moving through space. He could feel the tug of gravity in his arms and legs, and he could hear the roar of darkness sweeping toward him like a fist.

1982

My Public Service

Was it Kissinger who said that power's an aphrodisiac? The dictator with his cabaret dancer, the studio boss and the starlet, all the ruthless, puff-bellied, hairy-eared trolls with their creamy cupcakes . . . it's hardly a notion to inspire poetry, or pride of species. But the quest for power can be a search for love. This is what occurs to me now, years after I helped bring the senator down.

Like many before him, he required women. It was a compulsion, as drinking is for some men. He was a teetotaler, but he couldn't bear to pass a night alone. If he had fifteen minutes between appointments, he wanted to spend them in hot congress with a warm body. One of my jobs was to summon them, smuggle them up the back stairs, through the rear door, spirit them out in the service elevator just ahead of his wife if she'd taken the early flight. The blonde in the second row, the stewardess named Tami, the student who asked that interesting question about mental health. I would say that the senator was very impressed with her whatever—her question, her comment, her thoughts on the health-care question, her thorough and enlightening explanation of the safety features of the Boeing 747, her long blond tresses, her tits—and would like to meet her in his suite. At first I was embarrassed. A former fat boy who retained the doughy, pig-gaited self-image long after the lard had melted away, I was nearly incapable of approaching women on my own behalf, but as the senator's emissary, I'm ashamed to say, I became good at putting just the right spin on these invitations: It was important that candidates understand it wasn't actually their opinions on the health-care question that were being solicited, the senator not having time to waste on preliminaries, while it was also important to communicate all of this by implication, deniability being crucial in case the lady in question was unreceptive. I'm sorry to say there weren't many refusals.

There was a type: slim, no ass, big tits and long blond hair. Not that he wouldn't compromise his standards in a pinch, politics being the art of compromise, after all.

And now that I've given you every reason to despise the man, let me also say that I loved him. The women weren't drugged, or coerced. Neither were the voters. In a democracy, seduction replaces rape. He was the most magnetic individual I have ever met. When I arrived on the Hill during the dark days of the Republican ascendancy, all the young Democrats wanted to work for Senator Castleton, the fresh-faced, sandy-haired Solon of his day. At that time he was becoming known as a champion of comprehensive national health care and tax reform. The press liked him because he was young and photogenic—the same reasons for which they'd later dislike him.

He came out of the high plains, his exact origins obscured in a cloud of red prairie dust and self-invention. The campaign biography stated that his father had died in combat in World War II. That was the start of the trouble, when an enterprising reporter found the birth certificate that named his father as "Unknown." The fallout from this revelation was mixed, the senator perhaps gaining as much sympathy for his fatherlessness as censure for his mendacity. After the first disclosure, the second-day press coverage was somewhat cautious, accompanied by sidebars about compassionate man-on-the-street reactions, as well as a smattering of breast-beating editorials about the role of the press. Subsequent revelations about his background—the mother's lack of visible means of support, the hospitalizations—were handled gingerly, almost apologetically. The senator was perceived by many to be the double victim of an unfortunate childhood and an insensitive press. Trey Davis, the former administrative assistant who worked on the campaign, used to joke that this episode bought him an extra planeload of blondes.

The senator himself was reticent about his background, and in the end I'm not sure he could separate his own inventions from the facts. But one day in Georgia, during his first presidential bid, he told me about his mother. He'd just addressed a group of students at a private university and had been confronted by a shouting delegation from a nearby Bible college, whose members denounced his opinions on school prayer and abortion. Standing up to the protestors, he called them "narrow-minded religious bigots"; the event had ended in an uproar, with part of the audience chanting the Lord's Prayer to drown out the voice from the podium. Driving back to Atlanta, he was seething. After many miles of silence, he suddenly told me that his mother had been involved with a group called the Assemblies of God, to which she tithed much of what little money she was able to beg from relatives or collect from the state. His jaw clenched, the Styrofoam coffee cup in his hand shaking, he said she'd once driven him into a small Missouri town and made him beg money from strangers. Two days before, she'd signed over a Social Security check to a minister who promised her the Lord would provide. Later, he said, when his mother went back to complain, she was told that her wallet was possessed by Satan, who encouraged her spendthrift ways. The future senator had watched his mother perform an exorcism on the kitchen table, pounding on her wallet, chanting "Satan be gone." I tend to believe this story because of the clenched fury in his dripping face that day, the kudzu-strangled telephone poles ticking past the back window of the steaming Lincoln, and because I never heard him tell it again.

Between fits of religiosity, his mother drank, and as an adult he had little patience for drinkers, which made him something of an anomaly in the Senate. At any rate, she died when he was fifteen and he went to live with an aunt and uncle, attended the state university on a scholarship, married his first sweetheart, went to Harvard Law and joined the Kennedy administration.

These are the facts, the campaign bio. But try to imagine the distance between these points. Far easier to walk on your knees over broken glass from the state capital to Cambridge, Massachusetts, and Washington, D.C., than to do it as he did. Try to picture the days and nights devoted to work and study; you are obviously obsessed and driven to succeed, or you never would've made it so far. When finally you slump over on the desk, or turn off the light in your room in your uncle's basement, imagine the howling demons of fear and loneliness coming in off the plains like tornadoes and rattling the windows. Imagine those few moments suspended over the abyss between work and exhausted sleep. At dawn, the ordeal will begin again.

One morning—in New Hampshire, I think—I was due to wake him up. He had a breakfast speech with the Elks or the Moose, some antlered fraternity. I was just outside his door at the Holiday Inn when I heard the woman's voice, pleading, calling his name, and remembered her from the night before, the waitress from the cocktail lounge downstairs. When she started to cry, I used my key to open the door. They were in bed. She was on her side, facing out, and he was wrapped around her. She'd thrown the covers off but couldn't extract herself from his sleeping arms, which were clamped fiercely around her torso, his left hand with its wedding band clasping a breast that bulged pinkly between his clenched fingers. I managed to rouse him, and to free her. It would happen again, and even some of the women who managed to free themselves in the morning remarked on his tenacious reluctance, once asleep, to let go.

He graduated fifth in his class at Harvard Law and then signed on with Vista, the fledgling domestic version of the Peace Corps. JFK was his hero, and they became acquainted. I often wonder if he knew then about JFK's satyriasis, or if his later behavior was influenced by the eventual revelations. According to those who knew him back then, he was the straightest of arrows—like me, I like to imagine—and devoted to Doreen and their two children, avidly creating the family he'd never had.

On the anniversary of that infamous day in Dallas, I sat with him in a coffee shop in Iowa, where we were stumping for the caucuses, and he said he'd cried when he heard the news, sobbing uncontrollably as he hugged his secretary. Tears stood in his eyes as he told me this. "And then," he said without a trace of self-consciousness, "I decided I would take his place."

He had gone back home to run for Congress, then, after two terms, for the Senate. He took care of his state even as he refused to share its most conservative convictions. When he came out against the Vietnam War, early on, all agreed that his senatorial bid was ruined. His victory was seen by the national press as a signal event in the debate over the war; almost from the start, he was a national figure. He was, as unfashionable as it sounds, a hero of mine. Hero worship was especially unfashionable in the wake of the sixties, yet I was not alone. Most of us would've worked for him for nothing. In the end, some of us did.

I grew up in the sterile, fertile state he represented, not on one of its amber-waving farms, but in an aluminum-sided suburb rimmed with shopping malls. My father sold insurance. I was a 4-H captain, a stamp collector, an apple-polisher in white socks. A young nerd with aspirations to public service, I represented my state at a national high school conference on government, flying to Washington for three days of make-believe legislative sessions and inspirational speeches from lawmakers. Castleton spoke to our group and later invited me to his office. He had a face that seemed incapable of harboring deceit or insincerity, a visage like an open book. We chatted for ten minutes. His speech about the virtues of hard work and the joys of public service might have been lifted out of a civics textbook, but I believed every word. Unlike most of the other congressmen I'd met, who seemed to be speaking by rote, whose gestures and phrases sounded stagy and false even to a seventeen-year-old teacher's pet, he seemed absolutely genuine. Like a real person, talking man to man. What I sensed then was how much it actually seemed to matter that I liked him. I wanted to go to work for him then and there, but I had to wait five years. He wrote me a letter of recommendation to Harvard, and though I was accepted, my father made too much to qualify for financial aid and too little to pay for tuition comfortably, so I went to the state U. A week after my graduation, I was installed as an intern in his Senate office in the Dirksen Building.

The years I worked with him on the Hill seem, in retrospect, the best of my life. That first year, I shared a dormlike house near Lincoln Park with half a dozen other unpaid or underpaid press aides and interns. We walked to work, did most of our eating from canapé platters at nightly receptions and Capitol events. Later, when I became a legislative assistant, I moved to a two-bedroom apartment in Adams Morgan with Trey Davis, who also worked for the senator. Davis was a New Yorker, the first I'd ever met, and had a year's seniority and a world of experience on me. He'd grown up on Fifth Avenue, attended Buckley and Hotchkiss and Williams, where he'd been the protégé of James McGregor Burns. Initially I was put off by his dangerous good looks, his arrogant and cynical manner. As my immediate superior, he subjected me to a species of hazing the first few weeks and referred to me behind my back as "the lemur," an allusion to my putative wide-eyed innocence. His own eyes, beneath heavy bat-wing brows, seemed knowing and cruel.

At the end of the first week, he looked me up and down and said, "You're an aesthetic menace. The polyester has got to go." He took me to Brooks Brothers and picked out a pair of gray flannel slacks, a pair of chinos, three oxford-cloth shirts and a blue blazer, charging them to his own account. When I protested, he said I could pay him back in installments. Somehow, we became friends. I think I was like the plain girl who becomes the confidante of the beauty queen; he needed a protégé, an appreciative audience. When he moved to the apartment in Adams Morgan, he asked me to share it with him. Neither of us spent much time at home anyway. Mostly we worked. Trey would sometimes take the shuttle to New York for the weekend, returning, haggard, with tales of nightclubs and parties populated by dirty debutantes. He tried to explain the difference between downtown and uptown to me. I was content to stay in D.C., which was more than worldly enough for me. Occasionally I would have a beer at a neighborhood pub and attempt to impress ambitious young women in Talbot's suits. Though I didn't know it at the time, it was the heyday of the Pill, after Roe and before AIDS. I had a few dates and a brief, awkward romance with a Georgetown student who was interning in Senator Kennedy's office, during which I managed finally to shed my virginity at the age of twenty-three. But I wasn't very good with women. I think I was too earnest, even for serious young ladies with Phi Beta Kappa keys and Bass Weejuns who'd come to the Capitol to serve their country.

When the senator announced to the staff that he was going to make a run for the White House, we were ecstatic. We would all rise with him. But more than that, we believed in him, though by then I'd learned that heroes have a few warts. We all knew he'd had an affair with one of the assistants, whom he later placed in the office of the senior senator. And one night when I went back to the office late to retrieve some papers, I saw him emerge from the inner office with a disheveled female reporter. His face was flushed and glistening with a film of sweat. They were both giggling, until they spotted me and hurriedly donned their coats, the senator wishing me a curt good night.

Neat, housewifely Doreen had come to the office for the announcement. She smiled and hugged us, seeming more like the candidate's spinsterish sister than his wife. I couldn't help wondering what the campaign really meant to her. Bad enough to be the wife of a senator. But maybe he was a victim, too, married early to a woman he'd soon outgrown. She must have looked much different to an orphan at the state university than to a rising U.S. senator. After she left, several of us overheard Joe Cleary lecturing him from inside his office. "Goddamn it, you've got to keep it in your pants, or you're going to fuck the whole thing up," he roared. I couldn't make out the senator's response. Cleary was a tough old Boston politico who'd worked for Kennedy and alongside Castleton since his congressional days. Shambling red-faced out of the office, he turned to me and asked if I knew the three *b*'s. "The three whats?" I said, looking up at the craters and exploded veins on his broad, florid nose. I was afraid of him, of his caustic whiskey breath with its whiff of decomposition and corruption. He seemed to me the antithesis of the new political order we were trying to create. "Broads, bribes and boys," he said, then ran his sleeve under his nose. "Sooner or later . . ." Cleary shook his head and left the office, the sentence unfinished. I was glad to see him go. Although I might have concurred with the sentiment, it seemed out of place on this special day, the dawn of an era. I was full of liberal indignation at his crude and chauvinistic term for women, a word I'd certainly never heard on the senator's lips.

"What about booze?" Trey said from the next desk over, and we all had a good laugh.

I volunteered for the campaign staff. Within days I was on the plane with him to Iowa. Those first few months we were romantic underdogs, tilting at grain silos and cooling towers, drawing on a modest fund of skeptical goodwill. But the senator was charismatic, and if we could get five hundred people in a room, four hundred of them walked out believing. More often, though, it was forty. On one occasion four citizens came to hear him speak at a public library, one of them a reporter from the local weekly. But he reached out to those four as if they were convention delegates, turning his chair around backward and sitting among them, lingering to chat with the blue-haired librarian, who blushed and fussed with her hair as though sensing her womanhood for the first time in a decade. And the way I looked at it, that was five more in our column. Late at night, awash in lasagna indigestion and Trey's snoring from the next twin bed in the Ramada or the Holiday Inn, I would add them up in my head like a good little accountant—the number of mouths at the church supper, the number of hands shaken outside the factory gate. And one more late convert—

the receptionist who'd gone off duty at eleven and joined the senator in his room.

His close second-place finish in New Hampshire was interpreted as a win, given the large field and his last-minute gains against the polls. Suddenly money was pouring in, and the camp followers flocked: pollsters, consultants, volunteers, fund-raisers, local brokers, party leaders, single-issue nuts, social-climbing hostesses, reporters—and women. That was when it began to get out of control.

From New Hampshire, we flew straight to New York City, where they were waiting to shower Castleton with money and attention. That was where Carl Furst signed on, the most sought-after of Democratic political consultants, a red-faced left-wing assassin. He'd worked with the better-funded front-runner early on, but we'd been hearing he was unhappy with his candidate, and after New Hampshire, no dummy, he joined us. There were mixed feelings about this. On the one hand, it was good for the team, like signing a great pitcher. But some of us, particularly Trey, who had been practically running the campaign up to this point, resented this fair-weather friend, this bullet-headed mercenary. Since Furst would be stepping in at the top, everyone moved down a notch. And, in fact, the senator quickly became more and more isolated from those of us who'd started out with him, cocooned in the smoky scrum of Furst and his pollsters and spin doctors.

The night before the Furst meeting, we went to a Park Avenue party given by a fat man who owned a chain of stores and whose thin wife was a former lover of JFK. If you're wondering how I know this, they told us. That was my introduction to New York—a city I thought should be gerrymandered right out of the republic and bequeathed to France, or maybe Turkey. At any rate, I was part of the advance team, arriving at the apartment with Trey Davis and two Secret Service men. Our host and hostess greeted us with the special consideration that our association with the newly important senator conferred. They eagerly greeted Trey by name, reminding him that their son had been at Buckley with him, though he seemed distinctly cool about this. Giving us the tour, they pointed out the more prominent paintings, which were framed in gilt and had little museum plaques to identify the artist. Our host explained that he'd been a major supporter of the Democratic Party for years. "And Evie was JFK's lover when she was at Vassar," he said, nodding toward his wife—who was adjusting the lilies in a large crystal vase—and beaming as if he'd just commended her cooking or business acumen. I thought this was bizarre enough with his wife out of earshot, but later, with his arm around the tanned and beaming Evie, he repeated it to the senator. If she'd been any younger or prettier, I'm sure he would've been very keen on this admission.

That party was the beginning of the showbiz phase. Several movie stars were on hand; apparently, some of them lived in New York, though I can't imagine why. The writer Norman Mailer arrived with his beautiful new red-haired wife. As with most of the women in the room, she was much taller than her companion. Dressed like a banker, Mailer rocked back on his heels when he listened and jabbed his finger into Castleton's chest when he talked, while his wife smiled impishly. The senator was enamored. He kidded with Mailer as if they'd known each other for years, and flirted with Mrs. Mailer. It was hard to say which one he was more interested in, and it was the first time I'd seen him starstruck. Doreen was at the party, but, like most political wives, she had the gift for receding into the background, and after posing for photos, she left early to catch the last shuttle back to be with the kids.

I stood in the corner and watched the rich people. You could tell they were rich not only because of how they dressed but also because it cost a thousand dollars a couple to shake the senator's hand and exchange a few words. But since he was gifted at making that kind of encounter seem meaningful, I doubt anyone went away feeling cheated. Before he left, he did his best to make sure everyone in the room loved him. Yet, listening to his remarks, for the first time I heard in his voice the third-person self-consciousness of a politician addressing the masses. What he said wasn't new; I'd heard many of the same remarks a hundred times before, but each time he'd seemed to be speaking his mind and his heart directly, to individuals, no matter how large the group. This was one of his talents, that he didn't sound like a pol. Now, suddenly, he seemed insincere, as if his recent success had made him conscious of these sentiments as a winning formula. The phrase "what the American people want" was repeated a little too often for my taste.

That first night in New York, he started the liaison with Amanda Greer, which we all read about years later. Against everyone's advice, he accompanied her to a nightclub. Trey and I tagged along in our Town Car, trailing the actress's limo. Trey was furious. He explained that there were photographers outside these places and sometimes inside, that drugs were consumed openly on the premises; under normal circumstances, it was his kind of scene, but we could kiss the nomination good-bye if anyone got a good shot of the senator with his tongue in this actress's ear.

He jumped out of the car at a stoplight and ran over to the limo, rapping on the smoked window until it finally slid down. After a heated exchange, he finally negotiated a compromise. "Look," Trey said after he ran back to the car. "You go take her in the front door of the club. I'll sneak our hero in the side door—I know the owner—and we'll meet you in the VIP room." The senator emerged from the limo and jogged to our car, grinning sheepishly as I passed. In a daze, I walked to the limo and climbed in.

She was curled in the corner of the seat, her legs folded up beneath her. Regarding me quizzically, she appeared ready to burst into laughter. Tiny as she was, she had an enormous specific gravity; I could sense the car listing toward her side like a boat beneath us. She was more real than anyone I'd ever seen, her hair redder, her eyes bluer than anything in nature. Despite the unexpected wrinkles around her eyes, or maybe because of them, I thought nobody could be more beautiful. I imagined that others, those who worshiped her from the movies, would be surprised by the wrinkles, whereas I could look beyond them. She was smoking a cigarette, and when she spoke, her voice was husky and low.

"Wouldn't we like to play Mrs. Robinson to you," she said. She unfolded her legs and leaned forward to pour more Champagne in her glass. She seemed a little worse for wear, her words semislurred. All I wanted to do was to protect her from herself, and from all the people who wanted something from her. As we glided above the rutted streets of New York, she talked to me like an old friend and asked where I was from. I was astonished to learn she'd been born and raised on a farm not fifty miles from my home. She told me about her family, about leaving at seventeen to come to the city and study acting. When we disembarked in front of the club, she took my arm as the flashbulbs began to pop. There were perhaps a hundred people waiting outside, but right away a path opened up for us. I heard her name repeated like a mantra. Someone asked, "Who's the guy?" And at that moment I felt the envy of strangers and almost believed

I deserved it. Whatever the circumstances, I had become part of her world.

I was bereft when, at the door to the VIP room, I got separated from her by the ponytailed bouncer. Seeing her disappear inside, I was furious beyond reason, as if I'd been deprived of my rightful place by her side. I insisted that I was with her, to no avail.

I can't say what the VIP room was like, but what I saw in the bathroom and out on the dance floor gave me nightmares for days. After exploring the premises, I was waiting sullenly outside the door, when suddenly Castleton appeared, looking out into the crowd. Seeing me, he waved me in and the now-diplomatic bouncer stood aside. I glared at him indignantly. Then the senator put his arm on my shoulder and said, "I want you to take Amanda to her hotel suite and wait for me there. Don't let her out of your sight. And wait for me." Looking around the small, smoky room, I spotted her gliding toward us, a cigarette in one hand and a Champagne glass in the other, the eyes of the crowd tracking her as if attached by wires. Even in her cups she maintained a kind of dignity, her liquidity contained in a graceful vessel. "If it isn't my old friend Benjamin Braddock. My young friend. My new true-blue baby boy."

"Cal's going to take you home," the senator said.

"Home is where the hat is," she said, "and I don't wear hats. I don't wear hearts, either, except on my sleeve. Home is where you can't go again. It's in foreclosure." She kissed him on the cheek, then held her hand to her mouth in mock chagrin, looking around to see if the gesture had been noted. Then she took my arm and marched me out of the room, down the stairs and across the dance floor. If she had seemed tipsy, her stride was now quick and purposeful, a practiced gait that blurred her passage and left bystanders doing double takes, a just-short-of-running gait—like the rack of a Tennessee walking horse—which is unique to famous people who want to move between two points without getting dragged into contact with the spectating class. The senator resorts to it on occasion, when rushing for planes, though usually he's a glutton for handshaking, chats and photo ops.

She raced me out the side door, around the crowd. Her driver, spotting her, jumped out to open the door as a photographer snapped her picture. Suddenly she put her arm around me and posed, laying her head on my shoulder, then kissing my neck. Two other photographers materialized and someone shouted, "What's *his* name?" My vision was bleached out by the flashbulbs, and then we were in the limo, pulling away.

Laughing, she said, "I like to think about the photo editors and gossip columnists scurrying around tomorrow while I'm still asleep, trying to figure out who you are so they can run the picture. And the funny thing is, they'll never be able to figure it out."

My exhilaration vanished as I realized what she was saying—that in her world I didn't exist. She must have seen this, because the next moment she took my hand and said, "I didn't mean it like that. It's just so awful if you take it too seriously. Sometimes I want to drop my skirt and moon the silly bastards. But you *are* awfully cute." She leaned forward and kissed me, caressing my lips with her tongue. I had never been kissed like that. When she drew away and reached for a glass, I wondered what to tell the senator. She poured herself another drink. I saw myself rescuing Amanda Greer from this life of liquor and limousines and nightclubs and false adulation. I would take this fallen angel back home and plant her in the rich black soil of the heartland, buy a farm and raise children. I would run for Congress, and she'd campaign for me. I didn't see the contradiction between this vision and all the glamour that had dazzled me in the first place.

"The thing about fame," she said, "is you think everyone will love you, that it's a way to become close to people." She stopped and took a sip of her drink, and just when I'd decided she'd lost her thread of thought, she continued. "And then, when you are famous, it drives a wedge between you and the rest of the world. A wall of glass." She tapped the smoked glass of the window with her fingers. "I don't think your senator knows that yet." I wanted to tell her that I understood, but she reached overhead and punched a button that flooded the rear compartment with loud music, then laid her head back on the seat and closed her eyes, nodding lightly in time to the music, her lipstick, I noted happily, smeared from our kiss.

At the hotel, she carried her drink in with her, and the doorman greeted her reverently. She hadn't spoken another word to me. In the elevator, I asked how long she was staying there and she looked at me as if she didn't understand the question. Then she said, "I live here."

The suite was, to my eyes, a nest of luxury, with its pale peach floral carpet and antique furniture. It was nothing like any hotel room I'd seen on the campaign. She went to the bar and poured herself another drink, half of which she spilled on the carpet, then picked up a phone and dialed.

I sat down on the edge of a sofa. She was talking to someone named Gloria. I tried to imagine the course of the night, the course of my life. Should I go to her now, hang up the phone and take her in my arms?

Then there was a knock on the door. She put her hand over the receiver and pointed to it, kissing the air between us. The senator was waiting in the hallway with a Secret Service man. Somehow, I hadn't expected him this soon. I tried to think of something to say, thinking of what had happened in the limousine, but he nodded to me and said, "Thanks," then walked into the room, leaving his security guy in the hall. Amanda waved to him, the phone crooked in her arm. He paced around nervously, picking up a porcelain vase from a side table and flipping it over to check its provenance. When he saw me standing in the door, he looked irritated. "That'll be all, Cal," he said.

Emboldened by what I believed was love, frightened but firm, I said, "Senator, I think you should go back to the hotel."

He stared at me as if I'd just offered to shoot him.

"The lady's not herself," I said, "and I don't think we want to risk any scandal at this point."

"You little shit, how dare you—"

By now I was terrified, but I couldn't stop myself: "I would like to remind you, sir, that you're married."

At that moment, Amanda hung up the phone. From behind, she threw her arms around him, though he was glaring at me and looking as if he might charge, like a bull, but for her restraint. Peering over his shoulder, she saw me and smiled. But there was no recognition in her glazed eyes and it was a crooked, intoxicated smile, the kind she might flash at a fan who'd managed to catch her eye. She lifted her arms and pulled his face down to her own, locking him in the same embrace that I'd enjoyed only a few minutes earlier. I kept waiting for the kiss to end, waiting for inspiration. Finally I turned and walked out, my face burning, not wanting to be standing there when they finally broke apart. Crying with rage, I walked from the Carlyle to the midtown Sheraton, hoping I would be mugged or challenged, then lay sleepless in my bed till dawn, feverish with jealousy and yearning.

———

Two days later, a tabloid featured a smiling picture of the senator entering the nightclub and another of the actress, but the two were not linked. I bought all the New York papers that morning, foolishly hoping that a printed picture of Amanda and me might lend some substance to my folly. Anyway, that night marked a new level of recklessness on the part of my senator. And it changed me.

I suddenly felt the drabness of my own existence. The hour I'd spent with Amanda made me yearn for something I'd never known, or even missed, before. Not exactly beauty or money or sex or power, although all of these things, I realized, might be exchangeable for this thing. I can only call it brilliance, like a surfeit of light. For a brief moment, everything in my life was more vivid. And in that moment I felt a kinship with the senator and his quest for glory. I understood how he could risk everything for a moment like the one I'd shared in the limousine. I had risked quite a bit myself. I would have liked to discuss it with him, but we were never alone together again. After that night, my career with the senator was essentially finished. He didn't fire me, but I was sent to Chicago to work with the new office there in a clearly demoted capacity.

When he threw in the towel after Illinois, I had to pay for my flight back to Washington. While away, I'd been replaced on the Hill, and when I called the chief of staff, he told me there were no openings at that time. I wasn't really surprised. I was still living in Adams Morgan with Trey, to whom I confessed most of the details of my disgrace. Though disillusioned ever since the hiring of Furst, he was back at work on the Senate staff. Sometimes at night I heard the daughters of ambassadors and cabinet officers howling and moaning in his bedroom. For the first time in my life, I succeeded in picking up a girl at a bar, and later, back home, she had to plead with me to be gentle, although in all my scant amorous history, no one has ever accused me of excessive enthusiasm.

Three months later, Trey came home in a rage. After paying Furst and his people more than $200,000, the campaign committee declared bankruptcy. Like most of the staff, including Trey, I was owed four months in back wages. "Can you believe that bastard?" he said.

That night we went to an Ethiopian restaurant, and Trey told me the senator had flown up to New York twice in the last month to visit Amanda Greer. By this time I was working for a public relations firm. It was nothing I would've envisioned myself doing five months before, and I was hardly proud of the work. We represented, among others, a South American dictator who for years the senator had attacked for his appalling human rights record. I was, however, having more success with women. After my moment of glory with Amanda Greer, I felt slightly disdainful of mortal females, which seemed to make me more attractive. For six months I dated a legislative assistant from Texas, Deirdre Clark, who would've married me, and whom I probably would've been thrilled to marry a year before. She was coltish and sweet and smarter than I was. I cheated on her and let her find out about it, and she moved back to Houston a few months later.

Trey had increasing difficulties with Castleton and eventually went to work for Senator Moynihan. Three years after our campaign ended, Castleton officially announced he was making another run, and now he was the front-runner. According to Trey, fat-faced Carl Furst had agreed to take charge only after Castleton promised to stop fucking around. A week after he won New Hampshire, one of the supermarket tabloids published a story about his relationship with Amanda Greer. Lacking hard evidence, they published a picture of the two tête-à-tête at a fund-raiser. Unnamed sources said that the senator made frequent, unscheduled visits to New York and that his wife had given him an ultimatum. The issue of womanizing, the secret buzz of the press corps for years, was now out in the open. At a press conference in Florida, he was pelted with questions about marriage and infidelity. He indignantly denied the story, while acknowledging "an old friendship" with the actress. With Doreen standing at his side, he said, "I have always been a faithful husband and a devoted father," and refused to say more. He accused the press of conducting a witch-hunt and suggested this was the work of his rivals and the Republicans. The issue bubbled for a week, then faded with the lack of new disclosures.

A few days after the senator's Super Tuesday victories, Trey organized a reunion poker game for some of us who'd been involved in the previous campaign. We met at a saloon in Georgetown, where he'd reserved a private room in the back. He'd asked each of us to bring at least two hundred dollars. Gene Samuels, Dave Crushak, Tom Whittle, Trey and I drank beer and reminisced about the bad old days on the trail. All of us had been burned when the previous committee had declared bankruptcy, and not one of us was involved with the new one. If the American public had been listening in, they would've formed a highly unfavorable impression of Castleton's character. Old slights and grievances were revived, along with tawdry stories of broom-closet dalliances. We reviewed the specifications of "the type"—blond, big tits, no ass. Finally, Dave Crushak said, "I'm feeling lucky. Who's got the cards?"

"I've got a card," said Trey. From his blazer he extracted a five-by-seven picture of an attractive blonde, on which was printed the name Tamara, along with a set of measurements and the name and number of a Los Angeles modeling agency. We passed it around, making appreciative noises. We were all a little drunk by now. "Look familiar?" Trey asked. When no one could place her, he said, "The fucking archetype, boys."

It was true. She looked like a composite of all the stewardesses and receptionists and students.

Leaning forward and leering beneath the arched bat wings of his eyebrows, he explained: "The game, gentlemen, is one-card stud, no draw, two-hundred-dollar ante."

I had dim suspicions of the nature of the game, but I thought he must be kidding. We all fell silent. Trey looked smug. He had our attention.

"I met Tamara in New York, where she began her modeling career. Not only is Tamara a model; she's also—surprise, surprise—an actress. An aspiring actress. But it isn't easy to break into that business. Lots of competition, lots of pretty faces. Ditto for modeling. Tamara has to pay her rent. And she likes a good time. So she mixes business with pleasure. What the hell, you like a guy, you let him buy you dinner. Or a gram of coke. Why not let him pay your rent? Quid pro quo. Semipro."

"I'm a happily married man," Gene Samuels said nervously, misreading the intro.

"Ignorance is bliss, Gene. As usual, you're way behind the curve here. Now, let's say you're a young aspiring actress like Tamara. Wouldn't you kill to get invited to the house of a major studio head? Or even better, what if you had a chance to meet a handsome young senator?"

"If you're saying what I think you're saying . . . ," said Dave Crushak, who didn't finish his sentence.

Trey explained that Castleton would be attending a fund-raiser at a studio executive's home in L.A. the following week. A college buddy who owed him a favor had been invited. He proposed to send Tamara along as his friend's date and let nature take its course. Under skeptical questioning from the rest of us, he explained that Tamara would actively solicit and encourage the senator's attentions. Toward that end, we would pay her a thousand dollars. Another college buddy, a reporter at the *Los Angeles Times,* would be happy to watch Tamara's apartment in Santa Monica later that night, in case anything newsworthy took place. We all raised a dozen practical objections, though somehow we were unwilling to voice the moral ones. Like Castleton, Trey was a magnetic individual, whom the rest of us envied and feared. If anyone had raised his voice in indignation, the others would surely have followed, but nobody wanted to seem priggish. And we all felt betrayed. I think in the end I told myself the scheme was unlikely to succeed, thus absolving myself as I put my two hundred dollars on the table.

And that, basically, was how it happened. This was years ago, but I've never been able to forget it. Tamara was famous for a minute and a half, landing a role in a TV pilot that never aired. Trey married one of his debutantes, the daughter of a liberal philanthropist. Amanda Greer, whose screen career as a femme fatale had been fading for some time, did a well-publicized stint at the Betty Ford Clinic and was subsequently cast as the star of a TV series that's still running. I saw her two years ago in the Jockey Club at the Ritz-Carlton, where I was dining with a client and she was being feted by a large party. I'd read in the *Post* that she was in town to film an episode. She spotted me as she came in, and I guessed from her puzzled expression that she half-remembered me. Several times during dinner I saw her squinting over, trying to place me. When she excused herself from the table, I followed to where she was standing in front of the phone booth, waiting for me.

"Do I know you?" she demanded.

"I worked for Senator Castleton," I said, looking down, unable to hold her gaze. She was still beautiful, and, if anything, looked younger.

"Ah yes," she finally said. "Benjamin Braddock."

I nodded.

"You know the crazy thing?" she said. "He hardly touched me. Mainly, he just wanted to hold and be held. That was all. He'd fall asleep with his arms around me and hang on for dear life."

She looked very sad, although I'd grown old enough to wonder if it was genuine sadness or the mask of an actress.

"I felt so bad for him." She searched my face for a moment, her expression almost imploring, and I wanted to say something but suddenly didn't trust my voice. She sighed and nodded, then turned away and disappeared into the ladies' room. When she finally returned to her table, I was unable to catch her eye.

The former senator has an active consulting business, and as the scandal fades in public memory, he's called upon more often to comment on world and national events. He's writing his memoirs. Doreen stood by him, and by all accounts their marriage has actually flourished. I'm not nearly so cynical as to claim any credit for this, to suggest it was part of the plan or that it absolves me in any way. I don't know that Castleton could have won, or that having won he would've preserved any of the ideals of the man I went to work for, fresh from my American history seminars. At the age of thirty-three, I have lost or betrayed most of my own ideals. Having had so direct a hand in ruining him, I blame myself, as I'm sure he blames himself, though I'm pretty disgusted with everybody else, too.

Another election is upon us, and Trey's running for Congress from Manhattan, bankrolled by his father-in-law. They say he's settled down and is faithful to his wife. He's expected to win handily, and I'm confident that he will.

1992

The Waiter

"The problem with America," she said, "there is no context. Anyone can tell you anything."

"Exactly."

"You just don't know."

"*You* knew."

"Well, yes, *I* knew. But not until later."

I'd arrived in the middle of a story. Like my country, it seemed, I was lacking context.

"This is Seth," Cara said. The other woman was clearly foreign, possibly Italian; attractive in a windblown, careless fashion. Not as beautiful as Cara, who made me queasy with desire, but better-looking than I wished she were, since she had pretty much dismissed me at a glance. And her air of entitlement seemed to go beyond what her appearance would have merited. Though she was wearing jeans and a man's oxford shirt, her watch and jewelry probably cost more than my tuition for the next year, with plenty left over for room and board. She made me feel like a bumpkin, and I was already practically paralyzed with insecurity in Cara's presence. Between them, they seemed to present such an unassailable front of sophistication and beauty that I concentrated on the other girl's moles, one on her chin and another above her lip. It seemed to me, in my limited experience, that European women had more growths and marks than American girls did. I tried to hold hers against her, since she was clearly holding something against me. Cara on her own was daunting enough, with her casual aura of boarding school, country clubs and European vacations. I could hardly think of anything or anyone else that summer.

"Marella's just telling me a story."

"It is really not so interesting."

"I like a good story," I said.

"Well, of course," Marella said. "We all like a good story."

"Seth's a writer," Cara said.

Marella sucked hard on her cigarette and held the smoke in. "How *wonderful,*" she said, looking out toward the ocean. "What has he written?"

"I'm a student, actually," I said. "Studying to be a writer."

She was unable to suppress her contempt. "Only in America do they think that they can teach you this thing. To create literature. Do you think Proust studied—what do you call it?—'creative literature'? Or Kafka or Calvino? In Europe we don't believe a professor can teach you to have the soul of an artist. Even the English, they don't think this."

I could see and smell the ocean across the road from the café, and I was suddenly seized by the desire to run down across the beach and jump into the surf and swim far out into the waves. No, actually, that's poeticizing. Trying to be *writerly.* What I was actually seized by was the desire to hold Marella's head under the water while she thrashed and struggled for air. Still, I would've put up with far worse than this to be sitting next to Cara. I'd been insinuating myself into her presence for weeks. And if there was a story, I figured, I might as well hear it.

"We met him at that new place—what's it called?—it's owned by that terrible man who owns the one I like on Madison in the city. He started talking with Julia when I went to the powder room. Well, you know Julia. She would talk to the hat stand if it said hello. I mean, I *adore* her, really, but you *know* how she can be."

Well, of course I didn't know how she could be or even who she was, but that was the point. She wasn't talking to me, but to Cara, barely tolerating my presence. If I wanted to listen, then there wasn't much she could do about it, but she certainly wasn't going to go out of her way to make me feel included.

"I was just telling your friend about the meteor shower tonight," Marella said the man had said when she came back to the table. "It should be well worth staying up for."

"And you have some special place in mind where she can watch the meteors with you?" Marella said with a sneer. (Or so I choose to imagine—I'm sort of partly reporting and partly projecting, based on what she told us that day.)

"Well," he said, "I haven't entirely decided where I'll be watching from."

"You are keeping your options open," she said, "waiting for the best offer?"

"I think life is best viewed," he said, "as a linked series of improvisations."

"Maurice is renting the Condens' guest house for the month," Julia told her.

"I don't think I know them," Marella said.

"Sure you do," Julia said. "You remember, we were at their Memorial Day party on the beach."

Perhaps Marella let this pass, or else she muttered something about there being far too many parties in the season to remember every single one. She must have been softening up a little, because otherwise she would've frozen out the gentleman at the next table at this point. In fact, she'd already told us she thought he was handsome, his complexion suggestive of Latin blood. "Distinguished-looking," she said, his hair flecked with gray at the temples. He had an accent, but as a foreigner herself, she couldn't quite identify it. Of course, she could have just asked, but her innate snobbishness, I suspected, prevented her from being so direct. That was the funny thing to me—a few well-chosen questions could have removed the suspense and ended the story. Americans, at least the kind I grew up with, come right out and ask where you're from and what you do for a living pretty much in that order, but I guess this was too obvious for Marella. She wouldn't want to demonstrate that much interest, or perhaps it was considered rude where she came from. Anyway, Cara seemed fascinated with the story, and anything that interested Cara was sure to interest me.

"He told us he'd just gotten back from Dubai," she said. "Which, of course, is where all the Russian gangsters go to buy Cartier watches for their mistresses and all the Saudi princes go for dirty weekends, but he wasn't Russian and he certainly wasn't Saudi. It seemed he might have been traveling for business—he told us thirty percent of the world's cranes were in Dubai. And Julia asked him if he was a bird-watcher, and I didn't understand what she was talking about; I thought it was just, you know, more Julia craziness. And the guy, he says no, not bird cranes, but cranes for construction. And she says, 'Oh,' and I say, 'What are you talking about?' and they explain to me that a crane also is a kind of bird. Although it turns out, believe it or not, he really *is* a bird-watcher. He actually goes on holiday to look for birds. Or so he tells us."

"Seth's a bird-watcher," Cara said.

Pleased as I was to hear my name on her lips, it took me a moment to recall the basis for this claim. The first and only time Cara had visited the house I was renting with my buddies, she had picked up the well-thumbed copy of Roger Tory Peterson's edition of *Audubon's Birds of America,* which belonged to the owners of the house, and asked me if I was a bird-watcher. I'd said yes, the basis for this claim being that my parents kept a bird feeder and because I had recently met a man of letters, who was a big hero of mine, at a cocktail party and he'd told me, apropos of I don't know what, that he was "dead keen" on birds. I thought this sounded like kind of a good Waspy eccentricity to have if you were trying to impress a girl like Cara.

Marella, on the other hand, having zero interest in my hobbies, was determined to finish her story. "We were about to order a bottle of wine, and he asked us if we would mind a suggestion. He called the waiter over; he had this very casual but authoritative—what do you call it?—the way with the hand. You know how some men can't get the attention of the waiter. . . ."

"I hate that," Cara said. "You mean *wave.*"

"Yes, well this corrector, he knew how to *wave* to a waiter."

"What's a corrector?" I asked.

"You should know; you're the writer."

"Honestly, Seth. She means *character.*"

"Sorry, it took me a minute."

"He told the waiter to bring us a particular bottle of wine, without making too much of a fuss about it. You know, a man should know about wine, but you don't want to go on and on about it. Some of these American men can be so obsessive on the subject, trying to show off how much they know. Well, our friend, all he said was that the wine was made by a friend of his in Umbria and he thought it would go well with our food—he'd heard us ordering. So then Julia says, 'Oh, so you're Italian.' And he says, well, yes, on his mother's side. And so Julia asks him where in Italy, and after a long pause he names a little town not far from Lucca, which I happen to know because my friends own the place. So I said, 'You must know the Tamborellis,' and he says, 'Only a little,' because he moved when he was young and lived in France. So Julia asks him where in France, and it's the same thing when I ask him if he knows the d'Arbanvilles. He says he knows them, but not well, because he didn't stay there very long, either."

Over the hour they spent sitting next to him, Marella became obsessed with "placing" this guy while Julia flirted. Something about him set off an alarm for her. She must have thought he was some kind of con man, although she didn't say as much. When she said, "My suspicion was alerted," her glance at me made it clear that I hadn't quite passed the sniff test myself.

The way she told it, she was just looking out for her friend Julia, who'd accepted an invitation to a cocktail party the following evening before the main course arrived. By this time he'd joined their table. And it was the main course that eventually betrayed him, or so Marella believed.

"Julia had ordered the fish and it arrived at the table whole, with all the bones. And Julia is looking at this fish; she doesn't quite know where to start, and our friend says, 'Here, allow me.' And he takes the plate, and it's quite amazing; one two three, he has taken out the bones and made two perfect pieces of the fish, like two pages of an open book. Bravo, very nice. Julia was charmed. I am also impressed. But that's when I knew." She paused, a nasty smile of triumph deforming her face.

"Knew what?" Cara said.

"Darling, don't you see? The manners, the wine, the fish. I mean, it's very charming, being able to undress a fish like that. But what kind of a skill is that really? It was like a lightbulb on top of my head. How do you say? An epiphany. I knew who he was."

I looked suitably baffled and Cara shrugged. "Who was he?"

"Darling, he was a waiter."

It took us a moment to register this. I mean, I understood how she had come to the conclusion that the man might have been a waiter at some point in his life, but I couldn't see how it mattered, and, in fact, I was kind of waiting for Cara to say, "So is Seth." Because that's what I was doing in this little summer paradise, waiting tables at the best restaurant in town, collecting orders and tips from people like Cara's parents. I wasn't really a waiter, having already been accepted to grad school back in the city, and I was in the process of becoming, I hoped, a writer, although my father, the foreman of a maintenance crew in a paper mill, still hoped I would come to my senses and go to law school, and that, too, was possible. At that point in my life, almost anything was possible. At any rate, I knew I wasn't going to be a waiter for the rest of my life, and it didn't really occur to me to be insulted until I saw Cara blushing. I started to become embarrassed, whether for her or myself, I'm not quite sure. I mean, she could have made a joke of it. She could have said, "Well, Seth's a waiter, too," and proved her superiority to this silly woman. But the fact that she didn't made me feel that in her eyes I *was* a waiter, that on some level she accepted this woman's judgment about the social order. It was ridiculous. This was America, wasn't it? We weren't Europeans. I knew I was as good as anybody, that my father was every bit as good as her father, if not better. I believed it in theory anyway. But not in my heart, I realized as I watched her blush and felt myself blushing, as well. And I realized something that I'd only intuited up to that point, that there is a class system in America, even if some of us bottom-dwellers didn't realize it.

Somehow, we never got past that moment. Things had changed between us. She had a tennis lesson after lunch, and my shift started at four, and when I called her later, she was always busy and I knew it was no good. At least she didn't come into the restaurant again. I saw her once at the clam shack with some preppy asshole who was doing his best to look proprietary, but at least she had the decency to seem uncomfortable, nodding almost imperceptibly before turning away. I smoked sullenly, tragically—a *poète maudit* at the beach.

The days grew shorter, the nights cooler as September approached. On Monday nights, when the restaurant was closed, we had a staff clambake on the beach, and the following morning I awoke with cotton mouth, my fingers smelling like clams and butter and cigarettes. On the last Monday in August, I finally went home with the hostess, a bouncy nursing major from Stony Brook who'd been flirting with me all summer. I woke up with a nasty hangover at dawn and slipped out while she slept, carrying my shoes across the cold, dewy lawn to my car.

Then, on Labor Day weekend, I saw Cara again at a party. In her sleeveless turquoise blouse and her clam diggers, she looked like someone from a more glamorous era. I ignored her and threw back another Southside, nodding coldly when she came over to say hello.

"I was afraid I wouldn't see you before you went back to school," she said.

"You know where I work." I had meant to sound bitter, but my voice cracked.

"Don't be like that," she said. "Come on."

She took my hand and led me out back to the boathouse and started to kiss me. I realized she was drunk, but I didn't care. I could smell the sweet alcohol on her breath, along with the stale sea air trapped in the muggy confines of a shack that smelled like the inside of an old sea captain's trunk. Outside, the raspy ocean incessantly pounded the beach. I shoved my tongue in her mouth as she worked her hand down the front of my shorts.

"Fuck me like a waiter," she said.

And so I did.

2007

The Queen and I

As the tired light drains into the western suburbs beyond the river, the rotting pier at the end of Gansevoort Street begins to shudder and groan with life. From inside a tin-roofed warehouse, human beings stagger out into the steamy dusk like bats leaving their cave. Inside the shed, one can make out in the dimness a sprawling white mountain, the slopes of which are patched with sleeping bags, mattresses, blankets, cardboard and rafts of plywood. An implausible rumor circulates among the inhabitants of this place that the white mesa is made of salt that, back when there were still funds for municipal services, was spread on the icy city streets in winter; at present the rusting warehouse serves as a huge dormitory and rat ranch. At dusk the inmates rise to work, crawling out into the last light to dress and put on their makeup. Down on the edge of the highway along the foot of the pier, the shiny cars of pimps and johns wait alongside the beat-up vans from the rescue missions and religious organizations, ready to compete for the bodies and souls of the pier dwellers.

I watch as three queens share a mirror and a lipstick, blinking in the slanted light. One of them steps away a few feet, creating a symbolic privacy in which to pull up his skirt demurely and take a torrential leak. A second lights up a cigarette and tugs on a pair of fishnet hose. The third is my friend Marilyn, queen of Little West Twelfth Street. It's my first night on the job.

I ran into Marilyn in the emergency room at St. Vincent's a couple days before. I went in for gingivitis, my gums bleeding and disappearing up the sides of my teeth from bad nutrition and bad drugs. It's a common street affliction, another credential in my downward slide toward authenticity. Marilyn had a broken nose, three cracked ribs and assorted bruises from a trick tormented by second thoughts.

"I thought you had a pimp, Marilyn," I said, watching a gunshot victim bleeding freely on a gurney.

"The pimp, he get killed by the Colombians," said Marilyn. "He never protect me anyways, the bastard. He punch me hisself." Marilyn laughed through his nose, then winced. When he could speak again, he said, "Last time my nose got broke, it's my papa do the breaking. He beat the shit out me when he find me dressed in Mama's wedding gown. I'm holding the lipstick and he opens the door of my room. Smack me good, scream at me, call me a dirty little *maricón,* say he don't want no *maricón* for a son. The boy last night, he was like that, this big bulging muscle New Chursey boy. After I do him, he start hitting, calling me faggot. A lot them like that, they don't like what they want. Hey, man," he said, scrutinizing me with new interest. "Why don't you be my pimp? I give you five dollar every trick."

It was a measure of my prospects that I thought this was a pretty good offer. In fact, I'd been unemployed by another Colombian murder and was sleeping in Abingdon Square Park. I was dealing halves and quarters of coke out of a bar on Thirteenth when my man got whacked and I was left without a connection. Before that I'd been in a band, but the drummer OD'd and the bassist moved to L.A.

When I first met Marilyn, I was living in a cellar in the Meatpacking District. Marilyn worked all night, and I was up jonesing on coke or crack and trying to write. I'm a songwriter, you see, a poet. There is beautiful, ugly music inside me, which plays in the performance space deep in my mind. Walking the streets, doing the bars, I hear snatches of it in the distance, above the subliminal bass line of the urban heartbeat. I am most attuned to it in moments of transport, when I'm loaded on cheap wine or crack. Sometimes I'm dead certain that with one more drink, one more hit, I'll grasp its essence and carry it back with me to the other side. An aesthetician of ugliness, I am living here in the gutter like Prince Hal, biding my time, waiting to burst forth like a goddamn sun.

A refugee from the western suburbs, I used to skip school and take the bus into the city. I hung out on St. Mark's Place and the Bowery, copping the look and the attitude of punk, discovering Bukowski and the Beats in the bookshops. Returning to the subdivisions of Jersey was an embarrassment. The soil was too thin for art. No poetry could ever grow in the grapefruit rinds of the compost heap. Ashamed of my origins, neither high nor low, I dreamed of smoky bars and cafés, steaming slums. I believed that the down and dirty would lead me to the height of consciousness, that to conceive beauty it was necessary to sleep with ugliness. I've been in that bed for several years now. So far, nobody's knocked up.

Like Dylan says, "Someday, everything is gonna be diff'rent, / When I paint my masterpiece." I'll be rich and famous, photographed with models who will suddenly find me incredibly attractive—my goodness, where have I been all their short, naughty, long-legged lives?—and I will do a lot of expensive designer drugs and behave very badly and ruin my promising career and end up right back here in the gutter. And I'll write a song cycle about it. It'll be excellently poignant, even tragic.

Marilyn grew up in Spanish Harlem, where he was christened Jesús, a delicate boy with a sweet face who is a plausible piece of ass as a girl. He wants to get married and live the kind of life I grew up in. Except he wants to do it as a woman. At night he looks longingly out over the Hudson at the dim glow of suburban Jersey the way I used to look over from the other side at the lights of Manhattan. He wants a three-bedroom house he can clean and polish while awaiting a husband who works in the city. There's a huge Maxwell House sign across the river from the Gansevoort pier, and he told me once that when he wakes up at the end of the average American workday, he remembers the tuneful Maxwell House commercials he saw as a kid, dreaming about percolating a pot of coffee for a sleepy hubby.

The doctor who gives Marilyn his hormone shots says that more than half the—what shall we call them?—the people who get the operation get married, and that more than half of those don't tell their husbands about their former lives as men. I personally find this just a teensy bit hard to believe. But Marilyn doesn't, and he's saving up for the operation.

Poor Marilyn with his broken snout. In this business he needs to be able to breathe through his nose. I decide to give it a shot. Could be a song in it. Plus, I'm stone-broke.

So as the sun goes down beyond the river into the middle of America, where the cows are heading back to their barns and guys with lunch boxes and briefcases are dragging ass home to their wives, I'm trudging toward the Meatpacking District with Marilyn, who is wearing fishnet hose under a green vinyl miniskirt, and a loose black top. The Queen and I.

"How I look, honey?" Marilyn asks.

"Looking bad, looking good," I say.

"This my Madonna look. Those Chursey boys—they love it."

By now I'm sure you've guessed that Marilyn is currently a blond.

The smell gets worse as we approach Washington and Gansevoort, which is Marilyn's beat—the warehouses full of dead meat, the prevailing smell of rot inextricably linked in my mind with the stench of urine and excrement and spent semen. A sign reads VEAL SPECIALISTS, HOTHOUSE BABY LAMBS, SUCKLING PIGS & KID GOATS. Whoa! Sounds like that shit should be illegal, know what I'm saying?

With darkness falling, a slow and funky metamorphosis is taking place. Refrigerated trucks haul away from loading docks while rough men in bloody aprons yank down metal shutters and padlock sliding doors. The suffocating smell of rotting meat hangs over the neighborhood and, when the breeze blows east off the Hudson, infiltrates the smug apartments and cafés of Greenwich Village—which is the only good thing I can say about this stench.

As the trucks disappear toward New Jersey and upstate, strange creatures materialize on the broken sidewalks, as if spontaneously generated from the rotting flesh. Poised on high heels, undulant with the exaggerated shimmy of courtship, a race of lanky stylized bipeds commands the street corners. They thrust lips and hips at any cars that pass this time of night, the area not exactly being on the direct route to anywhere except hell or Hoboken. Motorists who find their way here cruise slowly down the unlit cobbled streets, circling and returning to scout the sidewalk sirens. Sometimes a car slows to a stop near one of the posing figures, who then leans toward the driver's window to consult, haggle and flirt, sometimes to walk around the car and slip in the passenger door, reappearing a few minutes later.

The girls of Washington Street come in all sizes, colors and nose shapes; and in this light, few of them are hard to look at. One lifts a halter top to expose a pair of taut white breasts as a red Toyota with Connecticut plates crawls past. It's just barely conceivable that some of these sports who transact for five minutes of sex believe they're getting it straight. But ladies, I wouldn't count on it. I mean if your fiancé gets busted down here, you might think about canceling the band and the tent and the cake. Or maybe not. They're probably good family men, most of them. And so long as clothes and makeup stay in place, no one needs to start parsing his proclivities. Sometimes the cops sweep through to meet arrest quotas; johns who find their pleasure interrupted by a sudden official rap on the window almost always act shocked when the cops expose the gender of their sexual partners with a playful tug of the waistband or the not-so-playful rending of a skirt.

The clientele is nothing if not diverse, arriving in limos and Chevys, Jags and Toyotas. Whenever a certain homophobic movie star is visiting New York—a comic renowned for obscene stand-up routines that outrage the gay and feminist communities—his white stretch limousine is bound to linger on Washington Street in the small hours of the morning.

I take up a post beneath a sagging metal awning, half-concealed in the shadows, while Marilyn takes out his compact to check on the goods. He frowns. "That salt terrible for my skin. Suck the moisture right out, sleeping every night on a big pile of salt. Even the rats don't like living on salt." Is that because the rats are worried, I wonder, about their complexions? Meantime, near the curb, Marilyn strikes a pose he borrowed from a Madonna video. Just up the street is Randi, who claims he used to play with the Harlem Globetrotters. Wearing a leather mini and a red halter, Randi stands six eight in heels beneath a sign that reads FRANKS SALAMI BOLOGNA LIVERWURST KNOCKWURST STEW MEATS & SKIRT STEAKS.

Down Gansevoort, at the edge of the district, the neon sign of a fashionable diner emits a pink glow. So very far away—this place where the assholes I went to college with are tossing back colored drinks and discussing the stock market and interoffice gropings. Like my former best friend, George Bing, who wanted to be a poet and works for an ad agency in midtown. We roomed together at NYU, which I dropped out of after two years because I was way too cool. After George graduated, we'd meet for drinks at the Lion's Head or the White Horse, where he thought he was slumming and I felt like an interloper among the gentry. So excited when he first walked in as a freshman—with a fake ID from a store on Forty-second Street—that Dylan Thomas had guzzled his final drinks practically where we were sitting, he gradually, over the years, decided that the Welsh bard had wasted and abused his talent. I mean, sure,

George admitted, he was great, but what was so bad about being comfortable, taking care of your health, eating sensibly and writing copy for Procter & Gamble in between cranking out those lyrical heart's cries? And I'm on my best behavior, nodding like an idiot coming down off something I smoked or snorted and hoping the bartender won't remember he threw me out three months before. And eventually, I think, it became too embarrassing for both of us. I stopped calling, and Lord knows I don't have a phone now, except maybe the open-air unit on the corner of Hudson and Twelfth. Actually, it's been a relief to quit pretending.

Farther down Washington Street, a trio of junkies builds a fire in a garbage can, although the night is hot and steamy—the heat of the day, stored up in the concrete and asphalt, coming off now, cooking everyone slowly like so much meat. These guys, after they've been on the street a few years, they never really get warm again. The winter cold stays in your bones through the long stinking summer and forever, like a scar. The old farts wear overcoats and boots in August. That way, you don't have to change clothes for winter.

I'm just fine in my black T-shirt and denim jacket, which doubles as a blanket, thanks. Be off the street before that happens to me. When I paint my masterpiece. Franks salami bologna.

A red Nissan slows to a stop. Marilyn sashays over to the car and schmoozes with the driver, turns and waves to me. I come out of the shadow to reveal myself in all my freaky emaciated menace, moon white face and dyed black hair, my yellow teeth in their bleedy gums. Marilyn zips around to the passenger side and climbs into the car, which makes a right and slows to a stop a half block down the street, where I can still see it. Farther on, a bum in an overcoat parks his overflowing shopping cart on the sidewalk and peers in the window at the brightly lit diners eating steak frites.

Eventually, Marilyn comes back from his date, adjusting his clothes and checking his makeup in a compact, just like a model. That's what he calls it—a date. He hands me a damp, crumpled fiver. I don't want to think about the dampness. I want to scrape the bill off my palm and throw it into the stinking street, but Marilyn's all excited about being back at work and planning for the future. He's talking about how it will be after the operation, when he gets married and moves to New Chursey. I want to slap him and make him understand that it's the land of the living dead. It's not real, not like this fabulous life we're living here on Gansevoort Street. The flesh they grill on their Webers out in Morristown comes out of the very warehouses against which we bravely slouch.

At least Marilyn will be spared the ordeal of having a rotten suburban brat who will grow up to resent and despise him for being a boring, submissive housewife.

As the night deepens, business picks up and I nearly become accustomed to the layered stench, the several octaves of decay. The old men sharing a bottle around the fire pass out and the fire dies. I skulk over to Hudson and buy myself a bottle of blackberry brandy to keep my motor running. A dealer strolls by offering coke, crack and smoke. At first I think, No, I'm on duty, but the second time he comes by I have twenty dollars in my pocket from Marilyn, and I buy a little rock and fire it up, tickling my brain, making me feel righteous and empowered—I'm here, I'm cool, I'm feeling so good, I'm back on my feet and the future is mine; if I can just smoke a little more of this, I'll keep from slipping back, just a little more to maintain, to stop this fading, this falling away from the perfect moment that was here just a minute ago, to hear that perfect tune in my deep brain, that masterpiece.

Franks bologna et cetera.

The buzz has slipped away like a heartbreakingly hot girl at a bar who said she'd be back in a minute, promise. Leaving me oh so very sad and cranky. Where is the goddamn dealer?

The traffic in and out of the diner picks up around four, when the clubs close, yellow cabs pulling up to dispense black-clad party people like Pez, the hip boys and girls who are not yet ready for bed. I buy a so-called quarter of alleged toot and snort it all at once, thinking it will carry me further but more slowly than smoking rocks.

Marilyn gets eleven dates for the night, a cavalcade of perverts representing several states, classes and ethnic groups, including a Hasidic jeweler with long Slinky side locks that bounce up and down as he bucks to fulfillment in the front seat of his black Lincoln, a construction worker still wearing his hard hat, in a Subaru with Jersey plates, a guy in a stretch limo who tells Marilyn he's in the movie business and tips twenty.

The Lambs of God van cruises up, pulls over beside us. The priest says,

"Top of the morning, Marilyn." He looks surprised, not necessarily happy, when I slink out of my vampire shadow.

"Hello, Father," says Marilyn. "You looking for some fun tonight?"

"No, no, just checking to see that you're not . . . needing anything."

"Fine thanks, Father. And you?"

"Bless you and be careful, my child." The priest guns the engine and pulls away.

"Very nice, the father, but shy," says Marilyn, a note of disappointment in his voice. "I think maybe you scare him off."

"The shy shepherd," I say.

"I stay at that Lambs of God shelter one night and he didn't ask me for nothing," says Marilyn, as if describing a heroic feat of selfless ministry. "That day he just cop a little squeeze when I'm leaving. Food pretty decent, too." We watch a car go by slowly, the driver looking us over from behind his sunglasses. He seemed about to stop, then peeled out and tore down the street. After a long pause, Marilyn says, "My very first date was a priest, when I was an altar boy. He give me some wine."

"Sounds very romantic," I say, recalling my own altar boy days in another life. In awe of my proximity to the sacred rituals, I didn't smoke or swear and I confessed my impure thoughts to the eager priest behind the screen until my thoughts transmuted themselves to deeds on Mary Lynch's couch one afternoon, which I failed to mention at my next confession, suffering the guilt of the damned as I slunk away from the confessional booth. When lightning failed to strike me through the days and weeks that followed, I began to resent my guilt and then the faith that was so at odds with my secret nature and, finally, to exult in my rebellion. And as I turned away from my parents and the Church, I created my own taboo-venerating cult. Which perverse faith I am stubbornly observing here at five in the morning at the corner of Gansevoort and Washington.

Another car cruises by slowly, a junkyard Buick with two guys in the front seat. Twos are potentially dangerous, so I decide I'll show my flag and talk to them myself. I tell Marilyn to stay put, then saunter over to the car. The driver has to open the door because the window won't roll down. Two small Hispanics in their fifties. "Twenty-five apiece," I say, nodding toward Marilyn. "And you stay on this block." Finally we agree on forty for two.

I wave Marilyn over and he climbs in the backseat, and I'm just leaning back against the building, lighting a smoke, when Marilyn comes howling and tumbling out of the car, crawling furiously as the car peels out, tires squealing on the cobblestones. Marilyn flings himself on me and I hold him as he sobs. *"Es mi padre,"* he wails. *"Mi padre."*

"A priest?" I say hopefully.

He shakes his head violently against my shoulder and suddenly raises his face and starts apologizing for getting makeup on me, wiping at my jacket, still crying. "I ruin your jacket," he says, crying hysterically. It's all I can do to convince him that I don't give a shit about the jacket, which started out filthy anyway.

"Are you sure it was . . . him?" I say.

Gulping air, he nods vehemently. "It the first time I see him in three years," Marilyn says. He's sobbing and shaking, and I'm more than a little freaked-out myself. I mean, Jesus.

Finally, when he calms down, I suggest we call it a night. I make him drink the rest of the blackberry brandy and walk him back to the dock in the grainy gray light. As the sun comes up behind us, we stand on the edge of the pier and look out over the river at the Maxwell House sign. I can't think of anything to say. I put my arm around him and he sniffles on my shoulder. From a distance we would look like any other couple, I think. Finally I suggest he get some sleep, and he picks his way across the rotting boards back to the salt mountain. And that's the end of my career as a pimp.

A year after this happened, I went back to look for Marilyn. Most of the girls on the street were new to me, but I found Randi, the former Globetrotter, who at first didn't remember me. I do look different now. He thought I was a cop, and then guessed I was a reporter. He wanted money to talk, so I finally gave him ten, and he said, "I know you. You was that crackhead." Nice to be remembered. I asked if he'd seen Marilyn and he said Marilyn had disappeared suddenly: "Maybe like, I don't know, seems like a year ago." He couldn't tell me anything else and he didn't want to know.

About a year after that, I spotted a wedding announcement in the *Times.* I admit I'd been checking all that time—perusing what we once called the "women's sports pages"—like an idiot, occasionally rewarded with the picture of a high school or college acquaintance, and then one fine morning I saw a picture that stopped me. Actually, I think I noticed the name first; otherwise, I might not have stopped at the picture. "Marilyn Bergdorf to wed Ronald Dubowski." It would be just like Marilyn to name himself after a chic department store. I stared at the photo for a long time, and though I wouldn't swear to it in a murder trial, I think it was my Marilyn—surgically altered, one presumes—who married Ronald Dubowski, orthodontist, of Oyster Bay, Long Island. I suppose I could have called, but I didn't.

So I don't really know how that night affected Marilyn, if it changed his life, if he is now officially and anatomically a woman, or even if he's alive. I do know that lives can change overnight, though it usually takes much longer than that to comprehend what has happened, to sense that we have changed direction. A week after Marilyn almost had sex with his father, I checked myself into Phoenix House. I called my parents for the first time in more than a year. Now, two years later, I have a boring job and a crummy apartment and a girlfriend who makes the rest of it seem almost okay. I'd be lying if I said there weren't times I miss the old days, or that I don't breathe a huge sigh of relief when I climb on the train after a few hours spent visiting my parents, or that it's a gas being straight all the time, but still I'm grateful.

You think you're living a secret and temporary life, underground, in the dark. You don't imagine that someone will drive up the street or walk in the door or look through the window—someone who will reveal you to yourself not as you hope to be in some glorious future metamorphosis, but as you find yourself at that moment. Whatever you are doing then, you will have to stop and say, "Yes, this is who I am. This is me."

1992

The Debutante's Return

The call came at six in the morning, as she was returning home from a party that had lasted far too long, if no longer than several others she'd recently attended. This one had started at a nightclub on Fourteenth Street and ended on a rooftop in SoHo. She counted ten rings while she was fumbling with the locks on her apartment door, and another two before she reached the bedroom. Messed up as she was, she had a pretty clear idea of what the call would be about.

"You best come home," Martha said. "You mama done had another stroke."

She didn't remember the rest of the conversation. She was sitting on the bed with the telephone cradled in her lap when a strange man appeared in the doorway. "Nice place," he said. "You got any vodka?" Apparently, she'd brought him home with her. He was wearing a pearl gray fedora and a white silk scarf. She was surprised to find herself with a man in a fedora, and even more surprised at the sudden impulse to tell him not to wear it indoors.

She led him to the kitchen, opened the freezer, and handed him the frosty bottle of Absolut. "Take it," she said, maneuvering him out into the hallway. Before he quite knew what was happening, she'd pulled the front door shut and locked him out.

Somehow, this time, she knew the party was over, that she was finished with all that. But she had second thoughts when she arrived that afternoon at the Nashville airport, where everyone seemed fatter and slower and the air was shockingly sultry with humidity. Stepping off the plane was like being enveloped in a steaming-hot towel. She remembered once again why she'd fled north in the first place.

She looked frailer than ever in the hospital bed, with onion-paper skin and protruding bones. One side of her face seemed to be frozen. "I'm here, Momma," Faye said when her mother's translucent eyelids fluttered open.

"Bunny, it's you."

"It's me, Momma."

"You look tired. Where's your father?"

"Daddy's not here, Momma. You're in the hospital."

"The hospital? But won't he be worried?"

"We're all worried about you. You gave us a scare. Now get yourself better so we can take you home."

"Who's feeding Bugsy?"

It took Faye a moment to recall Bugsy, a wheaten terrier run over when she was four.

"Martha's taking care of everything back home."

Faye moved back into her room in the so-called New House, a Tudor pile her grandfather had built in the twenties after subdividing the old family property. The old house, aka the Big House, completed a few years before the Union army took over the city and dispossessed her great-great-grandparents, was now a museum. Its replacement, Faye's childhood home, had once stood in splendid isolation on a sea of bluegrass, but in recent years the suburbs had engulfed the property, now a mere five acres, with ranch houses and split-levels. Her brother was all in favor of selling it, but their mother insisted on staying put, and Faye had strenuously defended her position, yet given this new turn of events, she didn't know that she could hold him off much longer. In fact, it soon became clear that he'd already begun taking the place apart.

Martha cataloged the missing pieces. "Mr. Jimmy come in with a U-Haul last night and took away three carpets, a chifforobe, the dining room table and all the chairs. He say Miss Jordan ain't gonna be givin' no dinner parties nohow."

Faye was glad she'd already decided to stay, knowing it would take all of her strength to protect her mother and to keep her brother at bay. They'd already had the nursing home discussion, and Faye adamantly refused to see her mother shut away like that. Her memory might be failing, but she had Martha to take care of her, and it wasn't as if they lacked the resources to keep the house running. While she sensed this debate would now turn ugly, Faye was determined. She realized her position was more than a little ironic, since more than once she'd expressed the wish that the stupid house, with all its bad plumbing and bourbon fumes and family secrets, would burn to the ground so they could all just get on with their lives. Here in the self-proclaimed Athens of the South, she hated all the nostalgia mongering, the pedigree parsing, and the casual racism of her brother and his friends. She'd gone to college in Massachusetts, which her grandfather derided as "the Yankiest state in the Union," and then moved beyond the pale to New York. She returned from time to time, but she'd truly believed when she left at eighteen that she was leaving for good. All of which saddened and mystified her mother, who was, to no small extent, the focus of Faye's apostasy.

Sybil Hayes Teasdale was everything the South expected its daughters to be, and everything that Faye wished to escape. She wore white gloves whenever she left the house, and on those rare occasions when she could be persuaded to speak ill of others, the worst curse she could muster was "common." The Hayes family had achieved prominence in South Carolina before Sybil's grandfather decamped to the more fertile cotton land of the Mississippi Delta, where he made and lost several fortunes and served two terms in the Senate. Her father attended Vanderbilt long enough to acquire a suitable bride, Dottie Trammel, whom he carried back to the Delta plantation. Sybil's most vivid childhood memories centered around the flood of '27, when she and her mother spent two days atop a levee outside of Greenville, waiting to be rescued. Eventually they were picked up in a rowboat and carried to safety. But her father, who stayed behind to help coordinate relief efforts, drowned trying to save one of his men, or so the story was told. Dottie took her daughter and moved in with her parents in Nashville, and while the Trammels always honored the heroic memory of their son-in-law, there was an almost palpable sense of relief that their daughter had returned to civilization.

Her father's death could only have exacerbated that innate southern consciousness of loss and nostalgia, while her mother's family, whose respect for the proprieties was profound, raised her with an exaggerated sense of the perils beyond the family threshold, as if she herself were in imminent danger of being sucked under by muddy torrents. Later, as she started to blossom, this peril was identified as male lasciviousness; she was sent to a finishing school in Switzerland. Returning to Nashville at the age of eighteen, she became the object of intense competition among the eligible men of her generation, who vied to be named one of the six escorts at her debutante ball, held the following spring at the Belle Meade Country Club. Faye's father was not among the chosen, the Teasdales having fallen out with the Trammels over a failed business venture—but he spent the next three years wooing Sybil. Theirs was a storied romance, the beauty with the tragic past and the scion of one of the town's great families, and they were inseparable for the forty-five years of their marriage, although Faye remembered her father as something of a tyrant when it came to his demure and fragile spouse. She'd loved him wholly but was glad she was his daughter, rather than his wife. Even with a staff of six at his disposal, Hunt had demanded constant attention and service from Sybil, and he'd seemed always to be pounding the table and raging against some perceived shortcoming on her part.

Faye had come away from her childhood less than impressed with the institution of marriage. These feelings were reinforced as the sixties gave way to the seventies and their minister at St. George's began railing against free love and women's lib, both of which sounded pretty appealing to teenaged Faye.

Sybil never seemed to feel her oppression as acutely as Faye thought she should, so instead of blaming her father, Faye blamed his wife for her slavish adoration, adding this sin to the tally of grievances against her mother, along with the injunction against blue jeans, and her constant endorsement of "ladylike" behavior. She would have liked to dismiss her mother as a hopeless prude, but on several occasions she had surprised her parents in the act. Saturday afternoons, after her father's golf game, were consecrated to conjugal sport; Faye and the staff were strictly forbidden to enter the master wing between two and four, and her mother inevitably emerged from her "nap" all glowing and kittenish.

After Hunt collapsed on the fourteenth hole at Belle Meade in the middle of one of his famous tantrums, Sybil seemed to shrink and fade. Faye had come home for the funeral and stayed as long as she could bear it. Though she knew she should feel greater sympathy for her mother and greater grief for her father, at that time all she could think about was getting back to her life in New York. But in the intervening years something within her had changed. Maybe she was simply tired of running. Or maybe her mother's helplessness, along with her brother's eagerness to stick her in a nursing home, had finally awakened her sense of filial duty.

When her brother arrived with the U-Haul that evening, she saw the car and trailer from her room upstairs and went down to confront him. He was in the entry hall with Walter, his longtime yardman, and they were examining the grandfather clock in the entry hall. He looked up, surprised, not having heard her descend the carpeted stairway. "Sis, you scared the shit out of me. Whatever brings you here?"

"Mainly the fact that Momma had a stroke."

"It's a damn shame is what it is," he said. "But I can't say it's a surprise. I saw this coming a mile away. She's been failing for the past year. I talked to the doctor this morning and he says she needs full-time care." Faye had forgotten how much she disliked his voice, the lazy pace and occasional crackerisms. Neither of their parents had ever spoken like that. But despite the trips to Europe and four years at a boarding school in Connecticut, Jimmy had somehow managed to become a good old boy, the kind of guy who attended cockfights and tossed the *N* word around. Perhaps that was his way of rebelling against his heritage and upbringing.

"Well, I'm here now. And she's got Martha."

"Well, sure, but what happens when you skip back to New York? I'm talking about professional care. What she needs is a real facility."

"I'm not skipping back to New York. And Momma doesn't want to go to a home. She's already got one."

"You're going to take care of her? Come on, now, sis. When did you get so damn interested? I can't even remember the last time you visited."

"It was last Christmas, actually."

"Well, we're deeply honored to have you back."

"What are you doing with the clock?"

"Just going to have it fixed. Damn thing hasn't worked right in years."

She watched as they wrestled the clock out the front door, feeling paralyzed and impotent, as if stuck in one of those dreams where speech wouldn't come. After all these years, she was still intimidated by her brother. He was twelve years older and had always treated her like a child, with a mixture of sarcasm and condescension. He had once, when Faye was seven, stuffed her beloved cat Twinkie in the dryer and turned it on, forcing her to watch as the terrified cat tumbled through what seemed to her like a hundred revolutions, until her screams finally brought Martha to the rescue. She watched now as the car rolled away down the long gravel drive, furious with herself for letting him steal the clock.

Over the years in New York, Faye spoke with her mother weekly and even more often with Martha, the housekeeper who had lived with the family for more than forty years and who had originally served as Faye's nanny. Sybil, she'd said, was living increasingly in the past, even before this latest stroke. The physical effects were blessedly minimal; she retained most of her mobility and speech. The doctors were less certain about her mental processes, though reluctant to speculate.

"But there's no reason we can't take care of her at home, is there?"

"She needs to be watched pretty closely," Dr. Cheek said. "I'd recommend hiring a nurse, at least for the first few weeks. But at this time I see no need for institutional care."

"I'd be happy to stop by and check up on her," the younger, good-looking doctor said. He seemed to be flirting, but she had to remind herself that this wasn't New York, that the mean temperature of normal social interactions was much warmer here. Quite possibly, Dr. Harrington was simply demonstrating the dedication and concern appropriate to his profession. Faye was so used to deriding the ritual politesse her mother so cherished, she had to remind herself good manners weren't necessarily insincere.

"Where are we going?" her mother asked for the third time, as they pulled off the interstate.

"We're going home, Momma."

"As soon as we get there, I want you to march up to your room and change out of those horrible dungarees. You look as if you're reporting for work on a road crew."

"They're called jeans."

"I know what they are. And they're not appropriate attire for a young lady."

"It's the eighties, Momma."

"I don't want your father to see you in that outfit."

Faye said nothing. She had decided to wait till they were settled in to address this subject.

But when they arrived home, Sybil wanted to see her roses. She seemed utterly lucid. "What's happened to the clock?" she said as soon as they walked in.

"Jimmy's taken it to be fixed."

"It hasn't worked in twenty-seven years," she said. "Why should he fix it right now?"

Her denuded dining room, meanwhile, was concealed behind pocket doors. Faye walked with her up to the master bedroom, which she hadn't entered in years. Everything was more or less as she remembered it from her childhood—the hand-painted wallpaper from Switzerland that offered up a series of fantastical Chinese vistas; the king-size bed with its upholstered headboard, the feather mattress and box spring ordered specially from the same firm that supplied Claridge's, which Hunt claimed had the most comfortable mattresses in the world; the white vanity where her mother had attempted to teach her the rudiments of makeup. On the other side of the room was her father's dressing table, with monogrammed leather stud boxes, a sterling cigarette lighter, an ivory comb, a tortoise-shell cigarette case, a souvenir ashtray from Augusta National, seven golf trophies and a small gallery of framed family photos. The silver was all bright and polished, as it had been during his lifetime. She wondered if the pearl-handled revolver was still in the top drawer.

"It's so nice to have you home," Sybil said.

"It's nice to be here."

"Have you been making friends at school?"

"More friends than I know what to do with."

"You can never have too many friends, Faye."

"Why don't you rest, Momma. I'll call you for dinner."

Sybil reached out and took her hand.

"I know your brother wants to put me in a home," she said.

To Faye, it seemed remarkable that her mother could have returned so rapidly to the present. "Don't worry. Nobody's going to put you in a home as long as I'm here."

"You know the Yankees, when they invaded, put your great-great-grandmother Eliza out of her home."

"I know, Momma."

"For five years she and your great-great-granddaddy Isaac had to live over a dry-goods store on Broadway while the Yankee officers slept in her bed and spit tobacco juice on her rugs. She died of a broken heart in those rooms over the dry-goods store."

No matter how many times Faye had heard this story, she'd never been certain what a dry-goods store was, or its significance in the story. Would it have been worse if it had been, say, a hardware store?

Sybil didn't mention her husband again until the following evening when Martha called her to dinner in the breakfast room.

"We can't sit down till Hunt comes home," she said. She was perched in her favorite armchair in the sunroom, looking out across the lawn, beyond which the orange Mediterranean roof tiles of a gated community called Tuscan Acres rose over the privet hedge.

Faye sat down across from her and took her hand, which was almost translucent, and freckled with age spots in spite of the white gloves she wore so often. "Daddy's not with us anymore, Momma. He passed away three years ago."

It was as if this was the first time she'd heard the news; tears welled in her eyes and her face contorted with grief.

Faye squeezed her hand as hard as she dared. "Don't you remember, Momma?"

She shook her head, the tears now rolling down her cheeks.

Faye had not been present when her mother learned of her husband's death, and she was witnessing now what she'd missed then. Her grief seemed utterly fresh and unbounded. She appeared to be almost literally melting, slumping lower and lower as the tears poured down her face, a woman devastated by loss. It was almost unbearable to watch.

"What will I do without him?" she finally managed to say.

"You've been doing without him for a while now, Momma."

This scene repeated itself twice more over the course of that week, and each time Sybil was inconsolable. Faye finally decided just to say that Hunt was on a business trip. In fact, she herself had started tearing up whenever she broached the subject of her father's death.

Dr. Harrington came by, as promised, dressed for tennis. If his legs were any indication, Faye imagined he was very fast on the court. He appeared to be in his mid-thirties, roughly her own age. He spent a good fifteen minutes with Sybil and then sat down with Faye in the library.

"Great room," he said, admiring the leather-bound volumes and the hunting prints. Faye had always found it oppressively masculine and studiously old-world.

"How does she seem to you?"

"She seems to be improving."

"She forgets things," Faye said.

"That's understandable."

"For example, that her husband is dead."

"It could be vascular dementia from the stroke, which may reverse itself. I think we also have to consider the possibility of Alzheimer's. I gave her a Mini-Cog—that's a little test where you ask the patient to remember a list of common household objects and draw the face of a clock. She drew the clock, but she couldn't remember the objects. There's a chance she may improve, but it's more likely we're dealing with progressive dementia. I wish I could be more optimistic. On the other hand, I can say with certainty that she's better off here at home, as long as she's properly cared for. Forgive me for prying, but I gather you live in New York."

She was reminded that there were no secrets here, and for a fleeting moment she was tempted to revise her plan and book the first flight back to New York. "I'll be here for as long as she needs me."

"That could be a long time," he said.

"I know."

"Well, I'm sure your mother is very happy to have you back," he said. "Although I imagine there may be some weeping and gnashing of teeth up in New York."

"I think they're thoroughly sick of me. I stayed too long at the party."

"I doubt that very much."

"There're a few boys up there in New York who wish I'd never left Nashville."

"Way I hear it, there're a few boys down here who wish the same thing."

Now she knew he was flirting, but she wasn't really in the mood. Just now she felt like she'd dated enough men for the next five or six lifetimes.

Over the course of the following week, Sybil inquired repeatedly as to the whereabouts of her husband, and the business trip story was wearing thin. Faye's next idea was to tape Hunt's obituary to her mother's bathroom mirror, hoping that the shock of seeing it there every morning might be partly alleviated by seeing her husband's accomplishments enumerated and praised. But the first morning, Martha came down from Sybil's bedroom to report that she was sobbing uncontrollably in her bed.

"I don't know what I'm going to do without him," she wailed when Faye went up to comfort her.

"Momma, you've been doing without him for three years."

"He was the only man I ever loved."

"There wasn't another like him," Faye said.

"You know, it was your father who fixed things when the colored people demonstrated at the lunch counters. He was president of the chamber of commerce and he convinced everyone that the time had come to integrate. The only reason so many went along with it was the respect they bore for your father's opinion. He said it was just good business."

The memory of her husband's civic heroism seemed to revive her spirits, and with Faye's help she dressed, then spent the afternoon tending her roses. That night they watched several episodes of *Upstairs, Downstairs* on video. But the next morning, Faye found her crouched on the bathroom floor, weeping. During the night she'd forgotten again, and the sight of the obituary had come as a shock. She spent the rest of the day in bed. Two days later, Faye removed the newspaper clipping from the mirror, and when Sybil asked about Hunt, Faye or Martha would reply that he was away on business, an answer that now seemed to satisfy her.

When Dr. Harrington came by a week after his first visit, Faye declined his invitation to dinner, suggesting instead that he join her for whatever Martha, an excellent cook, was rustling up. The dinner, chicken and egg bread with white gravy and collards, was a guilty pleasure, but the conversation seemed to flag whenever they veered off medical topics, and Dr.

Harrington tended to chew with his mouth open, a memory that put her off the idea of kissing him at the door.

When Faye returned from the gym the next morning, she found Martha in a state of agitation. "Mr. Jimmy come by," she said. "He tried to get your momma to sign a power of attorney. She's terrible upset. He try to sweet-talk her first, but she told him she wouldn't sign and he told her she was a foolish old woman and worse." Faye was ahead of her on the stairs, racing for Sybil's bedroom. "She say she don't want to sell her house and she don't want to go to no nursin' home. So Mr. Jimmy storm out, and your momma, she's in a state."

Sybil was a tiny dark figure in a great sea of linens, sitting upright against the headboard, her hands clenched on her thighs.

"I won't move to Broadway," she said. "I don't care what he says. He can tie a stick of dynamite to me like he did with that stray dog, but I won't sign that paper and I won't move to Broadway."

The next morning, a Saturday, Faye drove over to her brother's house, a sprawling ranch in a gated community called Elysian Hills, and rang his buzzer.

He came to the door wearing a shooting vest over a flannel shirt, his pink scalp glistening through the furrows of his brushed-back hair. "Sis, I was just about to call you. Come on in."

"I don't want to come in. I just want to say don't you dare come round and bully Momma like that again. You can say what you want, but I'm not letting you lock her away. And I'm not letting you loot the house."

He was taken off guard by this last remark; his face, always ruddy, turned a deeper shade of red. "You've really turned into a prime New York bitch, haven't you?"

"It's taken years, but I'm slowly getting there. I didn't say anything when you took Daddy's guns and his watch collection."

"What the hell good were they to you?"

"I could have sold them just as easily as you did."

"I've been taking care of Momma and that house for years while you were off gallivanting around New York with the beautiful people. Hell, I've even been paying your goddamn credit-card bills. Your Chanel and your '21' Club."

"Dad's estate pays my bills. And God knows what else the estate's been paying for. But if you persist in trying to lock Momma up, I'm going to send in a battalion of accountants and lawyers and it's all going to come out in the open. *New York* accountants and lawyers."

That night, Faye went through the family photo albums and found herself revising her memories, as if her childhood were an undervalued asset, like an anonymous painting suddenly revealed to be the work of a master. The cumulative impact of so many smiling faces was impressive. The pleasure her parents so visibly displayed in each other's company seemed to contradict her grim recollections. Looking through hundreds of travel snapshots reminded her of just how many trips they'd taken when she was younger. Jimmy, having gone off to college and marriage, was largely absent from the later pictures, while Faye looked remarkably happy, until she started to develop a pout around the age of thirteen, a sulky expression that said, *I can't believe I have to be here in Europe with my parents when I could be home with my friends.* The picture that eventually made her cry was at first a mystery, a blurry shot of what appeared to be a mermaid in a Venice canal. The woman, a Botticellian blonde in a blue bikini top, seemed to be sitting or lying on a submerged stone step or platform. Below the waist, just visible within the murky water, was a blue-green fish tail. Faye had been in a mermaid period then, sometime around her eighth birthday, and this had been the highlight of her trip. Years later, she learned that her father had staged the tableau. She had long ago forgotten the incident, which along with so much else suggested she had been the happy, spoiled child of loving parents.

After finishing the better part of a bottle of Campari, she called Cal, a former boyfriend, to whom she hadn't spoken in months.

"Was I so awful," she asked. "Was I just a total screaming bitch?"

"You were wonderful," he said. "The girl of my dreams."

"But you said yourself I broke your heart."

"You couldn't have broken my heart if you hadn't been so damn lovable."

"How could I be so wrong about everything?"

"Not everything," he said.

The next day she had dinner with Dr. Harrington at the club, and made a conscious decision to mute the critical inner voice that had found him wanting the last time out. She soon found herself telling him about her father, stories that she had told before, but never in such a fond fashion, his former flaws transformed now into lovable eccentricities. "He hated being alone," she said, looking away as the doctor masticated his steak. "He used to insist that my mother and I watch television with him, shouting for us to come downstairs and sit with him. He always seemed to be shouting and cussing, but now it seems funny to me somehow."

When he was driving her home after dinner, an ambulance flashed past with its siren screaming, and when they turned in, three Belle Meade police cars were parked in the driveway.

Faye panicked at the sight of the pulsing blue lights and the metallic, staccato walkie-talkie voices. "Oh my God."

"Let's not jump to any conclusions," Dr. Harrington said.

Not jump to any conclusions? She would have liked to have had the leisure to stay and ask him if he was fucking crazy, but instead she bolted out of the car and ran up the driveway to accost the nearest cop. "Please tell me what's going on. I'm Faye Teasdale."

"There's been an accident, Miss Teasdale," he said, taking hold of her forearm.

"Oh good Christ! Is my mother all right?"

"Your mother's fine. I mean she's not hurt. It's your brother. It seems your mother mistook him for an intruder."

"Where is she?" Without waiting for an answer, Faye rushed up the steps and through the open door, brushing past two more policemen in the hallway. Upstairs, she found her mother in bed, attended by Martha.

Sybil was sipping from a glass. She seemed remarkably calm under the circumstances, far more composed than her daughter.

"Momma, are you all right?"

"I'm fine, Bunny," she said, returning Faye's embrace.

"You didn't know," Faye said hopefully. "You thought it was a burglar."

"It was a burglar all right. He was walking off with the silver."

"She got Mr. Hunt's little pearl-handled Colt from the bedside table," Martha said.

"Your father used to take me to the shooting range on Sundays after church. I heard a noise downstairs, and I knew you were out."

Faye suddenly realized that she hadn't even inquired about her brother's condition. "Is he going to—"

"He gonna be all right. Your momma done shot him in the butt."

"Gave me a mighty big target," Sybil said.

"You couldn't tell who it was in the dark. Could you, Momma?"

"You know those damn Yankees turned Eliza Teasdale out of her own house."

Martha and Faye exchanged a look. "She confused," Martha said.

Sybil shook her head. "Jimmy says I'm losing my mind, but I'll tell you one thing. I can still recognize my own son. And I can recognize a thief."

"Momma, what are you saying?"

She looked up at Faye and stroked her hand. Her gaze was clear and direct. For the first time in weeks, she seemed fully present.

"Did I just say something?" she said. "Don't mind me. I'm a crazy old woman. My mind plays tricks on me. Just ask your brother. He'll be glad to tell you."

2008

Simple Gifts

By the time they dropped her off at Irving Place, it was nearly midnight. The thruway ride from Buffalo had been harrowing. The van was barely roadworthy under the best of conditions; between the ice and the wind, it was practically a miracle they'd made it home, especially when you considered that Lenny admitted somewhere around Utica that he'd dropped half a tab of acid. Rory had taken the other half, which disqualified him as a driver, and Zac had lost his license after the DUI in Cleveland, which left Lori as the only eligible pilot. Once again she was den mother to a trio of stoned Scouts. *Backup:* Wasn't that supposed to imply support, solidity, watching *her* back, if not massaging it on a nightly basis? When she'd hooked up with these guys, she hadn't imagined that it meant carrying amps and covering licks they were too stoned to remember.

She didn't think she'd ever been so tired in her whole life, between the drive and the partying last night, although the sight of the city had briefly revived her, the lights, the people, the improbable beauty of the snow on the streets.

"Hey, Merry Christmas, babe," Rory said as he slid across the seat to take her place at the wheel. He reached out the window and slapped a foil packet in her hands.

She watched the wheels spin as the van fishtailed up the street with its vanity plate: THE MAGI. They'd been the Magi before Lori signed on with them—Zac's girlfriend had given him a copy of a way cool novel, *The Magus,* which "had this, like, magician guy doing all this, like, crazy shit"—and since the band already had a local following, they'd just added to the name: Lori and the Magi.

Jeffrey was fooling with the lights on the Christmas tree when she came in. "Jesus, I thought you'd died on the thruway."

She detected the note of petulance in his voice.

"Almost."

Tired as she was, she wanted to lift his mood, and she bounded over to kiss him, tasting the sweet-sour tang of whiskey on his breath.

"You know, until I was about twelve I thought all men smelled like scotch. I thought it was a—what do you call it? A secondary sexual characteristic, like facial hair."

"How are the three wise men? Following any stars tonight?"

"I just hope they can make it to Brooklyn." She told the story of the trip—most of it anyway—trying to strike a fine balance between comedy and suspense.

"Jesus," he said, "when are you going to get rid of those clowns?"

The Magi were a source of some friction in the household. She kissed him again. "As soon as you learn to play bass and drums."

He turned away to adjust one of the lights on the tree. "So how was the last gig?"

"I would've called," she said, "but I didn't want to wake you. Forty-two Buffalo metalheads in a bar the size of this apartment."

"How do they compare to Syracuse metalheads?"

"A little hairier, I think."

"Ah, the glamour of the rock-and-roll life."

"How's the play?"

"Incomprehensible. But the lighting's going to be a killer."

She went into the kitchen and got a beer. "I am so fucking beat," she said.

"I was kind of hoping we could go out."

"Out? Tonight?"

"I sort of felt like dancing."

"Is this, like, a tradition in your family? Going to some club on Christmas Eve?"

"It's my answer to midnight Mass."

It was their first Christmas together, so they didn't have their own traditions yet. Well, why not dancing? Lori wanted to please him. He was practically the first guy she'd ever gone out with who wasn't a complete asshole. Or bi. Or a junkie. Who was, in fact, so far as she could tell after six months, a great guy. Just as she was starting to make a name for herself singing songs about what creeps guys were, she'd gone and fallen in love. Hooked up with a lover and a band at almost the same moment.

As much as she wanted to go right to sleep, she was conscious of the occasion. She liked to imagine they might be spending future Christmases together, and it seemed important to set the right precedents. He'd bought the tree and gone insane with the lights—it was his profession, after all. One of the first things she'd liked about him: *lighting designer.* The very concept—a man who taught light how to act. In the places she played, she felt lucky to get a spotlight. And how matter-of-factly he'd said it, like another guy would say *computer programmer.*

Seeing the lights and the wrapped presents beneath the tree, she suddenly felt guilty.

"Is that really what you want to do? Go dancing?"

"Don't worry about it," he said. "It was just an idea."

"It's not that I don't want to stay up with you," she said, moving closer to him on the couch and kissing his ear. "I think I could summon the energy to give you a special Christmas treat."

"A treat? Could it be . . . the Vulcan mind meld?"

"It's not your mind I'm interested in."

"That's good. For both our sakes."

"Maybe a shower will revive me."

"Don't worry about it. We can celebrate tomorrow."

Jeffrey seemed sincere, but she felt terrible about disappointing him.

In the bedroom, she lay down and dozed off almost immediately. Waking a few minutes later, she suddenly remembered the packet Rory had given her. That was the answer. Jeffrey was so excited about their first Christmas together, and she didn't want to let him down—especially now. In Syracuse she'd seen an old lover, Will Porter. He'd come to the gig and then she'd gone back to his apartment after, ostensibly because he didn't like to hang out in bars. A year out of rehab, he suddenly appeared to be everything she'd wished for back then. Was it possible to change that much?

Feeling a fresh stab of guilt, she fished the drugs out of her jeans and walked over to the dresser, opening the foil carefully, separating out two fat lines with a MetroCard and rolling up a bill.

The first line almost took her head off. Jesus, she thought, it's *crank.*

For some reason, she'd assumed it was coke. Like who wouldn't? At first she was pissed, but then she thought, What the fuck. If she wanted to stay up, she might as well *stay up*. She could sleep tomorrow. In the meantime, Jeffrey would have a dance partner. She did the other line for good measure, then stepped into the shower.

By the time she emerged, she was up for anything, though she was a little too jumpy to give Jeffrey his blow job just yet. Right at this moment the idea seemed kind of nauseating. But now they had the whole night ahead of them. She changed into her black vinyl skirt and the pink spandex top she'd bought at Patricia Field for her gig at CBGB.

Emerging into the living room, she found Jeffrey sitting on the floor in front of the TV, watching *How the Grinch Stole Christmas*. She stole up behind and tackled him.

"Whoa, what's gotten into you?"

"It's just your rock-and-roll girl, ready to dance." He fended off her attack and held her at arm's length, looking into her eyes. "Oh my God. You're wired."

"I wanted to stay up with my baby."

"I don't believe this."

"What's the matter?" She stopped wrestling with him. He'd never been judgmental about drugs before.

"You're fucking *wired*."

"I left some for you, if that's what you're worried about."

"This is rich."

"What's rich?"

He took her hands in his. "You looked so tired and I felt so sorry for you. I just took a Xanax and an Ambien."

It took a moment for this dart to lodge itself in her speeding brain. "Oh shit."

"Yeah."

She collapsed into his arms, laughing. "Merry Christmas," she said.

He kissed her. As much as she wanted to kiss him back, his lips felt strange on hers, which were slightly numb and had begun to take on a life of their own.

———

He managed to stay awake for another half hour, during which she regaled him with tales of upstate New York and Toronto, the quirks of the locals and the outrages perpetrated by her band mates, until he began to nod off on the couch.

"I'm awake," he said several times, snapping his head upright. In the end, she pulled off his shoes and put a quilt over him.

How was it that on this night, the first promising Christmas Eve of her life, she'd ended up alone again? She tried to think of whom she could call. Certainly not her parents, whom she hadn't spoken to in more than a year. She briefly considered Will Porter, her lost-and-found lover, who'd taught her how to play the blues like Bukka White and later how to live them. Waiting all night for him to come home, hiding her money in the toilet tank, one night dragging him into the bathtub and filling it with cold water and ice, just like he'd told her to. Will finally turning blue, if not black.

She was crying. To console herself, she did another couple lines, not that the first were wearing off, not that they wouldn't keep her buzzing into the dawn, but she wanted to get past the guilt about Will. She was entitled to that, surely, on a lonely Christmas Eve.

She called the loft in Brooklyn where the boys would be, but she only got the answering machine, which played a bar from the Sex Pistols' "God Save the Queen."

After watching *Carnal Knowledge* and sweeping the entire apartment, she tried to rouse Jeffrey, who was asleep on the couch, a thin trail of saliva running down his cheek.

"Honey?" She shook his shoulder. "Honey, are you awake?" She turned up the volume on the TV and then undid his belt and began to massage his cock. After a few minutes he shook his head and rolled over, burying his face in the cushions. She scratched at the skin on her arms, tormented by an invisible rash. If only Jeffrey would wake up long enough to scratch her back.

On one of many circuits through the kitchen, she decided to scrub the sink. She scoured and polished until the green Comet slush and the pink sponge had both disappeared; then she took an old toothbrush to the grout around the tiles. Jeffrey wouldn't be able to complain about her housekeeping when he woke up tomorrow. Afterward she took the toothbrush to the elusive itch beneath the skin of her arms and her neck. Lighting a cigarette, she looked down into the shiny white sink with the sudden conviction that she'd be sucked into the drain if she didn't move away immediately. She backed off and lit a second cigarette from the first.

She walked back to the bedroom and looked out into the courtyard, counting the lighted windows as she reached behind her shoulder to scratch her back. Twenty-three the first time she counted, twenty-four the second. As she watched, one third-floor window went dark. Walking back through the living room and past the Christmas tree, she stopped to look at the gifts underneath. Five packages, plus a bottle of Cuervo Gold with a ribbon around it. His presents to her were wrapped up in pages from *Interview* magazine. The square box, which she was pretty sure was a DAT recorder, showed Chrissie Hynde's face. Looking at the presents, she found herself remembering the Shaker hymn:

> *'Tis the gift to be simple, 'tis the gift to be free*
> *'Tis the gift to come down where we ought to be.*

That was all she could remember. As she walked into the kitchen, she wondered where she would be next Christmas, and with whom. She opened the refrigerator, though she had no desire to eat. Surely there was something she wanted to do, something that would fulfill this nameless compulsion, this desire without object.

Somehow it always ended up like this—solo at the edge of dawn. The stage was dark, the audience gone home. She tried to picture a lifetime of Christmases with Jeffrey and couldn't. It wasn't his fault. It was her. It was how she was. She shivered, feeling the chill from the open refrigerator on the prickly envelope of her skin. She tried to imagine herself rising away from her body skin and leaving the skin behind—like a snake's, like an empty shell of wrapping paper, then emerging strange and new.

That's what she really wanted to give him: a whole new girl.

"Wake up, honey," she would say. "It's Christmas."

2000

Story of My Life

I'm like—I don't believe this shit.

I'm totally pissed at my old man, who's somewhere in the Virgin Islands, god knows where. The check wasn't in the mailbox today, which means I can't go to school Monday morning. I'm on the monthly payment program because my dad says wanting to be an actress is a flaky whim and I never stick to anything—this from a guy who's been married five times—and this way if I drop out in the middle of the semester he won't get burned for the full tuition. Meanwhile he buys his new bimbo, Tanya, who's a year younger than me, a 450 SL convertible—always liked the young ones, haven't we, Dad?—plus her own condo so she can have some privacy to do her writing. Like she can even *read.* He actually believes her when she says she's writing a novel, but when I want to spend eight hours a day busting ass at Lee Strasberg it's like *another one of Alison's crazy ideas.* Story of my life. My old man's fifty-two going on twelve. And then there's Skip Pendleton, which is another reason I'm pissed.

So I'm on the phone screaming at my father's secretary when there's a call on my other line. I go hello and this guy goes hi, I'm whatever-his-name-is, I'm a friend of Skip's, and I say yeah and he says I thought maybe we could go out sometime. And I say what am I, dial-a-date?

Skip Pendleton is this jerk I was in lust with for about three minutes. He hasn't called me in like three weeks, which is fine, okay, I can deal with that, but suddenly I'm like a baseball card he trades with his friends? Give me a break. So I go to this guy, what makes you think I'd want to go out with you, I don't even know you, and he goes Skip told me about you. Right. So I'm like, what did he tell you? and the guy goes Skip said you were hot. I say great, I'm totally honored that the great Skip Pendleton thinks I'm hot. I'm just a jalapeño pepper waiting for some strange burrito, honey. I mean, *really.*

And this guy says to me, we were sitting around at Skip's place about five in the morning the other night wired out of our minds, and I say—this is the guy talking—I wish we had some women, and Skip is like, I could always call Alison, she'd be over like a shot, she loves it.

He said that? I say. I can hear his voice exactly, it's not like I'm totally amazed, but still I can't believe even *he* would be such a pig, and suddenly I feel like a cheap slut and I want to scream at this asshole, but instead I say, where are you? He's on West Eighty-ninth, so I give him an address on Avenue C, a rathole where a friend of mine lived last year until her place was broken into for the seventeenth time, and which is about as far away from the Upper West Side as you can get without crossing water, and I tell him to meet me there in an hour, so at least I have the satisfaction of thinking of him spending about twenty bucks for a cab and then hanging around the doorway of a tenement and maybe getting beat up by some drug dealers. But the one I'm really pissed at is Skip Pendleton. Nothing my father does surprises me anymore. I'm twenty-one going on gray.

Skip's thirty-one and so smart and so educated—just ask him, he'll tell you. Did I forget to mention he's so *mature*? Unlike me. He was always telling me I don't know anything. What I don't know is what I saw in him. He seemed older and sophisticated, and we had great sex, so why not? I met him in a club, naturally. I never thought he was very good-looking, but you could tell *he* thought he was. He believed it so much that he actually sold the idea to other people. He had that confidence everybody wants a piece of. This blond hair that looks like he has it trimmed about three times a day. Nice clothes, shirts custom-made on Jermyn Street, which he might just casually tell you some night in case you didn't know is in London, England. (That's in Europe, which is across the Atlantic Ocean—oh, really, Skip, is that where it is? Wow!) Went to the right schools. And he's rich, of course, owns his own company. Commodities trader. Story of Skip's life. Trading commodities.

So basically, he had it all. Should have been a Dewar's Profile. I'm like amazed they haven't asked him yet. But when the sun hit him in the morning, he was a shivering wreck.

From the first night, bending over the silver picture frame in his apartment with a rolled fifty up his nose, all he can talk about is his ex, who dumped him, and how if he could only get her back he would give up all of this forever, coke, staying out partying all night, young bimbos like me. And I'm thinking, poor guy, just lost his main squeeze, feeling real sympathetic, and so I go, when did this happen, Skip? and it turns out it was ten years ago! He lived with this chick for four years at Harvard, and then after they come to New York together she dumps him for some Rockefeller. And I'm like, give me a break, Skip. Give yourself a break. This is ten years after. This is nineteen eighty whatever.

Skip's so smart, right? My parents never gave a shit whether I went to school or not, they were off chasing lovers and bottles and rails of blow, leaving us kids with the cars and the credit cards, and I never did get much of an education. Is that my fault? I mean, if someone told you back then that you could either go to school or not, what do you think you would have done? Pass the trigonometry, please. Right. So I'm not as educated as the great Skip Pendleton, but let me tell you something. I know that when you're hitting on somebody you don't spend the whole night whining about your ex, especially after like a decade. And you don't need a Ph.D. in psychology to figure out why Skip can't go out with anybody his own age. He keeps trying to find Diana, the beautiful, perfect Diana, who was twenty-one when she dumped him. And he wants us, the young stuff, because we're like Diana was ten years ago. And he hates us because we're *not* Diana. And he thinks it will make him feel better if he fucks us over and makes us hurt the way he was hurt, because that's what it's all about if you ask me—we're all sitting around here on earth working through our hurts, trying to pass them along to other people and make things even. Chain of pain.

Old Skip kept telling me how dumb I was. You wish, Jack. Funny thing is, dumb is his type. He doesn't want to go out with anybody who might see through him, so he picks up girls like me. Girls he thinks will believe everything he says and fuck him the first night and not be real surprised when he never calls again.

If you're so smart, Skip, how come you don't know these things? If you're so mature, what were you doing with me?

Men. I've never met any. They're all boys. I wish I didn't want them so much. I've had a few dreams about making it with girls, but it's kind of like—sure, I'd love to visit Norway sometime. My roommate Jeannie and

I sleep in the same bed and it's great. We've got a one-bedroom, and this way the living room is free for partying and whatever. I hate being alone, but when I wake up in some guy's bed with dry come on the sheets underneath me and he's snoring like a garbage truck, I go, let me out of here. I slip out and crawl around the floor groping for my clothes, trying to untangle his blue jeans from mine, my bra from his Jockeys—Skip wears boxers, of course—and trying to be quiet at the same time, then slide out the door laughing like a seal escaping from the zoo and race home to where Jeannie has been warming the bed all night. Jumping in between the sheets and she wakes up and goes, I want details, Alison: length and width.

I love Jeannie. She cracks me up. She's an assistant editor at a fashion magazine, but what she really wants to do is get married. It might work for her, but I don't believe in it. My parents have seven marriages between them, and anytime I've been with a guy for more than a few weeks I find myself looking out the window during sex.

I call up my friend Didi to see if she can lend me the money. Her dad's rich and gives her this huge allowance that she spends all on blow. She used to buy clothes, but now she wears the same outfit for four or five days in a row, and it's pretty gross, let me tell you. Sometimes we have to send the health department over to her apartment to open the windows and burn the sheets.

I get Didi's machine, which means she's not home. If she's there she unplugs the phone, and if she's not she turns on the answering machine. Either way it's pretty impossible to talk to her. I don't know why I bother. She sleeps from about noon till like nine or so. If Didi made a list of her favorite things, I guess cocaine would be at the top and sunlight wouldn't even make the cut. So she can be hard to get hold of.

My friends and I spend half our lives leaving each other messages. Luckily I know Didi's access code, so I dial again and listen to her messages to see if I can figure out where she is. Okay, maybe I'm just nosy.

The first one's from Brian, and from his voice I can tell that he's doing Didi, which really blows me away since Brian is Jeannie's old boyfriend. Except that Didi is less interested in sex than any of my friends, so I'm not really sure. Maybe he's just starting to make his move. A message from her mom—Call me, sweetie, I'm in Aspen. Then Phillip, saying he wants his $350 or else. Which is when I go, what am I, crazy? I'm never going to get a cent out of Didi. And if I do find her, she'll try to talk me into getting wired with her, and I'm trying to stay away from that. I'm about to hang up when I get a call on the other line, my school telling me that my tuition hasn't been received and that I won't be able to go to class until it is. Like, what do you think I've been frantic about for the last twenty-four hours? It's Saturday afternoon. Jeannie will be home soon and then it's all over.

By this time I'm getting pretty bitter. You could say I am not a happy unit. Acting is the first thing I've ever really wanted to do. Except for riding. When I was a kid I spent most of my time on horseback, showing my horses and jumping, until Dick Tracy got poisoned. Then I got into drugs. But acting, I don't know, I just love it, getting up there and turning myself inside out. Being somebody else for a change. It's also the first thing that's made me get up in the morning. The first year I was in New York I did nothing but guys and blow. Staying out all night at the Surf Club and Zulu, waking up at five in the afternoon with plugged sinuses and sticky hair. Some kind of white stuff in every opening. Story of my life. My friends are still pretty much that way, which is why I'm so desperate to get this check, because if I don't there's no reason to wake up early Monday morning and then Jeannie will get home, and somebody will call up and the next thing I know it'll be three days from now with no sleep in between, brain in orbit, nose in traction. I call my father's secretary again, and she says she's still trying to reach him.

I decide to do some of my homework before Jeannie gets home—my sense-memory exercise. Don't ask me why, since I won't be going to class, but it chills me out. I sit down in the folding chair and relax, empty out my mind of all the crap. Then I begin to imagine an orange. I try to see it in front of me. I take it in my hand. A big old round one veined with rust, like the ones we get down in Florida straight from the tree. (Those Clearasil spotless ones you buy in the Safeway are dusted with cyanide or some shit, so you can imagine how good they are for you.) Then I start to peel it real slow, smelling the little geysers of spray that shoot from the squeezed peel, feeling the juice stinging the edges of my fingernails where I've bitten them. . . .

So of course the phone rings. Guy's voice, Barry something. I'm a friend of Skip's, he says. I go, if this is some kind of joke I'm really not amused. Hey, no joke, he goes. I'm just, you know, Skip told me you guys weren't going out anymore, and I saw you once at Indochine, and I thought maybe we could do some dinner sometime.

I'm like, I don't believe this. What am I—the York Avenue Escort Service?

I don't know where I get these ideas, but sometimes I'm pretty quick. I go, did Skip also tell you about this disease he gave me? That shrinks this Barry's equipment pretty quick. Suddenly he's got a call on his other line. Sure you do.

Skip, that son of a bitch. I'm so mad I think about really fixing his ass. First I think I'll call him up and tell him he did give me a disease. Make him go to the doctor, shut down his love life for a few days.

Then the phone rings and it's Didi. Unbelievable! Live—in person, practically. And it's still daylight outside.

I just went to my nose doctor, she goes. He was horrified. He told me that if I had to keep doing blow I should start shooting up, then the damage would be some other doctor's responsibility.

What's with you and Brian? I say.

She says, I don't know, I went home with him a couple of weeks ago and woke up in his bed. I'm not even sure we did anything. But he's definitely in lust with me. Meanwhile, my period's late. So maybe we did.

She has another call. While she takes it, I'm thinking. Didi comes back on and tells me it's her mom, who's having a major breakdown, she'll have to call me back. I tell her no problem. She's already been a big help.

I get Skip at his office. He doesn't sound too thrilled to hear from me. He says he's in a meeting, can he call me back? I say no, I have to talk now.

What? he says.

I'm pregnant, I say.

Total silence.

Before he can ask I say, I haven't slept with anybody else in six weeks. Which is totally true, almost. Close off that little escape hatch in his mind. Slam, bam.

You're sure? he goes, sounding like he's just swallowed a bunch of sand.

I'm sure.

He's like, what do you want to do?

The thing about Skip is that, even though he's an asshole, he's also a gentleman. Actually, a lot of the assholes I know are gentlemen. Or vice versa. Dickheads with a family crest and a prep-school code of honor.

I go, I need money.

How much?

A thousand. I can't believe I ask him for that much, I was thinking five hundred just a minute ago, but hearing his voice pisses me off.

He asks if I want him to go with me, and I say no, definitely not. Then he tries to do this number about making out the check directly to the clinic, and I say, Skip, don't give me that shit. I need five hundred in cash to make the appointment, I tell him, and I don't want to wait six business days for the stupid check to clear, okay? Acting my ass off. My teacher would be proud.

Two hours later a messenger arrives with the money. Cash. I give him a ten-dollar tip.

Saturday night Jeannie and Didi go out. Didi comes over wearing the same horrible surfer shirt she's been wearing all week and her slept-on, un-washed, really gross Rastafarian hair. But she's still incredibly beautiful, even after four days without sleep, and guys make total asses of themselves trying to pick her up. Her Swedish mother was this really big model in the fifties, and Didi was supposed to be the Revlon girl or something, but she didn't manage to wake up for the shoot. Jeannie's wearing my black cashmere sweater, her grandmother's pearls, jeans, and Maud Frizon pumps.

How do I look? she goes, checking herself out in the mirror.

Terrific, I say. You'll be lucky if you make it through cocktails without getting raped.

Can't rape the willing, she says, which is what we always say.

They try to get me to come along, but I'm doing my scene for Mon-day's class. They can't believe it. This shit won't last, they go. I say, this is my life, I'm like trying to do something constructive with it, you know? Jeannie and Didi think this is hilarious. They do this choirgirl thing where they both fold their hands like they're praying and hum "Amazing Grace," which is what we do when somebody starts getting religious on us. Then, just to be complete assholes, they sing, *Alison, we know this world is killing you,* which is kind of like my theme song when I'm being a drag.

So I go, *They say you're nothing but party girls, just like a million more all over the world.*

They crack up.

After they finally leave I open up my script, but I'm having trouble concentrating, so I call up my little sister at home. Of course the line's busy and they don't have call waiting, so I call the operator and request an emergency breakthrough on the line. When the operator cuts in I hear Carol's voice, and then the operator says there's an emergency call from Vanna White in New York. Carol immediately says *Alison* in this moaning, grown-up voice, even though she's three years younger than me.

What's new? I go after she gets rid of the other call.

Same old stuff, she says. Mom's drunk. My car's in the shop. Mickey's out on bail. He's drunk, too.

Listen, do you know where Dad is? I go, and she says last she heard it was the Virgin Islands but she doesn't have a number either. So I explain about my school thing and then maybe because I'm feeling a little weird about it, I tell her about Skip, except I say $500 instead of $1,000, and she says it sounds like he totally deserved it. He's such a prick, I go, and Carol says, yeah, he sounds just like Dad. And I go, yeah, just like.

Jeannie comes back around nine on Sunday morning, a shivering wreck. I give her a Valium and put her to bed.

She lies in bed stiff as a mannequin and says, I'm so afraid, Alison. She is not a happy unit.

We're all afraid, I go.

In half an hour she's making these horrible chain-saw sleep noises.

Thanks to Skip, Monday morning I'm at school doing aerobics and voice. I'm feeling really great. Then sense-memory work. I sit down in class, and my teacher tells me I'm at a beach. She wants me to see the sand and the water and feel the sun on my bare skin. No problem. First I have to clear myself out. That's part of the process. All around me people are making strange noises, stretching, getting their ya-yas out, preparing for their own exercises. I don't know—I'm just letting myself go limp in the

head, then I'm laughing hysterically, and the next thing I'm bawling like
a baby, really out of control, falling out of my chair and thrashing all over
the floor, a total basket case having some epileptic apocalypse, sobbing
and flailing around, trying to take a bite out of the linoleum. They're used
to some pretty radical emoting in here, but apparently this is way over the
top. I don't really remember all of it. Anyway, they take me to the doctor,
who says I'm overtired and tells me to go home and rest.

That night my old man finally calls. I'm like, I must be dreaming.

Pissed at you, I go, when he asks how I am.

I'm sorry, honey, he says about the tuition. I screwed up.

You're goddamn right you did, I say.

Oh, baby, I'm a mess.

You're telling me, I go.

She left me.

Don't come crying to me.

I'm so sad.

When are you going to grow up, for Christ's sake?

I bitch him out for a while, then tell him that I'm sorry, it's okay, he's
well rid of her, there're lots of women who would love a sweet man like
him. And his money. Story of his life. But I don't say that, of course. He's
fifty-two and it's a little late to try and tell him the facts of life. From what
I've seen, nobody changes much after a certain age. Like about four years
old, maybe. Anyway, I hold his hand and cool him out and almost forget
to hit him up for money.

He promises to send me the tuition and the rent and something extra.

He sends the check but then completely forgets my birthday. Not even a
phone call. His secretary claims he's in Europe on business. My sister tells
me he's in Cancún with a new bimbo. At this point my period's already
three weeks late. And if that's not, like, ironic enough, I see Skip Pendleton one night. He's with some anorectic Click model and pretends not to
know me. I'm trying to work out dates and guys, and I figure that if I'm
pregnant it could actually be his.

Of course with my luck it turns out I actually am pregnant. The rabbit
dies, so I have to visit the clinic for real. I can't believe it. I use the check

Dad sends for the month's tuition. They give me some Demerol—not nearly enough. I try to tell them I have this monster tolerance, but they say this is the dosage for your height and weight, and afterward it hurts like hell. While I'm getting my insides hoovered out, I swear off the so-called withdrawal method forever.

After it's over we have a party to celebrate, me and Didi and Jeannie and a bunch of other people. We start out at home, but it gets too small so we go over to Didi's place on Fifty-seventh, this zillion-dollar duplex that looks and smells like the city dump, but after a while nobody can smell anything anyway. No problem. The party goes on for three days. Some of the others go to sleep eventually, but not me. On the fourth day they call my father and he sends a doctor over to the apartment, and now I'm in a place in Minnesota under sedation, dreaming white dreams about snow falling endlessly in the North Country, making the landscape disappear, dreaming about long white rails of cocaine that disappear over the horizon like railroad tracks to the stars. Like when I used to ride and was anorectic and was starving myself and all I would ever dream about was food. There are horses at the far end of the pasture outside my window. I watch them through the bars.

Toward the end of the endless party that landed me here I was telling somebody the story of Dick Tracy. I had eight horses at one point, but he was the best. I traveled all over the country jumping and showing, and when I first saw Dick, I knew he was like no other horse. He was like a human being—so spirited and nasty he'd jump twenty feet in the air to avoid the trainer's bamboo, then stop dead or hang a leg up on a jump he could easily make, just for spite. He had perfect conformation, like a statue of a horse done by Michelangelo. My father bought him for me and he cost a fortune. Back then my father bought anything for me. I was his sweet thing.

I loved that horse. No one else could get near him, he'd try to kill them, but I used to sleep in his stall, spend hours with him every day. When he was poisoned, I went into shock. They kept me on tranquilizers for a week. There was an investigation, though nothing ever came of it. The insurance company paid off in full, but I quit riding. A few months later Dad came into my bedroom one night. I was like uh-oh, not this again. He buried his face in my shoulder. His cheek was wet and he smelled of booze. I'm sorry about Dick Tracy, he said. Tell me you forgive me. The business was in trouble, he goes. Then he passed out on top of me, so I had to go and get Mom.

After a week in the hatch they let me use the phone. I call my dad. How are you? he says.

I don't know why, it's probably bullshit, but I've been trapped in this place with a bunch of shrink types for a week. So just for the hell of it I say, Dad, sometimes I think it would've been cheaper if you'd let me keep that horse.

I don't know what you're talking about.

Dick Tracy, I go, you remember that night you told me.

He goes, I didn't tell you anything.

So, okay, maybe I dreamed it. I was in bed, after all, and he woke me up. Not for the first time. But right now, with these tranqs they've got me on, I feel like I'm sleepwalking anyway and can almost believe it never really happened. Maybe I dreamed a lot of stuff. Stuff I thought happened in my life. Stuff I thought I did. Stuff that was done to me. Wouldn't that be great? I'd love to think that ninety percent of it was just dreaming.

1987

Con Doctor

They've come for you at last. Outside your cell door, gathered like a storm. Each man holds a pendant sock and in the sock is a heavy steel combination lock that he has removed from the locker in his own cell. You feel them out there, every predatory one of them, and still they wait. They have found you. Finally they crowd open the cell door and pour in, flailing at you like mad drummers on amphetamines, their cats' eyes glowing yellow in the dark, hammering at the recalcitrant bones of your face and the tender regions of your prone carcass, the soft tattoo of blows interwoven with grunts of exertion. It's the old lock 'n' sock. You should have known. As you wait for the end, you think that it could've been worse. It has been worse. Christ, what they do to you some nights. . . .

In the morning, over seven-grain cereal and skim milk, Terri says, "The grass looks sick."

"You want the lawn doctor," McClarty says. "I'm the con doctor."

"I wish you'd go back to private practice. I can't believe you didn't report that inmate who threatened to kill you." McClarty now feels guilty that he told Terri about this little incident—a con named Lesko, who made the threat after McClarty cut back his Valium—in the spirit of stoking her sexual ardor. His mention of the threat, his exploitation of it, have had the unintended effect of making it seem more real.

"The association is supposed to take care of the grass," Terri says. They live in a community called Live Oakes Manor, two- to four-bedroom homes behind an eight-foot brick wall, with four tennis courts, a small clubhouse and a duck pond. This is the way we live now—on culs-de-sac in false communities. Bradford Arms, Ridgeview Farms, Tudor Crescent, Wedgewood Heights, Oakdale Manor, Olde Towne Estates—these capricious appellations with their diminutive suggestion of the baronial, their faux Anglo-pastoral allusiveness. Terri's two-bedroom unit with sundeck and Jacuzzi is described in the literature as "contemporary Georgian."

McClarty thinks about how, back in the days of pills and needles, of Percodan and Dilaudid and finally fentanyl, he didn't have these damn nightmares. In fact, he didn't have any dreams. Now when he's not dreaming about the prison, he dreams about the pills and also about the powders and the deliquescent Demerol mingling in the barrel of the syringe with his own brilliant blood. He dreams that he can see it glowing green beneath the skin like a radioactive isotope as it moves up the vein, warming everything in its path until it blossoms in his brain stem. Maybe, he thinks, I should go to a meeting.

"I'm going to call this morning," Terri continues, "and have them check the gutters while they're at it." She will, too. Her remarkable sense of economy and organization, which might have seemed comical or even obnoxious, is touching to McClarty, who sees it as a function of her recovering alcoholic's battle against chaos. He admires this. And he likes the fact that she knows how to get the oil in the cars changed or wangle free upgrades when they fly to Saint Thomas. Outside of the examining room, McClarty still feels bereft of competence and will.

She kisses his widow's peak on her way out and reminds him about dinner with the Clausens, whoever they might be. Perversely, McClarty actually likes this instant new life. Just subtract narcotics and vodka, and stir. He feels like a character actor who, given a cameo in a sitcom, finds himself written into the series as a regular. He moved to this southeastern city less than a year ago, after graduating from rehab in Atlanta, and lived in an apartment without furniture until he moved in with Terri.

McClarty met her at a Mexican restaurant and was charmed by her air of independence and unshakable self-assurance. She leaned across the bar and said, "Fresh jalapeños are a lot better. They have them, but you have to ask." She waved her peach-colored nails at the bartender. "Carlos, bring the gentleman some fresh peppers." Then she turned back to her conversation with a girlfriend, her mission apparently complete.

A few minutes later, sipping his Perrier, McClarty couldn't help overhearing her say to her girlfriend, "Ask *before* you go down on him, silly. Not after."

McClarty admires Terri's ruthless efficiency. Basically she has it all wired. She owns a clothing store, drives an Acura, has breasts shaped like mangoes around an implanted core of saline. "*Not* silicone," she announced virtuously the first night he touched them. If asked, she can review the merits of the top plastic surgeons in town. "Dr. Milton's really lost it," she'll say. "Since he started fucking his secretary and going to Aspen, his brow lifts are getting scary. He cuts way too much and makes everybody look frightened or surprised." At forty, with his own history of psychological reconstruction, McClarty doesn't hold a few nips and tucks against a girl—particularly when the results are so exceptionally pleasing to the eye.

"You're a *doctor?*" Instead of saying, "Yes, but just barely," he nodded. Perched as she was on a stool that first night, her breasts seemed to rise on the swell of this information. Checking her out when he first sat down, Dr. Kevin McClarty thought she looked like someone who would be dating a pro athlete, or a guy with a new Ferrari who owned a chain of fitness centers. She is almost certainly a little too brassy and provocative to be the consort of a doctor, which is one of the things that excite Kevin about her; making love to her, he feels simultaneously that he is slumming and sleeping above his economic station. Best of all, she is in the program, too. When he heard her order a virgin margarita, he decided to go for it. A week after the jalapeños, he moved in with her.

The uniformed guard says, "Good morning, Dr. McClarty" as he drives out the gate on his way to work. Even after all these years, he gets a kick out of hearing the title attached to his own name. He grew up even more in awe of doctors than most mortals because his mother, a nurse, told him that his father was one, though she refused all further entreaties for information. Raised in the bottom half of a narrow, chilly duplex in Evanston, Illinois, he still doesn't quite believe in the reality of this new life—the sunshine, the walled and gated community, the smiling guard who calls him "Dr." Perversely, he believes in the dream, which is far more realistic than all this blue sky and imperturbable siding. He doesn't tell Terri, though. He never tells her about the dreams.

Driving to his office, he thinks about Terri's breasts. They're splendid, of course. But he finds it curious that she will tell nearly anybody that they are, as we say, surgically enhanced. Last time he was in the dating pool, back in the Pleistocene era, he never encountered anything but natural mammary glands. Then he got married and, ten years later, he's suddenly back in circulation and every woman he meets has gorgeous tits, but whenever he reaches for them, he hears, "Maybe I should mention that, they're, you know . . ." And inevitably, later: "Listen, you're a doctor, do you think—I mean, there's been a lot of negative publicity and stuff. . . ." It got so he avoided saying he was a doctor, not knowing whether they were genuinely interested or just hoping to get an opinion on this weird lump under the arm: *Right here, see?* Despite all the years of medical school and all the sleepless hours of his internship, he never really believed he was a doctor; he felt like a pretender, although he eventually discovered that he felt like less of a pretender on one hundred milligrams of Seconal.

The weather, according to the radio, is hot and hotting up. Kevin has the windows up and the climate control at sixty-eight. High between ninety-five and ninety-eight. Which is about as predictable as "Stairway to Heaven" on Rock 101, the station that plays all "Stairway," only "Stairway," twenty-four hours a day—a song that one of the M.D. junkies in rehab insisted was about dope, but to a junkie, everything is about dope. Now the song makes McClarty think of Terri marching righteously on her StairMaster.

After a lifetime in Chicago, he likes the hot summers and temperate winters, and he likes the ur-American suburban sprawl of franchises and housing developments with an affection all the greater for being self-conscious. As a bright, fatherless child, he'd always felt alien and isolated. Later, as a doctor, he felt even further removed from the general populace—it was like being a cop—and that alienation was only enhanced when he also became a drug addict and de facto criminal. He wanted to be part of the stream, an unconscious member of the larger community, but all the morphine in the pharmacy couldn't produce the desired result. When he first came out of rehab, after years of escalating numbness, the sight of a Burger King or a familiar television show could bring him to tears, could make him feel, for the first time, like a real *American.*

He turns into the drive marked MIDSTATE CORRECTIONAL FACILITY. It's no accident that you can't see the buildings from the road. With homes worth half a million within a quarter of a mile, construction was discreet. No hearings, since the land belonged to the state, which was happy to skip the expense of a new prison and instead board its high-security criminals with the corporation that employs Dr. Kevin McClarty. He drives along the east flank of chain-link fence and triple-coiled concertina wire.

These guards, too, greet him by name and title when he signs in. Looking through the bulletproof Plexi, he sees the enlarged photo of an Air Jordan sneaker a visitor just happened to be wearing when he hit the metal detector, its sole sliced open to show a .25-caliber Beretta nesting snug as a fetus in the exposed cavity. *Hey, it musta come from the factory that way, man, like those screws and syringes and shit that got inside the Pepsi cans. I ain't never seen that piece before. What is that shit, a twenty-five? I wouldn't be caught dead with no twenty-five, man. You can't stop a roach with that fuckin' popgun.*

Dr. McClarty is buzzed through the first door and, once it closes behind him, through the second. Inside, he can sense it, the malevolent funk of the prison air, the dread ambience of the dream. The varnished concrete floor of the long white hall is as shiny as ice.

Emma, the fat nurse, buzzes him into the medical ward.

"How many signed up today?" he asks.

"Twelve so far."

McClarty retreats to his office, where Donnie, the head nurse, is talking on the phone. "I surely do appreciate that. . . . Thank you kindly. . . ." Donnie's perennially sunny manner stands out even in this region of pandemic cheerfulness. He says, "Good morning," with the accent on the first word, then runs down coming attractions. "A kid beat up in D last night. He's waiting. And you know Peters from K block, the diabetic who's been bitching about the kitchen food? Saying the food's running his blood sugar up? Well, this morning they searched his cell and found three bags of cookies, a GooGoo Cluster and two MoonPies under the bed. I think maybe we should tell the commissary to stop selling him this junk. Yesterday his blood sugar was four hundred."

Dr. McClarty tells Donnie that they can't tell the commissary any such thing; that would be a restriction of Peters's liberty—cruel and unusual punishment. He'd fill out a complaint, and they'd spend four hours in court downtown, where the judge would eventually deliver a lecture, thirdhand Rousseau, on the natural rights of man.

Then there's Caruthers from G, who had a seizure and claims he needs to up his dose of Klonopin. Ah, yes, Mr. Caruthers, we'd *all* like to up *that* and file the edges right off our day. In McClarty's case, from zero milligrams a day to about thirty, with a little Demerol and maybe a Dilaudid thrown into the mix just to secure the perimeter. Or, fuck it, go straight for the fentanyl. No—he mustn't think this way. Like those "impure thoughts" the priests used to warn us about, these pharmaceutical fantasies must be stamped out at all costs. He should call his sponsor, catch a meeting on the way home.

The first patient, Cribbs, a skinny little white kid, has a bloody black eye, which, on examination, proves to be an orbital fracture. That is, his eye socket has been smashed in. And while McClarty has never seen Cribbs before, the swollen face is familiar; he saw it last night in his sleep. "Lock and sock?" he asks.

The kid nods and then winces at the pain.

"They just come in the middle of the night, maybe five of them, and started whaling on me. I was just lying there minding my own business." Obviously new, he doesn't even know the code yet—not to tell nobody nothing. He is a sniveler, a fish, an obvious target. Now, away from his peers and tormentors, he seems ready to cry. But he suddenly wipes his nose and grins, shows McClarty the bloody teeth marks on his arm. "One of the sons of bitches bit me," he says, looking incongruously pleased.

"You enjoyed that part, did you, Mr. Cribbs?" Then, suddenly, McClarty guesses.

"That'll fix his fucking wagon," says Cribbs, smiling hideously, pink gums showing above his twisted yellow teeth. "I got something he don't want. I got the HIV."

After McClarty cleans up the eye, he writes up a hospital transfer and orders a blood test.

"They won't be messing with me no more," Cribbs says in parting. In fact, in McClarty's experience, there are two approaches to AIDS cases among the inmate population. Many are indeed given a wide berth. Or else they are killed, quickly and efficiently and without malice, in their sleep.

Next is a surly, muscled black prisoner with a broken hand. Mr. Brown claims to have smashed, accidentally, into the wall of the recreation yard. "Yeah, playing handball, you know?" Amazing how many guys hurt themselves in the yard. Brown doesn't even try to make this story sound convincing; rather, he turns up his lip and fixes McClarty with a look that dares him to doubt it.

So far, in the eleven months he has worked here, McClarty has been attacked only in his dreams. But he has been threatened several times, most recently by Lesko. A big pear-shaped redneck in for aggravated assault, he took a knife to a bartender who turned him away at closing time. The bartender was stabbed fifteen times before the bouncer hit Lesko with a bat. And while Lesko did threaten to kill McClarty, fortunately it wasn't in front of the other prisoners, in which case he would feel that his honor, as well as his buzz, was at stake. Still, McClarty makes a note to check up on Lesko; he'll ask Santiago, the guard over on D, to get a reading on his general mood and comportment.

Dr. McClarty makes the first official phone call of the day, to a pompous ass of a psychopharmacologist to get an opinion on Caruthers's medication—not that McClarty doesn't have an opinion himself, but he is required to consult a so-called expert. McClarty thinks Peganone would stave off the seizures just as effectively and more cheaply—which, after all, is his employer's chief concern—whereas Caruthers's chief concern, quite apart from his seizures, is catching that Klonopin buzz. Dr. Withers, who has already talked to Caruthers's lawyer, keeps McClarty on hold for ten minutes, then condescendingly explains the purpose and methodology of double-blind studies, until McClarty is finally forced to remind the good doctor that he *did* attend medical school. In fact, he graduated second in his class at the University of Chicago. Inevitably, they assume that a prison doctor is an idiot and a quack. In the old days, McClarty would have threatened to reach through the phone and rip this hick doctor's eyeballs out of his skull, ask him how he liked that for a double-blind study, but now he is content to hide out in his windowless office behind these three-foot-thick walls and let some other fucker find the cure for cancer. "Thank you very much, *Doctor,*" McClarty finally says, cutting the old geek off in midsentence.

Emma announces the next patient, Peters, the MoonPie-loving diabetic, then slams the door in parting. A fat man with a jellylike consistency, Peters is practically bouncing on the examining table. Everything about him is soft and slovenly except his eyes, which are hard and sharp, the eyes of a scavenger ever alert to the scrap beneath the feet of the predators. The eyes of a snitch.

McClarty examines his folder. "Well, Mr. Peters."

"Hey, Doc."

"Any ideas why your blood sugar's up to four hundred?"

"It's the diabetes, Doc."

"I guess it wouldn't have anything to do with that stash of candy found in your cell this morning?"

"I was holding that stuff for a friend. Honest."

Another common refrain here in prison, this is a line McClarty remembers fondly from his drug days. It's what he told his mother the first time she found pot in the pocket of his jeans. The guys inside have employed it endlessly; the gun in the shoes or the knife or the stolen television set always belongs to some other guy; they're just holding it for him. They never cease to profess amazement that the cops, the judge, the prosecutor, didn't believe them, that their own court-appointed lawyers somehow sold them out at the last minute. They are *shocked.* It's all a big mistake. *Honest. Would I lie to you, Doc?* They don't belong here in prison, and they're eager to tell you why. With McClarty, it's just the opposite. He *knows* he belongs in here. He dreams about it. It is more real to him than his other life, than Terri's breasts, than the ailing lawn outside these walls. But somehow, inexplicably, every day they let him walk out the door at the end of his shift. And back at Live Oakes, the guards wave him through the gate and inside the walls of that residential oasis as if he really were an upstanding citizen. Of course, technically he is not a criminal. The hospital did not bring charges, in return for his agreement to resign and go into treatment. On the other hand, neither the hospital administrators nor anybody else knew that it was he, McClarty, who had shot nurse Marcia DeVane full of the Demerol she craved so very dearly less than an hour before she drove her car into the abutment of the bridge.

Terri calls just before lunch to report that the caretaker thinks the brown spots on the lawn are caused by cat urine. "I told him that's ridiculous; they're not suddenly peeing any more than they used to—oh, wait, gotta go. Kiss kiss. Don't forget about the Clausens, at seven. Don't worry, they're friends of Bill." She hangs up before McClarty can tell her he might stop off at Unity Baptist on the way home.

Toward the end of the day, McClarty goes over to Block D to check the progress of several minor complaints. He is buzzed into the block by Santiago. "Hey, Doc, what you think about Aikman straining his ankle? Your

Cowboys, they gonna be hurtin' till he come back." Santiago labors cheer-fully under the impression that McClarty is a big Dallas Cowboys fan, a no-tion that apparently developed after the doctor mumbled something to the effect that he really didn't pay much attention to the Oilers. McClarty has never followed sports, doesn't know Cowboys from Indians, but he is happy enough to play along, amused to find himself at this relatively late stage in life assigned to a team, especially after he heard the Cowboys re-ferred to on television as "America's team." Like eating at McDonald's, it makes him feel as if he were a fully vested member of the republic.

"Hey, Doc—that strain? That, like, a serious thing?"

"Could be," McClarty says, able at last to offer a genuine opinion on his team. "A sprain could put him out for weeks."

Santiago is jovial and relaxed, though he is the only guard on duty in a cell block of twenty-four violent criminals, most of whom are on the block this moment, lounging around the television or conspiring in small knots. If they wanted to, they could overpower him in a minute; it is only the crude knowledge of greater force outside the door of the block that keeps them from doing so. McClarty himself has almost learned to suppress the fear, to dial down the crackle of active malevolence that is the permanent atmosphere of the wards, as palpable as the falling pressure and static elec-tricity before a storm. So he is not alarmed when a cluster of inmates moves toward him, Greco and Smithfield and two others, whose names he forgets. They all have their ailments and their questions and they're trot-ting over to him like horses crossing the field to a swinging bucket of grain.

"Hey, Doc!" they call out from all sides. And once again, he feels the rush that every doctor knows, the power of the healer, a taste of the old godlike sense of commanding the forces of life and death. This truly is the best buzz, but he could never quite believe it, or feel that he deserved it, and now he's too chastened to allow himself to really revel in the feeling. But he can still warm himself, if only briefly, in the glow of this tribal ad-miration, even in this harsh and straitened place. And for a moment he forgets what he has learned at such expense in so many airless, smoky church basements—that he actually is powerless, that his healing skills, like his sobriety, are on loan from a higher power, just as he forgets the caution he has learned from the guards and from his own experience be-hind these walls, and he doesn't see Lesko until it is too late, fat Lesko, who is feeling even nastier than usual without his Valium, his hand strik-ing out from the knot of inmates like the head of a cobra, projecting a deadly thin silvery tongue. McClarty feels the thud against his chest, the blunt impact, which he does not immediately identify as sharp-instrument trauma. And when he sees the knife, he reflects that it's a damn good thing he isn't Terri, or his left breast implant would be punctured. As he falls into Lesko's arms, he realizes, with a sense of recognition bordering on relief, that he is back in the dream. They've come for him at last.

Looking up from the inmate roster, Santiago is puzzled by this strange embrace—and by the expression on McClarty's face as he turns toward the guard booth. "He was smiling," Santiago will say afterward, "like he just heard a good one and wanted to tell it to you, you know, or like he was say-ing, *Hey, check out my bro Lesko here.*" Santiago will tell the same thing to his boss, to the board of inquiry, to the grand jury and to the prosecu-tor, and he will always tell the story to the new guards who train under him. It will never cease to amaze him—that smile. And after a respectful pause and a thoughtful drag on his cigarette, Santiago will always men-tion that the doc was a big Cowboys fan.

1996

Getting in Touch with Lonnie

Jared let his parched eyes slide across the soothing green lawns, watching the impeccable houses sail past the cab window. Colonials, mostly—the indigenous style here in Protestant-refugee country, some dating back to the exodus from the Old World. The twisty roads, paved and widened deer paths, the old stone walls, the deep green shade of oak and maple—all this was second nature to him. After two years, he wondered if he would ever become comfortable with palm trees and the architectural miscegenation of Los Angeles. In fact, he was thinking of moving back East. A town like this, maybe. He didn't have to live in Manhattan any more than he had to live in L.A. They would come to him now. Send a car (with a bar and a phone, please). He regretted not hiring a car and driver in Manhattan for the round-trip, but he had thought Laura would consider it ostentatious. He could've made some calls on the way up. One thing he had to do was call Lonnie. That was one thing you got used to in L.A., car phones. The phone he could live without, but this cab he'd picked up at the train station seemed to date back to the Frank Capra era. Jared felt he was suffering some kind of serious chiropractic malpractice, between the springs sticking through the backseat and the potholes, whose regular shocks seemed to travel directly up his spinal column without being even faintly absorbed.

Laura had tried to persuade him to move out to Connecticut a few years back, to the kind of place they'd both grown up in. And now she's finally made it back to the suburbs, he thought, feeling clever for just a moment, then guilty. The cabdriver kept looking up into the rearview mirror. Jared was becoming familiar with, but by no means tired of, that particular look.

"Hey, excuse me—but aren't you that actor?"

Jared nodded, his manner at once shy and weary.

"Yeah, I thought you were. Don't tell me. What's your name?"

Jared told him.

"Right, that's it. All right. You were in that movie."

"Been in a few," Jared noted.

"How about that? This is great. I woke up this morning, I had a feeling something was gonna happen today. You know what I mean?"

"I had the same feeling," Jared said.

"So, you checking into the Valley?" the driver asked.

It took Jared a minute to understand the question. Then he said, "Me? No, I'm not checking in. I'm just visiting my . . . I'm visiting someone."

"Hey, no offense. Lots of famous people come through here. In fact, this place is kind of famous for that. Of course, they come here so they can, you know, have their privacy. No publicity. I could tell you some names, man."

"I'm just visiting," Jared said.

"Okay, sure. Listen, do you think you could sign your autograph for my kid?"

They pulled up a long tree-lined driveway to a cluster of buildings that once might have composed the estate of a prosperous gentleman farmer, or a small New England prep school—a Georgian mansion surrounded by white clapboard satellites on several acres of blue-green lawn. Hard to believe this haven was just over an hour from the city. After only a day and a half back in Manhattan, he remembered how compressed and accelerated life could be. Exhausting. Living in New York was like being on location for a movie that never wrapped.

God, I'm wiped, he thought, which reminded him that he needed to call Lonnie. Of course he wasn't sure if Lonnie was even in town.

Signing his autograph on the back of a taxi receipt, he heard his name called out. Laura was waving from the door of one of the houses, a large black woman beside her. Jared strode across the striped lawn, the two women coming out to meet him. Thinner than ever, Laura threw her arms around him and squeezed as hard as she was able. When she finally came up for air, he saw that the worry creases across her forehead had deepened. It had been three months since he'd seen her. She was still beautiful in her distress, a tall and elegant, if rather too angular, brunette. Her eyes fastened on his, tugging at him, asking for answers to all of her questions. As a kid, Jared had been terrified by an old, supposedly bottomless quarry near his house, and that image often came to mind when he thought about the depth and vastness of Laura's need. She required so much love, her childhood stunted by some sort of emotional malnutrition, and he'd grown more and more unhappy and, finally, angry as he discovered his inability to deliver enough of it. Somehow, the worse he felt, the worse he behaved.

"This is Dorene," Laura said, drawing back to indicate the companion at her elbow. "Dorene's my special."

"Your what?"

"She's like my nurse. She stays with me."

Jared shook Dorene's hand, then glanced back at Laura. "All the time?"

"No, of course not. She's with me from seven to three, and from three to eleven another nurse comes on. Then there's the night shift."

"You have somebody sleep with you?"

"She sits in the chair beside the bed."

"This is all so . . ." Jared halted, then nodded and tried to smile.

Laura nodded and shrugged. "They think I'm still suicidal. I don't know. Some days I am." She looked down at the ground. "Sorry," she said. "I know it's tremendously expensive." Though her face and her voice had been animated for a moment with the excitement of seeing him, she spoke now in the barely audible monotone he had come to know over the phone this past month.

"Forget it," Jared said, happy that there was something he could feel noble about. The fact he was paying for this made him feel a little less guilty about everything that had happened. She had said it wasn't his fault, really, that all of the demons of her childhood had broken out of their cages at once, that it went back way before him. Her sadness over the dissolution of their marriage was just one more thing—not the sole cause of this acute depression, which had finally required hospitalization. Meanwhile, his friends told him that no one can be entirely responsible for the happiness of another human being.

Jared felt he should lighten the mood, particularly with a stranger hovering a few feet away. "You know, Dorene," he said in a phony-sounding drawl, "ever since I was a kid I've always thought I was kind of special. But it must be nice to *know* you're a special."

It was weak, he knew, but she rewarded him with a smile anyway.

"You want to see my room?" Laura asked.

"Great," he said, and together the three of them started across the grass back to the house. Suddenly remembering, Jared reached into the pocket of his jacket and handed Laura a small gift-wrapped package.

"I'm afraid I'll have to open that," Dorene said, reaching for it quickly. Suddenly she smiled a little sheepishly and returned the box to Laura. "Sorry, it's just rules. But I don't suppose just this once . . ."

"Thanks," Jared said, looking her in the eyes.

"I sure liked that movie of yours."

Laura stopped walking, bringing them all to an abrupt and awkward halt. "Take it," she said, holding the box out to Dorene. "Go ahead, take it. Rules are rules." Reluctantly, Dorene reclaimed it.

"This is my tiny little part of the world," Laura said to him. "It's not much. But the funny farm's all I've got right now. You have the rest of America. So please don't try to charm everyone right off the goddamn bat, okay?"

Laura had decorated the room with her old stuffed animals, a number of framed photographs, including two of Jared, and several painted baskets he'd never seen. Two windows overlooked the woods and a stream. A hospital bed with metal railings provided the institutional note.

Sitting on the bed beside Jared, Laura opened her gift, a bottle of Chanel perfume. "It's No. 19," she said.

"Your fave," he said.

"I can't stand No. 19. It's No. 5 I like."

"Are you sure?"

"Of course I'm sure. I hate No. 19." She threw the bottle down, and Dorene quietly retrieved it from the carpet.

"I'd swear it was No. 19 you liked," he said.

"One of your other girls," Laura said.

Jared had bought her the stuff for years, and couldn't believe he would forget. But there had been several Chanel purchases since he and Laura were together.

"Wait a minute, for Christ's sake. Remember a week ago, when I told you I was flying to London for that awards thing and we discussed how I should call Tony and Brenda and Ian and Carol and on and on, and when I called a couple nights later, you said, 'What are you doing in London?' After we'd talked about it for half an hour?"

"So? I'm sorry, my short-term memory's not so hot. The doctors said it was a symptom of the depression."

"So maybe you forgot what number perfume you like."

"Jared, you're unbelievable. You could talk yourself off death row and steal the warden's wife on your way out."

"Never worked on you," Jared said, wondering if the nurse was used to witnessing these sorts of scenes.

"Unfortunately, it still does," Laura said. "I want you back."

"What are you, crazy?" he said, unsure if he was trying to deflect the sudden seriousness of this meeting by hamming it up.

She held out her palms, indicating the room. "It would appear so."

"This is Wharton House," Laura said, stopping in front of one of the largest houses in the complex once they were back outside. "The substance-abuse facility."

Jared nodded.

"I wanted you to see it. It's modeled on Hazelden, and supposedly it's a really successful program. You'd like a lot of the people in there. Writers, actors, professors. There's this one guy I really want you to meet. Rob—amazing guy. He's made a fortune on Wall Street—"

"Why in the world would I want to meet a *stock*broker?" Jared said, gently tugging at Laura's elbow in hopes of accelerating their tour of the grounds.

"I don't know, I just thought of you the minute I met him. He's got these eyes like yours. Anyway, he's in for cocaine. Used to deal to all these stars, besides running his own investment firm. He's had an incredible life, lived with that model who's on the cover of *Cosmo* all the time and then—"

"You hate people like that, Laura."

"Eventually he started going to Colombia to buy quantity himself, so he gets busted and put in jail in Cartagena. But within two weeks he has these mercenaries blow up the jail and smuggle him out of the country. Anyway, *I* think you'd like him. He's really smart."

"If I told you about this guy, you'd say he sounds like an asshole."

"He's charming. And besides, I admire his courage in coming here. That takes even more guts than breaking out of jail."

"Sounds like love."

"No," she said. "Except insofar as he reminds me of you."

"That's one of the things I've missed about you," Jared said. "The way you use *insofar as* in conversation. Or *ergo*. We don't get that out in L.A. much. Anyway, I've never been to jail or to Cartagena, either one."

" 'Bout time we headed up for lunch," said Dorene.

On the walk up the drive to the main house, they were joined by some of Laura's housemates. Eric, whom Laura had mentioned several times on the phone, was a gentleman of sixty and a professor of religion at Yale. He was not visibly depressed or sedated.

"Has Laura told you she's our best basket maker," Eric asked.

"I'm an arts and crafts hero," Laura said. "I'm thinking of opening up a crafts boutique after I get out of here. Call it the Basket Case."

After they moved through the cafeteria line, Laura introduced Jared to those seated around the table.

"Just arrive today?" said Tony, a young man with a scimitar-shaped scar across his throat.

Jared nodded, his mouth full of cold, tough veal.

"Where are you, Wharton House?"

"I'm just visiting," Jared said.

"He's my husband," Laura explained.

"Oh, I see."

Jared wondered if the man was perhaps making a point by pretending not to know who he was.

The talk around the table was of the food and pharmacopoeia— prescribed dosages of antidepressants and lethal dosages of self-administered medication. Connie, a recently admitted middle-aged housewife—blond and seemingly cheerful—had tried to kill herself with Valium, thirty of the five-milligram yellows. But she threw up, and everyone told her it wouldn't have done the trick anyway.

"Thirty of the blues might possibly have done it," Jared added, eliciting a fairly general agreement around the table. "Thirty Seconals would do the trick. But for real sledgehammer results, Dilaudids are your best bet. Thirty of those would kill you and your two best friends, plus their household pets." That got a laugh. "Three thousand in the water supply would take out a medium-size city." Then in Ronald Reagan's voice, he said, "The hell with nuclear weapons, you damn Commies, we got the neuron bomb."

Everyone laughed except Laura, whose eyes he avoided.

Jackson, a Unitarian minister, told how he had closed his garage door, climbed into the Oldsmobile, inserted a tape in the cassette player and hit the ignition. When the tape turned over for the second play and he found himself still conscious, if nauseous, he gave up and went back into the house.

"It was a new car, a 1988," he said. "The new emissions-control systems are so good, you can't even kill yourself."

"What was the tape?" Laura asked.

"Pachelbel."

"Good choice. I love his chaconne."

"Thank you, Laura."

Laura's approach to the world had always been slightly skewed. Was that a function of the imbalances that had landed her here, or just her charming eccentricity? Jared loved her, was still unable to divorce her after almost two years of separation. Sometimes he suspected he was afraid to let go because she was the only person who wouldn't allow him to reinvent himself completely, turn himself into something bright and shiny and superficial. So many old friends had been replaced by new ones. Laura was perhaps his last chance to remember and preserve the best of what he had been. On the other hand, was success such a crime? Everybody changes, so why did she insist that he was both selling and destroying his soul? At worst, he was just visiting Babylon on a round-trip ticket. Which reminded him.

"Gotta make a quick call," he told the company. "Keep the veal patties cold for me, guys. I'll be right back."

Jared was directed to a phone booth, where he used his credit card to call Lonnie's New York number. He listened through ten rings, then another ten. Strange, he thought, that Lonnie didn't have his machine turned on, but he probably was still asleep and had the phone unplugged.

"What was the phone call," Laura asked as they were walking back to her house, Dorene trailing behind.

This, he remembered, was one of the things he hated—the suspicion.

"My agent," he said, "and I can never get right through to him."

"Just try to give me these few hours, Jared, will you? You'll be back in the world soon enough."

"You're right. Okay, I'm sorry."

She took his hand and squeezed it. "I'm sorry Rob wasn't at lunch," she said. "I really wanted you guys to meet."

"Who?"

"Rob. The ex–drug dealer."

"Next time, then."

"Can you come back soon?"

"Real soon. I gotta be in L.A. for a week or so, but I can get back right after that. It's for a part," he added, seeing her disappointment.

They sat on lawn chairs in front of the house, and Jared feared a serious talk was coming on. But Dorene's presence made that unlikely. Laura reached out to take his hand again, and looked into his eyes as tears welled up in her own.

"Oh, Jared, I feel like I'm just this insignificant speck on this rock that's spinning through cold space. If nobody cares about any of us, why should I keep on living?"

"I care."

"Not enough. Not more than anything. Not enough to come back."

"Your hand's trembling," Jared said.

"It's the lithium." She withdrew her hand and looked at his arm dangling over the side of the lawn chair. "So's yours," she said. "I noticed earlier."

He looked at it skeptically. "Jet lag."

"Oh, come on, Jared."

"I'm working too hard to be abusing myself," he said.

"You always tap your foot when you tell a lie."

"I'm trying to help with *your* problems," he said. "I'm functioning quite well out there, thanks."

After a sullen silence, they began to talk again, about her doctors and her therapy, and eventually, as the sun dropped in the sky and Jared became used to Dorene's presence and the suburban lawn came to resemble other suburban lawns, they talked about their families and the old friends, the people who'd been at the wedding five years before in her parents' backyard.

For a moment, Jared imagines that he and Laura might make a nice life of it, buying one of these big old white houses with fireplaces everywhere, starting a garden, cruising into the city for the theater and dinner. In a way, to surrender to the gentle yoke of domestic life would be such a relief. He knows Laura wants children—and he does, too, before very long. And she's told him about some decent fly-fishing water somewhere in the vicinity. But even now, another world is calling out to Jared from beyond the stone walls and shaded lanes. From down the railroad tracks, south across a river, he can almost hear the buzz that begins anew every night— the brassy clatter of silverware and female voices busy with praise. . . .

Laura's asking him a question—repeating a question, in fact—about when he will be back. But just then he sees someone coming across the lawn. And when Laura turns to look at the man, her face lights up. He is tall, and young, although his posture seems weary, his gait heavy. The face is familiar, yet in this unfamiliar context it takes Jared a moment to identify it.

He stands up. "Lonnie?"

"Hello, Jared," the man says.

"Lonnie? No, this is Rob," Laura says. "The guy I wanted you to meet."

"We've met," Rob says. And it's true. Jared's impulse is to flee across the lawn, but he doesn't feel he can move.

And the man he knows as Lonnie and has met many times, this man says, "Welcome."

1989

Summary Judgment

Everyone imagines it's all about blow jobs, or esoteric skills practiced in the more exclusive brothels of Europe and Asia. But other arts can be just as important to an ambitious woman who is determined to be the wife of a wealthy and powerful man. No one seems to consider how difficult it is to hold the interest of these demanding, distractable males, particularly after one has passed the first blush of youth.

Alysha de Sante was smitten with Billy Laube long before they met; she had already researched his family and his fortune in the days before Mary Trotter's dinner party, and after sitting beside him all evening she was fairly certain that she'd ignited a flame within his barrel chest. Knowing of his fondness for blood sport, she told him how much she loved shooting, and while she hated to brag, she was considered a very good shot indeed. Everyone said so. She had dropped the names of mutual acquaintances and other grandees and had also managed to convince him that it was his idea to invite her to his midtown corporate headquarters to see the art collection, which she had already researched quite thoroughly. She just adored Remington, she told him, so vigorous and masculine, naming qualities that, she hinted, she also appreciated in a tycoon. Remington was just so *American*—something that, as a European, she found terribly romantic. She had spoken knowledgeably as well about his business, while implying that she herself was burdened with the responsibility of tending to a significant family fortune.

Mary Trotter owed Alysha, who had gotten the Trotters invited to Blenheim the previous summer, and had been happy to seat her next to the recently divorced timber heir. After insisting that Mary recite the guest list, Alysha had decided against asking her to remember to use the title "Contessa" on her place card, after discovering that two European couples, including Lord and Lady Beecroft, had been invited. She had learned to be cautious in this regard; although she had two separate claims to the title, neither was quite beyond reproach. Alysha's mother had once been married to an Italian count and, furthermore, her second-to-last husband, Frederick de Sante, had also been a count, although, in fact, the elderly de Sante, it turned out, was still married to his second wife when Alysha called a priest to his sickbed to perform the wedding service. The prior wench had ended up with most of the count's estate, after an ugly legal battle; having lost three houses and two apartments, Alysha was damned if she'd give up the name, as well. She had continued to use it during her next marriage, to Sam Grossman, heir to an Atlanta-based retail empire. Sam himself had been perfectly comfortable with her decision to keep the name, even if certain third parties had chosen to be malicious. Everyone knew her as Alysha de Sante, and it would have been confusing were she to have changed her name. The fact that Sam was Jewish had nothing to do with it. Billy Laube, who'd recently moved east from Denver, knew none of this, and Alysha was eager to protect him from unpleasant gossip and give him an opportunity to form his own impressions.

Laube's grandfather was one of those giants who had won the West, a self-made financier with an uncanny knack for buying up vast tracts of wilderness that just happened to lie directly in the path of the advancing railroad. The Laube Corporation, of which Billy was president, was now a sprawling conglomerate with interests in timber, paper and chemicals. And unlike most of the local tycoons, he stood well over six feet, with a broad-shouldered athletic build, a thick mane of steel gray hair and—or so it seemed to Alysha—a kind of straight shooting, curmudgeonly frontier manner. His rough edges were charming—much as stubble can be attractive on the face of a younger man.

Like many rich men, he seemed to have a minor obsession with household economy. "My daughter spent four thousand dollars on a dress last month," he complained after she had asked him if he thought her own dress wasn't perhaps just a bit too low-cut. "Something she can apparently wear only once. I never in my life spent more than a thousand dollars on a suit, and I keep them for years." He held up the sleeve of his navy suit as if to demonstrate, and indeed the edge of the sleeve was frayed, the buttonholes fake. While the European men of her acquaintance tended to have their clothes custom-made, and often, she had learned to appreciate the shabby, frugal aesthetic that characterized a certain venerable subset of the American plutocracy. A mountain man by way of Deerfield and Yale, Laube had clearly taken his sartorial cues from the preppy New Englanders. It was all very charming; and later, she believed, she would have plenty of time to take him to Huntsman or Anderson & Sheppard.

"I don't believe there's any reason for young women to spend that kind of money on clothing," she told him, truly believing that the advantages of youth should be handicapped; it wasn't fair that an unlined face and buoyant bust should be further enhanced by a couture gown.

"It's ridiculous is what it is," he said. "Not so long ago, you could get a new Buick for less than that."

"I think it's important to set limits for young people," Alysha said with feeling, indignant at the thought of this girl squandering the family fortune.

"Maybe you're right," he said. "I'll have a talk with her, goddamn it. Four thousand dollars for a piece of cloth."

"Well, I'm sure it was lovely," she said.

In response, he made a noise somewhere between a growl and a grunt, a sound she would come to know well.

When he failed to call, she wasn't discouraged. Billy Laube was one of those busy, absentminded men who often got caught up in their own affairs. Alysha felt certain that she could succeed if given a second chance. She was on the board of the ballet, and it occurred to her that Billy would be the perfect honoree for their fall gala. Although the ballet was not among the many organizations to which his company doled out donations, he had yet to be adopted by any of the other high-profile charities since arriving in New York. The other girls thought it was genius, except for Laurie Greenspan, who was new to the board.

"But what has Billy Laube ever done for the ballet?"

"The point is," Trish Baldwin told her, "what can he do for us now? As the honoree, he'll buy at least two tables for fifty each and *tout le monde* is curious to meet him."

Now she just had to convince Billy. She went through the proper channels, having the ballet secretary call the vice president in charge of corporate giving at Laube, and eventually she followed up with Billy himself, calling from the ballet office to make it all the more official. She reminded him, briefly, of their recent encounter and then proceeded to the business at hand, her tone suggesting they were both very busy people and she wouldn't be bothering him except on a matter of great interest.

"The *ballet*?"

"Last year we honored Felix Rohatyn, and the previous year it was Bob Pittman," she explained. "It's one of the most important events on the social calendar."

"Well, I'm flattered, Miss de Sante, but I can't for the life of me understand why you would want to honor me. I'm hardly an aficionado of the ballet."

"Really? I never would've guessed. Over the years your company has been very generous to our organization."

"We have?"

"I don't suppose a man with so many corporate and charitable interests could possibly keep track of every single one of them," she said. Indeed, she was counting on that fact. "But we appreciate your support."

"There must be other fellows more—"

"I'd consider it a great personal favor if you'd consider it," she said, adopting an entirely different tone, which was meant to suggest need, vulnerability and promise. And by the time they hung up, she had his commitment.

After waiting a week, Alysha called to suggest a meeting to discuss the event. When it came time to pick the venue, he deferred to her. "Well, there's always Le Cirque," she said. When he didn't immediately make some noise of recognition, she reconsidered. Le Cirque might be a little flashy, a little Euro, a little feminine for a macho guy like himself—the realm of lunching ladies. Its masculine counterpart was '21,' the former speakeasy, exactly the kind of place where a lumber baron with a prep school tie would feel right at home.

"Let's go to '21,' " she said. "Bruce always gives me a good table."

Billy said he wasn't particular about where he sat and was delighted to let her make the reservation, which she did immediately. In fact, since the death of her last husband, she had been relegated to the middle or even the back room of '21,' but she certainly wasn't going to let that happen again. Normally, she would have her secretary make the call, but in this case she called herself and insisted on speaking directly to Bruce, the maître d'. It was all she could do to keep her voice pleasant after spending ten minutes on hold.

"Bruce, this is the Contessa de Sante. How nice to hear your voice. It seems ages since I've been in. I would like a table for two at one p.m. this coming Thursday. I will be dining with Billy Laube, who is very particular about where he sits. He would prefer one of the first banquettes, preferably the corner by the door."

"Of course we will do our very best to accommodate Mr. Laube."

At the restaurant, Alysha introduced the mogul to the maître d'. "This is my dear friend Bruce, who's one of the most important men in New York. I want you to promise me you'll take care of Billy now that he's a New Yorker."

Bruce took Billy's hand and said, "Good to see you again, Mr. Laube."

"Always a pleasure," said Billy.

After they were seated, Alysha pointed out to him that their table at the front of the room was the best in the house. She surveyed her surroundings from her privileged perch in the red leather banquette and waved to a handsome silver-haired man in a formfitting pinstriped suit at the center table.

"That's Curt Vetters, a very good friend of mine. He used to be terribly in love with me. When I was married to my late husband, he would always tell me he wanted to run away with me. He was a very naughty man, all hands. He just bought a football team—I forget which one. I'm afraid I don't know very much about American sports."

"Well, I don't know much about ballet," Billy said, "so that makes us even. I can't quite believe I let you talk me into this thing."

"Don't worry. I will teach you everything you need to know. You must be careful, when you come to New York, not to fall in with the wrong people. It's important to have the right advice," she said, reaching over and squeezing his hand.

"I believe I'm in good shape there," he said, smiling and looking her directly in the eye before turning away to take the menu.

The following week he invited her to La Grenouille for dinner. Moments after she put the phone down, it rang again, and she picked it up, her personal assistant having disappeared for the moment.

"Alysha, I've left you half a dozen messages," her accountant said, sounding exasperated. "It's absolutely crucial that we resolve the situation with the Southampton house."

"I'm sorry, Saul, I've only just returned from Paris."

"The bank's moving to foreclose. Unless we come back to them with some kind of plan, they'll file for summary judgment next month. We're four months overdue on the mortgage payments, and now they tell me the Realtor claims you've turned down three offers in that same period."

"They weren't offers, darling; they were insults."

"Alysha, we don't have the luxury of sneering, not when you owe the bank thirty million dollars. The Realtor says the last offer was for twenty-seven, and that you refused to counter."

"The house is worth at least thirty-five and you know it. It was designed by Stanford White, for heaven's sake. You know perfectly well we paid twenty-five for it three years ago, and look at what the market's done since then."

"You overpaid, Alysha. Sam got in a pissing match with Chip Rhodes."

"How dare you speak about my husband that way?"

"I apologize, but honestly, Alysha, we're running out of options here. We've got to liquidate something. What about the art?"

It was true: She had some valuable artwork, but she had already borrowed against the best pieces, and she continued to think of the rest as the cash in her sock drawer, the last line of defense between herself and destitution, and she wasn't ready to admit that things had reached that stage of crisis. The artwork had been bought at auctions in New York and in Europe, and what hadn't gone to the residences had been shipped to a warehouse in Switzerland, her hedge against the uncertainties of widowhood. Though her late husband had kept her on a rather tight leash when it came to personal expenses, he had relinquished to her the traditional female realm of household management and decor. She had formed a company, which she'd then hired to redo all of their houses. Sam had sometimes grumbled about the cost, but he'd left the details to Alysha. Some of the furniture and paintings that she and her decorators had acquired in Europe went directly into storage, a little nest egg she considered herself more than entitled to. After all, Sam's nasty children would be wildly wealthy in their own right, the income from the Grossman trust passing directly to the children upon his death. As things turned out, she only wished she'd put away more.

It had been war between Alysha and the children from the day their father proposed to her. They repeated all sorts of vile rumors and even dug up the certificate from her first marriage, to the polo player, which she hadn't told him about because it had been annulled. She only thanked God they hadn't found out about Riyadh.

Alysha wasn't one to leave an attack unanswered. She used to scrutinize their credit-card bills, which, naturally, came to her husband, and point out extravagant expenditures. Sonja was a tomboy who spent millions on horses—a mousy plain Jane, whom no one could accuse of spending too much on her wardrobe. She had a house in Millbrook, where all her horsey friends gathered on weekends. Her brother, Alex, was supposedly an art dealer, with a gallery in Chelsea underwritten by his father.

Alysha had liked to call Alex at some advanced hour, like noon, while her husband was in the room. "Oh, darling, I'm sorry, are you still sleeping? I'm so sorry I woke you. Go back to sleep." And she would hold the phone as Sam growled about the laziness of his offspring and Alex shouted, uselessly, that he'd been awake for hours.

She was still bitter about the trust agreement. She'd known about it, of course, but before the wedding she'd been blinded by love, not to mention the estates and the jet and the jewels. Somehow, she'd imagined the will could be changed once she was inside the walls of the castle. It really wasn't fair that Sam hadn't been able to dispose of his vast fortune as he saw fit, that his ungrateful children, who had no sense of style or elegance, should inherit almost everything. The little monsters hadn't been able to wait for their father to keel over, whereas Alysha had gotten him on a serious diet and exercise regimen, which made it seem all the more unfair that he died so soon after they found the Southampton house, or that he should have put so little money down. Her psychic had told her that Sam had at least five more years, at which point the house would've been paid off. Instead, in the middle of a session with the trainer she'd hired, he suffered a massive stroke and passed away twenty-four hours later.

"I just need a little more time, Saul. All will be well." What he didn't know was that she'd already taken out a loan against the art and the furniture, which had kept her going this past year.

"We don't have any more time. If we don't sell something, you could end up losing the co-op as well as the house."

"Then you must convince them, Saul. You're my savior, darling. We will look back on this someday soon and laugh about it, I promise you."

After their dinner at La Grenouille, she invited Billy up to her apartment for coffee, and he seemed every bit as impressed as she'd hoped. The doorman had appeared at just the right moment to help them out of the car, and said, "Welcome home, Contessa." She was almost impressed herself as they stepped directly from the elevator into her foyer, with its black-and-white marble floor and coffered ormolu ceiling. She pointed out the major paintings—the mortgaged Renoirs and the Monet—as they made their way to the living room, where there was no need to point out the view of Central Park. Billy walked over to the windows over Fifth Avenue and whistled. "Now that's what I call a view."

"One gets used to it, after all this time, but I suppose I am very lucky."

"It's really something."

"Come see the rest of the apartment," she said, taking him on a brief tour, which ended in the master bedroom.

"Oh, Billy, you must think I'm terrible," she said, burying her head in his shoulder after crawling up from a longish sojourn between his thighs.

"No, I think you're wonderful," he said.

"I couldn't help myself," she replied.

The next day she gave him a pair of cabochon sapphire cuff links from Cartier.

"I'm . . . speechless," he said after opening the little red box in his suite at the Carlyle. "I don't think anybody has ever given me anything this nice." He looked positively misty-eyed. "They're beautiful. I . . . I can't thank you."

"I'm so glad you like them, darling."

"I love them."

That night he made love like a teenager, and for the first time they stayed together until morning.

Three nights later she again spent the night at his suite. She was already up when the phone rang with his wake-up call.

"Darling," she said, "I can't find my jewels. When I went out to the living room, the door to the suite was wide open."

When they took inventory, it seemed that her earrings and necklace were missing, along with Billy's cuff links and several hundred dollars in cash.

She clutched him and buried her head in his chest. "It's terrifying to think they were right here in the room while we were sleeping."

Billy called the manager and demanded to know what kind of security they had in this goddamn hotel.

"I think their attitude is appalling," Alysha said after their initial interview with the hotel manager and the head of security.

"More worried about covering their asses than solving the crime."

That evening, the head of security knocked on the door and said they were still investigating. "Mr. Laube, can I ask you how long you've known Ms. de Sante?" Outraged, Billy threatened to move out that very night.

"Don't worry," Billy told Alysha later. "Between my insurance company and the hotel's, we'll reimburse you for your jewelry, if you can just give me an appraisal."

"Oh, darling, that's so sweet of you."

"No, it was sweet of you to buy me those cuff links. I'd just like to get my hands on the bastard who swiped them."

"There was a gentleman looking for you earlier," her doorman told her when she arrived home that night. "He wouldn't leave his name. I think he was trying to serve you with some kind of legal document. Of course I told him that you were out of town."

"There must be some mistake," she said, but Saul called the next day to confirm that she should indeed expect a subpoena.

"They're seeking a summary judgment of default and they want to depose you."

"I have no idea what any of that means," she said, "and I told you I just need a little more time."

"You can dodge the summons for a few days or a week, but sooner or later you'll have to give your deposition. And you're going to have to pay off the loan."

"Tell those nasty lawyers I'm far too busy at the moment for their silly deposition." The gala was only three days away, for one thing, and she was on the seating committee, which had to finalize the assignment of tables today, a very delicate operation that involved accommodating the large egos of major donors, separating enemies, and rewarding friends. And she had her final fitting at Valentino.

She instructed her doormen to tell all callers, except for Mr. Laube, that she was in Paris.

The night of the gala, Alysha wore the strapless white lace Valentino with a black bodice. And she had meanwhile taken Billy to Dunhill for a made-to-measure single-breasted tux with peaked lapels. He couldn't quite believe it cost three thousand dollars, but she told him that such a godlike build deserved custom suiting.

Lincoln Center's plaza, framed by the soaring columns of the opera house, Avery Fisher and the New York State Theater, seemed to Alysha a suitable stage for the great occasion. Billy took her arm as they disembarked at the drop-off area and escorted her up the steps. The photographers lining the red carpet began to stir, repeating her name as they readied themselves for her entrance.

They began to snap; then one of them stepped forward. "Alysha de Sante?"

"Yes?"

He handed her a yellow envelope. "You've been served."

"What the hell?" Billy said.

Alysha dropped the envelope, but on second thought, she realized that she could hardly leave it behind, and so she asked Billy to pick it up for her, the whole scene recorded as the cameras continued to flash, Alysha repairing her smile and leading the bewildered Billy through the gauntlet, turning to see Kip and Mary Trotter, who were right behind them, witnesses to the whole fiasco.

"What was all that about?" Billy asked, blinking and frowning, once they were inside.

"Oh, darling, I didn't want to bore you with my problems," she said in a quavering voice. She realized she had to present her own version of events before he heard any malicious gossip, or, God forbid, read an unflattering account in some column. But first she had to fulfill her role as gala cochair and escort of the evening's distinguished honoree.

"Whatever it is, it's nothing we can't fix," he said, squeezing her hand. The collective pronoun thrilled her even more than his compassionate expression; it was true—truer than he could possibly imagine—that with his help, her problems would simply vanish. It was all so simple, really. She would bare her soul to him and he would rescue her.

Mary Trotter took her by the elbow. "Anything wrong?"

"Everything is absolutely wonderful," Alysha replied.

And indeed it was. She and Billy circulated through the crowd, accepting compliments. Alysha knew everyone and introduced Billy to those dignitaries with whom he was not yet acquainted, including the director of the ballet and the mayor. At one point when they became separated, she introduced herself to Zach Hunter, the actor, who would be more or less a contemporary of Billy.

"Very nice to meet you," he said, looking over her shoulder.

"My gentleman friend, Billy Laube, is a big fan of yours," Alysha said. "I know he'd be delighted to meet you."

"Billy Laube? You mean, like, the Laube Foundation?"

She nodded, pointing to Billy, who stood a head above the crowd a few yards away. "Come say hello to Billy."

She led him over and introduced them. Billy seemed relieved to see Alysha and delighted to meet a movie star. It turned out they had a friend in common, someone in Los Angeles named Ray Stark. They engaged in an enthusiastic exchange, much of it relating to the Denver Broncos football team. When they separated to find their respective tables, Alysha said, "Who *was* that man?"

"You didn't recognize Zach Hunter? Are you that young? He's an actor, a movie star. At least he was. I thought you knew him."

"He introduced himself and told me I was the most beautiful woman in the room. I thought perhaps he did look familiar. But then he kept talking to me, so I thought I would introduce him to you so he would know I had a boyfriend."

"Wow," Billy said. "Zach Hunter was hitting on you. And you didn't even know it."

"Perhaps he *was* a little before my time, or else he is more popular here than in Europe," she said, taking his arm and leading him to the table.

The evening was an unalloyed triumph, and anyone expecting to see Alysha nervous or humbled was disappointed. She took the stage after appetizers and introduced Billy at some length, and he gave a very charming and self-deprecating speech that she had written for him with the help of her Wellesley-educated assistant. The performances were first-rate; even Billy seemed to enjoy the show, which at twenty minutes was just long enough to satisfy the faithful without alienating the banker husbands who had to be at work early the next morning. She knew there was a little buzz concerning the events out on the red carpet, but she chose to rise above it. All that mattered was what Billy thought. The rest of them would follow in his wake.

"You were wonderful," she told him, safely in the car shortly after eleven.

"You're the wonderful one," he said, throwing his big lumberjack arm around her and pulling her close. "I was worried about you."

"You're sweet," she said, "but I don't want you to worry. I'm used to these attacks. They are jealous of me, and they wish to see me suffer, but I won't give them the satisfaction." She buried her head in his shoulder.

"Who? Who's attacking you?"

"The children."

"Children?"

"My late husband's children. They hate me—they want to ruin me. They are contesting the beastly will and they have frozen my assets. My lawyers tell me we will win in the end, but before we do, I may lose my house in Southampton. Maybe even my apartment. Oh, Billy, I didn't want you to become mixed up in this nasty business."

"Well, it sounds like you need somebody to get mixed up in it. What was the summons all about?"

"It's about the mortgage. They're going to foreclose on my beautiful house."

"Nobody's going to foreclose on anything. Not if I have anything to say about it."

"I can't ask you to rescue me."

"You don't have to ask," he said, pulling her closer.

The next day, Billy canceled his lunch date and walked over to Cartier to look at rings. He'd almost proposed to her last night in the car, but he had old-fashioned ideas about propriety and presentation. He wanted to do it right. He wanted to have the ring and the proper setting for the proposal. Casting his mind about for a place, he realized that Alysha would be the person who would know the perfect location. In the past few weeks he had come more and more to rely on her. He realized that he liked this feeling of surrender, of being taken care of. She seemed to know everyone and everything. All he had to do was show up and be himself. They made a good team.

After fifteen minutes in the store, his head was spinning. Emerald cut, marquise cut, pear and princess . . . color and clarity. And he was shocked by how much you could spend on a fairly modest-looking diamond ring. Billy had little experience with jewelry. Most of the jewelry he'd given his first wife had originally belonged to his mother.

"I'm going on my break," the salesgirl said, "but my colleague will be happy to help you." She indicated a slim young man in a tight black suit, whose hair was combed to a peak in the center of his head.

"Mr. Laube, isn't it?" he said.

Billy nodded, surprised at being recognized by such an unlikely figure.

"Miss de Sante is a client," he said cheerfully. "A very fine lady. A very refined lady, I should say."

Billy nodded, wondering how this odd young fellow knew so much about him.

"I'm sorry you didn't like the cuff links," he said.

"I beg your pardon?"

"The cuff links. That Miss de Sante bought for you. She said they weren't your cup of tea."

"Cuff links? What are you talking about? You mean the sapphire cuff links?"

He nodded. "The ones she returned last week."

"That's impossible," Billy said.

"Perhaps I'm mistaken," the clerk said.

"She returned them?"

"That was my impression."

"This happened . . . recently?"

"Yes, last week."

"Could I see these cuff links?"

"You want to look at them again?" the clerk asked nervously.

"I think I need to see them," Billy said.

The day after the gala, the calls started coming in at eleven. All the girls agreed the night had been a big success. They assured Alysha that she and Billy were the cutest couple in town, and several wanted to know when they could expect an announcement.

When she hadn't heard from Billy by two, she decided to check in. His secretary said he was in a meeting.

"Did you give him my previous message?" she demanded the next time she called, told that he was still unavailable.

"I give Mr. Laube all of his messages." From the first time they'd spoken, Alysha hadn't liked her attitude, and she vowed to get rid of her, perhaps sooner rather than later.

"If you value your job at all, I strongly suggest that you tell Mr. Laube I'm on the phone."

"I'm sorry, Mr. Laube is unavailable."

This woman was simply intolerable, but Alysha was stymied. At one time, she'd found it charming that Billy was one of the last men on earth subsisting without benefit of a cell phone, but now it was simply infuriating. "Tell Mr. Laube it's urgent that he call me at home immediately."

At eight and again at eight-thirty she called the Carlyle, where the switchboard operator told her that Mr. Laube was not accepting calls.

"I'm his fiancée," Alysha said. "I demand to speak to him."

"I'm sorry, but my instructions were very clear."

"How dare you tell me I can't speak to my fiancé? I demand to speak to the manager."

But the buffoon of a manager was no more cooperative than the switchboard operator, and he seemed unmoved when Alysha told him that she was a very good friend of the owner and would have them both fired.

The next day, his awful secretary told her that Billy was out of town. Two days later, she heard from a friend that he was shooting at an estate in Norfolk. She couldn't understand what had gone wrong. He'd been so loving, so concerned, the night of the gala. Someone must have poisoned him against her. Someone had told him something, but what? Of course she knew she had enemies; a girl in her position was naturally a target of jealousy and resentment. Could someone have told him about Riyadh? If she had the opportunity, she would tell him that it wasn't her choice, that she was barely sixteen when her mother had arrived one day at the convent, after an absence of almost a year, and taken her away, promising a great adventure, reminding her about the prince, who'd seen her the previous summer in Monaco.

Billy was still traveling when she sat through her deposition a month later. Her lawyer prevented her from answering most of the questions, but once they were alone, he turned gloomy. "I can stave off a summary judgment for a few weeks at best," he said. "We've got to come up with some kind of plan."

That night, she called Mary Trotter and asked her to dinner the following Thursday, having heard that Mary was giving a party that night for Jake Taplow, the software billionaire.

"I'm so sorry," Mary said, "but I'm afraid we're busy that night."

"Perhaps we could combine our little soirees."

"I don't think so, Alysha."

"Well, you're actually the first couple I've called, so I could easily postpone my dinner and join you that night."

"I don't think you'd feel comfortable, darling." She paused. "Sonja Grossman's coming, and I know how you two feel about each other."

"That's silly. I don't have anything against Sonja." She was more than willing to be magnanimous about her former stepdaughter, if necessary.

"Well, I'm glad to hear it, but Sonja seems to be nursing some silly grudge. I certainly haven't ever discussed it with her, but I think it's safe to say she's not your biggest fan, and I'd hate to subject you to an awkward situation. And the fact is, she's bringing Billy Laube as her date. They met in London and apparently he gave her a ride home on his plane, and, well, honestly, Alysha, I wouldn't dream of putting you in that position. I think it's terrible the way he dropped you; everyone's saying it's practically a breach of promise. It's shameful, but honestly, what can I do? My hands are tied. I had no idea they were an item when I invited Sonja. But let's by all means get together this weekend in Southampton, just the three of us."

2008

How It Ended

I like to ask married couples how they met. It's always interesting to hear how two lives became intertwined, how of the nearly infinite number of possible conjunctions this or that one came into being, to hear the first chapter of a story in progress. As a matrimonial lawyer, I deal extensively in endings, so it's a relief, a sort of holiday, to visit the realm of beginnings. And I ask because I've always enjoyed telling my own story—our story, I should say—which I've always felt was unique.

My name is Donald Prout, rhymes with *trout*. My wife, Cameron, and I were on vacation in the Virgin Islands when we met Jack and Jean Van Heusen. At our tiny expensive resort we would see them in the dining room and on the beach. Etiquette dictated respect for privacy, but there was a quiet, countervailing camaraderie born of the feeling that one's fellow guests shared a level of good taste and financial standing. And the Van Heusens stood out as the only other young couple.

I'd just won a difficult case, sticking it to a rich husband and coming out with a nice settlement despite considerable evidence that my client had been cheating on him with everything in pants for years. Of course I sympathized with the guy, but he had his own counsel, had many inherited millions left over, and it's my job, after all, to give whoever hires me the best counsel possible. Now I was taking what I thought of as, for lack of a better cliché, a well-earned rest. I'd never done much resting, going straight from Amherst—where I'd worked part-time for my tuition—to Columbia Law to a big midtown firm, where I'd knocked myself out as an associate for six years.

It's a sad fact that the ability to savor long hours of leisure is a gift some of us have lost, or else never acquired. The first morning, within an hour of waking in paradise, I was restless, watching stalk-eyed land crabs skitter sideways across the sand, unwilling or unable to concentrate on the Updike I'd started on the plane. Lying on the beach in front of our cabana, I noticed the attractive young couple emerging from the water, splashing each other. She was a tall brunette with the boyish body of a runway model. Sandy-haired and lanky, he looked like a boy who'd taken a semester off from prep school to go sailing. Over the next few days I couldn't help noticing them. They were very affectionate, which seemed to indicate a relatively new marriage (both wore wedding bands). And they had an aura of entitlement, of being very much at home and at ease on this very pricey patch of white sand, so I assumed they came from money. Also, they seemed indifferent to the rest of us, unlike those couples who, after a few days of sun and sand in the company of the beloved, invite their neighbors for a daiquiri on the balcony to grope for mutual acquaintances and interests—anything to be spared the frightening monotony of each other.

In fact, I was feeling a little dissatisfied after several days, my wife and I having, more rapidly than I would have thought, exhausted our meager store of observations about the monotonously glorious weather and the subjects that we imagined we never had enough time to discuss at home, what with business and the social schedule. And after a relatively satisfying first night, our lovemaking was not as inspired as I had hoped it was going to be. I wanted to leave all the bullshit at home, rejuvenate our marriage and our sex life, tell Cameron my fantasies, pathetically simple as they were. Yet I found myself unable to broach this topic, stuck as I was in a four-year rut of communicating less and less directly, reluctant for some reason to execute the romantic flourishes—candlelight and flower petals in the bathwater and such—she considered so inspiring. And seeing her in her two-piece, I honestly felt that Cameron needed to do a bit of toning and cut back on the sweets.

But the example of the Van Heusens was invigorating. After all, I reasoned, we were also an attractive young couple—an extra pound or two notwithstanding. I thought more highly of us for our ostensible resemblance to them, and when I overheard him tell an old gent that he'd recently passed the bar, I felt a rush of kinship and self-esteem, since I'd recently made partner at one of the most distinguished firms in New York.

On the evening of our fifth day, we struck up a conversation at the poolside bar. I heard them speculating about a yacht out in the bay and told them whom it belonged to, having been told myself when I'd seen it in Tortola a few days earlier. I half expected him to recognize the name, to claim friendship with the owners, but he only said, "Oh, really? Nice boat."

The sun was melting into the ocean, dyeing the water red and pink and gold. We all sat, hushed, watching the spectacle. I reluctantly broke the silence to remind the waiter that I had specified a piña colada on the rocks, not frozen, my teeth being sensitive to crushed ice. Within minutes the sun had slipped out of sight, sending up a last flare, and then we began to chat. Eventually they told us they lived in one of those eminently respectable communities on the North Shore of Boston.

They asked if we had kids, and we said no, not yet. When I said, "You?" Jean blushed and referred the question to her husband.

After a silent exchange, he turned to us and said, "Jeannie's pregnant."

"We haven't really told anyone yet," she added.

Cameron beamed at Jean and smiled encouragingly in my direction. We had been discussing this very topic lately. She was ready; I didn't feel quite so certain myself. Still, I think we both were pleased to be the recipients of this confidence, even though it was a function of our very lack of real intimacy, and of the place and time, for we learned, somewhat sadly, that this was their last night.

When I mentioned my profession, Jack solicited my advice; he would start applying to firms when they returned home. I was curious, of course, how he had come to the law so relatively late—he had just referred in passing to his recent thirtieth-birthday celebration—and what he'd done with his twenties, but thought it would be indiscreet to ask.

We ordered a second round of drinks and talked until it was fully dark. "Why don't you join us for dinner?" he said as we all stood on the veranda, hesitant about going our separate ways. And so we did. I was grateful for the company, and Cameron seemed to be enlivened by the break in routine. I found Jean increasingly attractive—confident and funny— while her husband was wry and self-deprecating in a manner that suited a young man who was probably a little too rich and happy for anyone else's good. He seemed to be keeping his lights on dim.

As the dinner plates were cleared away, I said, "So tell me, how did you two meet?"

Cameron laughed at the introduction of my favorite parlor game. Jack and Jean exchanged a long look, seeming to consult about whether to reveal their great secret. He laughed through his nose, and then she began to laugh; within moments they were both in a state of high hilarity. To be sure, we'd had several drinks and two bottles of wine with dinner, and excepting Jean, none of us was legally sober. Cameron, in fact, seemed to me to be getting a little sloppy, particularly in contrast to the abstinent Jean; when she reached again for the wine bottle, I tried to catch her eye, but she was bestowing her bright, blurred attention on our companions.

"How we met," Jack said to his wife. "God. You want to tackle this one?"

She shook her head. "I think you'd better."

"Cigar?" he asked, producing two metal tubes from his pocket. Though I've resisted the cigar fetish indulged in by so many of my colleagues, I occasionally smoke one with a client or an associate, and I took one then.

He handed me a cutter and lit us up, then leaned back and stroked his sandy bangs away from his eyes and released a spume of smoke. "Maybe it's not such an unusual story," he proposed.

Jean laughed skeptically.

"You sure you don't mind, honey?" he asked.

She considered, shrugged her shoulders, then shook her head. "It's up to you."

"Well, I think this story begins when I got thrown out of Bowdoin," he said. "Not to put too fine a point on it, I was dealing pot. Well, pot and a little coke, actually." He stopped to check our reaction.

I, for one, tried to keep an open, inviting demeanor, eager for him to continue. I won't say I was shocked, though I was certainly surprised.

"I got caught." He smiled. "By agreeing to pack up my old kit bag and go away forever, I escaped prosecution. My parents were none too pleased about the whole thing, but unfortunately for them, virtually that week I'd come into a little bit of Gramps's filthy lucre and there wasn't much they could do about it. I was tired of school anyway. It's funny—I enjoyed it when I finally went back a few years ago to get my B.A. and then law degree, but at the time, it was wasted on me. Or I was wasted on it. Wasted in general. I'd wake up in the morning and fire up the old bong and then huff up a few lines to get through geology seminar."

He pulled on his stogie, shaking his head ruefully at the memory of his

youthful excess. He didn't seem particularly ashamed as much as be-
mused, as if he were describing the behavior of an incorrigible cousin.

"Well, I went sailing for about a year—spent some time in these waters, actually, some of the best sailing waters in the world—and then
drifted back to Boston. I'd run through most of my capital, but I didn't
feel ready to hit the books again, and somehow I just kind of naturally got
back in touch with my suppliers from Bowdoin days. I still had a boat, a
little thirty-six-footer. And I got back in the trade. It was different then—
this was ten years ago, before the Colombians really moved in. Everything
was more relaxed. We were gentlemen outlaws, adrenaline junkies, freaks
with an entrepreneurial streak."

He frowned slightly, as if hearing the faint note of self-justification, of
self-delusion, of sheer datedness. I'd largely avoided the drug culture of
the seventies, but even I could remember when drugs were viewed as the
sacraments of a vague liberation theology or, later, as a slightly risky form
of recreation. But in this era the romance of drug dealing was a hard sell,
and Jack seemed to realize it.

"Well, that's how we saw it then," he amended. "Let's just say that we
were less ruthless and less financially motivated than the people who eventually took over the business."

Wanting to discourage his sudden attack of scruples, I waved to the
waiter for another bottle of wine.

"Make sure it's not too chilled," Cameron shouted at the retreating
waiter. "My husband has very sensitive teeth." I suppose she thought this
was quite funny.

"Anyway, I did quite well," Jack continued. "Initially I was very hands-
on, rendezvousing with mother ships out in the water beyond Nantucket,
hauling small loads in a hollow keel. Eventually my partner and I moved
up the food chain. We were making money so fast, we had a hard time
thinking of ways to launder it. I mean, you can't just keep hiding it under
your mattress. First we were buying cars and boats in cash and then we
bought a bar in Cambridge to run some of the profits through. We were
actually paying taxes on drug money just so we could show some legitimate
income. We always used to say we'd get out before it got too crazy, once
we'd really put aside a big stash, but there was so much more cash to be
made, and craziness is like anything else: You get into it one step at a time

and no single step really feels like it's taking you over the cliff—until you go right over the edge, and then it's too late. You're smoking reefer in high school and then doing lines and all of a sudden you're buying AK-47's and bringing hundred-kilo loads into Boston Harbor."

I wasn't about to point out that some of us never even thought of dealing drugs, let alone buying firearms. I refilled his wineglass, nicely concealing my skepticism, secretly pleased to hear this golden boy revealing his baser metal. But I have to say I was intrigued.

"This goes on for two, three years. I wish I could say it wasn't fun, but it was. The danger, the secrecy, the money . . ." He pulled on his cigar and looked out over the water. "So anyway, we set up one of our biggest deals ever, and our buyer's been turned. Facing fifteen to life on his own, so he delivers us up on a platter. A *very* exciting moment. We're in a warehouse in Back Bay and suddenly twenty narcs are pointing thirty-eights at us."

"And one of them was Jean," Cameron proposed.

I shot her a look, but she was gazing expectantly at her counterpart.

"For the sake of our new friends here," Jean said, "I wish I had been." She looked at her husband and touched his wrist, and at that moment I found her extraordinarily desirable. "I think you're boring these nice people."

"Not at all," I protested, directing my reassurance at the storyteller's wife. I was genuinely sorry for her sake that she was party to this sordid tale. She turned and smiled at me, as I'd hoped she would, and for a moment I forgot about the story altogether as I conjured up a sudden vision: slipping from the cabana for a walk later that night, unable to sleep . . . and encountering her out at the edge of the beach, talking, both claiming insomnia, then confessing that we'd been thinking of each other, a long kiss and a slow recline to the soft sand. . . .

"You must think—" She smiled helplessly. "Well, I don't know what you must think. Jack's never really told anyone about all of this before. You're probably shocked."

"Please go on," said Cameron. "We're dying to hear the rest. Aren't we, Don?"

I nodded, a little annoyed at this aggressive use of the marital pronoun.

Her voice seemed loud and grating, and the gaudy print blouse I'd always hated seemed all the more garish beside Jeannie's elegant but sexy navy halter.

"Long story short," said Jack, "I hire Carson Baxter to defend me. And piece by piece he gets virtually every shred of evidence thrown out. Makes it disappear right before the jury's eyes. Then he sneers at the rest. I mean, the man's the greatest performer I've ever seen—"

"He's brilliant," I murmured. Baxter was one of the finest defense attorneys in the country. Although I didn't always share his political views, I admired his adherence to his principles and his legal scholarship. Actually, he was kind of a hero to me. I don't know why, but I was surprised to hear his name in this context.

"So I walked," Jack concluded.

"You were acquitted?" I asked.

"Absolutely." He puffed contentedly on his cigar. "Of course, you'd think that would be the end of the story and the end of my illicit but highly profitable career. Alas, unfortunately not. Naturally, I told myself and everyone else I was going straight. But after six months, the memory of prison and the bust had faded, and a golden opportunity practically fell into my lap, a chance for one last big score. The retirement run. The one you should never make. Always a mistake, these farewell gigs." He laughed.

"That waiter's asleep on his feet," Jean said. "Like the waiter in that Hemingway story. He's silently jinxing you, Jack Van Heusen, with a special voodoo curse for long-winded white boys, because he wants to reset the table and go back to the cute little turquoise-and-pink staff quarters and make love to his wife, the chubby laundress who is waiting for him all naked on her fresh white linen."

"I wonder how the waiter and the laundress met," Jack said cheerfully, standing up and stretching. "That's probably the best story."

My beloved wife said, "Probably they met after Don yelled at her about a stain on his linen shirt and the waiter comforted her."

Jack looked at his watch. "Good God, ten-thirty already, way past official Virgin Islands bedtime."

"But you can't go to bed yet," Cameron said. "You haven't even met your wife."

"Oh, right. So anyway, a while later I met Jean and we fell in love and got married and lived happily ever after."

"No fair," Cameron shrieked.

"I'd be curious to hear your observations about Baxter," I said quietly.

"The hell with Baxter," Cameron said. When she was drinking, her voice took on a more pronounced nasal quality as it rose in volume. "I want to hear the love story."

"Let's at least take a walk on the beach," Jean suggested, standing up.

So we rolled out to the sand and dawdled along the water's edge as Jack resumed the tale.

"Well, my partner and I went down to the Keys and picked up a boat, a Hatteras sixty-two with a false bottom. Had a kid in the Coast Guard on our payroll and another in customs, and they were going to talk us through the coastal net on our return. For show we load up the boat with a lot of big-game fishing gear, these huge Shimano rods and reels. And we stow the real payload—the automatic weapons with nightscopes and the cash. The guns were part of the deal, thirty of them, enough for a small army. The Colombians were always looking for armament, and we picked these up cheap from an Israeli who had to leave Miami real quick. It was a night like this, a warm, starry winter Caribbean night, when the rudder broke about a hundred miles off Cuba. We started to drift, and by morning we got reeled in by a Cuban naval vessel. Well, you can imagine how they reacted when they found the guns and the cash. I mean, think about it, an American boat loaded with guns and cash and high-grade electronics. We tried to explain that we were just drug dealers, but they weren't buying it."

We had come to the edge of the beach; farther on, a rocky ledge rose up from the gently lapping water of the cove. Jack knelt down and scooped up a handful of fine silvery sand. Cameron sat down beside him. I remained standing, looking up at the powdery spray of stars above us, feeling in my intoxicated state that I was exercising some important measure of autonomy by refusing to sit just because Jack was sitting. By this time I simply did not approve of Jack Van Heusen or of the fact that this self-confessed drug runner was about to enter the practice of law. And I suppose I didn't sanction his happiness, either—with his obvious wealth, whether inherited or illicit, and his beautiful and charming wife.

"That was the worst time of my life," he said softly, the jauntiness receding. Jean, who had been standing beside him, knelt down and put a hand on his shoulder. Suddenly he smiled and patted her arm. "But hey—at least I learned Spanish, right?"

Cameron chuckled appreciatively.

"After six months in a Cuban prison, my partner, the captain and I were sentenced to death as American spies. They'd kept us apart the whole time, hoping to break us. And they would've, except that we couldn't tell them what they wanted to hear, because we were just a couple of dumb drug runners and not CIA."

I sat down on the sand, finally, drawing my knees up against my chest, watching Jean's sympathetic face, as if her husband's tawdry ordeal, reflected there, would become more compelling. I couldn't feel very sorry for him—he'd gotten himself into this mess. But I could see she knew at least some of the ghastly details that he was eliding for us, and that it pained her. And for that, I felt sorry for her.

"Anyway, we were treated better than most of the Cuban dissidents because they always had to consider the possibility of using us for barter or propaganda. A few weeks before we're supposed to be shot, I manage to get a message to Baxter, who flies down to Havana and uses his leftist cred to get an audience with fucking Fidel. This is when it's illegal even to *go* to Cuba. And Baxter has his files with him, and—here's the beauty part—he uses the same evidence he discredited in Boston to convince Castro and his defense ministry that we're honest-to-God drug dealers, as opposed to dirty Yankee spies. And they release us into Baxter's custody. But when we fly back to Miami"—he paused, looked around at his audience—"the feds are waiting for us on the tarmac. A welcoming committee of G-men standing there sweating in their cheap suits. They arrest all four of us for violating the embargo by coming from Cuba. Of course, the feds know the real story—they've been monitoring this for the better part of a year. Out of the fucking frittata pan—"

"The *sartén,* actually," Jean said, correcting him impishly.

"Yeah, yeah." He stuck his tongue out at her, then resumed. "I thought I was going to lose it right there on the runway. After almost seven months in a cell without a window, thinking I was free, and then—"

"God," Cameron blurted, "you must have been—"

"I was. So now the FBI contacts Havana to ask for the evidence that led to our acquittal as spies so that they can use it to bust us for a smuggling rap."

I heard the sounds of a thousand insects and the lapping of water as he paused and smiled.

"And the Cubans say, basically, *Fuck you, Yankee pigs.* And we all walk. And Lord, it was sweet."

To my amazement, Cameron began to applaud. She was, I now realized, thoroughly drunk.

"We still haven't heard about Jean," I noted, as if I suspected, and was about to prove, Your Honor, that in point of fact they had never actually met at all.

Jean shared with her husband a conspiratorial smile that deflated me. Turning to me, she said, "My name is Jean Baxter Van Heusen."

I'm not a complete idiot. "Carson Baxter's daughter," I said, and she nodded.

Cameron broke out laughing. "That's just great. I love it."

"How did your father feel about it?" I asked, sensing a weak point.

Jean's smile disappeared. She picked up a handful of sand and let it slip through her fingers. "Not too good. Apparently, it's one thing to defend a drug dealer, prove his innocence and take his money. But it's quite another thing when he falls in love with your precious daughter."

"Jeannie used to go to my trial to watch her father perform. And that, to answer your question, finally, is how we met. In court. Exchanging steamy looks, then steamy notes, across a stuffy courtroom." Pulling her close against his shoulder, he added, "God, you looked good."

"Right," she said. "Anything without a Y chromosome would've looked good to you after three months in custody."

"After I was acquitted, we started seeing each other secretly. Carson didn't know when he flew to Cuba. He didn't have a clue until we walked out of the courthouse in Miami and Jean threw her arms around me. And except for a few scream-and-threat fests, he hasn't really spoken to us since that day." He paused. "He did send me a bill, though."

"The really funny thing," Jean said, "is that Jack was so impressed with my dad that he decided to go to law school."

Cameron laughed again. At least one of us found this funny. My response took me a long time to sort out. As a student of the law, you learn to separate emotion from facts, but in this case I suffered a purely emotional reaction I cannot justify in rational terms. Unfairly, perhaps, I felt disillusioned with the great Carson Baxter. And I felt personally diminished, robbed of the pride I'd felt in discussing my noble profession with an acolyte only a few hours before, and cheated out of the righteous condescension I had felt only minutes before.

"What a great story," Cameron said.

"So what about you guys?" said Jean, sitting on the moonlit sand with her arm around her husband. "What's your wildly romantic story? Tell us about how you two met."

Cameron turned to me eagerly, smiling with anticipation. "Tell them, Don."

I stared out into the bay at a light on the yacht we'd all admired earlier. Then I turned back to my wife, who was grinning beside me in the cold sand. "You tell them," I said.

1993

Philomena

The name of the party is the Party You Have Been to Six Hundred Times Already. Everybody is here. "All your friends," my girlfriend Philomena states in what can only be described as a tart, positively citric, manner. It seems to me that they are *her* friends, that is the reason we are part of this fabulous gala, which takes place in the waiting room of Grand Central, evicting dozens of homeless people for the night. We're supposedly on hand for the benefit of a disease, but we were comped, and so was everyone else we know. "I'm sick of all this pointless glamour," my glamorous girlfriend says. "I want the simple life." This has become a theme. Weariness with metropolitan life in all its colonoscopic intricacy. I wonder if her ennui is somehow related to that other unstated domestic theme: infrequency of sex.

We are accosted by Belinda, the popular transvestite, who I am nearly certain is a friend of my girlfriend's, as opposed to a friend of mine. Belinda is with an actual woman, an ageless one with striking dark eyebrows and buzz-cut white hair, who is always here at the party, and whom I always seem to recognize, and whose name is Hi Howareyou Goodtoseeyou. All the women lately have either three names or just one. Even the impersonators. "Oh, God, hide me," says the woman whose name I always forget. "There's Tommy Kroger. I had a bad date with him about five thousand years ago."

"Did you sleep with him?" Philomena asks, raising one of her perfectly defined eyebrows, which looks like a crow in flight in the far distance of a painting by van Gogh.

"God, I can't remember."

"If you can't remember—then you did," says Belinda. "That's the rule."

Ah, so *that's* the rule.

Later, as we are undressing for bed, Philomena announces preemptively that she is exhausted.

No nookie for you, buckaroo.

At Long Last, Sex

The narrator, the day after the party, is helping Philomena choose the outfits for her trip—a versatile taupe suit from Jil Sander, a Versace jacket and ripped jeans for the plane, a fetching little sheath from Nicole Miller for evening, plus an extra pair of ripped and faded jeans, plus three immaculate white T-shirts. If he were more attentive, the narrator might pick up certain clues from the packing, or from her behavior, that this trip is more than it has been represented to be, but he is not suspicious by nature and his powers of observation are swamped by a surge of hormones. When, after trying on the sheath, she slips out of it and asks him to fetch some panties from her dainties drawer, he is overcome with desire for the taut, tawny flesh beneath her teddy. "Please," he pleads. "Just a little slice." He reminds her that it has been nine days, five hours and thirty-six minutes. And they're not even married yet.

"No, we're not, are we?" Oh dear, a tactical mistake. Matrimony is a sore point. Luckily, the subject is not pursued, but still she makes him kneel and beg for it.

Craven, genuflective begging ensues, heartfelt and genuine. Please, please, please. He will do anything, he tells her. He will bark like any species of dog she can name, even roll over if necessary. Finally, she peels off the teddy and lies back on the bed like Manet's Olympia, ripe and haughty, a bored odalisque. She is a woman whose image is expensively employed to arouse desire in conjunction with certain consumer goods.

"Fast," she commands, "and no sweating."

The narrator takes what he can get, a grateful consumer.

Location, Location, Location

The narrator lives in the West Village, near the river, far enough west that he is spared the Visigoth invasions of provincial teens with boom boxes, just south and east of the Meatpacking District. A summer's-evening

breeze is imbued with a perfume that wafts from the scrap heaps of de-
caying flesh stacked outside the packing warehouses; after dark, the streets
are taken over by transvestites and the cruising vehicles of their johns;
many nights, the narrator is awakened by thick whispers and carnal grunts
from the stairwell just outside the bedroom windows. "It's always a trade-
off with Manhattan real estate," the agent cheerfully informed him, and
then demanded fifteen percent of the first year's rent.

Curriculum Vitae

The narrator's name is Collin McNab. That's me, thirty-two years old and
not really happy about it. Still waiting for my adult life to begin. Is this
my fault? I could blame my parents. *That* would be novel.

I have a job, of sorts. It is called Paying the Rent Until I Write My Original Screenplay About Truth and Beauty. The job description: writing
articles about celebrities for a young women's magazine. A branch of as-
trology. I'm planning to develop a computer program that will spit these
things out with the touch of a few keys, a simple program indeed, since
there are so very few variables. Already my word-processing program con-
tains macro keystrokes that instantly call up such revelations as "shuns the
Hollywood limelight in favor of spending quality time with his family at his
sprawling ranch outside of Livingston, Montana." (Control, MONT.) And
"There's nothing like being a parent to teach you what really matters in
life. The fame, the money, the limos—you can keep it. I mean, being a
father/mother is more important to me than any movie role could ever
be." (Alt, BABY.) And the ever popular "Actually, I've always been really
insecure about my looks. I definitely don't think of myself as a sex symbol.
When I look in a mirror I'm like—Oh God, what a mess." (Shift, WHAT,
ME SEXY?) Right now I'm trying to write a piece about Chip Ralston,
boy movie star, but cannot seem to track him down. Although Chip Ralston allegedly agreed to this piece, his agent, his business manager and his
publicist are all somewhat evasive at the moment. Is it possible that Chip
remembers a rather negative—all right, very negative—review in the *Tokyo
Business Journal* that I wrote about his second movie, in which I said that
the best acting was done by his car, a racing-green Jensen Healy with sexy
wire wheels and a deep, throaty voice?

Metropolis

After twenty-four hours, still no message from Philomena but one from the narrator's boss, Jillian Crowe, asking for an update on the Chip Ralston piece. There was a twinkling moment when Collin seemed to have the gift of pleasing Princess Jillian, a time when he detected an almost girlish interest in his person and his so-called work, culminating in the evening when he was her escort, a last-minute substitute but an escort nonetheless, to the Costume Gala at the Metropolitan Museum. This was the metropolis as it was meant to be seen, in the flattering aphrodisiac light of eminence, a brilliant republic compounded of wealth, power, accomplishment and beauty. The atmosphere of festive mutual regard extended even to tourists, like Collin, on the happy assumption that their applications for citizenship were pending. He was with Jillian Crowe, therefore he was. If he had first taken the whole thing more or less as a joke, secure in his self-knowledge as a flunky, toward the end of the night he started to feel remarkably comfortable in this new role. Infected by both a desire to please and half a dozen glasses of Krug, he regaled the table with colorful anecdotes about the sexual practices of the Japanese and with the untold story behind a recent celebrity interview. He didn't think that Jillian appreciated these stories quite as much as he'd hoped. But then again, he doesn't exactly remember. He does recall her saying, "Darling, when I try to show you the ropes, do try to pick up more than *just* enough to hang yourself." And then there was Philomena's reaction: furious at being left out, she was also irate at the datelike aspects of what Collin tried to present as a tedious professional obligation.

"Why don't you ask Jillian Crowe to fuck you?" became a late-night refrain in their bedroom for some time. It seemed to Collin that he paid dearly for this little outing. At work his novelty simply and immediately wore off, novelty being the cardinal virtue in the value system of the magazine; after that night, the frisson between Collin and Jillian Crowe fizzled.

Suspicious Information

Collin calls his girlfriend's modeling agency to ask for her hotel in San Francisco.

"San Francisco?" says the booker. "What's in San Francisco? I show no booking for Philomena in San Francisco. In fact, I'm showing no bookings at all. She booked out. Told me she was taking the week off."

Collin feels a painful outward pressure on either side of his skull, above and behind the ears, as if he were growing horns.

Fall

Yellow leaves fluttering down the face of the building across the street, like messages from a princess in a high tower. Another year going past.

Neutral Information, i.e., Raw Data

Philomena Briggs, born Oklahoma City, Oklahoma, July 13, 1963. Height: 5' 10". Hair: auburn. Dress size: 4. Shoe size: 8. Measurements: 34–24–34.

Interpretation

The above data comes from Phil's composite, the business card with pictures distributed by her modeling agency, and is in fact not raw at all but cooked to a turn. The actual birth year is 1961. The place of birth was a town too small to show up on any map. The measurements are obviously suspect. And the last time I bought her a dress, I had to return the four to Barneys and get the six. "The salesclerk told me they ran small," I noted helpfully as she tried it on, knowing that if she got upset with the way she looked in it I might not get lucky for days.

How I Got My Job

The joke around the office is that Jillian Crowe gave me my current job on the celeb beat after she heard that I was living with a model named Phil. Another point in my favor was what I wore to my interview, a vintage

Brooks Brothers gray flannel hand-me-down from my father; Jillian thought that I was fashion-forward enough to have anticipated the return of the three-button sack suit. She has since discovered her mistakes.

My contract is up in two months, and no one has approached me about renewal. In fact, my office was recently converted to storage space. I send in my copy via modem from my apartment: vanguard of the virtual office.

More on Phil

I met Philomena in Tokyo, on the Ginza Line between Akasaka-mitsuke and Shimbashi. I couldn't help noticing her, of course, the only other *gaijin* in the subway car, a head taller than the indigenous population, clutching her big black modeling portfolio to her ribs, nervously tossing her coppery hair. I was trying very hard not to stare. "Do you know which stop is Ginza," she asked. I looked up from my copy of *Heike Monogatari,* all innocence, my expression one that was meant to say, Whatever in the world leads you to assume that I speak English? At the same time I was thinking, Oh, Jesus, please don't get off the train and walk out of my life— you're the most gorgeous creature I've ever seen in it.

She was in Japan building up her modeling portfolio and her savings account. Aside from her modelish appearance, I was charmed by what seemed to me—after five years in Japan—her archetypal Middle Americanness, the curious alloy of wide-eyed curiosity and other-side-of-the-tracks street savvy. In that stranger-in-a-strange-land context, I, in turn, must have cut a rather striking figure, being able to order food right off the menu, count, ask directions and, when necessary, shout insults. Which is to say, I doubt she ever would've shacked up with me in the States. But in the context of adult males known to Philomena, I was practically a saint, just by virtue of nonviolently hanging around. Her father disappeared when she was three, and of her mother's several boyfriends the best that she could say of her favorite was that he was passed out most of the time. She has never really told me the worst of it, and I'm sure I don't want to know. Whenever Philomena, standing in front of the full-length mirror at five minutes to eight, tells me that she hates going out anyway, not to mention all of our so-called friends who are really only my friends, and that she is absolutely not attending the opening/screening/première/party/ dinner/wedding or whatever occasion has forced her to confront the imagined shortcomings of her wardrobe and her body, whenever she ignores my pleas for sexual relief or says, "Nobody really cares about anybody except themselves"—at these times I remind myself that she is still in a bad mood from her childhood. But this behavior did not manifest itself until we had been together for a year. And by then she was a relatively successful fashion model in New York, where such comportment was a professional prerequisite.

She moved into my tiny flat in Roppongi. We slept on a single futon that we laid out on the tatami floor each night and folded up each morning. Recently escaped from my official Ph.D. studies, I was keeping carcass and spirit together by teaching English and writing movie reviews for the *Japan Times* and the *Tokyo Business Journal*. Two evenings a week I took the train to Shinjuku and conjugated English verbs with Japanese businessmen:

I dump.
You dump.
He dumps.
We dump.
You all dump manufactured goods below cost on the American market in order to gain market share.

On my free nights, I bought mordant pickled vegetables, anthropomorphic ginger root, fat, white, talcy sacks of short-grain rice, shiny fish and skinny chickens with feet. I turned on the automatic rice cooker when I heard Philomena's key in the door. We made love when she returned home, and sometimes again after we had rolled out the futon for the night. We were always screwing in those days. Jesus, it was wonderful. Then we moved to New York, which is to monogamy what the channel changer is to linear narrative.

Celebrity Searches

I call Celebrity Searches. "Can you give me a current location on Ralston, Chip?"

"Still checking," the voice says after a long wait. Finally: "We show him in his Malibu house up until Thursday last week, then we pick him up last

Saturday at the Westin St. Francis in San Francisco. Checked out Sunday and we're not showing anything since."

"Can you work on that for me?"

"Sure. Meantime, how about Kiefer Sutherland? He's right here in town."

"Who I really need to find is my girlfriend."

"Actress?"

"Model."

"Supermodel?"

"Just model."

"Model, non super. Name?"

"Philomena Briggs."

After a search, he says she's not in their database.

Finally, a Message from Phil

"Hi, it's me. You there? . . . Guess you're out. I'm rushing to get a plane. We're off to L.A. to finish up. I'm not sure about the schedule. It's nuts. Call you when I know where I am. Big kiss." This message on my machine when I return from dinner. It's the tone of voice which is so disturbing. A false, heightened breeziness. The words strung together on a thin wire of nervous gaiety.

Collin's Reaction

The narrator has been able to suppress his anxiety until this moment. But hearing her voice, he knows that his suspicions were well founded.

Fruitlessly he dials the Chateau Marmont, the Sunset Marquis, the Four Seasons, the Bel-Air, the Bel Age and the Peninsula. Maybe it's not too late. Maybe if he can reach her in L.A., he can stop her from doing what he fears she has already done. Between calls he searches all the drawers for cigarettes—which he gave up a year ago—and finally finds a pack of horribly stale Newports that someone left in the apartment. He lights one from the stove and thinks, Wait a minute, who smokes Newports? No one he knows. And Phil has never smoked. Jesus, she's been entertaining black guys in the apartment? No—wait, it could be a girl who smokes Newports. One of Phil's friends. What friends? Who are her friends? He realizes that Philomena has very few girlfriends. Suddenly it seems dangerous to have so few friends. Who is your boyfriend supposed to call when he can't find you? Collin remembers something his sister once said: "Beware the woman who doesn't like other women; she's probably generalizing from her own character."

Flashback

"Why don't we ask Katrinka and her boyfriend for dinner?"

"*You* ask them. The three of you can go out. Or better yet, just the two of you. You and Katrinka."

"I thought you liked Katrinka."

"I used to. Till I found out she was a liar."

"What did she lie about?"

"Lots of things."

"Like what?"

"Like she said you were coming on to her, trying to get her to meet you and stuff."

"She said that?"

"Uh-huh."

At this point Collin was hard-pressed to speak up in Katrinka's defense. In fact, it had seemed to him that she was always flirtatious, and he had been aware at the time that he was not actively discouraging it. And so he did not really want to probe any deeper into the matter. And once again the two of them, Collin and Philomena, dined *à deux.*

Panic

The cigarette tastes so bad he immediately lights another one.

On a sudden inspiration, he rushes back to the bathroom and searches the cabinet beneath the sink, then the bedside table, then her lingerie drawer, scattering panties and bras to the winds. He looks under the bed, and in the soap dish in the shower, and finally admits that her diaphragm is not in the apartment.

Collin dials his sister, Brooke. Perhaps he hopes she will convince him that his fears are groundless.

She can only say she is sorry, though her concern is genuine enough to provide a momentary balm.

"I sit down," he says. "Then I stand up, and if I could I'd climb the goddamn walls and hang from the ceiling, but that wouldn't be any good, either. I don't want to be in the apartment another minute, but I don't want to leave in case she calls, and I don't want to be alone, but I can't think of anybody I could stand to be with, and I can't stand myself."

"Why don't you come over here?" Brooke proposes. Mercifully, she does not remind him that there are people far worse off than he is. Until recently she was doing postgraduate work in quantum physics at Rockefeller University, but she is on an extended hiatus, crippled by depression and an acute sensitivity to human suffering. She still has nightmares about Bosnia. Collin's sister is like one of those bubble children born with a defective immune system; she does not possess that protective membrane which filters out the noise and pain of other creatures. She is utterly porous. She told him recently that the average weight loss among adult residents of Sarajevo after seven hundred days of siege was twenty-five pounds, thereby giving her own dietary habits a symbolic dimension, but she's been starving herself on and off since the Vietnam War.

When Collin reaches his sister's apartment and sees her face, he comes apart like a three-dollar umbrella in a gale. Brooke scoops up the wrecked steel ribs and shredded black nylon and walks the whole mess inside.

When he has regained his composure, she is boiling water in the former coat closet that passes as a kitchen.

"I didn't know you knew how to boil water," he says.

"You're thinking of Mom," she says. "I learned this in prep school. Actually, it's not as difficult as it looks."

"Just please don't say I'm better off without her."

"Only because it would arouse your chivalrous instincts. I have no desire to provoke you into defending her." She looks like the poster child for anorexia, in the oversized Middlebury sweatshirt that Collin gave her about twelve years ago, with her hair swept back in a ponytail, her thin freckled hand resting on the handle of the kettle. If only he were allowed to fall in love with his sister, maybe they could save each other.

"She took her diaphragm, Brooke."

Brooke sighs, nodding gravely. "Could it be she was just anticipating the possibility that her plane might go down, stranding her in a remote snow-bound region with five or six male survivors who might force her to have sex? And, thoughtfully, she didn't want to be pregnant with some nameless homunculus when the snow finally melted and she was at last rescued and reunited with you, her only true love?"

"What about disease, for Christ's sake? If she was so concerned about me, she could have carried a gross of triple-strength condoms."

"It's possible she packed those, too. God, you smell like Lynchburg, Tennessee."

"I've been drinking."

"I'm shocked."

"It doesn't help."

"I wish you'd tell that to Dad."

She hands him a Beethoven mug full of steaming water floating a green herbal-tea bag. Collin slaps his hand against the wall. "I don't understand how she could be so eager to run off and fuck some other guy when I have to beg to get it once a week. It's not fair."

"I know."

A Parable

Later, Brooke strokes her brother's hair. "Remember how we could never get Rogue to eat his dog food? Remember the only thing that would get Rogue to eat? Clio. As soon as she stuck her whiskers in his bowl, he went wild. He'd bark and growl and run in circles around the bowl till she'd had her nibble, then he'd rush in and devour every last bit of it."

Collin takes the point, but is too unhappy to acknowledge it.

"When I talked to you in August, you said you supposed that you should get married but that *you* didn't really want to. Hardly the stuff of sonnets and *chansons*. But now that someone's got his nose in your bowl you're howling. I hate to say it, but this is a guy thing. You boys think you want virgins, but what you really want is to put your peepees where the other peepees have been."

"Why can't I just marry you," Collin asks.

A Call from Mom

"Hi, honey. How's every little thing with you?" The annual parental Manhattan pilgrimage commences the day after tomorrow.

"Swell," I say. Mom has such a dreamy and ethereal disposition that I try not to puncture the bubble. The last, miraculous child of ancient parents, she grew up in an atmosphere of benign and privileged neglect in Charleston, then wafted through Bennington until my father brought her to ground, briefly, after a mixer at Williams. When he graduated, a few months later, they married and moved into my paternal grandfather's house in Florida, where Mom resumed the life she'd led as a child—painting landscapes, tending the garden and riding. One hates to worry her.

"What do you want for Christmas," she asks.

I can't think of anything I want from central Florida, except maybe a lemon to suck on. "Just your own sweet self," I say, pouring myself another drink.

A Typical Morning in the West Village

10 a.m.: Collin wakes. Headache. Remembers that Philomena has abandoned him and is waking with someone else. Heartache. Back to sleep.

11:15: Wakes again. Realizes that Philomena is still gone. Guilt at sleeping so late. Crawls out of bed. Surveys disorderly, depraved bedroomscape. Vows to clean this up. Soon.

11:20: Showers. No shampoo. No soap. No toilet paper. Mental note to buy some. Files it next to yesterday's identical mental note.

11:45: Newsstand for the *Times* and the *Post*. The *Times* because Collin is a serious guy and the *Post* because he's not.

11:48 a.m.–12:30 p.m.: Bus Stop Coffee Shop, consuming coffee, bagel and newsprint. Peace talks in Dayton. Anna Nicole Smith redundantly in a coma. Whitney threatens to dump Bobby Brown unless he stays at the Betty Ford Clinic.

12:48: At his desk examining mail: Gay Men's Health Crisis, Amnesty International, second notice from the phone company, already ten days overdue, and—what's this?—a chain letter received about a week ago:

Chain Letter

WITH LOVE ALL THINGS ARE POSSIBLE

This paper has been sent to you for good luck. The original is in New England. It has been around the world nine times. You will receive good luck within four days of receiving this letter provided you send it on. This is no joke. Do not send money, faith has no price.

Do not keep this letter. It must leave your hands within 96 hours. An R.A.F. Officer received $470,000. Jon Eliot received $40,000 and lost it because he broke the chain. While in the Philippines, George Hish lost his wife fifty-one days after receiving the letter. He had failed to circulate the letter. However, before her death he had received $7,775,000.00.

Please send twenty copies. After a few days you will get a surprise. This is true even if you are not superstitious. Do note the following: Constantine Dias received the chain in 1953. He asked his secretary to make twenty copies and send them. A few days later he won the lottery of two million dollars.

Dolan Fairchild received the letter, and not believing, he threw the letter away. Nine days later he died.

Do not ignore this. It works.

The letter is signed "St. Jude."

Is this the source of Collin's calamity? He broke the chain? What if he had made twenty copies and mailed them out last week? This shrill imperative improbably strikes home. In his bereaved, pathetic, tenderized state Collin is almost prepared to believe in the capricious and personalized fate assigned to him by this otherwise innocent-looking piece of Xerox paper. "Collin McNab left the letter sitting on his desk. A week after he received it, his girlfriend packed up her diaphragm and disappeared. Two weeks later he was run over by a taxicab." Maybe it's not too late. Maybe if he sent it out now . . .

1:43: Calls Chip Ralston's manager in L.A. Secretary puts him on hold. And then over the receiver come the unendurable strains of Rod Stewart's "Da Ya Think I'm Sexy?" After Collin has listened to the song three times, a voice breaks in.

"Collin, how are you? Where are you, in New York? How's the weather? Snowing yet? Sleet? Seventy-eight degrees and sunny here. So how's it going with Mr. Chip? You guys hitting it off okay?"

He explains that it's not going, that he can't locate the greatest thespian of his generation, that his deadline is less than a week away and he hasn't even talked to his alleged subject. Ralston's manager evinces surprise and dismay. He explains that Chip has been terribly busy researching his new role, but he, the manager, will absolutely have Chip call him today. Tomorrow at the latest.

2:45: Shuffles to the newsstand for a pack of Seven Star. He hasn't really started smoking again, just a temporary thing till he gets through this crisis. It comes back to him, though, no question. Inhale, exhale. Like riding a bike. Suddenly worried he might be missing a phone call from Philomena. Hurries back.

2:51 p.m.: No messages.

3:13 p.m.: In an interlude of self-disgust, Collin wallows in shame at the sheer worthlessness of his life. All around him the city hums with purposive activity and commerce while he sinks into a slough of sloth and despond. His life has no purpose and no direction. No wonder Philomena has left him.

Chain Letter, Cont.

Collin McNab left the letter sitting on his desk. A week after he received it, his girlfriend packed up her diaphragm and disappeared. Two weeks later Collin discovered the letter. He sent out twenty copies and his girlfriend returned and said she loved him. It seems she had been hit by a taxicab in a foreign city and suffered a case of amnesia. The day after her boyfriend mailed this letter, she regained her memory and came home. The next day, Collin found a paper bag on the street containing $2,830,520 in cash. They were married a week later and now divide their time between St. Barts and Aspen.

Miscegenation Speculation

At last something Collin can use: the first high-profile marriage of a Hollywood sex goddess to a Japanese billionaire. Thinking that this particular prospect nicely combines his underutilized background in Japanese studies with his beat as celebrity chronicler, he tries to interest Jillian Crowe in an essay on this subject. Shades on top of her head, she asks, "Collin, darling, honestly, do I look like the editor of *The New York Review of Books* to you?"

The Parents Come to Town, but First . . .

Just leaving the apartment to meet my makers when I hear Philomena's voice on the machine: "Me. You there? Guess not." Sounding none too eager to find otherwise.

As rapidly as any gunfighter ever unholstered a Colt Peacemaker, I snatch the receiver from its cradle. "Where are you?"

The silence lasts long enough for me to fear I have lost her. "That doesn't really matter."

"Please come home."

"I need some time to think."

"You've already taken the better part of a week. Phil, what are you doing? Where are you?" God, my voice sounds pathetic, tremulous, quavering between tenor and falsetto.

"Things haven't been so great with us lately."

"I'll be better. I'll be so good you'll think I'm someone else. I'll be so sensitive you'll think I'm a girl. Shit. I mean *woman.*"

"Look, I've got to go."

"Who are you with?" I demand, desperately changing modes.

"I'm not with anybody." The rhythm and tone of this response are all wrong. I don't need a polygraph to confirm my suspicions.

"Why did you take your diaphragm?" I ask. "Who are you fucking while you're taking all this contemplative Virginia Woolf *A Room of One's Own* time to think?"

"Good-bye, Collin. I'll call in a few days."

"My parents are coming to town," I say lamely. As a logical fallacy this, I believe, is called appeal to false authority.

"Say hi for me."

And she's gone. It's impossible to present your best self—attractive, assured and desirable—when you are insane.

Deus Ex Machina

Not to be fooled twice, I go to the Spy store on Second Avenue to purchase one of those handy devices that tell you the phone numbers of incoming calls—something I have been meaning to acquire for a long time. Back at the apartment, I plug the little black box into my phone as per instructions and stare at it hopefully but discover that I still have yet to figure out how to will Philomena to call me.

Thanksgiving Cheer

Recently, in the *Times,* Frank Prial wrestled with that perennial question: What wine to match with your Thanksgiving turkey and traditional fixings? Some say Champagne, some chardonnay. Frank leans toward zinfandel, and there's even a case to be made for a young cabernet sauvignon. Be advised that my father recommends Johnnie Walker Black.

We're having Thanksgiving dinner in the restaurant at the St. Regis. Traditionalists that we are, Mom and I are working on a bottle of Champagne. My sister's current would-be consort, Doug Hawkin, M.D., is already throwing back the Diet Cokes like there's no tomorrow. He arrived before us, straight from the emergency room at New York Hospital. Mad Dog Doug is a trauma surgeon whose acquaintance Brooke made after she tumbled down a set of stairs at Rockefeller University. Brooke is stoned and sipping mint tea, like the hippie she once was, glaring at her food.

"I find it difficult to give thanks," she mutters, "when so many people in the world are suffering tonight."

"Give thanks you're not one of them," says Dad, tucking into a fresh scotch.

"In Ethiopia a family of four doesn't see this much protein in a month."

"You must see a great deal of suffering," Mom says to Doug. I still don't understand why he had to come. Doesn't he have his own fucked-up family to annoy?

Trauma Theory and Practice

"Is there a special season," Mom continues, "or month or anything when you get more traumas than other times?"

Dad snuffles at this question—the nasal declaration of a man who never ceases to be amazed by the eccentricity of his wife.

"No, actually, that's a good question," says Doug, answering both Mom and the snort. "The full moon is the worst. Emergency rooms are always extremely frenetic the night of a full moon. I don't know how to explain it scientifically, but the empirical evidence is fairly convincing. What's easier to account for is that sick children, particularly from economically disadvantaged neighborhoods, tend to be brought to the emergency room after eleven p.m."

Mom looks happily perplexed. "And why is that?"

"Because that's when prime-time television ends."

"The children wait until after prime time to get sick?"

"I believe," Dad says, "Brooke's, uh, friend means that the *parents* wait until after their favorite shows before bringing the kids in."

"That's dreadful." Mom turns to Doug. "Is that true?"

Doug nods sadly.

"The worst are the self-mutilators," says Brooke, rising out of her marijuana-induced stupor to do a brief promotional spot for her beau. "Can you imagine having a ward full of desperately ill and injured people to tend to, and having to spend two hours on some guy who, tell them about the thing yesterday . . ."

"Well," says Doug, "I wish I could say it was a unique case, but in fact we've seen it before. A patient arrived on the ward yesterday under his own power, clutching a towel to his groin. We estimate he lost more than thirty percent of his blood."

"Don't tell me," says Dad.

"Fortunately, I guess, he hadn't fully severed his penis. He seems to have lost—"

"Stop!" Dad shouts. "Is this any kind of dinner-table conversation?"

I don't know, I think I agree with my father, although I can't help feeling a twinge of sympathy for Doug, the outsider.

"Doug," says Mom, "are you sure you wouldn't like a *teeny* bit of Champagne?"

More Beverage Notes

One factor that Frank Prial doesn't take into account about holiday potables is their combustibility. When long-separated members of the same family are soaked in spirits and rubbed together, explosions almost inevitably result. This year it happens after I ask Mom how she met Dad. It's a story I haven't heard in years, certainly never with the kind of vivid dramatic detail she gives it this afternoon.

Boy Meets Girl, Spring 1955

"We used to think Williams boys were so square," she says, the stem of her Champagne flute pinched lightly between age-spotted pointer and thumb. "And, of course, they were."

A curmudgeonly harrumph from my father, still dressed in the square-college-boy uniform of his youth—blue blazer, blue oxford button-down shirt and regimental tie, his pink-pickled face unlined by the tussles of commerce or metaphysics.

"We used to think Bennington girls were artsy-fartsy dykes," counters the former captain of the debating team.

"And the Williams boys were so very tolerant of diversity," Mom continues, winking at us. "But we had to admit they were very good-looking." She smiles sweetly at my father. Beneath the sun-and-nicotine-cured skin, she is still girlish, pale blue eyes childishly bright, her hair long, just as she wore it at Bennington, the gold now ghosted with silver. "I drove down with Cassie Reymond and some other girls. Cassie was an actress, and she went to New York, and last I heard she was married to that actor who was in that wonderful play—what was it called—about the, it wasn't with Richard Burton but somebody like that?" She looks hopefully at my father, who coughs impatiently into his hand.

"*Camelot*?" proposes Doug.

Oh, do shut up, Doug.

Beside us, a Japanese family: father, mother, two solemn preteen daughters in severe white blouses and pageboy haircuts.

"Anyway, we got there, and it was awful, all these fierce, shy, hungry boys in their nice J. Press suits and their crewcuts, ready to pounce. We drove down in Cassie's car, thank God, but there was a bus that arrived from Smith or somewhere like that, someplace frilly and proper, maybe Holyoke, I don't know. Anyway, this bus came in just as we pulled up, and the boys were waiting outside it. They'd formed a kind of gauntlet, or gamut. What is it? I can never get those two things straight. Is 'gauntlet' the glove you throw down when you challenge somebody to a duel, or is that 'gamut'? Anyway, this was the other one."

" 'Gantlet' is actually the word you're looking for," says Doug. "I think," he hedges, for modesty's sake.

Here at the St. Regis they serve the fancy, lumpy kind of cranberry sauce with real berries, but I prefer the cheap, jellied kind. I seem to be the only one paying any attention at all to the food.

"Toward the end of the dance I spotted your father hovering. He was dressed exactly the way he is now. Could that be the same tie?" My father looks down at the neckwear in question, pennon of some lost regiment of the King's Army, and shakes his head. "He was kind of cute square," Mom continues. "And, oh, I remember—he was wearing white bucks."

"Not I," said my father, but I could see he was starting to enjoy this. "Tan bucks, maybe."

"You were. That was almost the cutest part about you, your nervous white feet. He kept circling us, getting a tiny bit closer each time, all nonchalant and pretending not to notice me. Well, he panicked when they announced the last song—I think it was 'Smoke Gets in Your Eyes.' "

My mother breaks off her narrative to warble a bar: " 'They asked me how I knew my true love was true . . .' "

"What's the matter with you?" my father demands, noticing my suddenly crumpled demeanor. Philomena and I used to love that song in its Bryan Ferry version.

"And when another boy asked me to dance," Mom resumes, "his face just collapsed."

My father snorts in disapproval. "Oh, come on."

"Well, after it ended, I dragged my feet on the way out. If I'd walked any slower I think I would have taken root in the pavement, and I was just about to give up on him when I felt a hand on my shoulder in the parking lot."

"What'd he say," asks Brooke.

"He asked me if I wanted a tour of the campus."

Brooke hoots with laughter. "At least he didn't ask you to see his etchings."

The Japanese family aim their solemn dark eyes at the strange, noisy *gaijin*. "I didn't say that," Dad insists.

"Well, I didn't really need to see the campus, but I told him I'd love to go somewhere where we could talk. So we ended up sitting in his roommate's Buick. And of course the talking led to kissing. I thought he was just a wonderful kisser, and after about ten minutes I realized he was just in agony, so of course I wanted to help him. It seemed like the least I could do."

"Lillie!"

"And the poor sweet boy was so grateful he proposed to me right there in the back of that Buick."

"What?" Brooke blurts. "You gave him a blow job?"

"Young lady!"

"Well," says Mom, "I just, you know, used my hand."

Dad Demurs

"This is not family conversation!" Dad thumps the table with his fist, making shimmery waves on our beverages.

"You got a proposal out of a hand job?" Brooke is impressed, Doug is nonplussed.

I am thinking back on a time when Philomena and I were still mad for each other and she gave me a hand job in a cab. Why didn't I propose to her then? Why didn't I ever? If only I had, she would be here now, having Thanksgiving dinner, comparing notes on post-ejaculatory proposals with my mom.

Word from Ralston

My phone rings. My caller ID shows an incoming call from Los Angeles.

"Hello?"

"Hello, could I please speak to Collin McNab?"

"You can and you are."

"What?"

"This is Collin McNab."

"Oh, this is Cherie Smith. Chip Ralston's assistant? Hello? What was that noise?"

"Nothing, really," I say as I write down the number. "It was probably a gasp of disbelief."

"Oh. Well, Chip just wanted me to tell you that he's changed his mind about the article. He doesn't want to do it after all."

"Wait just a New York minute. We had an agreement."

"I'm sorry. I don't know anything about that. He just told me to tell you, is all."

"Let me talk to him," I say. It's not that I'm dying to write a fucking article about Chip fucking Ralston, but I don't have enough money in my checking account to pay my half of the rent next month, let alone Philomena's.

"I'm sorry, but he's very busy right now. I'm sure it's nothing personal. Well, have a really nice day. Bye."

I'm not going to give up that easily. I wait fifteen minutes, then call the number I'd written down.

"Hello?"

I am stunned silent.

"Hello," says the familiar voice again. "Who is this?"

"Phil?"

"Collin?"

"What the . . . what are you doing there?" I demand, but the answer seems obvious enough, if somewhat incredible.

"How did you—"

"Jesus. I can't believe this is happening."

"I . . . didn't want to hurt your feelings," she says.

"You didn't *want* to hurt my feelings. So. That's why you're fucking Chip Ralston? To spare my feelings? What would you do if you actually *wanted* to hurt me and crush my spirit beyond repair?"

"I mean, that's why I didn't want you to know."

"And that's why he blew me off for the stupid fucking interview?"

"Well, you could hardly write objectively about him under the circumstances."

"I thought you were in Montana." I think I'm hoping that if I find a hole in her story, an inconsistency, the whole thing will turn out to be a joke.

"We were."

"We were."

"I'm going back up there in a few days."

"It must be just lovely."

"I told you I wanted a simpler life."

"Simpler life? You're moving to Livingston fucking Montana with Chip fucking Ralston. Do you have any idea what a cliché that is? I've got it in my computer. Control MONTANA CLICHÉ. It's not simple. It's just . . . stupid."

She is silent on the other end and, as for me, I can hardly speak. Finally I say, "This is a joke, right?"

"Collin, these things happen. You know? It's nobody's fault."

"Chip Ralston?"

"I can understand your being upset."

"It's pathetic."

"Don't make me say things you don't want to hear."

"That fucking midget," I say, then slam down the phone and regret it immediately. Scooping up an Imari vase, Philomena's prized possession, I hurl it against the wall, where it shatters gratifyingly. We bought the vase on a trip to Kyoto, and I remember wondering what would happen to it, the first durable object we purchased together. Would we look at it ten, twenty years hence and remember? Afterward, we went back to the *ryokan* in the hills, where a deep cedar tub was steaming in anticipation of our arrival, and blue-and-white striped robes had been laid out on the black-bordered tatami mats. Would I go back to that time, if I could? Would I relive it all to this moment, with foreknowledge? Or would I drown the bitch right there in the tub?

Parting Words from the Editor-in-Chief

"Please hold for Jillian."

I'd rather not, thanks.

"Whatever you did to alienate Chip Ralston and his people," my editrix says by way of greeting, "I'm afraid it's rather the last straw. At any rate, I don't think your heart was ever in this enterprise. I'm sure you'll find a position more worthy of your, uh, talents elsewhere, yes? Well, I think that covers it."

"What *I* did? The son of a bitch is fucking my girlfriend."

"Well, I think that's very democratic of him. *Droit du seigneur* and all. Quite an honor." She pauses to inhale. "You know, I keep thinking you've been hanging out for long enough—that you *ought* to be dry behind the ears by now. I kept waiting. Good-bye, Collin."

One Week Later, Theater District

We are clustered around the side entrance of the Ed Sullivan Theater, on West Fifty-third Street, home of the *Late Show with David Letterman*. Two blue police barriers make a corridor from the curb to the stage door. A security man stands nearby while we press up against the barricades, autograph books clutched to our chests, stamping our cold feet. We don't mind the cold. We're fans, real fans, big fans. We are the biggest fans. As in "Hey, Clint, I'm your biggest fan." (Most of us are, anyway, although one is an impostor.)

Clarence, for instance, with his huge, fur-hooded Army-surplus parka, his scholarly thick black glasses, has the unabashed air of a man engaged in an important pursuit: "I just got Brooke Shields, man. She's a real nice lady. Not like that Richard Chamberlain. Richard Chamberlain, he comes through here, he shakes your hand. That sucks, man. What I'm gonna do with a handshake?"

"Can't sell it," says Charlie, an incongruously sane-looking gentleman in a Mets warmup jacket who is probably a plumber in Patchogue, Long Island, when he isn't here outside the Ed Sullivan Theater or in the lobby of NBC headquarters in Rockefeller Center. He and his friend Tony are armed with five-by-eight index cards and the squeaky-wheel, Me-Me-Me manners of born New Yorkers. If they can get three cards signed, they will sell two to a dealer.

Suddenly the throng goes taut and silent, a lovestruck jellyfish, as a shiny black stretch fins up to the curb and stops, its cargo invisible behind the smoked glass.

The stately, plump driver marches around and opens the door.

"Chip!" screams one of the photographers. "Over here!"

"Hey, Chip!"

"I'm your biggest fan, Chip."

"How about an autograph, Chip?"

"Look over here! Smile!"

Chip hesitates, framed in the open door of the limo, before he launches himself toward the stage door, hunched over, his head retracted into the shell of his jacket, moving quickly, but not quickly enough to dodge me as I slide under the police barrier and cut him off.

"Hi, Chip, I'm Collin McNab." Savoring for a nanosecond the infusion of fear in his much admired and, indeed, very striking, hazel eyes, I then nail him with a hard right jab, aimed at the bridge of the nose, that actually connects with his temple as he tries to duck away. Solid contact, nonetheless. Solid enough to hurt the shit out of my hand.

"I'm your biggest fuckin' fan, Chip," I say as he wobbles and then sinks to his knees just as a security guard tackles me and smashes my face against the grainy concrete.

Good news, Clarence and Charlie: I see stars!

The Lemon Light

By the time my name is called, Brooke is waiting for me by the front desk at the Eighteenth Precinct. So is a reporter from the *Post*. A sallow man, ancient by newspaper standards—easily forty—he pushes back the bill of his cap, which bears the logo *New York—It Ain't Over,* and flips open his steno pad.

"Why'd you do it?" he asks as I finish signing at the desk.

"I didn't like his acting choices."

"Is it true you've been stalking Chip Ralston for months?"

Brooke takes my arm as we bolt for the door. Outside, we are ambushed by three photographers.

"Collin, look here."

"Is that your girlfriend?"

"How about the two of you kissing for a picture?"

They follow us down the street, yipping and snapping. So this is what it's like, I think.

Finally we are alone and anonymous again on the sidewalk. The next day the *Post* will run a photo of me and Brooke, who is identified, half correctly, as my girlfriend.

"So," Brooke says. "What do you want to do? Go to Rockefeller Center and watch the skaters?" For some reason I find this hilarious. "Then maybe check out the windows at Saks." She's laughing now.

"Catch the Christmas show at Radio City," I suggest.

"I don't know if they let felons in to see the Rockettes." Brooke's demeanor turns earnest. "Maybe if we act like we just got off the bus and it's our first day ever in the city, and we've come from really far away to see the lights on Fifth Avenue and the tree . . ." She shrugs, takes my hand and begins to lead me east on Fiftieth.

And, walking through the slanting secondhand light toward Rockefeller Center and Fifth Avenue, I remember that the city used to seem to me like a giant advent calendar with a thousand doors. Prowling the streets at night, you felt that every luminous tower was a glittering enigma that might secretly bear your name. I remember the joy, not so very long ago, of waking up newly arrived in the city, believing that everything I wanted in the world was waiting outside the door of my apartment, right down the street. Just around the next corner, or the one after.

1995

I Love You, Honey

1.

The first time it happened, Liam blamed the terrorists. He assumed that his wife, like all the other sentient residents of the city, was traumatized by the events of that September day. Deciding that this was no world into which to bring another child was a perfectly rational response, though he knew many people who'd had the exact opposite response. This, too, was understandable: affirming life in the face of so much death. He could name several children who were born nine months later, and he assumed there were hundreds, maybe thousands, more around the city—in fact, he'd read something to that effect. But Lora's was the opposite response. He didn't really begin to suspect until much later that her motives might have been more complex, less cosmic and more personal, than he had imagined.

2.

Her friend LuAnne had called to say something had happened, and she'd started surfing channels with the remote in one hand and the phone in the other, seeing the same image on all the stations. She called Liam at work and his assistant said he had a meeting scheduled out of the office. Lora then tried his cell, but the call went directly to voice mail. She kept punching the redial button every few minutes. After the second plane hit, she called the office again to ask where, exactly, the meeting was, frantic with worry, trying to remember if Liam had ever mentioned any business in the World Trade Center, but now she got the assistant's recorded message. In fact, Liam's office was in TriBeCa, only seven or eight blocks from the towers, and after the first one collapsed, she could imagine any number of scenarios that might have put him in harm's way. After the second tower fell, she was convinced he was dead. And then he called, his greeting incongruously blithe.

"Hey, babe, it's me."

"Liam. Oh my God. Where *are* you?"

"At the office. Just out of a meeting. What's up?"

"Thank God," she said.

"What's wrong?"

"I thought you were dead."

"Why would I be dead?"

"Jesus, God, Liam, haven't you *heard*? Turn on the TV. Look out the window, for God's sake."

3.

Liam arrived at their apartment on Waverly Place ten minutes later—less time than it would have taken him to walk from TriBeCa, but he didn't realize until later that the subway service was knocked out and that cabs had vanished from the downtown streets—so everyone later agreed—within minutes of the second plane hitting. In fact, he'd been a few blocks away at his girlfriend's apartment on St. Mark's Place. They met there every Tuesday morning, between nine and eleven, turning off the phones, doing it exactly twice, and there had been no reason to suppose that the world would be turned upside down on this particular Tuesday. After talking to Lora, he turned on the TV, shushing Sasha as she stepped out of the bathroom, trying to figure out what the hell was happening to his city. His horror was compounded with guilt as he realized how implausible was his claim of being at the office.

"My God, I can't believe this," Sasha said, throwing her arms around him as she slumped beside him on the couch. He squirmed free and stood up. He knew it was unfair, irrational even, but somehow he blamed her for what had happened and felt an overwhelming desire to be with his wife. Walking back across the Village, looking up warily at a looming apartment tower on Broadway, he struck on the perfect alibi.

4.

Until she actually saw and touched him, Lora couldn't quite overcome her earlier conviction that he'd perished in the disaster, and he seemed just as emotional as he hugged her in the foyer, nearly crushing her ribs in his emphatic embrace. When he finally let go, she saw the tears in his eyes.

"I thought I'd never see you again."

"I was in a screening," he said. "I had no idea."

"I thought I was going to raise our baby alone."

5.

The days that followed were the most vivid of his life. In retrospect, though, they sometimes seemed reduced to a set of experiences that came to sound almost clichéd by virtue of their resemblance to those of their friends, repeated endlessly over numerous cocktails: the mind-numbing hours in front of the television; the sense of disbelief; the missing friends and acquaintances; the nightmares; the acrid electrical-fire smell in the air; the spontaneous weeping, the excessive drinking. And yet they both agreed—as did everyone else—that they'd never been so conscious of the lives of others, of their own turbulent stream of consciousness, of their own mortality. And they discovered that life was never quite so precious as it was in the proximity of death. From that first night they fucked as if their survival depended on it, and with a passion neither had felt in years.

Liam was mortified at his own infidelity and brimming with the resolve to honor his marriage vows forever more. He'd felt the same resolve three weeks earlier when he learned Lora was pregnant, but somehow he hadn't managed to break it off with Sasha. He kept meaning to, but it seemed like something he had to do in person rather than over the phone or in an e-mail, and then she would greet him at her apartment door, wearing that aquamarine kimono, the mere sight of which aroused him even before she kissed him.

It was a time of lofty resolutions, of vows and renunciations. He felt incredibly lucky to have escaped this recent peccadillo unscathed, with his marriage intact, although he sometimes wondered if Lora didn't harbor suspicions, and he felt the occasional twinge of guilt about Sasha, who had no one to comfort her in this moment of collective trauma.

6.

For her part, Lora was too relieved to have her husband back to inquire too deeply into his precise itinerary that day. She told herself that the clock had been reset on the morning of September 11 and that whatever happened before didn't really matter. But she couldn't help noticing that Liam seemed almost allergic to his cell phone, jumping whenever it rang over the next few days. He also seemed uncomfortable whenever the subject of people's whereabouts that morning arose, as it did constantly in the days and weeks that followed.

They were inseparable those first few days, staying in or near the apartment, clinging to each other in the aftermath, until Saturday morning, when Liam said he was going to the gym.

"Maybe I'll go with you," Lora said.

He shrugged. "If you'd like."

"No, you go ahead," she said.

She waited exactly sixty seconds and then followed him out the door and down the two flights of stairs to the double doors leading to the street, the second of which was just wafting shut. It was one of those days when the wind had shifted uptown, carrying the burned-plastic smell of smoke from Ground Zero. Her fellow pedestrians seemed skittish, the brusque, purposeful tunnel vision of the natives having been replaced by a new caution that made everyone seem like tourists. Lora didn't really have a plan, but the gym was only a few blocks away, and if she lost him on the street, she could just turn up, and if she found him there, she'd say she'd changed her mind. She watched him walking west and followed, catching sight of him at the end of the block as he turned left on Sixth—the opposite direction from the gym. She ran up Waverly and saw Liam at the next corner, waiting for the light.

He crossed the avenue, turned right and went up the steps of St. Joseph's Church, disappearing inside through the big double oak doors. She could hardly believe it. She approached stealthily and stood watching for a few minutes on the sidewalk across the street. She felt almost giddy with relief when she realized this was his secret destination. But her relief was almost immediately replaced by a sense of irritation at how cowardly it was to have lied about where he was going.

Liam had been raised as a Catholic on Long Island, and they were married in the church where he'd received his First Communion. Their wedding day was the last time she agreed to accompany him to church. The daughter of a Jewish father and an Episcopalian mother, Lora had enjoyed a thoroughly secular childhood. A staunch agnostic, she used to tease him about his residual Catholicism, which she saw as a tribal habit, like his fondness for corned beef and cabbage, rather than an active belief system. She supposed it made sense that he would seek out the faith of his childhood now, in this moment of extremis. Part of her envied him this reserve source of consolation, and part of her thought he was weak for surrendering, when the going got tough, to the superstitions of his ancestors. What the hell was he doing in there anyway? It was probably a reflex, like the desire for comfort food and retro music that had swept across the city. She waited for another five minutes and then returned to the apartment, where she flipped restlessly from one news channel to another, watching the towers fall over and over again as she waited for Liam to come home.

7.

Liam knelt with his head in his hands, finding the familiar darkness of the confessional, redolent of furniture polish and stale perspiration, unexpectedly comforting. When he heard the wood panel slide open, he looked up to see the silhouette of the priest behind the screen.

"Bless me, Father, for I have sinned. It's been, well, more than a year since my last confession."

"How much longer, would you say?"

"It's been . . . I think it's about four years."

"Go ahead, my son."

"I'm not sure where to begin."

8.

When he returned home, Liam seemed like a different man from the twitchy neurotic who'd left the apartment a half hour before. For the rest of the day he exhibited a maddening serenity. Lora wanted to challenge him, to crash his spiritual buzz, if that's what it was, but it seemed peevish to chide him for being in a good mood, and she couldn't think of how to engage him in an intellectual debate without acknowledging that she'd followed him. She took another Xanax, her third of the day.

"I'm thinking about going to Mass tomorrow," he said, while they waited for the check at their local bistro. "I don't know, somehow, with everything that's happened, I think it would be, you know, comforting. Of course you're welcome to join me."

"I think it's sweet," she said, pinching his cheek, "and totally understandable that you can find comfort in your old rituals, but I might feel a little hypocritical suddenly going to church just because I'm feeling emotionally needy. But that's just me. You do what you need to, honey."

That night, for the first time since Tuesday, they failed to have sex. Lora wasn't really in the mood, and was almost looking forward to letting him know she wasn't. But within moments of turning off the television set, she heard him snoring from the other pillow. Lora lay awake in the dark, feeling abandoned, thinking about the chaos outside, and the life growing within her. Though she wished she had some kind of faith, after what had happened she was hard-pressed to imagine a moral order in the universe.

9.

The churches were packed that Sunday. Liam arrived fifteen minutes early for the ten o'clock Mass and even so he had to stand in the back. He felt the force of Lora's implicit admonishment, along with a kind of sociological embarrassment. Ever since he'd made his way to Stanford, he'd done all he could to distance himself from his heritage and to regard religion as an academic subject. Seeing himself now through the eyes of his friends, he felt ashamed, as if he were standing naked in a room of fully clothed adults, but at the same time he felt the exhilaration of surrender, as if he were a naked infant lying in the sun, absolved of the responsibilities of higher consciousness. For the first time since Tuesday, he felt at home and at peace in his city. He was unexpectedly moved when it came time to exchange the peace of the Lord—a folksy ritual inspired by the Second Vatican Council—which had always seemed artificial to him, the congregants stiffly shaking hands and wishing one another the peace of the Lord, but that day, he found himself clasping the hands of neighbors with special vigor and warmth, looking into their glistening eyes as he uttered, "The peace of the Lord be with you," the voices of his neighbors swelling and filling the church around him. And when the priest intoned, "Lift up your hearts," he seemed to feel his own heart swell and rise as he responded, "We have lifted them up to the Lord." And when, finally, he took the host on his tongue, letting it dissolve on the roof of his mouth, he imagined his inner being infused with light, like a cave suddenly illuminated by a torch.

After Mass he didn't feel he could return directly to the apartment. It would be like smoking a cigarette after running a marathon. He knew he couldn't face Lora in this state, any more than he'd been able to face Jenny, his last girlfriend, the teetotaler, after doing a few lines of coke. Instead, he tested this new lightness of spirit as he walked down to Canal Street, to the edge of the blue police barricades sealing off the zone of destruction from the rest of the city, and stood with his fellow citizens watching the plume of smoke that rose like a white pillar into the blue sky and tilted off to the east before diffusing into the cumulus over Brooklyn. From this distance it was an incongruously beautiful sight.

10.

That night, they walked over to Norman's loft in Chelsea, where everyone was telling their stories. "I'm walking down Greenwich Street and suddenly this plane is practically on top of me," their host said, passing a joint to Jason, "this huge jet flying just above the tops of the buildings."

Jason took a hit. "Do you guys remember Carlos, the guy who used to cook for our parties?"

"The cute one with the scar above his eye?"

Jason nodded. "Missing. He was a line chef at Windows on the World."

"Jesus."

"Speaking of Jesus," Lora said, "Liam has rediscovered his faith."

"What's this?"

"He went to Mass this week." Lora walked over and ruffled his hair as if he were a child who'd just done something cute. "Didn't you, my love? I think it's sweet."

"That's great," Jason said.

"Yeah, really," Norman said. "I wish I had one to rediscover."

"Confession," Jason said. "That's what I've always envied about Catholicism. The idea that you can go into a little booth and cleanse your soul."

"I don't think I could go and tell some stranger my sins."

"Oh come on. We Jews have that, too. It's called psychoanalysis."

"But it doesn't help. I've talked to my shrink twice this week. What can he tell me? That I have every right to feel bad? That I have survivor's guilt? That I should refill my Paxil?"

Norman looked at Liam. "Did it help?"

"I suppose so," Liam said. He didn't feel he could go into it with this group. It would be like discussing sex with his parents.

Lora took his cheek in her fingers, putting her face close to his and smiling sweetly, or so it appeared, though he'd come to suspect the sincerity of this particular gesture. "We love you, honey," she said.

As soon as he could, he retreated to a neutral distance; at that moment his phone rang and he answered it, happy for the interruption.

"Liam, it's me," Sasha said. "Don't hang up. I'm so miserable. I need to see you."

He shouldn't have looked to see if Lora was watching him, because she was. "I'm sorry, but you've got the wrong number," he said, feeling the heat in his cheeks. He turned off the ringer before slipping the phone back in his pocket.

"The phones are still completely screwed up," Jason said.

11.

"So you've become a believer?" she asked, smiling brightly. It was the second Sunday of the new era and he'd just asked her if she wanted to join him at Mass. He shrugged. "I just . . . at this particular moment in time, I'm feeling a sense of, I don't know, spiritual yearning. Is that so surprising, really?"

"If that's what you need, then I think you should by all means go to Mass."

"Look, I know you feel differently, but I don't want to argue about this."

"Who's arguing?" She reached over and stroked his cheek, pinching it between her thumb and forefinger. "I love you."

"Maybe I'm weak, maybe I'm being hypocritical, but just indulge me in this, okay? If you don't want to go, I'll understand."

Lora assumed Liam's recrudescence of faith would fade along with the initial shock of that terrifying day. She was kind of assuming the same thing about her own Xanax consumption; she'd cut back again once things returned to normal, but right now it seemed impossible to get through the day without forty or fifty milligrams.

After Liam left, she turned on the TV again, another escalating addiction that would surely subside in the weeks to come. She was watching the Taliban spokesman, defiant in his black beard and black robes, when she heard Liam's phone vibrating on the coffee table. She noticed that he'd turned off the ringer days ago, but now it was buzzing like a big flat beetle on the glass. She picked it up. "Hello?"

There was silence on the other end.

"Did he tell you I'm pregnant?" Lora said, then snapped the phone shut and went to the bathroom and took two more Xanax.

For some reason, she remembered the conversation at Norman's loft. She'd almost forgotten about the whole confession thing, but suddenly she wondered if that had been the point of Liam's new faith: to clear his soul of mortal sin before the next plane hit.

12.

Liam's office was inside the restricted zone south of Canal, and for the first week or so he didn't even think about going to work, but then a friend invited him to use his space in Chelsea. He went back to work the second Monday, not that he foresaw a big demand anytime soon for the kind of edgy independent films he produced. When he got home that night, he could tell that something was wrong. His first thought, on seeing her stony expression, was that somehow she'd learned about Sasha.

"Any thoughts about dinner?" he asked.

"I'm not hungry."

"Shall I cook something?"

"I told you: I'm not hungry."

"I brought some DVDs from the office. *Hedwig and the Angry Inch* and *Riding in Cars with Boys.*"

"I don't think so," she said. Tears were pooling in her eyes, though she looked more angry than sad.

"What's wrong?"

"The baby's gone," she said.

"Gone?"

The tears were coursing down her cheeks, but her manner was defiant. When he tried to embrace her, she pushed him away and said, "I ended it."

13.

Eventually, in his mind, it seemed, the abortion became subsumed into the narrative of the collective trauma. Liam went out and got drunk that night, but in the succeeding days he seemed unwilling to confront her about her motives, as if he was afraid their marriage couldn't survive the revelation of certain facts. At some point, after telling her that he believed in the sanctity of life from the moment of conception, he made the decision to forgive her, just as she, in turn, forgave him, though neither of them ever acknowledged his transgression. But he had presumably confessed his sin, and she sometimes wondered how he squared his own faith with her action, and her own unshriven state. Apparently, in his mind, she had committed murder. But divorce, too, was a mortal sin. As much as she despised his faith, she kind of liked the idea that Catholicism protected her matrimonial monopoly.

Most of the noble resolutions of that period gradually faded away, but Liam continued to attend Mass, without making a big deal of it. The fact that he stopped talking about it had convinced her of his seriousness. For her part, she tried not to give him a hard time.

The following spring, Lora was pregnant again. The days between the morning the stick on the home pregnancy test turned blue and the evening their son was delivered in December were among the happiest of their marriage. After a long period of apartment hunting and soul-searching— both of them of an age to have used the phrase "bridge and tunnel" to denote those living in the hinterlands—they bought a town house in

Brooklyn's Boerum Hill. Like most converts, they became strident prose-lytizers, declaiming the virtues of the restaurants on Smith Street and in-sisting that it was only ten minutes by subway to the Village. They loved telling not only their friends but also each other how much they didn't miss Manhattan, though eventually this became something of a moot point when Liam started spending half his time in Los Angeles after one of his scripts was picked up by HBO shortly after Jeremy's second birthday. Lora couldn't pretend that it wasn't hard on her, being left behind to take care of the baby. And she couldn't help wondering what he was doing when he wasn't working, despite his declarations that every waking mo-ment was consumed by the show. But he was an attentive father and lover during his sojourns in Brooklyn, and one morning she woke him at his hotel in Los Angeles to tell him that she was pregnant.

"That's fantastic," he said.

"You're happy?"

"I couldn't be happier. Aren't you?"

"I don't know. I'd be happier if you were here right now."

"I'll be home the day after tomorrow. We'll celebrate."

Unpacking his suitcase two mornings later while he slept in, she found, mixed in with his shirts, a baby blue silk teddy trimmed with black lace.

14.

When Liam woke up that morning, he was alone. Sitting up in bed, he saw his suitcase, propped open on the floor, and recognized the light blue undergarment on top as belonging to his production assistant. For years he'd behaved himself and remained faithful to Lora, but recently he and Lanie had been working late, and one night she'd kissed him and he'd been unable to resist. He'd gone to confession the next afternoon, but it had happened again several times since. He didn't know how her nightie had gotten into his suitcase, but the more troubling question was why it was so flagrantly displayed, when he was ninety percent certain he hadn't opened the bag when he came in the previous night. What the hell was he supposed to do now? He finally decided to bury it beneath his shirts and hope that it never surfaced again.

He descended the stairs with trepidation, but he couldn't read anything unusual in Lora's demeanor when he found her in the kitchen with Jeremy in her arms, attached to her breast. That she was still breast-feeding Jeremy at two and a half was a point of contention, but he wasn't about to get into it now. Lora seemed delighted to see him. "Here's Daddy," she said. "And we love Daddy, don't we? Yes, we do." She shuffled across the floor in her slippers, clutching Jeremy to her chest, and took Liam's left cheek in her fingers, pinching and pulling his face close to hers. "We love you so much, Daddy."

All weekend he waited for the accusation, but it never came. After two days at home, he would almost have welcomed a confrontation, but Lora seemed to have finely calibrated her chilliness to a degree or two above the freezing point, and when they had another couple over for dinner on Saturday, she was overly effusive, gratuitously declaring her love on several occasions. Before the Robertsons arrived, he'd suggested they tell them about the pregnancy, feeling that the announcement would make it more real, might lodge the fetus more firmly in Lora's uterus, but Lora said it was way too early for that.

While Liam was mixing the margaritas, Lora told her new joke: "What's the biggest drawback to being an atheist? Give up? No one to talk to during orgasm."

Shortly after she put dessert on the table, she stabbed him with a fork. She was talking to Donna about private schools when suddenly she brought her clenched fist, clutching her fork, down on his thigh, impaling him through his jeans.

If Liam, in his surprise, had been able to suppress a shriek of pain, it's possible the attack would have passed unnoticed. As it was, Lora made the whole thing seem like an unfortunate accident, an absentminded gesture.

"Oh my God. Oh, Liam honey. You know how I'm always grabbing your thigh. It's like, shit, I forgot I had a goddamn fork in my hand. Poor baby, you're bleeding. I'm so sorry." She showered him with apologies and first aid, and even after the Robertsons had left, she maintained an air of concern and contrition. For his part, Liam was too frightened to confront her. He only hoped that she'd gotten it all out of her system at once. Maybe now they could go on as if nothing had happened.

Back in L.A., he told Lanie that it was over between them, citing the pregnancy, and she seemed to understand. In retrospect, he found it remarkable that communication between a man and woman with a sexual history could be so straightforward.

A few nights later, they were crashing a script, four of them working in the office till midnight, when they decided to move to his hotel suite, where they could order up a room-service supper. Liam was in the bathroom when the phone rang, and he rushed out in a panic. He knew who was calling.

Lanie was still holding the receiver. "Hello?"

He grabbed the phone away from her and heard only the dial tone. It was three-ten in the morning; it wasn't hard to guess what Lora, if it had been Lora, was thinking. There was no way of verifying the incoming number on the hotel phone.

"What's the matter?" Brodie asked.

He dialed his home number in Brooklyn. After a half dozen rings, he heard his own voice explaining that no one could come to the phone right now. "Honey, it's Liam. Listen, I thought you might have called just now and I wanted to make sure everything's okay out there. We're all here just finishing up on the script for tomorrow, me and Brodie and Issac and Lanie. I guess you're asleep. Just wanted to make sure everything was okay. Big kiss."

He called throughout the day, but Lora never answered. When he still couldn't reach her the following afternoon, he told his colleagues he had an emergency and caught the red-eye to New York.

15.

She was in bed with Jeremy when he came in at seven. She said she wasn't feeling well, that she had cramps and was bleeding.

"Are you all right?" he said, breathlessly.

"Not really," she said.

"The baby?"

"There is no baby."

"You had a miscarriage?"

"No." She shook her head. "Not a miscarriage."

Having arrived all tense and alert, he seemed to deflate before her eyes, slumping to the foot of the bed. "How could you do this?"

"It's just a procedure," she said. Of course, she knew it was more than that to him. To him, it was a mortal sin.

"It's a life," he said. "Is this what happened the last time, too? You were punishing me?"

"Punishing you for what, my love?" Despite the pain, she managed a bright smile. "I just wasn't ready for another child. I didn't think *we* were ready."

"But you know how I feel about this," he said. "How am I supposed to live with you after this?"

"Of course you'll live with me. With us—your wife and son. What else would you do? You know I love you, honey."

2008

Sleeping with Pigs

"Wait a minute," my shrink says. "Stop. Go back. Did you say *in the bed*?"

I nod cautiously. Actually, my mind was drifting off on a tangent. Even as I was droning on about my failed marriage, I was wondering, not for the first time, why she had a picture of John Lennon in her office and whether it was an Annie Leibovitz. You know, the one where he's in a sleeveless New York City T-shirt with his arms crossed.

"The pig was sleeping in the bed. With you. In the marital bed. With you and your wife."

"Well, yes," I say.

"You've been coming to me for more than a year, trying to come to terms with your guilt about the breakup of your marriage, and this is the first time it's occurred to you to mention that the pig was sleeping with you in the bed?"

I can see her point. I don't know why I didn't mention it before. It was actually a big point of contention at the time. On the other hand, I was behaving so badly by then that I didn't really feel I was in a position to make demands. Blythe used to have all kinds of jokes about sleeping with two pigs. No, actually, it was the same joke over and over. Plus, McSweeney's my surname and she liked to call me McSwine.

"Was this a nightly occurrence? How long did it go on?"

"Pretty much every night for a year or so. Two years maybe. Mostly at the end."

"And where did the pig sleep?"

"Between us."

"Between you. *In the bed.*" Apparently, she wants to make sure she's clear on this point.

"Sometimes it would burrow under the covers and sleep down at the foot."

"Didn't you think this was relevant to our enterprise here? To the whole question of the fate of the marriage? That you were being asked to sleep with a pig between you. Am I safe in assuming this wasn't your idea?"

"Of course not." About this at least, I can be emphatic. "It was hers."

"And you didn't object?"

"Well, yeah, sometimes. In the beginning."

"And then?"

"Well, you get used to things."

She sighs and shakes her head. "I think we need to talk about this."

I can see her point. In retrospect, here, on the Upper West Side of New York, sitting in this book-lined office across from my shrink, who is literally and figuratively framed within a constellation of diplomas and portraits of Carl Jung, Hannah Arendt and Anna Freud, I can imagine how bizarre this sounds. Now that it's come up, I'm kind of amazed myself that I let my ex-wife talk me into sharing the bed with her potbellied pig. Over time almost anything can come to seem normal in the course of a marriage: food fetishes, sexual kinks, even in-laws. First you get talked into a pet pig, and the next thing you know it's sleeping with you.

"How did it get up on the bed?"

"She built a ramp. With carpeted steps."

"And you didn't think this was . . . unusual? And, in terms of your marriage, unhealthy? How did you manage to have sexual relations with a— How big was the pig?"

"By then? Hard to say, really. Too big to lift anyway. I threw my back out the last time I tried. Hundred and sixty, hundred and seventy pounds. About my weight. Plus, the shape's kind of awkward and it's not like they're going to hold still and stay quiet when you try to pick them up." Normally, her expression is pretty imperturbable, but for the first time in our association I get the impression that she's looking at me like I'm a crazy person. "They're actually very clean," I add. "And they're smarter than dogs." I realize I'm quoting my ex. I can anticipate my shrink saying something to the effect that we were enabling each other in our respective fantasy worlds.

She nods slowly, drinking this in, and regarding me with what seems to me an air of wonder mixed with disappointment, as if she now has to reevaluate our relationship and start again from the beginning. It's the kind of expression that leads me to wonder whether psychiatrists ever fire their patients. I want to point out, in my defense, that her cat's purring away in my lap and she didn't seem to think there was anything weird about that.

"Well," she says. "We certainly have a lot to talk about next week, don't we?"

Having thought I was marrying a southern belle, I hadn't counted on getting Ellie May Clampitt in the bargain. I met her at one of the most fashionable watering holes in Manhattan, where she made an unconsciously grand, fashionably late entrance on the arm of a movie star. It was a birthday dinner for my friend Jackson Peavey, and the chair next to mine had been empty for half an hour. When I asked someone about my absent dinner partner and was told the seat belonged to Blythe, Jackson's aunt, I imagined a blue-haired southern dowager. I certainly wasn't prepared for the leggy, luminous blonde who finally alighted beside me with the ease of someone effortlessly mounting a horse. Though she has since denied it, I could've sworn the movie star leaned over and whispered, "See you later" as he took his leave. She should have been thoroughly daunting, except that somehow she wasn't.

"Hey there, Blythe Peavey, delighted to meet you. If I'd known what an excellent seat I had, I would've absolutely come sooner. That's a beautiful shirt. Is it linen? I love that color with your eyes. Have I missed any bon mots or bad behavior?"

She dispensed compliments with a liberality that would have seemed insincere in anyone I found less attractive and made me feel as if we were dining alone, tête-à-tête. She seemed to know quite a bit about me, which I found gratifying, considering how little there was to know at that early moment in my life, and what she didn't know, she seemed to be in a desperate hurry to learn. Eventually I admitted that I'd been expecting someone much older.

"My brother Johnson, Jackson's dad, is almost twenty years older than I am," she explained. "Jackson loves calling me 'Aunt Blythe,' which seemed funny when he was ten and I was twelve, but now that he's followed me to New York, I'm thinking of offering him lots of money to quit it."

Later she told a self-deprecating story about having lunch, in her early days in the city, with Leo Castelli and an artist named John something—she hadn't caught his entire name. She found him rather attractive and confessed to possibly flirting with him a bit, frequently repeating his name and touching his arm. The artist became more and more remote, until he finally said, "My dear, I've been called a john before, but never by a woman." Castelli later told her that she'd been flirting with Jasper Johns. "You can imagine," she said, "that I've never been able to show my face at a Castelli opening again, for fear of running into him."

I thought her story was a kind of wonderful spoof of the name-dropping that passed for anecdote in the world I was then aspiring to enter.

She slipped away around midnight, whispering that she hoped to see me again and disappearing at a raucous moment, so that I was the only one to actually observe her departure. I would learn later that this was her habitual strategy, that she didn't believe in saying good-bye.

After that, I followed her career as a girl about town, watching for her at parties and in the gossip columns. She was one of those women who conquered Manhattan for a few years, who seemed to be everywhere and to know everyone interesting, although even the most brilliant and articulate among her admirers had a hard time defining the qualities that made her so popular, in part because her greatest gift was the ability to reflect and magnify the attributes of those around her, particularly with men, a talent that was much rarer in New York than it was in Tennessee. She had a way of identifying and admiring the traits you liked most in yourself, no matter how recessive, so that as long as you were with her, you could imagine you were the person you most wanted to be. "Tony is the most extraordinarily talented tax accountant." "Roger has the most exquisite taste of any heterosexual in the city." "Collin was without a doubt the most popular man in Savannah before he chose to break a thousand hearts and move up north." She added to the collective sense of self-esteem. And though it wasn't obvious at the time, it became clear after she left that she wasn't terribly invested in the whole scene—and that was another aspect of her charm. Unlike the rest of us, her lack of vaulting ambition gave her an aura of grace. As it turned out, she was just visiting from another world. Several admirers tried to get her to stay. I knew of three spurned marriage proposals—from a publishing mogul, a playwright and a tennis player—and two book dedications.

One theory about Blythe's elusiveness, propounded by her nephew, was that she would never marry anyone while her father—a former Tennessee governor and doting domestic tyrant—was alive. I never met the man, but he left a big footprint on his native soil. In Nashville, a street and two buildings, including the tallest skyscraper, were named for him. As the president of the chamber of commerce, he'd gone up against the prohibitionist lobby to legalize restaurant alcohol sales, reaping a whirlwind of calumny and death threats; for more than a year, Blythe had been attended by full-time bodyguards. He had not approved of any of Blythe's suitors, Jackson told me, not even the English lord who'd brought him a present of matched Purdey shotguns. And he certainly wouldn't have approved of me. Another of her expatriate kinsmen speculated it was the death of her beloved brother in Vietnam that had made her so skittish about long-term attachments. At any rate, she left the city before anybody had a chance to get tired of her, and before she became coarsened by it or embittered by watching younger women take her place.

Blythe went home to Tennessee to care for her ailing parents, but she kept her apartment in the city and returned for brief visits every couple of months. I saw her at parties with a poet or a CEO, or, once, with a ridiculously good-looking guy who, she said, was a carpenter from Tennessee. One night, at a cocktail party in an Upper East Side penthouse, I stepped outside to smoke a cigarette and found Blythe standing alone, her blond hair billowing in the breeze from the river. Against the backdrop of the downtown skyline—with her head slightly tilted to the right, it looked as if she were leaning up against the Chrysler Building—she seemed like the embodiment of all my cosmopolitan fantasies.

"Well," she said, "you've certainly made good since I last saw you."

It was true. My first book had been a success and I was currently adapting it for the screen. Perhaps this emboldened me enough to ask her out, something I would have been too intimidated to do a few years earlier. I couldn't believe my good fortune, and not long after finding myself in her bed at the end of our third date, I proposed. Why she accepted me, having turned down so many others, I can't really say. Maybe it was because her father had died the year before, or maybe she'd just gotten tired of fleeing. Sometimes I think she agreed to my proposal on a whim, marriage being one of the few adventures she hadn't essayed. Or it's possible I was just at the right place at the right moment. At the time, I never really asked the question, being more than a little full of myself and my own success, but in retrospect, I have to wonder. Better-looking, more successful, richer and funnier men than I had failed to drag her to the altar.

A childhood friend of Blythe once dropped a clue that I didn't initially pay much attention to, saying that I reminded her of Blythe's deceased older brother. "I don't know what it is, something about your smile, the way you carry yourself. But damn if you didn't make me think of Jimmy just now. They were really close. Blythe was just devastated." Later, I cautiously tested this theory on my wife. We were in bed, flipping through the on-screen cable guide, looking for movies. *Platoon* was coming up on HBO.

"I never really thought about it," she said in response to my question. "I suppose it's possible. Maybe, subconsciously, you do remind me of Jimmy."

"Do you think about him often?" I asked.

"No, not very," she said.

"Really?"

"You know, one of the things I hate about the South is the backward-looking aspect, the obsessive dwelling on the past. Nostalgia is like our regional disease. All that longing for the lost cause, lost plantations, Dixie. All those odes to the Confederate dead. That was one of the things I wanted to get away from when I went north. I try not to look back. Ever."

After our city hall wedding, we split our time between Manhattan, where I taught a spring semester workshop at Columbia, and Tennessee, where we bought an antebellum farmhouse outside Nashville with sagging wide-board floors, tilting barns and ragged pastures. Early on it became clear that she was happier on the farm than she was on Park Avenue. I came to think of her as Persephone, who stoically suffered her six months in Hades in exchange for another six in the sunlight of the surface world. Which would make me the king of the underworld.

For a long time I was happy enough with the contrast between our two worlds. After a decade in the city, I was ready for a change—and I was in love. Honestly, I would have followed her anywhere, although there was something particularly romantic for me, student of Faulkner and Welty that I was, about seeing her in her natural environment. For me, the South was mysterious and exotic, and the sense of nostalgia for a lost Eden, the deeply ingrained social hierarchies and the polite insincerity of public discourse were all endlessly intriguing. I studied the local population with the detachment of an anthropologist and the passionate intensity of a man attempting to decode the mysteries of his wife.

In those early days, Blythe's menagerie consisted of six cats, one of which deposited a dead bird on my chest the first morning I woke up in her bed. "A welcome offering," she said. "You should feel very honored." But once we moved to the farm, the animal population exploded, starting with goats, eventually five of them. Blythe left the table in the middle of a dinner party to check on the pregnant goat that was confined in the laundry room and returned forty minutes later, her white peasant blouse thoroughly stained with blood. "We have a new member of the household," she said, sitting down to resume her meal as if she'd just stepped out to go to the bathroom. "Topsy just gave birth to a fine young billy goat. What did I miss?"

The chickens came next, although the foxes eventually took care of those—except for the one clever enough to move in with the goats. Our first horse was adopted from the local polo club after it came up lame; she took the second, a stately black Tennessee walking horse, in trade for a Parker side-by-side shotgun inherited from her father.

I took to the role of country squire, even going so far as to buy a secondhand John Deere tractor with a bush hog in order to cut the fields myself. At times I could almost imagine leaving my life in the city forever. In the spring, before the heat became unendurable, we would sit on the back porch and observe the sunsets, which could be positively lurid across the back pasture. I would fix a pitcher of martinis and we'd sit and watch the horizon flare up pink and orange. The air was laced with the sweet herbal tang of fresh-cut grass and horse manure and you could feel it grow cooler as the fireflies became visible in the failing light. If we lacked anything at all, it was hard for me to imagine what it might be. Blythe, however, had plans.

I would always claim later that the pig was foisted on me through trickery, particularly after it had just eaten an entire coq au vin, or destroyed a cashmere coat in search of the packet of cashews in my breast pocket. She'd talked before about getting a potbellied pig, but I'd quashed the idea, or so I thought. Her strategy was to buy one for the movie star, whose fortieth-birthday party we'd been invited to, and for some reason couldn't attend. So in our stead, Blythe sent a baby potbellied pig to the event—at the Beverly Wilshire—dressed in a bridal veil. The pig was presented to the movie star shortly after the cake and was a big hit, especially with his kids, who apparently were pretty upset when he decided he couldn't keep it; he was about to go off on location for three months and his ex-wife wanted nothing to do with a pig, potbellied or otherwise. I think Blythe had been counting on this all along. In her birthday note she offered to raise the foundling if it didn't prove convenient for him to do so. A week later the pig was back in Tennessee.

If I'd known it was meant to be an indoor pet, I might have protested from the start, but in its infancy, when it was about the size of a football, it had the inherent charm of all baby mammals, and the fact that it was so easily trained to use a litter box was an added bonus. But somehow I assumed that when it got bigger and fatter, it would take its place outdoors with the other farmyard creatures as God and nature had intended. At any rate, I was led to believe that it would always remain a shrimp among pigs. "Potbellies don't get really big," Blythe assured me. "She's definitely fully grown," she said, a few months later, when she was already too heavy for Blythe to lift. "No way will she get any bigger than this. The breeder showed me pictures of her parents."

I don't quite know what compelled Blythe to surround herself with animals, even in the face of fierce and protracted human opposition. After two miscarriages and one round of in-vitro fertilization, we had both resigned ourselves to the fact that we weren't going to have children. This certainly played a role, but I think it was a preexisting condition. Her friends told me about the raccoons and squirrels of her childhood, and a previous boyfriend, with whom she was still on good terms, confided to me one night over bourbon that he thought she cared more about animals than people. At any rate, a week after Sweetheart arrived, Blythe discovered she was pregnant again. We might have been spared the pig if our son had been born a little earlier.

The pig was, if anything, cuter at first than the baby. Blythe certainly thought so. For three months after Dylan came home from the hospital, after a long bout with a staph infection, she seemed strangely indifferent to him, and far more absorbed by the piglet. Eventually her maternal impulses kicked in, for which I was grateful, although our sex life never really recovered. We would hardly have been the first couple to have experienced postpartum celibacy, but I couldn't help wondering if the pig, by now sleeping in a little box beside our bed, didn't bear some of the blame. Dylan gradually grew hair and developed recognizable human features, while Sweetheart, whom Blythe referred to as his older sister, soon sported long black bristles and a vast sagging belly. To me, she resembled a boar who'd come in from the wild in order to live the good life. I don't think it was ever Blythe's intention that her name would seem ironic, but it was hard not to see it as such.

Many of our friends were horrified once the pig got big enough to knock them over if they happened to be standing between it and a food source, or after it rooted through their purses or their luggage to snack on soaps and cosmetics. It didn't help that Blythe would inevitably blame the victims.

"Well, you could hardly expect a red-blooded pig to resist a delicious and highly aromatic Cadbury bar that just happened to be lying within easy reach, practically begging to be eaten. It's not fair. Really, Karen, you should watch where you leave your purse. Now she's going to have a tummy ache all night."

Pity the houseguest who made the mistake of leaving his suitcase on the floor and then tried to complain about the destruction. "You don't have to tell *me* she ate your prescriptions—she's been up all night puking her guts out. What the hell kind of pills did you bring into this house anyway? You could have killed little Sweetheart McSwine."

The houseguest proved to be too flabbergasted to point out that there was nothing little about Sweetheart, too flummoxed by Blythe's righteousness to press his grievance—the fact that hundreds of dollars of pharmaceuticals were consumed and that he would be suffering from acid reflux, insomnia, high cholesterol and high anxiety until he could replace them. Instead, he stammered an apology. He came from across the seas, after all; he'd heard about the eccentricity of southerners.

Blythe used to say pigs were smarter than dogs, and this one certainly showed great ingenuity in the pursuit of anything edible. Sweetheart learned to open the refrigerator door before her first birthday. She would feign sleep, only to lunge at a bag of potato chips or a bowl of popcorn when she sensed we'd let our guard down. Dylan was regularly robbed of his snacks and his bottle. If we failed to clear the table after a dinner party, she would inevitably pull the tablecloth to the floor in order to get at the leftovers. On the first such occasion we lost a fair portion of the antique crystal and china that Blythe had inherited from her parents. We heard the crash and went running downstairs from our bed—neither the first nor the last time the pig would interrupt coitus.

She was busy rooting in the remains of the cheese plate, becoming frenzied as Blythe tried to separate her from the feast, snorting and grunting as she engaged in a tug-of-war for the last of the Manchego. Then she bolted for the living room, sliding and nearly falling over as her hooves hit the bare floor beyond the dining room carpet as Blythe jumped to her feet empty-handed. "Bad Sweetheart," she shouted. "Bad girl!"

"I don't believe this," I said, surveying the wreckage—the shards of Waterford and Worcester, the linen tablecloth soaked in red wine.

"Cheese is just so bad for her," she said.

"That's your big concern? That cheese is bad for her?"

"Well," she said, "at least there wasn't any chocolate on the table."

It was trying enough to have the pig in the house in Tennessee; weirder still when Blythe decided it should go with us to New York. She felt Sweetheart would be too lonely in Tennessee for six months without us. During our New York sojourns, we lived in one of the snootier co-op apartment buildings on the Upper East Side, where capital was only the most obvious of the entry requirements, and I certainly wouldn't have passed the co-op board if not for Blythe's venerable family name, which even graced the Declaration of Independence. I still couldn't believe they'd let me in, but I was pretty sure they'd draw the line at Sweetheart. "What they don't know won't hurt them," Blythe told me.

I pointed out the impracticality of transport, of sneaking Sweetheart into the building and keeping her existence a secret, but it was no use.

Blythe had a friend who designed handbags, and she had him construct a special carrying case with a sturdy plywood bottom. "She has to fly in the cabin with us," she insisted. "She'll be traumatized flying in the hold." I said that even if Sweetheart could fit under the seat, which I doubted, it was probably illegal to take a pig into the cabin of a passenger plane. "Then we'll just have to smuggle her aboard," she said.

Because the beast was now tipping the scales at eighty pounds, this scheme required my participation. On the morning of our departure, I staggered into the Nashville airport carrying a heavily reinforced black canvas shoulder bag. Blythe was carrying Dylan, who then weighed about eighteen pounds.

"What's in the bag?" the guard asked at the security checkpoint.

"Actually, it's a potbellied pig," Blythe said.

"A what?"

The other guards gathered around, more excited than alarmed, while I unzipped the front of the bag and Blythe expounded on the habits of the domestic pig.

"They're actually very clean. She loves to eat soap; she had a bar of Crabtree & Evelyn lemon verbena that she relished the other morning. A free-range pig will always go to the far corner of her enclosure to do her business, and Sweetheart has a litter box. . . . Well, yes, it's a big litter box. They eat just about anything, but we try to keep her on a vegetarian diet to help her retain her girlish figure."

In the end, the security supervisor couldn't recall any official ban on pigs, and Sweetheart marched through the metal detector on her leash while her bag went through the X-ray machine. A small crowd had gathered before we managed to stuff her back in her bag.

Blythe was addressing a young brother and sister. "Of course she knows her name. They're very smart—way smarter than dogs."

With no small difficulty, I hoisted the bag up on my shoulder and started toward the gate, moving deliberately, like a conscientious drunk. When our group number was called, I threw a jacket over my bulging carry-on and followed Blythe past the stewardess checking boarding passes—hoping Dylan might distract her—and lurched into the plane, located our seats and swung the bag into the space in front of them, though it didn't quite fit and its occupant was grunting indignantly. When I straightened up, I felt the sharp bite of a pulled muscle in my lower back. I pressed the top of the bag, the pig squealing away, and finally slid it under the seats. Glaring at my wife, who was standing in the aisle behind me, I indicated the window seat. She climbed in and perched, her feet resting on the bag; I eased myself into the aisle seat, grunting as I felt the hot stab of back pain. I'd just settled in beside her when a fat woman clutching a violin case tapped my shoulder. "I'm sorry, but I think this is my row. Twelve A. That would be the window seat."

"This is row thirteen," I said.

She pointed to the illuminated number over my head. "Twelve, see? You're in the next row back."

"Oh shit," I said, rolling my eyes and glaring at Blythe, who seemed to find the whole situation hysterically funny. From a certain point of view, I guess it was funny. But from seat 12B, it was incredibly frustrating. It wasn't the pig, per se, although that was a major component. A year ago, even a month ago, I'd shared a frame of reference with Blythe; we lived within the same marriage. Her idiosyncrasies were charming and her faults, in the early years of our marriage, virtues. That she insisted on living with a pig and treating it like a member of the family was amusing enough, especially when we were still having sex on a regular basis. But now for the first time I felt myself looking over at her as if from a great distance, from outside the rosy bubble of our shared existence. At that moment I felt something turn cold inside of me.

With an almost palpable sigh of relief, I resumed my life in New York. For the next six months I was back on my own turf, among my friends and living in a beautiful apartment, which I now shared with a potbellied pig— a pig that, by the end of the year, was well over a hundred pounds and far too big to be lifted. Blythe had taken one of the doormen into her confidence, but we had to hide her from our fellow shareholders and especially from the super, a cranky tyrant who certainly would have reported us to the board. To prevent her detection, Blythe designed a secret compartment underneath the platform bed, where Sweetheart could be hidden on short notice.

As she grew, we had to get increasingly bigger litter boxes, which we concealed beneath a round side table draped in a floor-length cloth. Our occasional dinner parties would sometimes be interrupted by the thunder of hooves on the parquet floor as a black shape shot across the floor, disappeared under the table and then, after a pause, unleashed a hissing torrent. The contents of the litter box became something of an obsession for Blythe. Because our garbage was sorted by the super and his minions down in the basement, she believed it had to be disposed of outside the building. She solicited her friends and kept a collection of shopping bags—Barneys, Bergdorf, Chanel, Armani—that would seem appropriate on the arm of an uptown girl, and once a day she would venture out with one of these, a beautiful woman carrying a bag of pig shit out to Park Avenue. She chose a different street-corner trash receptacle each day, fearing, irrationally, that the garbage collectors might become suspicious of agricultural waste and locate the illegal animal unless extraordinary measures of concealment were taken.

Blythe had her Sweetheart and I found mine.

With her I could talk about how I felt underappreciated and unsatisfied at home; many were the justifications with which I mollified my conscience, although the pig wasn't necessarily one of them. To me, it was now merely a fact of life, albeit one that signaled Blythe's increasing distance from social conventions, especially as practiced on the island of Manhattan. Whatever the rationalizations for my affair, it would hardly have been possible if Blythe hadn't grown increasingly withdrawn, frequently sending me off into the night on my own while she stayed in the apartment with Dylan and Sweetheart and her needlepoint.

After all those years of being a virtual dervish, Blythe seemed to have lost her curiosity. "I think I've already been to that party," she would say when I would run an invitation past her. "Like about three thousand times." I don't know, maybe we're all born with certain quotas and she'd hit her limit of parties. A jaded friend of mine likes to say that God allows us all a swimming pool full of vodka and a bathtub full of cocaine, and that he finally quit the latter after realizing he'd started in on his second bathtub. Blythe had burned pretty bright and steady in her early days in New

York. Maybe some filament had burned out. She'd gone to more parties, on the arms of more men, than most people even read about in the course of their lifetimes.

She preferred to sit on the couch, a bowl of popcorn within reach on the coffee table, reading a book, one foot rubbing the belly of the pig lying beneath her, our son crawling around on the floor. "Besides, somebody has to watch Dylan." I pointed out that we had a nanny to watch Dylan, not to mention that he'd be asleep anyway by the time the party started. "Well, somebody has to watch the Sweetheart."

Perhaps she'd evolved to a higher plane of consciousness and no longer required the shallow distractions of small talk and flirtation, of voyeurism and self-display. But I did and I wasn't ready to retire. Even though I'd sworn off the bathtub, I still had several feet of vodka left in my swimming pool and I was still drawn to the music of the night. And inevitably I was drawn to a face across the room, the flash of a provocative smile.

My affair with Katrina lasted for the duration of that Manhattan sojourn, almost six months. It seemed incredible that Blythe didn't question me more closely about my late nights and midday disappearances. With each successful tryst, I became more emboldened, more entitled, less guilty about my transgression. I didn't really have a plan or a specific ambition for the affair. Katrina was funny and sexy, and she also seemed to be happy with a part-time lover, with the stolen hours and midnight departures. I often went to sleep on the daybed in my office so as not to wake Blythe and Sweetheart, although I would often, after a late night, return to the master bedroom for a restorative nap; on these occasions, Sweetheart liked to join me, shoving her nose into my armpit and stabbing me with her hooves. Actually, it was strange how well we got along during this period, after almost two years of uneasy coexistence.

Katrina and I had been friends for years, a fact that helped to mask the drift into physical intimacy, to make it seem innocent even to ourselves, right up until the irrevocable moment—the kiss in the back of the taxi, my hand sliding down her shoulder to her breast, her hand sliding up my knee.

"This is probably a terrible idea," Katrina said as she unfastened my belt. After the night we moved from her couch to her bed, we fell into a pattern of twice-a-week trysts.

I probably would've been satisfied with this arrangement indefinitely, but eventually Katrina's conscience started to bother her; she wanted more, yet was loath to demand it, and I wasn't nearly ready to leave Blythe. But I was crushed when Katrina ended our affair, and in order to console myself, I embarked on a crime spree of serial infidelities. Or perhaps I'm being too easy on myself; maybe I'd just developed a taste for it.

I must have been exuding some kind of scent that telegraphed my debauched availability and my intentions, because there were willing women wherever I looked. I had never noticed them in the early years of my marriage, but suddenly I was awash in opportunity: the dental assistant who held my gaze as she suctioned my gums; the librarian who helped me find Peter Quennell's *Byron in Italy;* the studio executive I met on the plane to L.A. I was compulsive and insatiable. It reminded me of one of Blythe's folksier aphorisms—that once a dog starts sucking eggs, there's no stopping him. In her part of the world, where guns were standard household equipment, the implication was that the dog needed to be shot. Yet in the end she was surprisingly forgiving.

The tipping point was reached back in Tennessee, where I was spotted emerging from a hotel at midnight with the wife of one of Blythe's cousins. At that point, the community, which teemed with friends and relatives, took it upon itself to advise Blythe that enough was enough.

The showdown was surprisingly muted.

We were lying in bed, Sweetheart splayed between us, her sharp cloven hooves thrust toward me. She grunted interrogatively, hoping for a tummy rub, just as Blythe launched her interrogation.

"They say people are calling me the Hillary Clinton of Tennessee."

Scared and guilty as I was that we were finally addressing the elephant in the room, I tried to delay the inevitable. "Down here, I guess that's a bad thing to be."

"This isn't the time for you to be a smart-ass Yankee. They mean I'm a fool who's turning a blind eye to your flagrant and relentless philandering."

"I know," I said. I was, I realized, actually relieved that we were finally discussing this.

"This can't go on. I can't go on."

"I know."

"You realize my father would have had you shot. And I'm not even exaggerating."

"I guess I could only say I deserve it."

"Now you're exaggerating. You don't believe that, so stop bullshitting me. Stop bullshitting yourself. You've been lying to both of us. And don't you dare say *not really*. Not telling isn't the same as not lying. Now listen, I'm not going to give you a real hard time about this, though I probably should. People think I'm crazy, that I should cut your balls off and have done with it, but I just don't have it in me to yell and scream and cuss. I can't say I'm not hurt. I am. You really stabbed me in the heart and turned the blade. But nobody can help falling out of love with someone else."

"It's not that," I said. "I still—"

"Shut up and listen," she said. "All I ask is that you tell me everything— and everyone. I'm serious about this. You owe me that much at least. And if I think you're not being honest, you'll end up wishing Daddy was still around to shoot you and put you out of your misery."

So, I told her. About Katrina. About the dental assistant and the librarian and the studio executive, about her cousin-in-law and the neighbor two farms down who'd come over to dinner one night and flirted across the table, then ridden her horse over a couple days later after seeing Blythe drive into town.

"That sneaky cunt! Goddamn her. I saw her shaking her cleavage under your nose. But I hardly thought she'd come riding right over here like Annie Oakley and fuck my husband."

It was curious how she seemed to blame the women more than me; she hated every one of them from that day forward. I have no idea why I largely escaped blame. It was like the time when Sweetheart ate our houseguest's Dopp kit. She didn't find fault with me so much as with the women who'd tempted me, who'd waved treats in front of my face. Over the years she managed to cut most of them dead, to let them know that *she* knew and was pissed. This is another southern trait—cutting people—and she's good at it. She didn't forgive and she didn't forget, except in the case of Katrina, who, she felt, had at least shown remorse and done the right thing by breaking up with me. Years later, at a play opening in New York, she went out of her way to let her know that it was okay. As to her treatment of me, I eventually remembered the conversation we'd had about her brother, when she'd said she never looked back.

Even by her own admission, Blythe's postmarital dating life was somewhat compromised by the presence of Sweetheart. "I've become familiar with a certain facial expression," she told me. "These guys walk in and look at Sweetheart and what they're wondering is, How long does a pig live? They're wondering if they can outlast her. Sometimes they ask. But even when they don't, I still know that's what they're thinking. I see that look, I just up and say, 'About fifteen years is the answer to your question. And she's eight.' Some of them turn tail right away."

I was living in the city with my new girlfriend; Blythe had stayed in Tennessee. I visited every month to spend time with Dylan, staying with them for a week, an arrangement that made perfect sense to us, if not always to the girlfriends and boyfriends. In the end, though, I think Sweetheart scared away more suitors than I did, which was only one of the reasons I was astonished when Blythe told me she was getting another pig.

"Are you crazy?" I said. We were sitting on the back porch, watching Dylan splash in the pool, and looking out at a vermilion slash of sunset bleeding through the storm clouds above the roof of the old barn.

"Probably," she said.

"Explain this to me."

"I'm not sure I can."

"It's perverse."

"Look, I know it's going to be a disaster for my love life, but somehow I don't care."

The afternoon's intolerable heat was finally subsiding, the cicadas shutting down their tiny chain saws, the fireflies just waking up under logs and eaves, checking their switches. It was a moment of hiatus, of stillness between the activities of the day and those of the night. Sweetheart lay on her side, catching the last rays of the sun. Even Dylan seemed to pause for a moment, standing at the edge of the pool, gazing out over the pasture as it turned from pink to gray as the sun slipped beneath the treetops at the far end of the field. The air was heavy with the promise of rain. All at once

I felt myself projected back in time, the light and the temperature and the scent of the air exquisitely and precisely mimetic of a previous June evening some four or five years ago, when I was a better and a happier man.

"I already paid the breeder," she said. "He's arriving at the airport tomorrow. It's a boy. Another McSwine."

"What the hell," I said. "I'll drive you."

It was no crazier, I realized, than certain aspects of my own life. And it was no longer my fight.

The next day we dropped Dylan off at preschool and then drove to the airfreight terminal. After several inquiries, we were directed to a door with plastic flaps and a gravity wheel conveyor. As we watched, three big cardboard boxes with holes punched in them parted the flaps and rolled out, GRASSMERE ZOO stamped on each one.

"What are those?" Blythe asked the men who were retrieving the boxes.

"Mice 'n' rats, I reckon," one of them said in a slow country drawl.

"Chow for the reptile house," said the other.

"I would've thought frogs," Blythe said.

"Frogs, too," said the country boy. "Frogs was last week."

As they wheeled the rodents away, a large red-and-white-striped box appeared between the flaps.

Blythe saw it before I did, and a pained expression crossed her face as she lifted her hand to her mouth. I looked again as the box emerged, sliding toward us on the steel rollers. Then I saw the blue field of stars at the other end of the box—an American flag wrapped neatly around a coffin.

"Oh my God," Blythe said.

I looked around. "Shouldn't someone . . . be here?"

For the moment we were alone.

I looked at her. "Maybe we should . . ."

"I don't know."

"Me, neither."

At that moment a uniformed baggage handler holding a small animal carrier approached us.

"Are you the pig parents?"

Blythe nodded, gingerly taking the carrier. Tears rolled down her cheeks as she bent down to look in through the slats. "Look at him—he's so scared," she said, wiping her eyes with the back of her hand. "The poor baby."

"Maybe you should tell someone about . . . this," I said to the baggage handler, gesturing toward the coffin.

He shook his head and sighed. "Second one this week."

Back in the car, the little pig squealed like a banshee when Blythe took him out of the carrier and held him in her lap. He was about the size of a beer bottle, with black-and-white bristles, stubby legs and a straight tail that twitched incessantly. "The sweet thing," Blythe said, stroking his back. The tears reappeared as we drove down the exit ramp. "That poor boy," she said. "Why wasn't anybody there for him?"

I shook my head, not trusting my voice.

"It's so awful," she said, rubbing the piglet. "All alone, nobody to welcome him home. Oh God, my poor Jimmy."

It was, I realized, just the second time I'd heard her say her brother's name.

We drove in silence until I finally found my voice. "I'm so sorry, Blythe," I said, my voice a hoarse whisper. "I'm so goddamn sorry." It was some time before I could speak again. "Please forgive me. I never even said I was sorry."

"It's okay, McSwine," she said, turning to me and wiping my cheek. "You know my motto: 'Don't look back.'" I took her hand and lifted it to my mouth. Kissing the back of her wrist, I could smell the sweet, milky, barnyard tang of her fingers. As I squeezed her hand and pressed her fingertips to my lips, I believed there was still time and hope for me, if I could only remember always exactly how I felt at that moment.

2007

Everything Is Lost

Sabrina decided to throw Kyle a surprise party for his thirty-fifth. Her biggest concern was that she wouldn't be able to keep it a secret—so pleased was she with the whole idea. She liked to say she shared all her thoughts and feelings with Kyle. "I tell him everything," she would say. And Kyle would say the same.

She'd been talking to the owner of the Golden Bowl—the hottest new place in TriBeCa—telling him she expected maybe forty or fifty people for the party, dropping some names in hopes of getting him down a little on the price, when Kyle walked into the bedroom and threw himself across the duvet.

"Who was that?" he asked, stroking her knee after she quickly hung up.

"Just a fact checker."

Much to her relief, he didn't seem to notice she was blushing; at least she assumed the heat in her cheeks had to be visible. She felt so transparent that she could hardly believe he didn't sense something amiss.

She suddenly realized that her preparations would be complicated by the fact that the bedroom walls stopped six feet short of the ceiling in their loft. She didn't usually think about it, except when Kyle was being particularly loud on the phone in the other room or the time her brother had spent the night on their sofa and she'd been self-conscious about having sex. When they'd first seen the loft and the Realtor had suggested the walls could be extended up to the ceiling, Sabrina had remarked, rather smugly, that they didn't need privacy. Walls were for people who weren't really in love.

"What was that you were saying about Toby Clench?" he asked.

"Toby Clench?" She was trying to buy a minute to think of what to say.

"I thought I heard you mention his name."

"He collects Brancott's work."

"Who's Brancott?"

"The artist I'm writing about."

"Oh, right. God, I can't believe that son of a bitch is collecting art," he said, again not noticing that she was blushing. He was stroking her knee, moving in the direction of her thigh, pursuing his own secret agenda. If she hadn't been so flustered, she would already have realized he'd come into the bedroom in search of nookie. She could have two jugglers and three elephants in the room and he wouldn't notice when he was in this particular state of anticipation. It was so simple—sweet, really. All she needed to do was administer a quick blow job. Sometimes it was so much easier than the full production. And she'd never heard him complain.

She reached down, unbuttoned his jeans, and slipped her hands inside his boxers. He moaned and lay back on the duvet. Spontaneous sex—one of the perks of the freelance life.

Sabrina worked at a desk in the bedroom. Kyle taught writing at NYU and had an office there. On Tuesdays and Thursdays he had classes and office hours, but most other days he liked to work at home at the kitchen table. Sabrina had been his student a couple years ago and now was writing articles to help pay the bills while intermittently working on her first novel. She loved that they shared a sacred vocation—literature, he liked to say, was their religion—and one that allowed them to spend so much time together.

When she was working, she'd hear him pacing around on the uneven old wooden floors. Sometimes she could hear him humming, or even singing, when concentrating deeply, and she loved the idea that he was working on some short story that might appear in *The Paris Review* or *The New Yorker*. And while he must have been able to hear her on the phone, he didn't seem to mind. They'd check up on each other, intermittently, in one room or the other, and if she didn't hear him for a few minutes, she would go out to see what he was doing. Sometimes, irrationally, she was afraid that he wouldn't be there. He often came into the bedroom with that earnest, hungry look on his face, and if she wasn't too busy, they'd fall into bed and devour each other. This routine had seemed wonderful until she needed a little privacy. Was it her imagination, or was he more housebound than usual this week? She kept waiting for him to leave so she could make her calls. Though she knew it wasn't fair, she grew increasingly irritated as he failed to do so.

"How do people who live in lofts have affairs?" she asked her friends one night over drinks at the Odeon.

"They have offices," Daisy said.

Kyle's office, she recalled, was the first place they'd ever had sex.

The next day she told Kyle she had to go out to conduct an interview, hoping she sounded casual enough to be convincing. He was sprawled on the sofa, reading a manuscript. "Have fun," he said.

In the elevator she wondered, somewhat peevishly, if he ever even thought about her whereabouts. She could be on her way to some assignation, though in fact she was going to check out the restaurant for his party.

The owner, Brom Kendall, had offered to show her around. She recognized him from his picture in *New York* magazine, where he'd been included in a feature on hot restaurateurs. He was wearing a black leather jacket over a white T-shirt, and his cleft chin and a slightly crooked nose just barely saved him from being too handsome. For some reason, she felt awkward. She had a notion that he would be conceited, although in fact he seemed a little shy as he shook her hand.

"How about a drink?" he said after they'd completed their short tour of the restaurant, which, in broad daylight, without its glittering clientele, seemed to her interchangeable with a dozen others in the neighborhood. Kind of an Armani palette: taupe walls, black wood trim, gray leather upholstery and moody vintage black-and-white photos of scantily clad women.

Not wanting to seem unfriendly or uptight, she said she'd have a Ketel One and tonic. He went behind the bar to mix the drinks while she took a seat on the other side.

He told her that for years he'd been an actor but that then one day he'd realized it was never going to happen. Besides, he liked people; he liked food. . . .

It wasn't a terribly original story—she was glad she didn't have to write it—but his obvious sincerity made it interesting. She was expecting him to be glib. "Sometimes that's what I think about my writing," she said, "like I should give it up for something practical."

"I thought that piece you did for *Black Book* was really insightful," he said, surprising her. "The one about the new chick lit."

"Wow, I'm, like, amazed." So much so that she was suddenly talking like a moron. It didn't occur to her until later that he'd probably Googled her the night before, after she first called. Still, it felt good, knowing that someone besides friends and family had read it.

He asked how she'd gotten into writing, which led her to explain that Kyle had been her writing teacher.

"Huh. How long have you two been together?"

"A little over a year."

"It's very cool of you to throw a party for him. I'd be so blown away if someone did that for me."

"Nobody's ever thrown a surprise party for you? You don't seem like the kind of guy who's been totally deprived of female attention."

"Not the *right* anybody," he said, looking at her with an intensity that made the remark seem significant.

Once again she found herself blushing. "I guess I should be getting back," she said, swilling the rest of her drink and rising to her feet.

"If you have any questions, just call," he said, handing her a card.

Kyle went to his office on Monday, giving her a chance to make some calls. She sent the invitation out by e-mail at noon, and though she'd requested RSVPs by the same means, some of their friends, knowing they had separate lines, started calling her with acceptances just as he returned from campus. She had to keep her voice down and keep the conversation general while he puttered in the next room.

She was pleasantly surprised when Toby Clench called, having doubted he would come. One of Kyle's students at NYU a few years ago, he'd gone on to publish a wildly successful novel, and since then his teacher's feelings had oscillated between pride and jealousy. Kyle's own novel, published six years before, had been a critical success, but it hadn't been featured on the cover of the *New York Times Book Review,* as Toby's had, nor had it been optioned by Brad Pitt's production company. But Toby's meteoric debut had certainly raised Kyle's profile, because he routinely cited his mentor in interviews.

"I'll be coming in from London that afternoon," Toby told her, "but for sure I wouldn't miss it."

"Kyle will be so pleased," Sabrina said. "I'll put you by someone sexy and smart."

"I hope that means I'll be sitting next to you," he said.

She heard Kyle's footsteps approaching the bedroom door. "We'll just have to see," she said, lowering her voice.

Kyle appeared in the doorway as she put down the receiver. "S'up?"

"Nothing." Her voice sounded high and false—the squawk of a seabird.

He smiled. "Need anything? I'm going out for a pack of smokes."

"I'm fine." How could he not notice her discomposure?

"See you in a few."

She was relieved that he hadn't noticed anything, but after the elevator door closed behind him, she wondered if he'd always been so unobservant. In class she'd often heard him invoke Henry James's prescription for writers: "Try to be one of the people on whom nothing is lost." He also had it on a typed index card tacked on the bulletin board over his desk.

She was pleased, though, to nab Toby for the party. That was a coup. And she'd definitely seat him next to her; after all, he'd asked. And as the hostess, she figured she was entitled to sit beside the smartest and most entertaining guy at the party. She'd loved his book. Sure, it had become fashionable to say Toby's novel was overrated—she'd heard Kyle say it—but in her opinion that was just jealousy talking.

The answering machine was a problem. She kept meaning to get the service from Verizon, but for now she turned down the volume whenever she left the bedroom, worried that Kyle might overhear something about his birthday. She kept the RSVP list in the bottom drawer of her desk. Suddenly she wondered if he ever looked through her things, or, for that matter, wondered about her life beyond the sphere of this loft. She considered the few stories he'd written since they'd been living together: The women in the stories weren't terribly complex, really. There was a recurring neurotic, mendacious, narcissist type that represented his old girlfriend. And then there was the nice girl, presumably her, who the angst-ridden protagonist struggles to be worthy of. Nice, but hardly subtle or interesting. Which said more about his lack of curiosity than it did about her. She couldn't remember the last time he'd asked her about her desires and dreams and fears. She hadn't said anything at the time, reading the last couple of stories, but he actually wasn't very good with female characters.

While Kyle was out getting cigarettes, George Brasso called to accept. "But I'd rather be having an intimate dinner with you," he said.

"I'm not sure Kyle would like that."

"Does that mean you told him about us?"

"To tell you the truth, I forgot about us until just this minute," she said. They'd been classmates at Yale and they'd had a fling their first year in the city.

"You've never told him?"

"A girl needs a few secrets," she said.

"I couldn't agree more."

She heard the elevator. "I've gotta go. Kyle's back."

"Call me."

Sabrina went out to make a cup of tea, and Kyle was in the kitchen, flipping through the mail. While she stood at the counter, waiting for the water to boil, he came up behind her and wrapped one arm around her waist, groping her breast with his free hand.

"What say we take a little break?" he said.

"From what?" For some reason, she wasn't really in the mood. But as he stroked her breast, she relented. "Okay," she said, turning off the kettle and walking back to the bedroom.

"Wow," he said when they'd finished. She was almost surprised to hear his voice, so absorbed had she been in her own orgasm. She felt a little guilty, realizing she'd been thinking about George. They'd never really had any resolution to an affair that had lasted only a few months before George went off to Paris for *Newsweek*. Was she keeping her options open? George had, upon his return to New York, become a mutual friend, but somehow she'd neglected to tell Kyle about their history. Then again, she wondered why he'd never asked. She'd always been afraid the sexual tension between her and George was conspicuous, but Kyle had never once commented on it, which suddenly seemed incredibly weird. Was he that unperceptive, or did he just not care?

Two hours later she found herself increasingly irritable as she waited for him to leave for his weekly department meeting. She had a lot of party-related calls to make. With each passing minute she became more agitated. Finally she went out to see what he was doing. As nonchalantly as she could, she asked about the meeting.

"Postponed," he said cheerfully. "Haddon and Maselli are sick."

The next day, Sabrina had to fly to D.C. She worried herself sick about the phone, then decided it was better to say something than to have Kyle pick up her phone or turn up the volume on the answering machine.

"Listen," she said, "I've ordered this birthday present and somebody might be calling about it. That's why I turned down the volume on the machine."

"You don't have to get me anything," he said.

Which struck her as a silly thing to say.

"Of course I do. And you sure as hell better get me something for mine. Now promise me you'll stay away from the phone."

"Cross my heart and hope to die."

The next evening, the night before the party, they stayed home and watched *Le Mépris,* Godard's adaptation of the Moravia novel. Kyle was in a Moravia phase.

"Do you ever get jealous?" she asked, lying on the couch with her legs in his lap.

He shrugged. "Not really. I trust you."

"I trust you, too," she said. "But I wouldn't want you sharing a villa in Capri with Brigitte Bardot."

"Don't worry," he said. "She must be in her seventies by now."

"Wouldn't you be worried if I were on an island with some hunky guy?"

"Probably," he said.

In the end, Kyle was surprised. He was expecting dinner *à deux,* tickled that the restaurant was named after a Henry James novel. When everyone jumped up from behind the banquettes, he was flabbergasted.

"You really didn't have any idea, did you?" she said.

"Not a clue," he said before happily throwing himself into the scrum of his friends, many of whom had originally been her friends.

Brom, the owner, materialized at her side with a drink. "Ketel One and tonic," he said.

"You remembered."

"It's part of the job."

"So I'm just another Ketel and tonic to you."

"I wouldn't say that."

This wasn't like her, this silly flirtatious banter. But he *was* cute. When they were finally seated, he leaned over and whispered in her ear that he'd be upstairs in the office if she needed anything. She nodded, then leaned toward Toby. "Do you think that a great writer, by definition, is someone who can't be surprised? Who notices everything?"

"Someone on whom nothing is lost."

"Exactly."

"Are you trying to decide whether Kyle's a great writer?"

"Maybe."

"I think you know the answer to that question."

"I do?" But he was right, of course.

As the dessert plates were being cleared, she thought it was only proper to go up and thank Brom for everything. He rose from behind his desk when she appeared in the doorway. It would seem quite wonderful later, when she recalled the moment, that he hadn't even hesitated. He'd just walked right over and taken her by the shoulders and kissed her so violently that her lips felt bruised the next day. Standing in front of the mirror that morning, she studied her swollen lips and wondered if Kyle would even notice.

As it turned out, he did eventually ask about the hickey on her collarbone, but by then it was too late.

2008

Reunion

The early-morning silence of the graveyard is broken by the approach of a car. I duck behind a stone as the sound of the engine rises toward the gate and falls away among the streets of the town. Sitting on a flat marble slab, Tory continues cutting pieces of masking tape, which she attaches to the back of her hand. The cemetery grass is brown and worn, as if it has been grazed by sheep. The last shreds of morning haze cling to the old stones, which tilt at eccentric angles.

I stand up again but remain hunched, feeling conspicuous among the squat headstones, while Tory seems right at home, though she has warned me this is illegal. The old cemetery is surrounded by the town; although it is wooded and on a rise, I feel exposed. A seagull cruises overhead with an inquisitive squawk. My eyes are dry and itchy from waking too early.

"Stretch this as tight as you can across the face of the stone," she says, holding out a big sheet of newsprint from the tablet we picked up at a hobby store last night. I kneel as Tory directs me to raise and lower the paper until finally it's just where she wants it; then she secures it with masking tape and rubs the crayon across the paper. Crayons, drawing tablets, masking tape. I find it strange that we have come to visit the dead with children's art supplies. "Not too hard," she says. White, archaic letters rise to the surface of the paper. The letters gradually become words. HERE LYES emerges, then BODY OF. I think of it as ghostwriting. The inscription states the facts: name, age and parents. The stone is a triptych, the outer tablets bearing images of a grinning skeleton on one side and Father Time on the other. A skull appears under Tory's crayon, then ribs. "This guy was very rich," she says. "The stonework's amazing. Look at these details—you can even see the anklebones on Father Time." Tory nods toward the tablet of newsprint. "Give it a try," she says.

I stalk the uneven avenues for a likely stone. In the corner near the savings bank, I find one dated 1698, with the name NATHANIEL MATHER. A winged skull presides over the inscription: AN AGED PERSON WHO HAD BEEN BUT NINETEEN WINTERS IN THE WORLD. I sit down on the grass and touch the stone. What does it mean? I once read about a disease that accelerates the aging process so rapidly that its victims die of old age in their teens. Or is it just a metaphor—a young man worn down by troubles?

"Michael, come here," Tory calls.

I get to my feet and look around. "Where are you," I ask in a loud whisper.

"Over here." She raises her hand and waves from behind a cluster of stones. I watch the cemetery gate as another car passes, then scuttle over.

"Look at this." She points to a lichen-covered stone. The engraving has a crude, homemade look. THE CHILDREN OF CHARLES AND SARAH . . . The surname is unreadable. EMILY, TWO YEARS. CHARLES, SEVEN MONTHS. ETHAN.

"There's no age for Ethan," I say.

Tory looks up at me. She doesn't say anything at first. She holds the crayon like a cigarette and touches it to her lips as she stares at me. Finally she says, "He died in childbirth." She says this as if she holds me responsible.

"Where are the witches?" I ask.

"They didn't bury them in the cemetery. This is hallowed ground. They put the witches in unmarked graves on Gallows Hill in Salem Village."

"I wanted to rub a witch's stone."

"You can do the guy who sentenced them to death. Judge Hathorne's right over there. That would be a good one for you to get. A fellow pillar of the legal profession." Tory is on her third rubbing of the children's stone. The first two were black. This one's red. I pick a stone near hers, keeping an eye on the entrance.

"There was one man named Giles Corry, who refused to confess or to implicate anyone as a witch, so they put a beam on his chest and started piling rocks on top to force a confession. But he refused to speak. They piled more rocks on. His ribs broke and finally he died."

"That's a lovely story," I say.

Tory's a little morbid these days. But she says this grave rubbing is something she's been doing since she was a kid. This is the first time we've come up here. Though we've been living together in New York for over a year, Tory hasn't been eager to come home for a visit. Her parents separated shortly before she and I moved into our little apartment. Her mother hung on to the house, but things are strained between her and Tory. I suspect Ginny's unable to live up to the high standards that Tory sets for those she loves, although I'm not sure, because we seldom talk about it. Tory is furious with her father for leaving with another woman; yet she also seems to blame her mother for letting him do so, for not being the kind of woman that no man would ever walk out on.

Shortly after we arrived, Tory gave her mother a lesson in makeup. Ginny submitted patiently as Tory demonstrated the uses of blush and mascara. Ginny has the skin of a tennis player and the hair of a swimmer; the makeup seemed to disappear without a trace moments after it was applied. Later, Tory worked on her mother's taxes; Ginny has an antiques shop that was operated for years on the principle of losing money to write off her husband's taxes. But with the division of property hung up in the courts and two years' worth of taxes due on the house, Ginny now is faced with the new and baffling imperative of making money.

The family, sans patriarch, has ostensibly gathered for Bunny's graduation. There are four sisters, spread over ten years, all conspicuously blond. Carol, her new husband, Jim, and her daughter by a former marriage are here from California. Carol's pregnant. Jim's a Christian. Under his tutelage, Carol has been born again. She is the eldest, and, according to Tory, she has been exemplary, doing all of the stupid and illegal things that her younger sisters might've been tempted to do. Bunny, who just turned twenty-four, is able to seem merely adventurous by comparison. She started Radcliffe but dropped out to marry a cocaine dealer. When the marriage broke up, she moved back in with her parents. In two days she'll graduate from a local state school, where she's dating a married professor twice her age. Tory is the third child. Mary, the youngest, still lives at home and mostly is into cars and boys. I'm not sure whether she likes the boys because they have cars, or the cars because the boys have them. She speaks confidently about horsepower, engine displacement, biceps and pectorals. She doesn't think much of me—I drive a Toyota and wear a thirty-eight regular. Last night at the supper table she noticed me long enough to

ask if I would make a lot of money now that I've graduated from law
school.

This family reunion might be the last one in the old house. Ginny can't
afford to keep it. I'd love to live in a house like this one, an old post-and-
beam saltbox core that has been added to in various directions over the
last couple hundred years, jammed with primitive furnishings of scarred,
fragrant wood; crude iron implements; cloudy bull's-eyed blue-green glass.
I like the outbuildings, the sagging, disused stables and greenhouse; even
the pool, cracked and covered over with a green scum, has the aspect of
an ornamental pond.

I grew up in houses that were vague, standardized descendants of those
in this neighborhood. Since arriving yesterday I've conceived an indeterminate fantasy of saving the old homestead with my legal skills, distinctly
featuring the gratitude of this family of attractive females.

But for several weeks now I have felt helpless in the face of Tory's medical problems. She has been bleeding erratically. Her gynecologist in New
York has several hypotheses. In two days she will check into Mass General
for tests, and I'll drive back to New York to start an associateship at Cra-
vath, Swaine & Moore.

On the way home from the cemetery, we stop at a package store, where
Tory waits in the car. A red Camaro is idling in the parking lot, heavy metal
blasting from the open windows. Inside the store, a kid with an Iron
Maiden T-shirt hefts three cases of beer up to the counter. His denim
jacket has the sleeves ripped out, BILLY embroidered above one pocket,
HEAVY CHEVY over the other. He asks for three bottles of Jose Cuervo
tequila. The clerk checks his ID doubtfully. "Frank Sweeney?" he says.

"Yeah, right," the kid says. The clerk sighs and hands the ID back.
Coming out of the store, I spot Mary, Tory's younger sister, inside the Camaro. She waves. The kid with the ID is loading the stuff in the trunk.

"How do you like my wheels?" Mary says. "Don't tell Mom you saw
me, okay? I'm supposed to be at Laura's house." The kid comes around
the side of the car and looks me over. Mary doesn't introduce anyone.
They leave in a roar of exhaust.

Back in the car, I describe the scene for Tory, who has been reading.
"She's young," Tory says, then goes back to her magazine. Mary is the only

member of the family who escapes Tory's censure. Tory's still able to see her as the baby. It seems to be something she clings to, this idea that there's still a baby in the family after all that has happened.

In the kitchen, Carol and her daughter, Lily, are playing with Barbies. Carol has four months to go on her next, but she's already huge. Between her religion and her fertility, she's bursting with contentment. Ginny, the aproned matriarch, is fixing lunch.

Lily lifts her Barbie toward me and waves it from side to side as she speaks in a high, squeaky voice. "Look, Barbie, it's Ken."

"That's not Ken," Carol says. "Who is that?"

"That's Michael," Lily says in her own voice, hiding her face in her mother's arm.

"You like Michael, don't you?" Carol says, doing a Barbie voice.

Lily shakes her head back and forth. She won't look up.

"Don't teach her to be a dumb blonde, Carol," Tory says.

"And who's that?" Carol says, directing Lily toward Tory.

Tory kneels beside Lily's chair and points her finger at herself. "Do you remember my name?"

Lily shakes her head and hides it again in her mother's shoulder. She can't remember Tory's name but has the others down cold.

"That's Tory," Carol says. "Isn't that a pretty name? *Tory* rhymes with *story* and *glory*, doesn't it?"

Tory says, "And *gory*."

"Do we have a kiss for nice Aunt Tory?"

When Lily shakes her head against her mother's shoulder, Tory stands up and leaves the room.

"Sandwiches are ready," Ginny says. "Grilled cheese, tomato and bacon." Ginny's one of those people who believe that there is very little that can't be fixed by putting a meal on the table.

"Jim doesn't eat bacon," Carol says.

"I thought he was a Christian. Isn't it Jews who don't eat bacon?"

"We eat low cholesterol."

Ginny puts the hot tray down on the counter. She takes off the oven mitt and lights a cigarette. "You eat low cholesterol. You don't smoke. You don't drink. You don't swear, and you don't like it when other people do. Is there anything else I should know as your innkeeper? Would you maybe like some more hay in your manger?"

"Jesus loves you, Mom."

Jim, the born-again husband, comes in, looking sleepy. "Is that bacon I smell?" he says.

"I was going to do fishes and loaves," Ginny says, "but I couldn't find a good recipe."

I find Tory in her room, lying on the bed with a stuffed tiger in her arms.

"I brought you a sandwich," I say.

She shakes her head. I sit down beside her on the bed. A framed grave rubbing hangs over the headboard: HERE LYES THE BODY OF . . . The bedside table displays a collection of handmade dolls. I pick up a porcelain doll in peasant costume, then put it back.

"This was my room all the time I was growing up," Tory says.

"Maybe one of these days we'll buy ourselves a big old house like this," I suggest. I wish I hadn't said "maybe," but I feel uncertain of the future. Tory and I have talked about marriage, though everything seems to be changing. I don't really know what I want. Everything has become so gloomy and difficult lately.

"I don't want a big old house," Tory says. "A big old house needs kids in it."

"Don't be so pessimistic. The doctor said that was a worst-case scenario."

"Doctors have been treating women like children for centuries."

There's a knock on the door, and Bunny comes in.

She throws herself down on the bed beside Tory. "And now the graduate, exhausted from rehearsal in the hot sun, takes a load off her feet," Bunny says. "Also, by avoiding her own room, she hopes to escape interrogation at the hands of the mother of the graduate."

"What interrogation?" Tory says.

"She wants to know whether Bill's going to be at the ceremony."

"Is he?"

"Of course."

"You could introduce him as the father of the graduate," Tory says. "He's even older than Dad. Is he going to bring his wife with him?"

"He's not older than Dad. They're the same age."

"That makes it perfect."

"He's in terrific shape. He works out and plays tennis every day."

"You're going to ruin the graduation for Mom if she sees him there."

"She won't see him."

"Is Dad coming?"

"I didn't invite the bastard."

The sisters fall silent, both bouncing lightly on the bed, as if responding to some signal I can't hear. The resemblance of the two sisters lying on the bed is eerie and exciting. They seem to lend each other beauty, their juxtaposition creating a context for appreciation. In silence, they exercise a lifetime of intimacy. I hear the clop-clop of a horse outside on the road. Dust swarms in the wedge of sunshine coming in through the curtains; a shaft of yellow light catches the edge of Bunny's hair and appears to ignite it. Both women have their eyes closed. I watch them. They seem to be asleep.

When I go downstairs, Ginny is sitting at the kitchen table, reading a magazine. The TV is on, a game show. Ginny looks up and smiles. "My *Gourmet* arrived, so I'm happy," she says. "I hardly ever cook anymore, but I love to read the recipes." I take a seat at the big round table that is the hub of family activity. The house has dens, living rooms and I'm not sure what else, but everyone hangs out in the kitchen. I wonder if it was always this way.

Ginny closes the magazine and looks up at the television. Then she looks at me. "Do you think in this day and age it's possible to win an alienation of affection suit?"

"I believe it's very difficult," I say. "But I'm afraid it's not my area." I wish I could tell her something encouraging, save the farm, stay the execution. I imagine myself flat on my back while a hostile jury piles stones on the beam across my chest. I went into law school with a vague notion of righting wrongs. "I don't know much about divorce law," I say. "Corporate marriages are my field. But I could look into it for you."

"No, that's okay. I've got a lawyer. I shouldn't be bothering you for advice." She reaches over and pats my hand. "It's good to have you here. I'm so pleased that Tory has someone like you to take care of her. You're great together." She lights up a cigarette. "Carol—I'm just relieved that she's not in jail or the nuthouse. If Jesus is what it takes, fine. Although I must say having those two around makes me want to curse and smoke and drink just out of spite." She looks at her watch.

"How about a drink, Ginny? I picked up a bottle of vodka."

"Well, I suppose, since it's the weekend. . . ."

"It's an occasion," I say. "I think we're well within our rights here." I fix the drinks. We were pleased to discover, last night, that we both like vodka on the rocks with a splash. Tory, less pleased, thinks her mother drinks too much.

"I'm so glad you're a sinner," Ginny says. "I can't tell you what a relief it is. Carol and Jim were here for two days before you arrived, and it felt like two weeks. Cheers."

The phone rings. Ginny jumps up and catches it on the second ring. She says hello three times and hangs up. "That could've been one of three people," she says after she's back at the table. She raises her hand and holds up a finger. "It could've been my husband, calling to see if I was out so he could sneak over and steal the silver. He tried one afternoon, but Bunny came home and caught him." She lifts a second finger. "It could've been Bill, Bunny's aging lover. He hangs up if I answer, because he knows I won't let him talk to Bunny. Can you tell me what a young girl would want with a fifty-five-year-old man? And he's married. He keeps telling her he's going to divorce his wife, but he certainly hasn't told the wife yet. Although she knows all about it." Ginny raises a third finger. "Bill's wife is the other mystery-phone-call candidate. She calls sometimes when she doesn't know where her husband is, to see if Bunny's home. She disguises her voice when she asks for Bunny."

Ginny takes a long sip of her drink. "You know, I almost feel relieved when I think of Mary drinking beer with boys her own age."

While I freshen our drinks, Ginny starts dinner. Mary calls to say she's having dinner at Laura's house. I wonder if Ginny knows about Heavy Chevy Billy. I feel uneasy, vaguely responsible for her. What if she's in an accident tonight? Lily cautiously enters the kitchen, without parents, self-conscious and pleased when Ginny and I compliment her on her new dress. She tells us her mommy made it. "Your *mommy* made it?" Ginny says.

Lily nods.

"Christ really does work miracles," Ginny says.

Tory comes down. "Why didn't you wake me up?" she says.

"For what?"

"I don't know. What have you been doing?"

"Saying bad things about you," Ginny says. "Want a drink?"

I can tell Tory's looking her mother over to see how much she's had.

"I'll have a beer."

The phone rings again and Ginny grabs it. She says hello several times. Then she says, "I know it's you," and hangs up.

"Who?" Tory says.

"Who knows," Ginny responds.

Supper is chicken Kiev, cranberry muffins and asparagus. Carol and Jim take turns scolding Lily for her table manners. He seems very uncertain of his surroundings, and his discomfort makes me feel more at home. Although he has been here two days longer, I feel he's the outsider, the rude interloper. I hate his clothes and his mustache. I also hate the way he snaps at Lily. She's not even his kid. I wink at her across the table. Bunny announces she isn't going to eat anything and makes good on her threat, though she filled her plate to stop the argument. She's upset because her mother yelled at her about the phone calls. The news is on TV. A group in Boston is in front of a hospital, protesting abortion.

"Jim and I belong to a right-to-life group back home," Carol says.

"A woman should have the right to do whatever she wants with her body," Bunny says.

"No one has the right to murder the unborn."

I find it annoying how everyone bandies around the concept of *rights.*

"It would be nice," Bunny says, "if you people were as concerned with living women as you are with fetuses."

"Murder," Carol says. "That's what you're talking about."

"Is this dinner-table conversation?" Ginny asks.

Tory stands up and excuses herself, then leaves the room.

"That was lovely, girls," Ginny says. "Tory's going into the hospital on Monday."

"Excuse me," I say. "I'll go see if she's all right."

Tory's in her room, lying facedown on the bed. I sit beside her and stroke her hair. "It's going to be all right."

She flips over to face me. "All right for you. You don't want children. You're glad about all of this."

"That's not fair."

"I wouldn't even be having these problems if it weren't for you. I'd be a mother already if it weren't for you."

"We weren't ready yet. It would've been a mistake."

"Carol is right. It's murder."

"You don't believe that."

Carol's inside the room before she knocks on the open door, then stands right beside the bed. "I don't mean to barge in," she says. "But I thought maybe I could be of help." She lowers her ponderous form onto the mattress. "None of us is strong enough to bear his burden alone."

"All of us," Tory says, "are strong enough to bear the misfortunes of others."

"Jesus wants to lighten your load. All you have to do is ask." Carol stretches out her hand to Tory, who examines it and its owner with mild distaste. "Do you love Jesus, Tory?"

"Do I look like a necrophiliac to you?"

I expect Carol to be shocked, but her smile is indelible. "You can run from Jesus, but you can't hide."

Tory says, "But can you get a restraining order, is what I want to know."

The evening passes in the kitchen in front of the TV. The women are skilled at dividing their attention between the television and one another, so while never seeming to watch, they will suddenly comment on the action on the screen. The conversation has a casual, intimate rhythm. I listen from outside the circle, a privileged observer. I enjoy studying Tory on her home ground, and am eager to pick up the family lore. I feel a renewed interest, seeing her in this context. More than bone structure and habits of speech, I can see aspects of character I was never quite able to bring into focus suddenly illuminated and framed in their genetic setting. I feel like someone whose appreciation of an artist has been based on a single painting but who then is suddenly admitted to his studio.

My role of licensed connoisseur is compromised by the presence of Jim. Awkward and out of place, he butts into the conversation to ask who or what. He looks resentful, worried that a joke is being perpetrated at his expense. Mercifully, he heads up early after yawning pointedly at his wife.

She tells him she'll be up soon. Bunny is up and down. At one point she disappears for most of a sitcom. I find myself sharing Ginny's anger at the old bastard who's stealing her youth.

Ginny keeps saying how nice it is to have everyone home, until, with her fourth drink, she begins to foresee the end of the reunion and slips into sullenness. "Mary's been out every night since she got her license," she complains to Carol and Tory. "She's no company. She doesn't have time to sit down with her old mom. She's always coming or going, and everything's a big secret. She doesn't tell me anything. And then Bunny. She hates me because I don't want her to throw her life away."

"She doesn't hate you," Tory says impatiently.

"Of course she doesn't," Carol says. "She *loves* you. We *all* love you."

Ginny looks at Carol through tears and says, "Spare me this indiscriminate love. The trouble with you religious types is that you're promiscuous. Love, love, love. But then, you always *were* a cheap date."

"Stop it," Tory says. "That's no way to talk to your daughter."

"That's all right, Tory," Carol says. "I understand Mom's anger."

"No, you don't," Ginny says, slapping her palm down on the table. "You can't begin to understand my anger."

I feel I should leave, but right now that would only make my presence more blatant.

"Between your sloppy L-U-V and Tory's Ice Queen judgment, I'm dying for a little daughterly affection." She shakes her head. "What a brood. And Bunny. As if I need to be reminded about old letches and young bimbos."

Ginny lights a cigarette. "And where the hell is Mary? She's supposed to be in at eleven o'clock." We all turn to the clock above the range: It reads 10:40. "All right," Ginny says, "so she's got twenty minutes." They all laugh at the same moment, like synchronized swimmers executing an abrupt, graceful maneuver, their anger dispersed.

"Do you think she's still a virgin?" Ginny asks suddenly.

"Of course she is," Tory says.

"Mary's a sensible girl," Carol says. "She's not going to let herself be talked into anything."

I remember Tory told me that Carol had her first abortion when she was fifteen.

"She's only sixteen," Tory says.

"She's so cute," Carol says.

"She is," Ginny says.

Tory turns to me and says, "Isn't she a cutie?"

I could get very inspired on this subject. Instead, I just say, "She sure is."

Carol says, "Remember that time she stuck the key in the electrical socket?"

At eleven o'clock, Tory announces she's tired. "You don't have to come to bed yet," she says to me. I would like to stay up with the others, to sit quietly and listen to three women talk, but I say I'll go up with her. Ginny lets us share a room. Everyone kisses good night. Bunny, who has come back down, presses close enough for me to feel her breasts as she kisses me. Carol's breath smells chemically sweetened. Ginny folds me in a long motherly hug. She says she's going up, too.

After she takes off her shirt, Tory points to the small protuberance on her left side. It is the size of a BB, only slightly darker than the surrounding skin. "Do you know that this would have been enough evidence to convict me of witchcraft in the seventeenth century?" she says.

I do know, because she has told me several times, but I say, "Really?"

"It's what they call an 'auxiliary nipple.' A devil's teat. Proof that I've been suckling demons."

"Rules of evidence have advanced a little since then," I say cheerfully.

"Wouldn't it be strange if in former lives you were a prosecutor at the witch trials and I was a witch?"

"I'm on your side, Tory," I say, putting my arms around her. As her face disappears against my chest, I see that she is looking not at me but at some region inside herself. "Everything will be all right," I say. I can still see the sadness in her eyes and mouth. "We'll have children together." Maybe I say it because I want to sleep with her sisters and I feel guilty about it, or because she thinks that, like her father, I'll leave and I'm afraid she's right.

Lying there after Tory has fallen asleep, I conjure up the image of Bunny and Tory sleeping side by side on this same bed, and think about how I felt then, how I wanted to crawl between them and have both. What I really imagined, seeing these two women who look so much alike, was a single woman who was Tory leavened with Bunny's careless grace. As I drift toward sleep, I superimpose Mary's face, which in the liquor-store parking lot seemed fearless and flushed with sexual anticipation, and to that I add Carol's womb. Then I see Ginny alone in the bed in which the four of them had been conceived. And I think of my own mother, who is dead, and my father, whom I haven't seen in eight months, and imagine myself as a pinprick of life, floating whole in the dark, before all of these divisions and divorces and separations.

1986

Putting Daisy Down

Life was good. It was one of those April mornings when the warmth of the sun on your skin seems miraculous after the deep freeze of winter and you can almost feel the hair on your arms turning golden, the vivid physicality heightened by the lingering trace of a hangover. Bryce was two over par and he'd just hit the green on thirteen with his six iron. The supernaturally verdant fairway was fringed with cheerful yellow forsythia, some of which concealed the ball Tom McGinty had just hooked with his five wood.

Bryce was playing with the big boys—Tom, Bruce Pickwell and Jeff Weiss. That night, at the club dance, they would share a table with their wives, and after dinner Bryce would be officially welcomed as a member of the club, something he'd been working toward for the past two years.

"What the hell?" Tom said, shading his eyes, looking back down the fairway at the cart barreling toward them.

Bruce removed his finger from his nose and crossed his arms over his chest, girding for confrontation. "Looks like—"

"My wife," Bryce said as the cart bounced ever closer, the baked skin on his arms tingling with a sudden chill. Even from a distance there was something in her posture, and the speed she was traveling, that spelled trouble.

"Carly," Tom said. "To what do we owe the pleasure?"

Ignoring the greeting, she jumped out of the cart and marched over to Bryce, holding a lavender envelope in one hand, the other clutching her swelling belly, just visible beneath her pink warm-up suit. Glaring at him, she held the envelope at arm's length, between thumb and forefinger, until he took it from her. Her stony visage told the story, even if he hadn't recognized the stationery and the handwriting, the ropy loops spelling out his wife's name and their home address.

Without a word, she turned and drove away. The men watched silently until the cart finally disappeared behind the rise of the thirteenth tee, and then resumed their play, Bryce's partners respectfully somber, their fraternal compassion compounded in equal parts of selfish relief and empathetic dread. Their goodwill seemed only to increase as his game fell apart.

"That's a bitch," Jeff said, patting his back, when Bryce missed a three-footer for par on fourteen.

Bryce drove to Julie's apartment on the Upper West Side directly from the course. He was fond of her, and might even have convinced himself he loved her at one point, but she'd just committed an unpardonable offense, and for the first time in months, underneath the anger swelling into rage as he raced down the Henry Hudson Parkway, he felt a welcome sense of moral clarity. His righteousness was only bolstered by the miraculous parking space a few spots down from the entrance to her building on Ninety-sixth Street. He couldn't believe she would actually write a letter to his wife. Was she out of her mind? he wondered as he held down the buzzer for 4F.

Her voice over the intercom sounded tentative. "Who is it?"

"It's me," he said, his hand clutching the doorknob.

"Come on up," she said in what seemed to him a false singsongy tone, buzzing him in.

Julie could see that her gambit had backfired as soon as she opened the door. He ignored Cocoa, her longhaired dachshund, who swirled affectionately around his ankles.

"How dare you?" he said.

She claimed that she'd done it as much for him as for herself, that she knew he wasn't happy with the status quo.

"*I* was perfectly happy with the status quo," he said, no longer needing to maintain the fiction that he was trapped in his marriage and desperate to be with his mistress. He no longer had to pretend that only fear of his wife's unpredictable behavior and compassion for her precarious emotional state kept him from leaving her. Not that Carly couldn't be unpredictable and volatile, but he'd never really intended to leave her. He could see that clearly now. He was about to have a baby with her.

"But you said—"

"I said a lot of shit. I said what you wanted to hear."

It had been more than this, of course; but she had broken the rules, had violated the sanctity of his marriage, and now he wanted to hurt her.

She appealed for compassion and forgiveness, but all her justifications and her tears failed to move him. Her mascara ran, collecting in the little wrinkles and crow's-feet around her eyes, lines that he'd never noticed before. Looking away from her, he was confronted with the evidence of his folly, framed pictures of the two of them—in front of the Rodin Museum in Paris, on the beach in Montauk and in this very apartment, standing amid the bronze Buddhas, ceramic dragons, hexagonal shards of quartz and amethyst. Incense was burning in a little bronze urn on the coffee table. Julie was a believer in meditation, pyramids and crystals, whereas Bryce was feeling very Catholic at this moment. With all the zeal of a newly reformed sinner, he rejected her pleas for forgiveness. Strangely, he felt most sorry for Cocoa, who couldn't possibly understand why his old friend was giving him the cold shoulder. He was genuinely moved by the dog's doleful expression.

His confidence and his clarity ebbed as he approached his own driveway. If only Carly were the screaming and crying type, he might be able to imagine an eventual diminution of the crisis. But as it was, he had no idea what to expect.

Daisy greeted him at the door, rubbing her head against his shin. He crouched down and rubbed her head, scratched behind her ears. Daisy thrummed with appreciation and followed him as he reconnoitered the first floor. Carly was sitting in the sunroom, looking out over the back lawn. The fact that she was neither reading nor knitting didn't seem like a good sign.

He knelt down before her, took her hand in his, and laid his head on her rounded belly. "I don't know what to say—except that it's over. I'm so sorry." As he waited for a response, his head on her taut tummy, he felt Daisy massaging herself on his calf.

"This can't go on," she said.

"It's done," he said.

"She's got to go."

"I've taken care of it."

"I can't have this in the house."

"It was never in the—"

"Not in my condition."

Confused now, he looked up at her, at the lips drawn so thin and tight across her face that it was hard to believe they'd ever kissed his, and then followed her gaze down to the floor, to the dead robin on the carpet.

He could hardly contain his relief as he jumped to his feet, ready to deal with this discrete and tangible problem. He'd picked up dozens of dead birds in his long association with Daisy, whom he'd discovered as a kitten in the garbage room of his building on Ninth Street seven or eight years ago, when he was living in his first apartment in the city. It was the work of a moment to pick up the robin by its tail feathers, swing open the French door and fling the thing out into the yard.

Turning back to his wife, he found her regarding him with a distaste bordering on horror. "You picked it up with your bare hands," she said.

"I can wash them."

"I can't believe you picked it up with your bare hands. Don't imagine for a minute you're going to touch me with those hands."

"I was just about to—"

"I can't have this. I simply can't. I won't live with this."

"She's just being a cat."

"It's unsanitary. It's a health risk for the baby."

"After I wash my hands, I'll shampoo the rug."

"That won't help," she sobbed, lifting her hands to her face. "It's not enough."

"What do you want me to do?" he asked.

"It's your cat," she said. "You figure it out." She lifted herself from the couch with that new, slightly labored motion he had noticed of late, an exaggerated series of pushes and lifts whereby she seemed to be anticipating a larger and more pregnant future, cradling her tummy to support it, although in this case the gesture seemed not only protective but also defensive, as if he constituted a possible threat to the fetus.

———

The guys in his foursome didn't seem surprised by Carly's absence from the club that night, although they eagerly corroborated the alibi.

"You remember that first trimester, honey."

"Kate was puking like a freshman pledge."

"Don't remind me."

"Actually," Bruce's wife said, "I was lucky that way."

"Still," Bruce said, "it wasn't like you felt like going out every night and painting the town."

"Speaking of which," Jeff said, "let's get another round here."

The windows of the master bedroom were dark when he pulled into the driveway. He congratulated himself on his stealth and silence when he stepped into the guest room, which is where he awoke the next morning, on top of the duvet, fully dressed. A baby bird was lying on his chest, Daisy sitting beside him on the bed, the proud huntress.

"Oh shit," he said. He'd almost forgotten this hazard of the suburban springtime—the baby bird menace. Even with arthritis, she could still catch the fledglings. In his muddled state, he couldn't quite separate out the different components of the guilt that was oppressing him—about the affair, about Daisy's murderous habits, about having overindulged the previous night. Had he come on to anyone at the club? No, not really; he was clean on that score.

Bryce flushed the bird down the guest room's toilet, wondering if he hadn't closed the door the night before, or if Carly had opened it that morning. He showered in the guest bath and crept down the hall to their bedroom, where he fortified himself with four Advil and two Zantac, then dressed and girded himself for the inevitable confrontation.

She was sitting at the kitchen table, reading the paper.

"Good morning," he said, sitting down across from her.

She stood up from the table, cradling her belly, and busied herself at the sink.

"You always try to sound bright and chipper when you're hungover. As if that will somehow fool me."

He didn't feel quite bright and chipper enough to think of a response to this. On the other hand, he was happy to keep the focus on the lesser sin of drinking. "Kate and Serena send their love," he said.

"That's ridiculous," she said. "They don't even know me."

"You met them at the Winter Frolic," he said.

"The Winter *Frolic*."

"Well, anyway." It *was* a little weird, how everything at the country club sounded like high school. A few years ago, when he still lived in the city, he would've sneered at the previous night's event. The term *Winter Frolic* would have been a source of mirth. Everything about it would have aroused his urban cynicism.

"And I suppose last night was called the Spring *Fling*."

He was about to refute this charge before realizing he couldn't.

"Rather appropriately for you," she said.

He went to the refrigerator in search of liquids.

It hadn't been his idea to move out of the city. At least not entirely. He'd been happy enough in the one-bedroom on Columbus. But Carly began complaining about the friction of urban life. First it was the dry cleaner's losing her Marc Jacobs top. Then the guy in the wine store who kept hitting on her, which was totally plausible—she was a beautiful woman, after all. Plus the garbage trucks at three in the morning and the homeless guy who followed her in the park. After the planes had crashed into the towers, she'd had nightmares for months. Wasn't that the sequence of events that had led to their finding themselves in the suburbs? The idea had already been raised before that day, inextricably related to the decision to have children. They would have needed to find a bigger place in the city anyway, as she'd pointed out. No, it definitely hadn't been his idea. But he had wanted to alleviate the anxiety and dissatisfaction that seemed to have taken hold of her even before that terrible day in September.

Somehow, three years before, they'd both believed that marriage would be the cure for a malaise they'd never named or spoken about, for the dark moods that descended upon her and the memories of childhood deprivations—most particularly her vanished father. Later, it seemed that graduate school would be just the thing. Moving to the suburbs was, as he saw it, the latest attempt to make her happy. If he hadn't discovered golf, he would have hated it out here, almost an hour from Grand Central. The pleasure he discovered in the game raised his tolerance for certain cultural clichés, although he maintained enough of his urban-hipster sensibility to forswear the kind of brown-and-white footwear that looked like saddle shoes, as well as certain shades of pink and green. And he was probably the only guy at the club with a Celtic cross tattooed on his left shoulder. And what would they think if they knew about Carly's tattoo? Even he had been a little shocked when she first proposed it.

Much as he would have loved to escape to the green refuge of the course that morning, he knew he had to cancel his game. The problem then became how to get through the rest of the day without a confrontation.

Carly went to the stove and returned with a plate, which she dropped on the place mat in front of him. "Your breakfast," she said.

On the plate were two raw eggs, two strips of raw bacon and two pieces of white bread.

A chilly truce prevailed through the afternoon. He trimmed the box-woods, something he'd been promising to do for two weeks, and later took her to the Barnes & Noble at the mall, where she picked up a book called *Taking Charge of Your Pregnancy.*

That night, they sat in the den together and watched *The Sopranos* and then *The Tudors,* a ritual that suddenly seemed fraught with peril. Carly tended to take her movies and TV shows very personally, to generalize the behavior of individual characters. As a married man, Bryce didn't want to be represented by Tony Soprano and Henry VIII. When Tony had been sleeping with the Russian babe back in season three, Bryce somehow got blamed for Tony's behavior. "You guys are just slaves to your dicks," she said. And, yes, okay, he'd been guilty as charged back then. Fortunately, Tony wasn't screwing anyone this week, although, astonishingly, he killed his nephew Christopher.

"I can't believe he did that," Bryce said. "I mean, how could he do that?"

"He was a hopeless drug addict," Carly said.

"Well, yeah, but still."

"Not to mention a cold-blooded killer."

"I guess."

Bryce was comfortable dealing with the major crimes and mortal sins of others. He tried to remember whether adultery was a mortal sin. *Thou shalt not covet thy neighbor's wife.* It didn't seem like it should be right up there with murder. Carly didn't have much to say about Tony's latest offense, but she pitched a fit when Daisy jumped up on Bryce's lap. "Get her away from me!" Under normal circumstances, Bryce might've stuck up for his cat, but tonight he put her outside without protest.

Shortly after Anne Boleyn professed to be insulted by Henry's offer to make her his one and only royal squeeze, Carly said she was going to the kitchen to get a snack. Bryce said he'd see her upstairs.

He raced through his ablutions in the master bath and managed to slip between the sheets and pick up his book before she ascended the stairs. For a moment, as she paused in the bedroom doorway, he was certain she would challenge his presence there, but when he finally allowed himself to look up from his book, she was standing in front of the mirror, rubbing her belly and observing her reflected image, as if trying to verify and fathom the great mystery of her condition.

Ten minutes later she climbed ponderously into the bed beside him. "I can't have Daisy dragging mice and birds all through the house in my condition," she said.

"She's a cat," he said. "That's what cats do."

"I can't have it."

"Maybe we can keep her inside for the next few months."

"No," she said. "She has to go."

"Go?"

"I'm having a baby, in case you haven't noticed."

"You want me to give her away? She's been with me for ten years."

"She's had a good life. You said yourself she's getting old. Didn't the vet just tell you she had arthritis?"

"You want me to put her down?" He could hardly believe it. But when he looked over at her, her face had a hard glaze of implacability, with which he was all too familiar.

"I don't think this is too much to ask when I'm carrying your child."

"Maybe I could find a home for her."

"If you can't do this one thing for me, after what you've put me through . . ."

Seeing the tears welling in her eyes, he realized she was serious and he understood that it would not be enough to find another home for Daisy. "Don't cry," he said, sliding across the bed to take her in his arms. She tried to pull away, but eventually she buried her head in his shoulder, sobbing inconsolably.

He could have tried to find a home for her—that was what haunted him later. But he was genuinely sorry for his betrayal and felt bound to honor Carly's wish, cruel and unnecessary though it seemed to him. This, apparently, was the price of his transgression.

He postponed it a few days in the hopes that Carly might soften, but he could feel the tension whenever Daisy entered the room, and then again at bedtime. After he found a baby chipmunk in the hallway, he called and made an appointment for the following day.

He gave his name to Susanna, the vet's receptionist, a freckled blonde, whose normally bouncy manner was appropriately subdued on this occasion; it was she who'd given Bryce the appointment after he'd explained its purpose.

Despite his previous diagnosis of arthritis, the vet was somewhat reluctant. "We've been getting good results with glucosamine," he said. "Unless you think she's been suffering."

"I really think it would be best," Bryce said.

Given the choice, he opted to stay with Daisy and hold her to the end. The vet shaved a patch of fur on her foreleg before injecting her. Bryce would never forget the way she looked at him as the vet inserted the needle into her vein. She hissed in protest and tried to squirm out of his grasp, as if she knew what was about to happen. It was over in seconds. Daisy relaxed in his arms as the light faded from her eyes. He felt her exhale and then she was suddenly heavier in his arms.

The vet excused himself and told Bryce he'd give him time to regain his composure.

A few minutes later, Susanna came in, opening the door gingerly and tiptoeing forward. "I know how hard it is," she said, placing a hand on his cheek and wiping the tears away. "I went through it myself last year."

———

That night, Carly made love to him for the first time in weeks. As bad as he felt about Daisy, he believed that he had atoned for his transgression and righted the imbalance between them. After all that had happened, they were tentative and tender with each other, and he woke up the next morning feeling as if they had weathered their crisis. He was certain that with time he would forget about the grim transaction. But in fact, as Carly grew larger with their baby, his sense of injustice and of guilt about his own cowardly acquiescence seemed to intensify. Sometimes when they were watching television and she would rub his hand over her belly, he would wonder why he couldn't have found a home for Daisy, why Carly'd been so brutal as to close off that option. What kind of a person was he married to? Hell, he could have asked Julie to take the cat. His anger toward her had faded in recent weeks, and he had to resist the urge to call.

For years, even before she was pregnant and had the excuse of hormones, Bryce had lived in fear of his wife's dark moods, but now he found himself losing patience with her complaints and her piques. "Jesus Christ, you'd think you were the first person to have a baby," he snapped one day after she moaned yet again about her swollen ankles.

He waited until after the baby was born to call Susanna, from the vet's office, who'd given him her number that day.

2007

The Business

I'd heard all the jokes before I moved out here. But still, you think Hollywood will be different for you. You say to yourself, Sure it's a jungle, but I'm Dr. Livingstone.

I graduated from Columbia with a degree in English lit and went to work for a newspaper in Bergen County, just across the river from Manhattan, keeping my cheap apartment on West 111th Street, where I lived with my girlfriend. My thesis was a poststructuralist analysis of film adaptations of major American novels, and within a year I'd wangled the job of movie reviewer and entertainment reporter. I love the movies, always have. The idea of being a screenwriter came to me during a group interview with a writer-director who was in Manhattan flacking for his new picture. It wasn't the fact that he didn't seem particularly bright, or that he made his ascent sound so haphazard and effortless, but something more visceral—the way he looked sitting there smoking a cigarette with the light coming through the window of the fortieth-floor corporate tower. I could see the pores in his skin and the stubble of his beard, and there was something green stuck between two of his teeth. And I suddenly thought, That could be me sitting there with two days' growth and a green thing on my teeth.

I didn't quit my job that day or anything, but I did start writing screenplays, renting films I loved and studying their structure, thinking about what they had in common. I was abetted in this by my aunt Alexis, who once had been a contract player at Paramount. She'd been in a couple of Westerns with John Wayne and was briefly married to a director. After the divorce she moved to New York; the director had made her quit the movies, she said, and it was too late to go back, but she still talked as if she were a member of a warm extended family called "the business." She claimed as friends some relatively famous folks, and she read *Variety* and the *Hollywood Reporter* faithfully. I knew from our actual family that she'd been somewhat badly used out there, but she wasn't bitter. Now she gave acting lessons and occasionally did community theater. When I moved to New York, she more or less adopted me. My parents were divorced, receding into the orange sunsets of Arizona and Florida, respectively.

Alexis lived in faded elegance in a grand prewar building over near Sutton Place, a duplex she'd occupied for years, the first couple with her third husband, and which she couldn't have afforded if not for rent control. Even with a severely depressed rent, she'd had to sublet the more luxurious lower floor, which was separated by two doors from her own quarters upstairs. The centerpiece of the downstairs apartment was a spectacular canopy bed replete with rose-colored chintz drapery. Alexis herself slept in the upstairs parlor on a pullout sofa. The lower floor was occupied by the manager of a rock group, who was burning holes in all the upholstery. Alexis knew because she sneaked down and snooped around whenever he wasn't home.

Alexis encouraged my screenwriting ambitions and read my earliest attempts. She also provided the only good advice I've ever gotten on the subject. "Dalton Trumbo once told me the secret of a screenplay," she said, mixing herself a Negroni in the closet that served her as kitchen, pantry and bar. At six in the evening the dying light was slicing through the mullioned windows at a forty-five-degree angle—that second-to-last light thick and yellow with doomed bravado—and making the dust swimming through the apartment seem like movie mist. "He was a lovely man, much misunderstood. That McCarthy stuff—terrible. But as I was starting to say, Dalton said to me one night—I think we were at the Selznicks'—and I said, 'Dalton, what's your secret?' and he whispered something in my ear, which I won't repeat. I gave him a little slap on the wrist, not that I really minded. I was flattered and told him so, but I was still married to the fag—before I found out, of course. So I said to Dalton, 'No, no, what's the secret of a great *screenplay*?' And he said, 'It's very simple, Lex. Three acts: first act, get man up tree; second act, shake a stick at him; third act, get him down.' "

When she was really in her cups, Alexis told me she'd call Swifty Lazar or some other great friend of hers and fix me up, the exquisitely carved syllables of her trained speech softening, liquefying like the cubes in her glass. But the fact is, she didn't have any juice in the industry. I didn't mind. I eventually landed an agent on my own, at which point I figured it was time to make the leap of faith. Plus, my girlfriend announced that she was in love with my best friend and that they'd been sleeping together for six months.

I sublet my apartment and rented a place in Venice, three blocks from the beach. This was in February, and I loved exchanging the frozen, crusty city for a place smelling of flowers and the ocean. At the same time, more than anywhere else in Southern California, Venice reminded me of New York, with its general shabbiness. There were plenty of bums, just so I wouldn't get too homesick, and the crime rate was also pretty impressive. But basically I felt the same way about California that Keats did about Chapman's Homer. I quit smoking, ate plenty of fruit and vegetables, started sleeping regular hours.

One thing I didn't do was rush out to join AA, which was just then becoming really hip. If I had, I probably would've met some girls. But I was still under the thrall of the writer-as-holy-lush idea. Who could imagine Raymond Chandler sober? One of my favorite stories involved Joseph Mankiewicz, the other genius behind *Citizen Kane,* who arrived drunk one night—not uncharacteristically—at an elaborate A-list dinner party. He then got drunker, and finally evacuated the contents of his stomach all over the table. As the other guests looked on, horrified, Mankiewicz turned to his hostess and said, "Don't worry—the white wine came up with the fish."

In Venice, my second-story studio had a little terrace off the back. I'd wake up early most mornings and take my computer out there, overlooking a tiny courtyard choked with cacti, palms and flowering bushes. Having grown up in the intemperate zones, I'm still a little thrilled by the sight of a palm tree. My landlady believed that nature should be allowed to take its course and she just let it all grow. The couple across the way believed in nature, too; they fucked at all hours with the shades up, and I couldn't help seeing them, usually her bobbing up and down on top of him, facing me. I guess she was performing. Maybe she thought I was a casting director. . . . Anyway, I appreciated it, since that was as close as I was getting to carnal knowledge.

My second screenplay opens with this very long scene, close on couple making love, girl on top, camera pulling back out the window, reverse angle on the guy watching from his terrace. Eventually, the girl and the guy on the terrace—a writer, of course—meet and have this incredible affair. She decides to leave her boyfriend, but of course he turns out to be a coke dealer involved with some very heavy Colombians, and the girl knows enough about the gang to implicate them in a murder. Except she doesn't realize it until . . .

Believe it or not, this screenplay attracted the interest of a fairly important producer. That was when I first met Danny Brode. The producer had a first-look deal with the studio where Brode was the new vice president of production. The meeting Brode scheduled for me was my first with a studio executive. I spent about three hours that morning trying to figure out what to wear and whether to shave. Finally I shaved and put on a white shirt, tie, blazer and jeans. Brode made me wait an hour, and when I was ushered into his dazzling white office, he shook my hand and said, "What, you got a funeral or a wedding today?" When I looked baffled, he said, "The tie, dude." So I knew I'd worn the wrong thing, and knew he knew I'd worn the tie for him.

Brode was wearing jeans and a work shirt that barely held him in. Standing about five six, the man weighed three hundred if he weighed an ounce. He had D-cup cheeks, and his chin would've made another man's potbelly. Not exactly the guy to be handing out advice on appearances. Anyway, he told me he'd been running late all day and had to drive out to the Valley to check on a film in postproduction, and asked if we could take the meeting in his car.

We went out to the parking lot and got in his car, which was this four-door Maserati sedan. I didn't even know Maserati made sedans, but I figured Brode was too big to drive around in one of the sports models. On the drive out to the Valley, he spent most of the time on his car phone, but in between he listened as I pitched like crazy. Finally he said, "Instead of a writer, how about if this guy's an artist? We move the thing from Venice to San Francisco, and he's got a humongous studio filled with canvases— and right out the window he sees the couple screwing. The art thing's very hot right now, and this way we'll get a lot more visuals." I don't know, I probably would've made him into a female impersonator. I was dying to get into the game, my savings were exhausted, my Subaru needed new brakes and I had yet to meet a girl who wanted to go out to dinner with an unemployed screenwriter. My ex–best friend had just written to say he and my ex-girlfriend were getting married and that he hoped I didn't have any hard feelings. After pretending to think deeply about Brode's suggestion for a minute, I said, "I like it. I think I could make it work."

He dropped me at the gate of the soundstage and gave me a business card from a car service. "We'll work it out with your agent." I stood around baking in the sun for an hour before the car finally came to take me back to the studio. That night I bought a bottle of Spanish bubbly, which I knocked back on the terrace while my neighbors traded orgasms.

I called Alexis in New York, and she told me that I was part of the big family. We talked for an hour, and for once I believe I matched her drink for drink. Then I thought about calling my old girlfriend, imagining her chagrin when she realized what she'd given up, but passed out instead.

"Martin, babe, I'm going to make you a rich man," my agent told me a week later. She'd grown up on Long Island and had been out here only a couple years, but she talked just like something out of *What Makes Sammy Run?* They must give you a copy at LAX or something, I don't know why I never got mine.

The deal was two drafts, plus revisions at scale, which, if not a fortune, was more money than I'd made in a year at the newspaper. And I was thrilled to have a foot in the door. "Danny Brode's really big," my agent said without a trace of irony. "That man is going places, and he can take you with him."

"I don't feel like going to the fat farm," I said.

"You better start watching your mouth around this town," my agent said. "It's a small community, and if you want to be part of it, you've got to play by the rules. Bill Goldman and Bob Towne can afford to be smartasses, but you can't."

"Could you send me a list of these rules?" I was so happy, I couldn't help being full of myself. The next week she took me to lunch at Spago and introduced me to several people she described as "important players," calling me "Martin Brooks, the writer."

Then I started writing the draft that would transform my hero into a painter. I flew up to San Francisco for atmosphere, talked to gallery owners and artists. Just dropping the studio's name opened doors, and I implied that a major star was interested in the lead. Back home I was able to get an interview with an LAPD narcotics detective, who filled me in on the inner workings of the drug cartels.

Ten weeks after the papers were signed, I handed in my new draft. The next day I got a FedEx package with Danny Brode's card attached to a bottle of Cristal. Only his name—no title, studio, address or phone number—was printed on the card. *Danny Brode.* No need to wear a tie around here. Anyway, drinking that bottle of Cristal was the high point of the whole experience.

The hangover set in a couple weeks later, when my agent called. "Basically they're thrilled with the script. Ecstatic. But they want to talk to you about a couple of little changes."

"No problem," I said. "We're contracted for two drafts, right? I mean, I make another ten grand or so for a rewrite."

"Don't worry your genius brain about it. Just take the meeting and we'll see what they want."

What they wanted was a completely different story. Having fallen in love with his idea of the art-world backdrop, Brode now wanted a movie about how commerce corrupts artists. Columbia had an art project in development, and he was determined to beat its release. We could keep the drug element—the big-shot gallery owner was also involved in the coke trade. I sat in Brode's huge white office, trying to figure out where the white walls ended and the white leather furniture began, trying to see the virtues of this new story and to recognize some shred of my own script.

Nodding like an idiot, I practically called him a genius and said I didn't know why I hadn't seen all this potential in the first place. Back home, though, I called my agent and screamed at her about the stupidity of studio executives and the way art was corrupted by commerce. She listened patiently. Finally I concluded, "Well, at least I get paid to be a whore."

She said, "Try to pick out the virtues in his concept. I'll work on the money."

"What do you mean, 'work on the money'? It's in the contract."

"Of course," she said.

I sat down again and tried to be professional about the whole thing, which is to say I tried not to give a shit. Three weeks later I delivered the new draft. I'd just bought a new car, a little Beamer, with my first check. When my agent called one morning to talk about another project, I said, "When do I get paid for my second draft?"

"We're calling that a polish instead of a draft."

"A *polish*? It was a *whole new story,* however stupid. I knocked myself out. Are you trying to tell me I'm not getting paid? What about the contract?"

"Look, Martin, you're new at this. Brode says it's a polish, and he wants you to do one more polish before he shows it to the head of production."

I was beginning to understand. "You mean I get paid for a second draft, but it's not a draft unless Brode says it is."

"Let's just say it behooves us to give Danny Brode some slack at this point. You don't want to get known as a difficult writer. Give him one more polish and I promise you it'll be worth your while in the long run."

When I threatened to go to the Writers Guild, she said she'd hate to end our professional relationship.

Maybe you've heard the one about the devil who goes to the agent and says, "I'll give you any client you want—Cruise, Costner, Pacino, you name it—in exchange for your immortal soul for all eternity." And the agent says, "What's the catch?"

I stopped trusting my agent from that moment on, but I followed her advice. I wrote three drafts, got paid for one, and the project was in turnaround within six months. Though I didn't see Brode for a couple of years, in a sense my agent was right. I was bankable because I'd had a deal, and that led to other deals, and within a couple years I had my first movie in production and moved into a house in Benedict Canyon. And whenever I needed a villain for a story, someone rich and powerful to harass the protagonists, I had vivid impressions to draw on.

Danny Brode became even more rich and powerful. He married into a Hollywood dynasty and shortly thereafter was running the studio his in-laws controlled. Consolidation of power through marriage was established procedure in this particular family. Brode's father-in-law was supposed to be affiliated with a major crime family. In the film community it was whispered that in a premarital conference Brode had been made to understand cheating on his wife would constitute his precipitous fall from grace. This was considered slightly bizarre, since everybody fucked around in proportion to their power and wealth, most of all people who owned studios and casinos. But the old boy was apparently overfond of his first daughter.

"Some nice Faustian elements in this situation," I said to the lunch partner who first filled me in on this story. I once heard someone say there are only seven basic stories, but in this business there's only one. In Hollywood the story is always Faust.

"Some nice what?" he said.

I smiled. "I was just thinking of an old German film."

Brode got even fatter. In a town where everybody had a personal trainer and green salads were considered a main course, there was something almost heroic about his obesity. From time to time I would see him at Morton's or wherever, and after a while—once CAA took over my representation, for example, and I started dating actresses—he even began to recognize me. I heard stories. My first agent was right—the bitch. It's a small town.

One of the stories I heard was about a novelist I knew from Columbia. After his first novel made him famous, he star-tripped out here to soak up some of the gravy. Success came on him pretty fast, and he ran so fast to keep up with it that he got out in front of it. He bought a million-dollar co-op on Central Park West and a beach house in Maine, plus he had a little coke problem. He'd sold his book to Brode's studio outright, which is to say he got paid the same no matter whether it went into production or not. By the time the second payment was due, this writer was pretty desperate for money—he was overdue on both his mortgages, his girlfriend had an insatiable wardrobe and his wife was socking him for a big settlement. Brode knew about this. So when it came time to pay off, he called the writer up to his house in Malibu and said, "Look, I owe you a quarter mil, but at this point I don't know if we're going to go into production. Things are tight and your stock's gone down. Let's just say either I could give you seventy-five and we could call it even or I could tie you up in court for the next ten years." The writer started screaming about the contract, his agency, the Writers Guild. And Brode said, "Talk to your agent. I think he'll see it my way."

Even in Hollywood, this is not standard procedure, but the writer's stock had dropped; after being hot for a season, he'd cooled off fast, and the agency, after a lot of thought, decided to go with Brode and advised the writer to take the seventy-five and shut up.

By the time I heard this story, I wasn't even surprised. I'd learned a lot in three years.

I was doing well by local standards, and that I found myself doing business with Brode again wasn't really surprising. Several production companies were tracking an idea of mine when Brode told my agency he wanted to work with me. CAA packaged a deal with me, a director and two stars for a story about—well, let's just say it was a story of betrayal and revenge. This was the one I'd been wanting to do from the beginning. "A Yuppie *The Postman Always Rings Twice*" was the one-liner devised by my agent. For a variety of reasons, some of them aesthetic, it was important to me that the movie be shot in New York. Brode wanted to do it in Toronto and send a second unit to New York for a day. Toronto was far cheaper, and thought to resemble Manhattan. I knew I couldn't change any producer's mind when two or three million dollars was at stake, so I worked on the director. A man with several commercially successful films behind him, he was dying to be an auteur. He couldn't understand how the kind of respect that Scorsese and Coppola got had thus far eluded him, so it wasn't hard to convince him that New York's critical fraternity would take his film much more seriously if it was *authentic;* that is to say, if it was shot in New York. You couldn't fake these things, I said, not even in the movies. You think Woody Allen would shoot a movie in Toronto, or that they'd publish him in *The New Yorker* if he did? Or consider Sidney Lumet, I reminded him.

That did it. Though Brode kicked and screamed, the director was adamant and very eloquent; besides, his clout far exceeded mine, commercially. In the end, after I'd handed in the third draft, they headed off to New York with long lines of credit and suitcases full of cash for the friendly local Teamsters.

I went along for preproduction, since the director'd decided he liked having me around; so long as I didn't ask for a consulting fee, the studio was happy to pay my expenses. Brode's assistant, a woman named Karen Levine, would be on location, while he would fly out once in a while to check in. Levine was so petite, blond and terribly efficient that at first I hardly noticed her. In Los Angeles one can become accustomed to thinking of beauty as something languid, sexiness as a quality that adheres only to the slow-moving, self-conscious forms of actresses and professional companions. And while Karen was no odalisque, I began noticing her more and more. Despite the legendary informality of Southern California—the indiscriminate use of first names, the gross overextension of the concept of friendship—it was unusual to encounter someone who could sail straight between the whirlpool of craven servility and the shoals of condescension. Karen did, and I liked her for it. That she was doing more than working for Brode had occurred to me, but my discreet inquiries suggested they were strictly business associates and that Brode was living up to the contract with his father-in-law.

Then I heard Karen say she was looking to rent an apartment for the three months of filming. I thought of Alexis, who had finally thrown the rock manager out, losing several thousand in the process. I figured the studio would pay a bloated-enough rent to make up some of what Hollywood had taken out of her in the old days. Alexis would be thrilled by her renewed proximity to "the business," and I liked the idea of doing Karen a favor.

We were both staying at the Sherry-Netherland, and one afternoon I walked Karen over to Sutton Place. She'd grown up in Pasadena and was a little nervous about Manhattan, so I wanted her to see the city at its best. On a cool day at the end of April, the air was crisp, swept clean by a light breeze. Across the street, the Plaza glowed white in the sun. The daffodils on Park Avenue were blooming in the center median, and the doormen stood guard at the entrances of the grand old buildings. Karen looked casually tremendous in an Irish sweater and jeans; I felt like a boy returning to his homeland after making good in the colonies.

Alexis greeted us in a flowing caftan, kissed Karen on both cheeks and ushered us into the upstairs parlor, where she'd laid out a tea service that would've done Claridge's proud. She then took us on a tour, pointing out pictures of herself with the Duke, and Bogie, a signed first edition from Faulkner, a set of candlesticks given to her by Red Skelton, the love seat on which she'd traded confidences (here she winked) with Errol Flynn. Some of this stuff even I hadn't heard before. She was laying it on a bit thick, but Karen seemed both attentive and relaxed. When we went downstairs, I knew Karen was hooked as soon as she saw the big canopy bed floating in the middle of the big paneled bedroom, wreathed in rose-colored chintz. Before Alexis had mixed her second Negroni—"I don't usually drink in the afternoon, but this is an occasion. Are you sure you won't have one?"—it was decided that Karen would move in for the three months and that Alexis would introduce her to the landlord as her niece; the rock manager had been her "nephew."

When we finally left at six, I asked Karen out to dinner. She said she had a lot of work to do but would love to some other night.

When shooting started, I hung around and visited the set every couple days. Brode flew in most weekends, which surprised me, though he seemed to be taking an excessive interest in the project. Each of his visits managed to make someone miserable. Three weeks into shooting, it was me. Having decided he didn't like the ending, he wanted an upbeat rewrite. I kicked and screamed about the integrity of the story. Then I tried to go through the director; but Brode had worked on him first, and he was impervious to my warnings about what *The New Yorker* would think of the new ending. Apparently, he was more concerned about his two points of the gross.

"It comes down to this, Martin," Brode said as he sawed into a veal chop one night at Elaine's. "You write the new ending or we hire somebody else. I'll give you another twenty-five, call it consulting." I watched him insert half a pound of calf's flesh into his maw, waiting for him to choke on it and die. It occurred to me that he was too fat for anybody to perform the Heimlich maneuver successfully, so I could say to the police officers, *Hey, sorry, I tried to get my arms around him, but no go.*

I rewrote the ending. For me, it ruined the movie, but the American public bought sixty million dollars' worth of tickets, a big gross at the time.

I visited Alexis frequently and used these occasions to knock on Karen's door. One night, she finally allowed me to take her to dinner. I told her what I'd never told anyone before, about how my ex–New York girlfriend ran off and married my best friend. Karen was appalled and sympathetic. By now she'd adopted the Manhattan uniform of nighttime femininity, looking very sexy in a small tight black dress. At her door we exchanged an encouraging kiss, but when it began to develop into something else, she pulled back and announced she had to be up at five.

A week or so later I went over to visit Alexis. As she was mixing the Negronis, she said, "Who's Karen's boyfriend anyway? I take it he's some big shot."

"I don't think she has a boyfriend," I said, somewhat alarmed.

"I can't understand how someone as pretty as Karen could let that fat man touch her."

I felt relieved. "That wasn't Karen's boyfriend; it was her boss."

Alexis snorted. "Call it what you want. I know all about girls and their bosses."

"It's not like that with Karen."

"Don't tell me what it's like," she said. "I have to listen to them. And now I have to buy a new bed."

"What're you talking about?"

She put a finger to her lips, walked over to open the stairway door and listened. Then she motioned for me to follow her down.

The canopy bed was wrecked. The box spring and mattress, which had previously floated a couple feet off the floor, were now earthbound, the bedposts and chintz draperies tangled and splayed.

"I've had bosses like that," Alexis said. "But thank God I never had that one. The poor girl's risking her life every time she climbs into bed with that whale."

Brode had flown back to the West Coast that morning, so I had a whole week to plot my strategy. I called a meeting as soon as he got back to town. The only time he could meet me was breakfast: the Regency, at seven-thirty.

When I arrived at eight, he was just finishing off a plate of ham and eggs. "I'm just leaving," he said. "What's up?"

"I have another movie. You might like this one."

"What's the pitch?" he said. "I've got exactly three minutes."

"It's a mob story."

"That turf's pretty well worked," he said.

"You'll like this one," I replied. "In my story, a young mobster's career takes off when he marries the don's daughter. But there's a catch: If he ever screws around, the don tells him, he'll be a piss-poor scuba diver, fifty feet under without oxygen. At first the son-in-law does very well. However, a young wise guy within the organization happens to live in the same building as this very attractive girl, and there's a farcical scene involving this broken bed. The broken bed leads to very dire consequences for some of the parties concerned."

Brode's face turned dark red as he listened. At the end of the pitch he looked into my eyes to see if he might've misheard me. Then he said, "What do you want?"

"I want another movie with you. Okay, maybe not this one, but something else. And I want to coproduce."

"I could have you . . ." He didn't finish.

And that's how I became a producer, on terms that were highly satisfactory from my point of view. I don't think Danny felt it was the best deal he'd ever made, and I knew I'd have to watch out for him. But the project I eventually developed made money for both of us, which made me feel a little safer when falling asleep at night.

A year after this breakfast, I flew back to New York for Alexis's funeral. One of ten mourners, I cried when they lowered her coffin into the ground out in the cemetery in Queens. The last time I remembered crying was on a day that should've been one of my happiest. I'd just gotten a call from an agent in Los Angeles who'd read my script and decided to represent me. I'd waited two hours for Lauren, my girlfriend, to come home from work. I'd bought flowers and Champagne and called everyone I knew. Finally, Lauren got home, and I almost knocked her over in my excitement. We'd talked about moving to California together if anything happened for me. I sprayed Champagne all over us and talked about our future in the promised land. "We can live near the beach," I said, following her into the bathroom, where she rubbed a pink towel back and forth across her dark hair. "We'll drive up to Big Sur on weekends." That was when she told me. One minute I've got Champagne streaming down my face, and tears the next. I thought about that as I listened to the words of the minister at the cemetery, and felt the wetness on my cheeks. I remembered that day years ago in a one-bedroom apartment on West 111th Street as being the last time I'd cried. Somehow, I don't think it will happen again.

1988

Penelope on the Pond

Sometimes it helps if I think about all the women in world history who've been in my position, of Anne Boleyn waiting for her Henry, or what's-her-name waiting for Odysseus to come back from the Trojan War. (I've been reading a lot since I've been here, in case you can't tell, browsing through these paperbacks mildewing on the bookshelves here in the cabin.) Sometimes it feels like I've been here forever. But some mornings I wake up with a dreamy feeling of being outside of time, of being able to wait as long as he needs me to. And I think that's one of the things he loves about me—his own time's so regulated and regimented and subdivided into little pieces, while I can just go with the flow. I try to get him to see that it's all an illusion anyway, that we all have to live in the moment, and not get too attached to outcomes, but for now he has to do what he has to do. It's his karma; I understand. I can wait. This morning I woke up and found myself in that still, gray moment right between night and morning. The sun hadn't showed through the trees yet, but the clearing around the pond was visible and a beaver was carving a V into the silver surface of the water, and I realized this phase of my existence is as fleeting as the beaver's wake.

Now it's almost eleven o'clock and I'm wondering where he is and what he's doing. I mean, I know he's at some grange hall in Iowa, according to the schedule, but I wish I had a constant video feed so I could see him and hear him all day long, like I used to when I was working with him. As for the nights, it doesn't take a genius to figure out what I wish for then. I still can't believe how good it is. How good it was, I should say, since I haven't seen him in almost three weeks.

I should take up knitting or something. What do you call it? Needlepoint. Knit him a scarf, or a hat, or a pillow with a slutty slogan. Give me something to do with my hands besides texting him and touching myself.

Last night I made myself come four times. I try to keep the texting to a minimum, though, 'cause it's risky. (The touching, on the other hand, is healthy.) And e-mail's out of the question. If I could, I'd send him naked pictures every few hours. But he calls me every day, sometimes more if he can slip away. And sometimes I get to see him on TV. Last week he was on *The View,* and he was so fucking cute, I almost died. I could tell the girls thought so, too, even that Republican blow-up doll Elisabeth Hasselbeck. She was ready to put her ideological differences aside, along with her panties. It's a good thing I'm not the jealous type. I love it when other women think he's hot. They're right: He is. If they only knew.

To clear my mind, I chant and meditate. Sometimes I get frustrated, though, being sidelined like this, not being able to share it with him and help him, or tell him who's totally full of shit and when he's full of shit himself. For three months we were together every day, and it was great. I was on staff as a "media consultant." Of course, we had to be careful. We had separate hotel rooms and all, and PDAs were strictly prohibited, but we still managed to steal time alone together. Like I said, we tried to play it really safe. But once in a while we just couldn't help risking it all—the quickie out behind the restaurant in Des Moines, the blow job in the back-seat of the taxi in D.C. I know it's crazy, but when the stakes are that high, the sex is unbelievable. Anybody who's ever been married can tell you what happens to the thrills when there's no risk.

It was one of those love-at-first-sight things. We locked eyes at a restaurant in New York. I thought he was incredibly good-looking and I could tell from the way people were fussing and coming over to his table that he was a big deal, but honestly, I didn't recognize him. Even so, looking into his eyes convinced me. It was only after I'd been picturing him naked for twenty minutes that my girlfriend turned around and said, "Oh my God, don't you know who that is?" What can I say—I don't spend my waking hours glued to C-SPAN, but of course it clicked as soon as she said it. I knew he looked familiar. He was still eating when we walked out, and I couldn't catch his eye—he told me later he'd deliberately not looked over when I was leaving, pretending to be all into what the people he was with were saying, even though he was totally distracted and had no idea. He waited till I was gone and then excused himself, supposedly to go to the men's room.

He caught up with me on the sidewalk a block away from the restaurant. He introduced himself and asked for my number, and I was really happy I hadn't just imagined it—our intense chemical connection, I mean—and an hour later he called me and, what can I say, I agreed to meet him at his hotel room. I mean, sure, it wasn't exactly subtle of me, going straight to his room for our first date, but I figured it might be a little weird for us to be seen sitting all tête-à-tête at the bar downstairs.

Later I couldn't help thinking how me and my girlfriend were supposed to go to Elio's that night, but when we got there, our table wasn't ready and there were about a thousand people crowded around the bar waiting for a table, and my friend said, "Let's try Elaine's; it's only a few blocks up," and I said sure, what the hell, I hadn't been there in a couple of lifetimes. And that's where I met Tom. And later, when he came running after me down Second Avenue, I'd almost jumped in a cab that was waiting right outside—a homeless guy hoping for a tip was holding the door open—but at the last minute I decided to walk, get some air instead. And that's the only reason Tom caught up with me. Otherwise, I would have been long gone in the cab. I heard what sounded like a gunshot up the street, and when I turned around to look, there was Tom.

It's amazing, the connection we have. I think because I was so far outside of his world, I had a perspective on it that he really needed. Obviously, he's incredibly smart, but he's also been living inside this bubble for so long that he can't always see beyond it, and before that he was a small-town boy, which he still is, in a way. As smart and successful as he is, he's never gotten over being the son of a shit-kicking tobacco farmer, feeling like he had to go to the back door of the big house, and people sometimes think he's slow because of his accent, and even though I'm a lot younger, in some ways I'm way more sophisticated. I mean, I've lived in New York and Ibiza and Paris and I've dated actors and artists and rock stars—yeah, I know, big thrill, I'm so cool. The key to Tom is that he's really smart and knowledgeable and he's also, in his own mind, still a boy picking tobacco on his father's farm. It makes him insecure when he's having tea with some fucking aristocrat, but he also totally uses it. Like, check out his stump speech, where he basically makes it sound like he didn't have shoes till he got to Duke on scholarship.

I read about the Great Man theory, which is basically the idea that in-dividuals can change history. But I have my own theory, call it the Little Man theory, which just basically says that if you want to understand any Big Swinging Dick, you just have to figure out who he was when he was a ten-year-old boy. Tom seems pretty honest about how his childhood made him who he is. In his mind, he's still wearing hand-me-down overalls. And I love that about him. But sometimes I worry that he needs constant re-assurance as to his lovability and general wonderfulness, and what hap-pens if I'm not there to give it to him?

Practically the first thing we did was jump into bed, and we've been jumping ever since. When I walked in the door of his hotel room, he said, "You're so hot," and I said, "You're so hot," and the next thing I know, we're ripping each other's clothes off. And God, it was good. It was even better the second time, an hour later, because we weren't in such a rush.

Afterward he looked in my eyes and said, "You're amazing," and I said, "You're amazing." I told him he was awake, and he said, "I feel like I'm dreaming, actually," and I said, "No, I mean you're awake in the Bud-dhist sense. You're aware and you see yourself reflected in other people. You see beauty and the goodness in other people because you have it within yourself. I felt that about you the minute I looked across the restau-rant. I could see you were awake. And it was like everybody else in the place wasn't."

It wasn't really like I taught him anything he didn't already know: I just made him more aware of his own powers. Officially, I was listed as a media consultant, but really I was more like his spiritual adviser. Not in any for-mal sense, and of course he still goes to the Methodist church when he's home, the same one he grew up going to with his parents. But, like, the other day, I quoted him the sutra that says a person who doesn't aim for enlightenment is like a spoiled child who plays obsessively with a toy while the house is burning down around him. And that night he was on CNN, and the sound bite is Tom saying the president is like a child playing with his toys while the house is burning down around him.

I was on staff for almost three months, mostly on the road, before I met his wife, three months before the Iowa primary. She took one look at me and didn't like what she saw. Even though she doesn't really love him, that doesn't mean she wants to look like a fool. And there are the kids to con-sider. So that was it; I was off the bus. I understood, of course. I didn't like it, but I couldn't really see that he had much choice. If he hadn't loved me, that would have been the end of it; he would have had the perfect excuse to just dump me.

They haven't had a real marriage in years, and even in its heyday they weren't exactly setting the sheets on fire. I mean, this is the kind of southern girl who wore a surgical glove when she finally gave him a hand job. The last time they had sex was during the Clinton administration.

Twenty years ago it wouldn't have been possible to run for president under these circumstances, but I guess we've come a long way since Bill Clinton creamed on Monica's dress. Not that Tom or anybody on his staff thinks that we've come far enough to elect a president who's getting divorced and fucking a younger woman with—well, let's just say a colorful past. We're not living in France, dude. Which is why I'm here, in the cabin on the pond. Well, actually, I'm here because rumors started to spread, and reporters started coming around to my house. There was a story in the *Star* about Tom and an unnamed former female staffer. Lots of innuendo and a claim by an unnamed source—true, actually—that we'd been caught in the shower together. Basically it was decided that I better just drop out of sight for a while.

I try not to get attached to any particular outcome, but it's a struggle to stifle my desire. Once Tom's in office, I can come out of hiding and he can get a divorce. If he doesn't get elected, then everything's that much easier, really. Not that we allow ourselves to consider that possibility. Tom wants to be president more than he wants anything in the world, except for maybe me. That's what he said one night, and you won't hear me contradicting him. But it's hard being this far away and knowing that it will be months before we can really be together. Sometimes I get frustrated. Just now I tried to call him, but he's not picking up, so I call Rob, his right-hand guy, who's also not picking up, which is pretty weird.

The cabin belongs to a buddy of his, a big supporter. I don't know why they call it a cabin, because for all its down-home rustic pretensions, it's pretty damn luxe, the kind of place you see on a hillside in Aspen or Telluride, with that sort of Daniel Boone meets Frank Lloyd Wright look. A kind of contempo mission theme inside, with big leather club chairs,

Navajo rugs, and lamps made out of antlers, paintings of English setters and ducks in flight on the walls. *Très* macho, but everything a girl could need is here, except for male companionship—a six-burner professional Viking range to boil water, fully equipped gym, spa and sauna, plasma screens in every room. The views are pretty great, taking in a ten-acre pond and, beyond that, a pasture spreading out to the base of a wooded ridge. I've been out walking every day, but yesterday Tom called and told me not to go in the woods 'cause it's deer season. And to wear orange if I take out the garbage or whatever, which I thought was sweet. When I told him I didn't look good in orange, he got all Big Daddy on me. "Alison, this is for your own protection," he said in that voice he sometimes uses to lecture journalists. Any minute I expected to hear him say, *What the American people want is for Alison Poole to start wearing protective orange clothing during deer season.* "I'm kidding," I said. "Joke." Poor Tom was working on about two hours of sleep a night, plus yesterday this fucking political blog called Below the Beltway printed my name: *Who, exactly, is Alison Poole? And why doesn't the Phipps campaign want to talk about her?* Jerk-offs.

After two days of deer season, even yoga can't quite quell the restlessness. I'm getting a little stir-crazy, and I'm down to my last cup of yogurt, so I decide to go into town for groceries. It's almost a mile from the cabin out to the paved road. I have to stop short of the gate, get out, open the padlock and unchain the gate, get back in the car, drive through and lock it all up again. On the front of the gate is a big PRIVATE PROPERTY, NO TRESPASSING sign. A really determined snoop could just climb over the fence and walk down to the cabin, but he'd be trespassing and I could call the local sheriff, who's been instructed by Skeet Jackson, the owner of the property, to keep an eye on me. From the gate, I drive the three miles into town, if that's the word for a grocery store, a post office, a firehouse and a BP station.

I wave to Cassie, the checkout lady at the Piggly Wiggly, who's my new best friend since last week. "Your boyfriend come by looking for you this morning," she says, causing me to crash my shopping cart into a stack of rock-salt bags. For just a second I'm all excited, and then I think, Wait a minute. How does she know who my boyfriend is? If she does, she shouldn't. And why would he be looking for me, when he knows exactly where I am?

"Boyfriend? I don't have a boyfriend," I say, trying to sound nonchalant.

"Pretty girl like you? This fella was awful cute."

"What'd he say?" I ask. "What makes you think he was looking for me?"

"Showed me your picture."

I'm like, "What'd you tell him?"

"I didn't say nothing," she says. "I figured if you wanted him to know where you was, you would of told him. Whatever's going on between you-all, it ain't none of my business."

"Did he tell you his name?"

She shook her head. "Said you was friends. Asked me how to get to the Jackson place."

I say, "You didn't tell him, did you?"

"Like I said," she says, "I don't stick my nose in other people's business. I said I wasn't rightly sure where it was. But I saw him talking to Pete over to the BP. I don't know, like I said, it ain't none of my business, but he seemed awful nice. Whatever he done, I'm sure he's sorry."

"Thanks, sweetie," I say. "I appreciate you covering for me."

"You don't have any reason to be scared of him, do you?"

"No, I don't think so," I say. "Not physically anyway."

"Tell you what. You take my mobile number," she says, scrawling it on an old receipt. "You can call me anytime. If he gives you any trouble, my husband'll straighten him right out. Jake's already got his buck, so now he's just sitting around on his big ol' butt waiting for turkey season."

So I give her a hug and pick up a few groceries and think about who could have followed me here. Back by the freezer case I call Tom, but he's not picking up. Then I call Rob, who says Tom's speaking to a Rotary Club. I fill him in on the situation here. He thinks it might be somebody from one of the other campaigns. If it were one of the tabloids, he says, they would have offered her cash right up front.

"So what am I supposed to do now?" I say.

"Just go back to the cabin," he says. "If you see anybody, call the sheriff. Then call me."

There's nobody waiting at the gate and no cars visible at the cabin when I pull up. I'm putting the groceries away when I look out the kitchen window and see a man in a camel-hair coat standing on the back porch. He jerks his head in my direction after the jar of Ragú smashes on the kitchen tiles. The only thing that saves me from a full-scale myocardial infarction is the fact that I recognize him. He's standing out there, not sure what to do, probably wondering what I'm going to do.

When I catch my breath, I walk over and pull open the sliding glass door. "What the fuck are you doing here?" I say. "This is private property, and if you don't get your ass out of here, I'm calling the sheriff."

"Sorry," he says. "I didn't mean to scare you."

"What did you mean to do?"

"I just wanted to talk."

"I already told you. I've got nothing more to say."

"Yeah, well," he says. "I wanted to see you."

"Okay, here I am. Get a good look, and then I'm calling the sheriff."

"Please," he says, with this pathetic look on his face. "Can I come in?"

"Hell no," I say.

"Well, you come out, then. Just give me five minutes."

"It's freezing," I say. "Just come in."

"Thanks," he says.

I walk out to the great room and plunk myself down in one of the big club chairs with my arms folded across my chest. "What are you doing here?"

"My job?" He shrugs.

"Harassing me is a job?"

"Actually, I'm not entirely sure why I'm here."

"What does that mean?"

"I wanted to see you again. You wouldn't return my calls."

"How'd you find me?"

"I can't tell you that."

"Protecting your sources?"

"We all have our secrets."

"Not me. My life's an open book."

"Which is why you're hiding out in the middle of nowhere?"

"Not hiding. I just needed some time by myself."

"Must get a little lonely down here."

"I was enjoying the solitude. Builds character. You should try it sometime."

"I don't think I'd like it. I'm a people person."

"I can't believe you just said that."

"It was supposed to be funny."

"It was, trust me."

"So?"

"So?"

"This is the part where I ask you if Skeet Jackson's a good friend of yours."

"Why would you ask that?"

"Because according to county records, he owns the place."

"Oh, right," I say. "Skeet's an old friend of the family."

"So he just lent you his house? Help me out here. *Why* did he lend you his house?"

"I told you. I just needed to get away. Do some thinking. A little writing. Skeet offered."

"Awfully generous of him."

"Skeet's a generous guy."

"He's been very generous to Senator Phipps."

"Let's cut the shit," I say. "Why don't you just come out and say what it is you want?"

"I wanted to see you again."

"Right. And I'm here for the deer hunting."

Of course, as soon as I say that, I realize I'm sort of dropping the pretense. We both know why I'm here. I first met Frank about six months ago, when I was working on the campaign, at a party in D.C., although I didn't know he was from Below the Beltway at first; some fucking media consultant I turn out to be. I'd had a couple of cocktails and he asked me where I worked and I'm telling him about the senator, and when he finally gets around to telling me he writes a political blog, I'm worrying that maybe I've said a little too much—that I was a little too free and easy about my closeness to Tom, partly because he was cute and I wanted to impress him at the same time that I wanted to keep him at a distance and remind myself that I was totally taken. All of a sudden he asks flat out if I'm dating Tom, and I say, of course not, so he says, "Well, then, will you come to dinner with me tomorrow night?" So I end up having dinner with him just to throw him off the scent, although it's not like it's such a chore, since he's about as hot as a habanero and Tom's been at the lake house with his family the last four days.

I realize if I'm not careful, I could get into a sticky situation, so I have the genius idea of telling him that as much as I like him, I'm seeing someone else. When he asks again if it's Tom, I say, "No, it's another staffer, but I can't talk about it." He dropped me off that night at the condo I was borrowing and gave me a semi-innocent kiss good night. The next day he posted something sweet about me being the best-looking girl on any campaign staff, and that was that. Except that he calls me every couple of weeks to chat, and then again last month when the *Star* printed this nasty piece insinuating that Tom was having an affair with an unnamed former staffer whose description fit me like a pair of True Religion jeans. Of course I denied everything, and of course he didn't believe me, and then he asked me if we could get together for a drink. I said I didn't think that would be such a great idea, and after that I stopped taking his calls.

"You drove all the way down here?" I say.

"Except for the last mile or so, which I walked."

"I didn't see your car up at the gate."

"I parked up the road a little, out of sight."

"You're lucky you didn't get shot."

"Folks around here seem friendly enough."

"If I were you, I'd think about hitting the road before it gets dark."

"How about a glass of wine before I go?" he says, taking a bottle out of his backpack. "This is the one you liked so much when we had dinner that night."

It's true, we had an amazingly delicious bottle of wine that night. He hands me the bottle, a 2001 Châteauneuf-du-Pape. "I remember," I say. "The wine of the Popes."

"Also reputed to have aphrodisiac qualities," he says.

"That didn't really pan out for you, did it?"

"Hope springs eternal," he says.

"Although I guess it worked for those old guys. From what I hear, Popes were like the rock stars of their era in terms of pussy. Oh my God, you're actually blushing. That's so sweet."

"Well, I'm a Catholic. I mean, I used to be."

Part of me knows I should get him out of here as soon as possible, but another part of me's dying for company. So we open the wine and I put out a rock-hard wedge of Brie and Carr's water biscuits—it's actually kind of amazing what you can buy these days at the Piggly Wiggly in East Jesus—and he tells me about what's going on with the various campaigns. I mean, who knew what a hound that Bill Richardson was, but then again, who knew fucking anything about Bill Richardson? He tells about his last girl-friend, who scarred him for life by sleeping not only with his best friend but also with his best friend's wife; then he asks me about my life. I'm telling him about my year at the ashram, pursuing enlightenment and try-ing not to lust after my guru, when I suddenly think, Wait a minute. He's getting background for his story. I can, like, visualize the blog post: *The for-mer party girl then sought enlightenment at an ashram run by controversial guru Darpak Lalit. . . .* "Are you going to write about this?" I say.

"I don't know," he says. "You do realize it looks kind of incriminating, you staying in a big house owned by one of Phipps's best friends and biggest donors. *Are* you having an affair with Phipps?"

"Why don't you ask me if I'm having an affair with Jackson?"

"Sounds like a nondenial to me."

I hear what sounds like a gunshot somewhere in the distance and then my text tone sounds, the first three bars of Gnarls Barkley's "Crazy." I flip open my phone, to find a text from Tom: *Whassup Sugar Plum?*

I don't know why, I'll probably always wonder, but I can't decide whether or not to tell him what's going on. I don't want to worry him. I feel like I could go either way. I can see reasons for both. I stare at the screen until Frank finally says, "Are you okay?"

"I'm fine," I tell him.

I text back: *Blogger found me. Here now.*

Call Sheriff.

That will b big drama/story.

Dont say anything.

I wasnt born yesterday.

It bothers me, him telling me not to say anything. As if I haven't been the soul of discretion for the last year. Frank is looking at me, puzzled. He glances down at his watch.

Get rid of him.

Dont worry.

I decide to turn my phone off. His tone really bugs me.

"I should probably be heading back," Frank says, downing the last of his wine.

"I guess you should," I say. "I can give you a ride out to the gate."

"Thanks," he says.

When I let him off up by the main road he says, "Don't worry, I'm not going to write about this."

"I really appreciate it," I say.

"Call me sometime." He closes the door, climbs over the gate and walks off down the road.

Driving back to the house, I feel kind of bad for Frank. I mean, he doesn't get the story and he doesn't get laid. He turned out to be a pretty decent guy. And I can't help wondering how far Tom would go to keep us out of the papers. Would he still say he wants me more than he wants to be president? Would he screw somebody to protect our secret? Like, for instance, his wife?

When he calls an hour later the wine's wearing off and the sun is setting and I am sinking into a swamp of doubt.

"What happened?" he says. "Did you get rid of him?"

"Sort of," I say.

"What does that mean?"

"He's gone for the moment."

"What did he ask you? Did my name come up? Please tell me you didn't say anything."

"I told him you fucked like a stallion."

"Jesus, Alison."

"Of course I didn't tell him anything."

"Thank God."

His tone is really pissing me off.

"Listen," he says, "I'll call back in five minutes."

But instead it's Rob who calls back and asks me what happened with Frank. "I handled it," I say, and when he insists on details I tell him I'll give those to Tom, then hang up.

When Tom finally calls I've had almost an hour to brood.

"Sorry," he says. "We got a call from Fox and I had to run down to the affiliate for a live feed. So what happened with the blogger? Please tell me we don't have a problem here."

If he'd just asked about me, or sounded concerned and sympathetic, the conversation might have gone in a whole different direction. "I don't know," I say. "That depends."

"On what?"

"He wants to come back for dinner."

"What the hell? I hope you told him to go fuck himself."

"I could have, but that would've pretty much guaranteed a highly incriminating post on his blog tomorrow."

"What the hell does he want?"

"I could be wrong, but I think he wants your girlfriend."

"What are you saying?"

"I'm saying I think he wants me more than he wants the story." When he doesn't respond, I go, "Tom?"

"Did he say that?"

"Not exactly."

"What *did* he say exactly?"

"Well, I can't recount the whole goddamn conversation verbatim. But he made it pretty clear he was interested. And he basically kind of indicated that if I wasn't interested in him then he'd take that to mean I was involved with somebody else."

"What do you mean, he *indicated*?"

"I'm summarizing like ten minutes of back and forth. I'm interpreting."

"You told him you were involved with somebody else, right? We agreed that Rob's our cover story."

"He knows Rob's not straight. I mean, come on, Tom."

"What did you say?"

"What do you want me to say?"

"I want you to get rid of him."

"I can do that."

"Does he have anything solid?"

"He claims he has a source for us getting caught in the shower in Manchester."

"Then why doesn't he just go with it?"

"He may."

"You really think he likes you enough to kill the story?"

"It's possible. He wants to come over here and cook dinner for me tonight. What do you want me to do?"

"I don't know, I have to think about this. Let me talk to Rob."

"You're going to talk to Rob about this," I say, incredulous. "I don't want to know what Rob thinks, Tom. I don't *care* what Rob thinks. I want to know what you think. I want to know what you want me to do."

"Shit, Rob's at the door and I'm late for the VFW."

"What do you want me to do about Mr. Below the Beltway?"

"I don't know. You're going to have to handle this one, honey."

"I don't know what that means."

"It just means you should do whatever you think is best."

"You mean whatever I *have* to do."

"I have tremendous faith in you, darlin'. I love you. I know I can count on you."

Up until that moment, I'm still hoping. But the way he says he knows he can count on me—that tone of voice, that public speaking inflection he uses in his speeches—it broke my heart. Even the way he said "darlin'" was stage southern. It wasn't an endearment so much as an imitation of an endearment.

"Alison, honey, I gotta get going. I'll call you later."

He was walking out the door. I couldn't help trying to picture that room, even though it would look pretty much like all the other hotel rooms along the campaign trail, like one of the many rooms I snuck into in Franconia or Nashua, in Cedar Falls or Gastonia—those rooms that conveniently seemed to have no personality and no history, with a vinyl-covered ice bucket flanked by two cellophane-wrapped plastic glasses—without ever really wondering too much about all the people who had been there before us, about what had happened in these rooms. Maybe every room deserves its own bronze plaque, if we only knew. I would never see that room at the Hampton Inn in Dubuque, but I couldn't help wondering if he would remember it, out of all the hundreds of hotel rooms that year, as the place where he traded his soulmate for something he loved more.

2008

The March

Corrine had agreed to meet Washington and Veronica at the diner on Fifty-second Street, a place they'd come for hamburgers on Saturday or brunch on Sunday when they were living in the neighborhood back in the eighties. It had been more than a decade since she'd set foot there, and the glazed apple pies and coconut cakes under their plastic domes seemed like museum displays from the distant era of her lost youth. But now it was jammed with cops—she hadn't seen this many uniforms since her days at the soup kitchen downtown, feeding cops and firefighters and san men and the steelworkers who had come together in the smoking ruins. She'd gotten to know several cops then, but the cohort here today seemed less benign, their faces tight, closed and bolted against fraternization. That moment of solidarity, of strangers comforting one another in the streets, of stockbrokers hugging firemen and waving to cops, had already faded into history. The citizens of the metropolis were changed, though less tangibly than they might have imagined or hoped back in the time of anthrax and missing-person posters. They had, most of them, been given a glimpse of their best selves, and told themselves they wouldn't forget, or go back to the old selfish, closed-in ways. But then they'd gone back to work and the rubble had been carted away and the stock market had recovered. You woke up one morning not thinking about that terrible day, not remembering it had happened until perhaps seeing the tattered remains of an old poster on your way to lunch. And it felt good not to think about it all the damn time.

She stepped outside to wait. Already, at ten-thirty, the street was jammed with people bundled against the cold and carrying signs. ALL WE ARE SAYING IS GIVE PEACE A CHANCE. A little kid holding one that said WAR IS TERROR and his sister in a red snowsuit with her own sign: DRAFT

THE BUSH TWINS. Russell had stayed home with the kids, who were working on a play for her birthday. While he shared Corrine's feelings about the imminent war, Russell was not a joiner. "I don't march," he'd said earlier that morning, showing the same kind of contrarian pride he sometimes brought to his traditional refrain of "I don't dance."

Looking south down the sidewalk for Washington and Veronica, she felt her chest tighten as she picked out a familiar figure—the loose, loping stride beneath the camel polo coat, the flopping sandy forelock, a garment bag hanging on his shoulder like a vestigial wing. She waited, paralyzed at his approach, and watched the changes ring on his unguarded visage as he recognized her, the rapid modulation from shock to wistful chagrin that preceded his public Isn't-this-a-pleasant-surprise mien.

"I might've known you'd be here," he said as he kissed her cheek.

"Actually, I was just thinking about you," she said, a statement that to her ears sounded false in its implication of surprising coincidence; it would have been true on almost any given day, despite the fact that they hadn't seen each other in more than a year—not since that snowy night in the plaza outside the New York State Theater when they'd both been on their way to see *The Nutcracker* with their respective families. By now he had occupied more time in her thoughts than he had in the flesh. They'd exchanged e-mails and he had called from Tennessee and left a message five months ago, on September 11.

"I mean, I was thinking about those days downtown, at the soup kitchen. This whole thing . . ." She waved her arm to indicate the milling crowd with their signs. "For me, it all kind of loops back to that time. The demonstration—the war."

"Yeah, I guess so," he said. "At least that's the question, isn't it? They'd have us believe that what happened back then justifies their war." He sighed. "I didn't know this was happening, actually. The march, I mean. I was just on my way to the airport and I kind of waded into this thing. I was staying up the street at a friend's place." He pointed behind him, as if to lend credence to the claim. "We sold the apartment as part of the separation agreement."

She tried not to react to this last phrase, the confirmation that he'd parted from his wife.

"You're heading back to Tennessee?"

He nodded. "Ashley's really settled in—she's going to a girls' school in Nashville and seems to love it."

"That's good."

"Your kids?"

"They're fine. They're great." It seemed important to emphasize their well-being, since the children, after all, had probably been the fatal obstacles to their romance.

"How's your mom?" It felt as if she was staging these remarks for the benefit of unseen observers, but she didn't know how to break out of the formulae of polite conversation.

"Well, that's the other thing," he said. "Not so good. She's been ill. Cancer."

"Oh my God, Luke. I'm so sorry."

"It's been rough, but the prognosis is somewhat encouraging."

"She must be glad to have you there."

He shrugged and pushed his hair off his forehead—a gesture so familiar, it made her feel faint. "Making up for lost time."

"Good for you. Are you working?" He'd been between things back when they were working downtown at the soup kitchen together, trying to decide what to do with the second half of his life.

"I'm running a little fund."

"What about the book?"

"Oh God, I'd almost forgotten about that. Maybe someday. And you? What about the screenplay?"

She told him about the actor who'd optioned it, without adding that the option had just expired the week before.

"That's great. I'll be watching for it at the Cool Springs Multiplex."

The strained formality of this exchange was exhausting her. She had been ready to change her life for him, and for the last year she'd been struggling to convince herself they'd done the right thing.

For better or worse, the arrival of Washington and Veronica rescued them from the peril of intimate revelation. Corrine made the introductions, realizing as she did so that they'd been present outside the theater the night when their affair had effectively ended. Seeing her with her husband and children had awakened his conscience, and dampened his ardor. He'd told her later that he couldn't bear to be the reason for her breaking up her family.

"Sorry we're late," Veronica said. "Traffic on the Hutch. Then we had to find parking."

"The perils of the suburban couple," Washington said, still embarrassed at being yet another commuter—that, too, a result of the attack. They'd started looking at houses in Connecticut the week after.

"You look great," Veronica said to Corrine.

"So do you."

"I'd better get on out of here and try to find a cab," Luke said.

She didn't want him to leave; as awkward as this public posturing might be, she'd hoped they might find a few more minutes to talk. Suddenly she was afraid they'd never see each other again.

They stood for a moment on the sidewalk, the bitter cold infiltrating the soles of her shoes, uncertain of the form their parting should take.

He leaned over and kissed her cheek, the brush of his unruly forelock across her face excruciatingly familiar. If she'd had any doubt about his state of mind these last few minutes, she saw now that he was as miserable as she was. He managed a rueful smile before turning away and walking west. She watched as he slowly disappeared into the flow of the converging marchers.

"What's with all the fucking heat?" Washington said, nodding as four cops exited the coffee shop. Sullen, wide-bodied white guys girdled with hardware, pulling up their pants and avoiding eye contact with the civilians, they exuded the grim camaraderie of an army in enemy territory.

Corrine shook her head. Nothing seemed real to her right now, her resolve evaporating along with an animating sense of indignation about the war soon to take place six thousand miles away.

"I don't like the look of this shit," he said. "Maybe you should make your own damn sign: MY SISTER MARRIED A COP."

For a moment she didn't know what he was talking about; then she realized it was true. Her sister *had* married a cop, another improbable result of that improbable time.

It was reassuring being a part of a crowd, surrendering to its volition. They merged with the throng flowing east toward Second, marching beside a sign that said FREEZING MY ASS OFF FOR PEACE. The air was cold enough to show their breath as they pressed forward, trying to see up ahead. The Roosevelt Island tramway rose up in the distance. Corrine got clunked by a CHILDREN AGAINST WAR sign being carried by a little girl right behind her. Maybe it would have been good, she thought, for the kids to see this.

Luke had been stricken at the sight of her twins outside the theater that night. She'd seen it in his eyes. At that moment she'd known this chance encounter had doomed them, though they'd struggled to recover from it for several days of agonized discussions. It wasn't rational really, since he'd known from the beginning about her family. In fact, the plan had been to tell their spouses after Christmas.

When they finally reached Second Avenue, the march turned north, although their destination, the UN, was some ten blocks south and east.

Washington was jumping in the air, trying to get a look ahead. "Why the fuck are we going uptown?" he said.

"They've blocked Second," a kid in a tasseled ski hat explained. "We have to go north and circle back down."

"That doesn't make sense," Corrine said.

"It makes lots of sense," Washington said, "if they're trying to keep us away from the UN."

At times the sound of car horns was deafening. The marchers overflowed the sidewalks, filling in the gaps between vehicles like mortar, blocking the traffic aimed in the opposite direction. This was now completely unreal.

A voice from a megaphone was directing them to proceed north.

"They're trying to scatter us," said the man beside her, whose EMPTY WARHEADS sign featured caricature heads of Bush, Cheney and Rumsfeld, each one of them open, the crowns of the skulls rising on hinges.

"I like your sign," she said.

"They're trying to keep us from getting there, the bastards."

"Is this fucked-up or what?" Washington said.

Veronica said, "I'm glad we didn't bring the kids."

"Hey, it would've been educational," Washington said. "A lesson in the trampling of our motherfucking constitutional right of assembly."

"Why are they doing this?"

"A Republican governor and mayor sucking up to our president is what's going on," Washington said.

Corrine and Veronica fell into step behind him, having barely spoken in two or three months.

Veronica squeezed her glove. "How are you?"

"Fine. The kids are great."

"And you two?"

"Well, Russell took me to Bouley last night for Valentine's." She wondered where, and with whom, Luke had been last night—if there was someone in his life now, a question she'd been afraid to ask: a childhood sweetheart, some southern girl with pouffed-up hair and a syrupy accent.

"Washington cooked his famous Szechuan chicken and we opened a bottle of sparkling cider."

"That sounds nice."

"It sounds boring. But boring is better than all-nighters and strange panties, I guess. I don't know, I hate the commute and I miss the city, and those stay-at-home moms are just clones. I can't make up my mind which scares me more—the possibility that my kids won't be accepted by their peers or the possibility that they'll grow up just like them."

Corrine, meanwhile, was wondering if Luke was happy, and if she wanted him to be. Yes, of course she did. Only she wanted him to think of her and to wonder sometimes, as she did, whether they had really done the right thing after all.

At Sixty-third Street they were greeted by a phalanx of cops, a line of barricades blocking the street. A red-faced policeman with a crescent scar on his cheek pointed his billy club north.

"What's the point of pushing us uptown?" Corrine asked him.

"Just keep moving," he said.

The next street, when they reached it, was also blocked off.

"Hey, man," Washington said, "we live on this block."

"We need ID," the cop said.

"Officer, I don't understand," Corrine said. "We're not trying to cause any trouble. We're just exercising our constitutional right of assembly and free speech."

"Just keep moving."

Washington took her arm and eased her away from the barricade.

"Why are they doing this?" she demanded. "Why are they *being* like this? They don't act this way at the Saint Patrick's Day parade."

"Exactly," Washington said, his hand still on her arm.

"Even if they're enforcing some ridiculous order," Veronica said, "they could at least be civil."

The faces of these cops reminded Corrine of the old pictures of Selma and Birmingham.

"It's an outrage, that's what it is." The speaker was a Waspy middle-aged blonde with a black velvet hair band and a three-quarter-length mink. A bit of an anomaly in this crowd, she put Corrine in mind of an older version of Luke's ex, Sasha, whose picture she occasionally saw in the party pages of magazines.

Up ahead, the crowd was chanting raggedly, the chorus moving fitfully down the column, picked up by the marchers and passed along before it spluttered and died as they reached Sixty-fifth Street, which was also blocked off.

"This is ridiculous," Corrine said.

"It's all part of the plan," Washington replied.

"What plan?"

An old guy who was wearing a camo jacket and had long gray hair and a beard was shouting to her over the din. "They don't want us anywhere near the UN, or the cameras."

"Who doesn't? This is America. This is New York, for God's sake. Who ordered this? The police commissioner? Our squeaky mayor? That asshole in the White House?" The injustice of it infuriated her. The idea that the attack on the city was being used to justify this dubious war was outrage enough.

Glancing up ahead, she could see a huge globe borne aloft by the crowd. About ten feet in diameter, it appeared to be made out of soft fabric.

"*Whose streets? Our streets!*"

Corrine took up the chant. Her anger was righteous and liberating. She was cold, her ears and toes prickly with numbness. If the cops were trying to incite the crowd to violence, they were doing a good job of it.

"*Whose streets? Our streets!*"

She was a peaceful person, the mother of two, but she felt like throwing something, breaking something, running amok.

"*Whose streets? Our streets!*"

Seeing all the angry faces, she had a sudden vision of chaos spreading through the city, smoke rising from the brownstones. . . .

Finally at Seventy-first Street, they were herded east. As they approached First Avenue, word filtered through the crowd that it was sealed off, which made their progress seem completely futile.

Up ahead, cops on horseback towered over them. She still hoped she might find a level head, establish a dialogue, explain the purpose of their collective mission.

But she sensed anxiety rising around her, an increasing edge of anger and hysteria.

"They're making arrests!"

"Get back! They're charging!"

"You *bastards*!"

"They hit him!"

The mounted cops started moving forward as the crowd ahead of her fell back, reversing the momentum of the march, until she felt herself pushed back, up against the crowd bottled up on the sidewalk on the south side of the street. A plastic water bottle arced through the air and sailed past the head of one of the cops, shouts of distress, curses and screams rising from the intersection.

Three mounted policemen floated toward them, looming against the sky, and Corrine recognized one of them. All of a sudden the name came to her: Spinetti.

She thrust herself forward against the tide of retreat.

Sitting atop a huge chestnut mare, Spinetti held his billy club aloft, like a torch, the reins held loosely in his left hand, his eyes fixed on a point above or even beyond the crowd.

"Officer!" she shouted. "Officer Spinetti!"

The cop looked around, scanning the faces, holding his club at the ready.

A space had opened up on the street ahead of her. A boy in a puffy blue parka was lying facedown on the pavement, a dark stripe glistening on his flaxen hair, which was so similar in color to her son's that despite the obvious difference in ages, she had to fight back the notion that it was her son, Jeremy, lying there, bloody, on the pavement.

She waved at Spinetti from the edge of the circle that had cleared around the boy and the horse, feeling ridiculous as soon as she did so, not sure what she intended. "It's Corrine," she said. "From the soup kitchen."

He regarded her without obvious emotion.

She didn't know what to say. She wanted to break through his blood lust and recall him to his humanity, ask him how this could happen, to remind him that when they met, their country was under attack and the citizenry looked to him and his kind to defend them. She was shivering and it felt as if her jaw were wired shut. "We fed you," she said finally. "We were proud of you."

Spinetti stared down at her implacably. Finally he lowered his club, turning his horse and moving back toward the intersection, where a dozen of his comrades were clustered.

Two women knelt down to examine the boy, who was moaning. Perhaps he had been moaning before and she hadn't noticed. Voices behind her cleared the way for a doctor coming through, and he emerged from the crowd wearing a bright orange thermal suit, silver tufts of gray hair on either side of his balding head.

Washington suddenly appeared beside her, holding her close as she shivered violently in the midday sun.

"He gave us a ride home one night," she said. "Me and Luke. He took four sugars in his coffee. I used to make him a fresh pot. I mean, what were we doing down there anyway?"

Washington was steering her west, away from the march. "Maybe so on a cold winter day you could prevent a full-scale riot from breaking out."

She was still shaking. "I want to go home," she said. "Do you think it would be okay if I just went home now?"

They offered her a ride downtown, but she didn't think she could bear even the company of friends. Finally, Washington found her a cab all the way over on Fifth. Veronica hugged her before she got in, and the cabdriver lurched manic-depressively down the avenue, braking and accelerating. She thought about the boy with the cracked head and about all the boys who would soon be bleeding and dying on the distant streets of foreign cities, and she wanted to scream at the senselessness of it all. She wanted to slap Spinetti. She wanted to draft the Bush twins. But most of all, she wanted to see Luke. She had tried to do her civic duty, but she was tired of trying to do the right thing, of always trying to be a good person and a good mother and a good wife. She wanted to live for her own de-sires and forget, if only for a little while, about the needs and wants of oth-ers. She wanted what *she* wanted. She wanted Luke. She wanted to be fucked senseless. She'd always hated the expression, but now, suddenly, she understood it. At this moment, being fucked senseless was the only thing that seemed to make sense.

"You say West Broadway, miss?"

"West Broadway, yes. At the corner of Reade."

As they approached her building, a shaft of sunlight pierced the wind-shield, momentarily blinding her. For years, this part of the city had been gloomy at this time of the afternoon, entombed in shadow. This was what they called "a silver lining."

2004

The Last Bachelor

Emerging from the surf, Ginny was amazed to discover A.G. sitting cross-legged on her towel, chatting up her niece. Her first reaction was entirely self-conscious—wondering how she looked dripping wet in her ratty blue Speedo—her first impulse to flee. She hadn't seen him in—what, a couple of years? That night after the Alzheimer's ball, when he'd drunkenly asked her to go with him to Saint Barts. After a quick inventory of her own imperfections, she noticed his paunch. When had that happened? Watching him hit on her niece, interpreting the casual slouch of his posture as he leaned on his elbow, she decided that what was interesting wasn't the belly per se but his lack of self-consciousness, that he'd probably never stoop to suck it in or even count it against himself when he was tabulating his own defects. He still had the same boyish, timeless shock of blond hair—she was quite sure he'd taken it very much to heart when she told him, early on, that he looked like Robert Redford. She could read, even from this distance, the old sense of entitlement, the ease and confidence as he turned his charms on a beautiful young woman half his age. This is what had always, in her mind, saved him from being a caricature, that he deviated just enough from the type—even if it was only a question of scale. In this case, the way that his vanity was larger and more impregnable than that of other middle-aged men who obsessively chased younger women, spent hours at the gym, or, failing that, risked herniation trying to, at crucial moments of presentation, inhale that extra flesh around their middles. Perhaps she was reading too much into what could be a simple, innocent tableau, but that, too, was A.G.—the fact that he inspired this kind of hermeneutics. This speculation on Ginny's part was the work of an instant, the interval between two waves breaking around her ankles. Before the second had retreated beneath her feet, she felt angry at herself for the intricacy of her speculation, for caring that much. Wasn't it far more likely that he *was* a type, and that the supposed complexity was her own embroidery on a standard pattern? Hadn't he disappointed even the modest hopes she'd invested in him?

She had reason to chastise herself again, approaching them, when she realized that she was the one sucking in her own stomach, but this was mitigated by the pleasure of seeing his reaction when she sat down beside him and shook the salty water from her hair.

"A.G., this *is* a surprise. I see you've met my niece."

For a man who prided himself on his composure, he was comically discomfited, though he made a valiant recovery, kissing her on the cheek, doing his best to convey the impression that he'd practically been expecting her at any moment. He then excused himself as quickly as one with his exquisite manners could. Ginny had the satisfaction of watching him retreat down the beach, slightly duck-footed as he struggled for purchase in the dry sand. Yes, she remembered that, chasing after him one day through the snow in Aspen—seeing his splayed tracks, thinking it made him even more endearing.

"What was that all about?" she asked Lana, who blushed.

"I don't know. He was like, you know. He was just kind of . . ." She shrugged.

Well, actually, yes, Ginny did know. But she wasn't feeling entirely collegial toward her niece at this moment, appraising her as she imagined A.G. had, and she conjured a strange conceit—that the concavity of a young woman's tummy was precisely calibrated to the paucity of her wisdom. God, she was young. Of course Ginny had watched A.G. pick up women who were no older than her niece. But until this moment she would never have thought of her niece—her little Lana—as having anything in common with those girls. "Kind of what?"

"Well, you know. Friendly."

"You mean he was hitting on you."

"Well, he just kind of sat down. Actually, he walked past me a little and then came back and introduced himself. He asked me if this was Gibson's Beach, and I told him I wasn't from here, and then we just started talking."

"Did he ask you out?"

"Well, he said he was kind of busy this coming week but he'd call me next Monday."

Ginny nodded. She told herself it wasn't Lana's fault. She counted to ten. She tried to tell herself she took no pleasure in this, in feeling, suddenly, so very worldly-wise. "I expect he *is* fairly busy," she said, shaking a cigarette from the pack. "Unless I'm very much mistaken, he's getting married this weekend."

Approaching the house on Gin Lane, the so-called cottage with its sprawling wings, white porches and shingled gray gables, A.G. saw the white tent rising up above the perfectly squared green privet battlements that surrounded the property of his future in-laws. The gates were open. As he drove in, he was presented with a scene of furious activity. He stopped the car in the middle of the driveway and watched. Painters and window washers on ladders had stormed the big house. Three maids waddled like white ducks up the path to the guest house, bearing linens. Half a dozen young men who looked like camp counselors were setting up the tables beneath the tent. Gardeners were scattered about the property, planting and deadheading flowers; still more flowers were coming out of a van from a Manhattan florist. And an anonymous tradesman was taking a leak against the side of the pool house. All of this had been set in motion by his proposal to Pandora Bright Caldwell Keirstead, of Chattanooga, Palm Beach and Southampton, several months before. It wasn't exactly a spur-of-the-moment decision. He'd actually purchased the ring at Graff more than a month before and carried it with him on two dates with Pandy, somehow losing his resolution each time. Finally, he'd invited her to One If by Land, which practically forced his hand, it being notorious as a setting for proposals. Before their appetizers had arrived, two other swains had dropped to their knees in front of their dates. Pandy blushed deeply the first time; the second proposal she pretended not to notice. If she was disappointed that A.G. had stayed seated when he popped the question, she wasn't about to show it.

The announcement, the planning, the registry of gifts—all followed inexorably but somehow insubstantially, like scenes constructed from pixels. A.G. sat in his car in the driveway and tried, at this late hour, to reconnect himself to this series of events. He knew he should feel elated, or scared—or both. He listened for the chuffing sound of the ocean waves. He wondered why you could always hear the surf from the yard at night but never during the day.

A rabbit rocketed across the driveway and disappeared into the privet, closely pursued by Woofter, the Keirsteads' retriever. The dog barked twice at the hedge before turning away and trotting back toward the house.

Leaving the Meadow Club after her tennis lesson, Ginny Banks caught a glimpse of a scene she'd never expected to witness: the rehearsal dinner for A.G.'s wedding. She stood at the edge of the doorway, looking in on the assembled company. Besides family, there was the table of best men— A.G. having assembled a team of five, rather than leaving anyone out. Tommy Briggs, Wick Seward, Nikos Menzenopoulus, Cappie Farquarson and Gino Andreosa. Back in the day, they had all been known as ladies' men. Nikos and Gino were among the last of the old school playboys in the mold of Agnelli and Rubirosa, race car–driving Euro sybarites. All of them had eventually married at least once—most of them twice, although Gino and Wick were currently between. They'd chased, and bedded, many of the same girls, initially women their own age and later their younger sisters. A.G. was the last of his kind, the last unmarried man of his generation. For two decades he had been a kind of prince of the city, gliding between the social clubs of the Upper East Side and the nightclubs downtown, an intimate of artistic circles as well as the world of inherited wealth. He belonged to the Racquet Club, the Brook Club and the Century Club, was an early investor in a famous SoHo art gallery and a patron of several literary magazines. He was also a famous lover, a playboy who cut a wide swath through Manhattan and Europe, faithfully alternating between models and debutantes. For years he conducted an affair with a married screen idol, while continuing to pursue an international serial-dating career. His fortieth-birthday celebration, which took place on Nikos Menzenopoulus's yacht, *Dionysus,* inevitably appeared on subsequent lists of "Parties of the Decade." Cappie Farquarson went into rehab three days later, and Nikos eventually became involved in two paternity suits, both plaintiffs citing A.G.'s party as the date of conception. A.G. himself managed to escape these kinds of entanglements, although at some point in the years that followed his name began to be invoked as a synonym for a certain kind of arrested development. He'd been eligible for so long that he ceased to be plausible. Married couples, seating their dinner parties, began to think of him as a hopeless case—a quaint relic of their wild youth. "Who can we put next to Celia?" "There's always A.G." "Do we really want to do that to Celia? I mean, even if she hasn't already slept with him, I think she's had enough of the bad boys for one lifetime."

Ginny turned to see Lori Haddad with her daughter Casey in tow, looking in on the scene. "Can you believe this?"

"I'm actually seeing it," Lori said, "but I still don't believe it."

"What don't you believe, Mommy?"

"He's still got twenty-four hours to leave the country."

"Maybe we're being too cynical."

"Mom, what don't you *believe* in?"

"Mommy doesn't believe in fairy tales, honey."

"What do you suppose it is about *her*? I mean, is it just that she happened to be the one sitting in the chair next to him when the music stopped?"

"Well, besides that she's young and pretty and thin and rich. And she's from his hometown. That seems to count for a lot with these southerners."

"Good point. So what does she see in him?"

"Well . . . He's charming and smart and he has a D-I-C-K the size of Florida."

"That sp—"

"We know what it spells, honey," said Lori, covering her daughter's mouth.

A. G. Jackson had grown up on Lookout Mountain in Chattanooga, although his own father was an émigré from Birmingham, by way of Vanderbilt. As the vice president of the local bank, he was a respected member of the community, although their circumstances were more modest than those of the native oligarchy. A.G. distinguished himself as both scholar and athlete, joined his schoolmates on bonefishing expeditions to Islamorada and quail-hunting jaunts at their south Georgia plantations while his father managed their trust funds. A.G. was raised to believe there was no higher title a man could aspire to than "gentleman," and this Episcopalian epithet was so constantly attached to Jackson *père,* often accompanied by the words *old school,* that his son couldn't help but sense an almost imperceptible undercurrent of condescension from those whose secret faith was more Darwinian. The old man's rectitude was in part a reaction to the flamboyance of his own father, who'd made and lost two fortunes, one in stock speculation and one in real estate, while he was growing up. A.G.'s father did all he could to temper his son's fearless and exuberant character, so reminiscent of his grandfather's, while his wife secretly undermined this program, instilling in him a sense of confidence and entitlement. Her own family was among the first families of Charleston and she saw no reason to defer to the local gentry. Her husband would scold her for saying, as she so often did, "Who's the handsomest, smartest little man in the whole wide world?" "Please, Kate," he'd say. "You'll spoil the boy." While A.G. absorbed from his father a respect for tradition, position and inherited wealth, his mother taught him to believe in his own secret superiority. Their marriage, from his vantage point, was a happy one, although his mother sometimes believed that she'd sold herself short, that her husband lacked the necessary fire and grit to advance her ambitions.

No family loomed larger in Chattanooga than the Keirsteads. They had made their original fortune in land and later compounded it with an interest in a soft-drink empire based in Atlanta. In the past half century their holdings had spread from the Southeast throughout the country and around the globe. A.G. had gone to school with Burton Keirstead III, aka Trip, whose father had taken a benign interest in A.G.'s career, even writing him a letter of recommendation to Harvard. They had stayed in touch after A.G. moved to New York, occasionally dining together when Keirstead was in the city, and the old man sometimes steered some business his way. As a young investment banker, it certainly didn't hurt to be acquainted with Burton Keirstead, Jr. Trip, meanwhile, married a girl from Savannah, built a house on Lookout Mountain and took an office downtown, next door to his father's, which he visited when he wasn't following the salmon from Nova Scotia to Russia, or the birds from Georgia to Argentina. Their friend Cal Bustert, to nearly no one's surprise, burned through his trust fund, bouncing between fashionable resorts and rehab facilities; marrying, spawning and divorcing; wrecking cars and discharging firearms at inappropriate targets, including, finally, himself. A.G. had flown south for the funeral, a somber yet lavish affair that lasted for three days.

Most of their former classmates, after forays into the North, settled within a few miles of their parents and married girls they'd known for years. A.G. always returned for the weddings—five of them the year he turned thirty—and always brought a different date, and in time he returned to stand as godfather to the children. He visited his parents on Thanksgiving and Christmas. Only rarely did he bring a girl along for these family holidays, and when he did, she was inevitably from what he called, without self-consciousness, "a good family." But his parents learned in time not to get too attached to any of them.

Despite his increasing success in New York, he maintained a deep loyalty to his hometown. Chattanooga, Tennessee, the South—this was part of him, and distinguished him from the mass of rootless Yankees with whom he associated in Manhattan. He always told his drinking buddies in both cities that he would return one day, although as the years passed it became harder and harder for his friends in either place to take this threat seriously.

Within a few years he was making more money than his father, although he did not announce this fact—except to his mother—and continued to seek his father's advice on matters large and small, although they did not discuss A.G.'s love life.

Ginny was reading in the living room of the little cottage in Sagaponack she rented every August, half-conscious of the wistful susurration of the waves from the beach. The yard, which had once enjoyed unobstructed views of the potato fields, had over the years been hemmed in by houses, first by Lego-like boxes and later by vast shingled mansions that mimicked the old cottages of Southampton, but at night she could still imagine herself as a lonely beachcomber. Emma Wodehouse was just realizing how badly she had misjudged both Mr. Knightley and her own heart, when the phone rang, startling her. She was hardly less startled by the identity of the caller.

"A.G.?"

"Sorry to call so late. But I know you've always been a night owl."

"If you're looking for my niece, she's gone off to sleep over at a friend's house."

"No, actually I was looking for you. Wanna get a drink?"

"Now? Tonight?" Her watch said 1:45.

"We're not getting any younger."

"Don't you have a big day tomorrow?"

"That's probably exactly why I want to drop by."

She paused. She knew, of course, that she was going to say yes, but it irritated her that she was so pleased at the prospect of his coming over. Naturally, he was drunk and probably high. She'd been the recipient of many such late-night phone calls back in the day. She couldn't help feeling an illicit satisfaction in the fact that she was, after all these years, getting another, and on this of all nights. He was probably just feeling sentimental in his cups, but whatever his motivation, she had unfinished business with A. G. Jackson, and this might well be her last chance to close the account.

He was flushed, and his speech, always slower and more elided than that of his northern peers, was just a little slurrier than usual. But for all the nights they'd partied till dawn, she'd never really seen him lose control of his faculties.

He hugged her just a little longer and harder than he might have in a public encounter. "Hey, little darlin'. I can't tell you how glad I am to see you." She pointed him toward the living room couch. He set up camp on the couch and proceeded to lay out a pile of coke on the coffee table. "You don't mind, do you? I just need to settle my nerves."

"Oh, that should definitely do the trick," she said. "You're *so* mellow on coke."

"Well, you know. Old habits die hard."

Though it had been years since she'd done blow herself, it seemed perfectly normal to watch him chopping lines, since that's what they'd always done. Being transported back a decade wasn't such a bad thing for a girl. Plus, she was morbidly fascinated with his recklessness on the eve of his wedding. She couldn't help wondering just how far he would push it.

"Is that how you'd describe me? 'An old habit'?"

"I'd describe you as an old . . . a *close* friend." He laid out four identical lines with his Soho House membership card. He always prided himself on this little skill.

She sat down beside him and accepted the rolled-up twenty. Always the gentleman, letting her go first. She felt a thrill of recognition as he held her hair back while she leaned over the table. And then the other familiar thrill, the chilly tingle in her sinuses that turned warm as it spread out toward the follicles of her scalp.

"Feels like old times," he said.

"Not exactly," she said.

"I can't believe it's been . . . God, how long *has* it been?"

"Seven years."

"No way."

"Yup."

"Well, it's not like we haven't seen each other around town."

"No, though you probably would have preferred me to just disappear into thin air."

"Oh, come on, darlin'. Don't be ridiculous. I'm always happy to see you." He leaned over and snorted his two lines.

"You weren't so happy to see me today at the beach."

"Well, not my best moment."

"So you admit you were hitting on my niece."

"It's a reflex. What can I say? She's a very pretty girl."

"I understand that. What I don't understand is tomorrow."

"Yeah, well. I'm not so sure I do, either."

"Don't you think you'd better figure it out?"

"I hardly think there's time for that," he said.

"Are you in love with her?"

"I suppose so. I'm not sure."

"Have you ever been in love?"

He nodded his head and looked off through the bay window, out across the invisible ocean, his eyes turning glassy. She realized with a start that he was on the verge of tears. When she slid across the couch and embraced him, he virtually collapsed in her arms. "Once," he said.

———

At Harvard, A.G. had fallen in love with Eve Garrigue, who was a class ahead of him and who, by the time they met, had already published several poems in *The Paris Review*. He was aware of her legend—brainy, beautiful and hard-drinking—even before he arrived on campus, and he already knew her family, from New Orleans, in the way that all southerners know one another. A.G. had discarded his virginity at fifteen and never looked back. At first she found his boundless self-confidence absurd—a freshman wooing the most popular woman in the sophomore class—but eventually it won her over. He was precocious intellectually as well as sexually, and he was also a willing student. He wrote her a sonnet cycle, twelve strictly constructed love poems modeled on Wyatt's and Shakespeare's. And there was the tribal connection—they had a common set of cultural references and a common enemy in the subtle prejudice of all those who assumed that a southern accent was a sign of slow-wittedness.

Under Eve's influence, A.G. began to write poetry in the runic, oracular manner of Merwin and Strand; her own was high-pitched and baroque, reminding some of late Plath. Eventually he gave up verse, after realizing that he was a better critic than a poet, and a lesser poet than his girlfriend. He would provide the intellectual framework for her creation. In fact, he would've done almost anything for her. Accustomed to being intellectually and emotionally dominant, he happily acceded to her whims and opinions. He started smoking Gauloises and briefly abandoned the preppy wardrobe of his youth in favor of colorful long-collared shirts and flared pants. Eve, who had a breathtaking figure to show off, hid it beneath drapey vintage dresses and scarves. His devotion was extreme; he couldn't believe his luck in finding, so early in life, all the answers to his desires in one woman. They shared a destiny. While they gathered around them a group of friends and admirers, they were often criticized for being a universe of two.

They spent their second summer together backpacking in Europe; her family had offered to pay for a deluxe version of the grand tour, but Eve refused their money on principle. They bought Europasses and stayed in youth hostels, dined on bread and cheese and vin du pays and screwed like minks. By day they retraced the lives of the poets and sought out ancient churches. One afternoon in the cool, musty interior of a Romanesque church near Saint Paul de Vence, Eve knelt down on the stone floor and gave him a blow job. It was the most shocking thing that had happened to him in his life, though he didn't say anything, more fearful that she'd think him prudish and stop before she finished than he was of discovery or blasphemy.

They worried about what to do after graduation, which would come a year earlier for Eve. Marriage was discussed, but they agreed—or rather, Eve assured him—that they didn't believe in it. Finally she decided to go to Columbia for her master's. She'd take the four-hour train ride to see him every weekend, and in the meantime she could scout out Manhattan, a territory they planned to conquer together. Her senior year, Eve was invited to be a Fellow at Bread Loaf. A.G., interning in Chattanooga at a law firm, couldn't understand the diminishing volume and ardor of her letters and phone calls. She herself was almost impossible to reach. Frantic, he drove one Friday night from Chattanooga to Vermont, arriving at the mountain outpost of literature sixteen hours later, just in time to find a tousled Eve walking to breakfast, hand in hand with a middle-aged poet A.G. recognized from dust-jacket photos. Her surprise turned almost immediately to defiance. A.G. punched the poet, knocking him down. Eve jumped on his back and scratched his face as a small crowd of aspiring writers looked on.

In his young man's heart he believed he could never forgive her, but she astonished him by refusing to ask him to. Back in Chattanooga, he waited for the letter or the call, in his mind conducting the dialogue she refused to initiate. How could she? After all that time, after all they'd been through together. For all his intelligence and eloquence, the sentiments and even the words were the same as those of all spurned lovers. He spent hours engaged in this furious debate, but his side amounted to the repetition of a simple question: "How could you stop loving me?" This was his first experience of rejection. He had never been in love before, and some of his friends wondered if he ever would be again.

At his father's insistence, A.G. had taken half a dozen economics classes already, and having finished most of his course work in English, he decided to do a double major in literature and economics. He took up with a new set of friends, avoiding most of those he and Eve had known. He had no idea what he wanted to do. After graduation he went to China to teach English, which he envisioned as a kind of romantic exile. The following year he enrolled in business school, and then, after a grueling year as an analyst at an investment bank, he found his calling as a closer—the guy who entertained the clients and held their hands as they signed the checks.

"So she broke your heart and drove you to banking?"

"I don't suppose it was quite that simple. I've probably simplified it in retrospect. Mythologized it in my mind."

"So how does this lead us to the present? To your imminent nuptials?"

He shook his head and chopped up more coke. "I don't know. I guess it just seemed like time." He folded the coke and chopped it again.

"That's it? It 'seemed like time'?"

He shrugged. "She's a nice girl, from a good family. You know, we have a lot in common. So, what about you?"

"What about me?"

"Have you ever been in love?" He was rubbing his face as if to wash off a spot—a tic that was terribly familiar to her.

"Once," she said, taking a cigarette from his pack and holding it to her lips while he lit it.

"Tell me about it."

"You know most of the story," Ginny said. "You were there."

"I was there?" He seemed determined to be obtuse.

"You were the one."

"Jesus. Are you—"

"Yes, I am serious. All those years, all those nights. I couldn't help it. I knew it was supposed to be fun, but I fell in love with you."

"I didn't know."

"You don't remember the last night we spent together?"

"Not exactly."

"You asked me to marry you."

"I did?" He looked horrified.

"You did. You asked me to marry you and you told me you wanted me to have your babies. We stayed up all night planning our future. We were going to spend our summers in Provence. And the next day you said you'd come to my parents' house for Thanksgiving. But later that same day you said you had a late meeting on Wednesday and you would take the train up to Bedford Thursday morning. And that was the last I ever heard from you."

He slumped back on the couch. "That was terrible, really the worst—I know. I just didn't know what to say to you." He leaned forward and snorted another line. "I was going to go up to Bedford. Except I went out for a drink that night. And I met a girl. And one drink led to another. And the next thing I knew, it was noon the next day and we were finishing the last of the coke. I couldn't very well face your family in that condition. And, you know, letting you down like that . . . I knew I needed to call and apologize, but somehow I couldn't."

Well, at least now she knew what had happened. She bent over the coffee table and snorted another couple of lines. "It used to kill me to see you at parties," she said finally, "and you acting so casual, as if nothing had happened. With some babe on your arm. For a long time I hated you."

"I guess I can't really blame you," he said. "I wish there was some way—"

"Make love to me," Ginny said. In her own mind, she wasn't being sentimental so much as practical. She felt he owed her that much at least. Either it would be as good as she remembered it or it wouldn't, and she would've gotten it out of her system.

Up in the bedroom, he was smart enough, or considerate enough, to kiss her long and hard before he began removing her clothes. In the middle, for all his skill, and all her desire to be transported, she began to come back to herself and feel awkward and sad. And after what seemed like a very long time, she just wanted him to finish. She realized now that what she'd really wanted was to believe that he still wanted her and that he cared enough for her to betray his future wife.

Afterward, she wrapped herself in the bedspread and walked out to the deck. The sky had turned gray in the east and the dark surface of the ocean was stippled with silver sunlight. The coke was wearing off, and her eyeballs felt as if they were being pricked with tiny needles. She hated herself.

Eventually, A.G., in his paisley boxer shorts, holding a cigarette, joined her on the deck.

"What are you going to do?" she said.

"I don't know." He took a drag. "Probably the correct thing."

"What's the correct thing?"

"It's what we do when we don't know what the right thing is."

He put his arm around her and held his cigarette to her lips. She inhaled greedily, as if she believed the smoke could save her, the ember blazing and crackling between A.G.'s fingers before it faded and dimmed within a cocoon of gray ash and he tossed it away, the last sparks dying on the dewy lawn below.

2008

A NOTE ABOUT THE AUTHOR

The author of seven novels and two collections of essays on wine, Jay McInerney is a regular contributor to *New York, The New York Times Book Review, The Independent* and *Corriere della Sera.* His short fiction has appeared in *The New Yorker, Esquire, Playboy* and *Granta.* In 2006, *Time* cited his 1984 debut, *Bright Lights, Big City,* as one of nine generation-defining novels of the twentieth century. He was the recipient of the 2006 James Beard Foundation's M.F.K. Fisher Distinguished Writing Award, and his novel *The Good Life* received the Grand Prix Littéraire de Deauville in 2007. He lives in Manhattan and in Bridgehampton, New York.

A NOTE ON THE TYPE

The text of this book was set in Simoncini Garamond, a modern version by Francesco Simoncini of the type attributed to the famous Parisian type cutter Claude Garamond (ca. 1480–1561). Garamond was a pupil of Geoffroy Tory and is believed to have based his letters on the Venetian models, although he introduced a number of important differences, and it is to him we owe the letter that we know as old style. He gave to his letters a certain elegance and a feeling of movement that won for their creator an immediate reputation and the patronage of Francis I of France.

Composed by Creative Graphics
Allentown, Pennsylvania

Printed and bound by Berryville Graphics
Berryville, Virginia

Designed by M. Kristen Bearse